What could frighten a monster's daughter?

Nod growled and crawled out from under the table and I stood up without quite knowing why. Ghosts could be frightened, but they couldn't really be hurt unless they allowed it, and they couldn't be destroyed at all. But still—why frighten a ghost? And how?

He smiled dreadfully and stretched out his hand to catch the ghost's arm, like somebody playing tag in slow motion. It had just that air of a game being played. But when he touched the ghost, the ghost screamed.

It wasn't like any mortal scream I'd heard before. It wasn't a noise. It was a blow, straight down the spine. It raised Nod's fur and the hair on the back of my neck, and every mortal in earshot paused and looked around. The expression on the ghost's face was terror and agony. And then the ghost just... disintegrated into wind, and his scream was the last thing to go.

Praise for the Senyaza Series:

"Lovely worldbuilding and an unusual heroine surrounded by strong relationships and good intrigue kept me reading *Matchbox Girls* until well past my bedtime. Tzavelas has created a winning story universe and I'm impatient for the next book!"

—CE Murphy,
author of *Urban Shaman* and *The Queen's Bastard*

"Tzavelas writes genuine, interesting characters with voices that feel real. Well worth your time."

—*Fantasy & Science Fiction* magazine

also in the Senyaza Series:

wolf interval

Chrysoula Tzavelas

dreamfarmer press

First edition published 2014.
Second edition published 2015.

Copyright © 2014 by Chrysoula Tzavelas
All rights reserved.

For information, address

ISBN: 978-1-943197-07-1
eBook ISBN: 978-1-943197-03-3

Cover art by Ravven
www.ravven.com

Book design and composition by Kate Sullivan
Typeface: Adobe Caslon

Editor: Kate Sullivan

Proofreader: Aliza Becker

www.dreamfarmer.net

Hey, Persephone.

Each time you come out of the dark,
you bring the spring.

We're waiting for you.

-one-

O h, AT," sighed my mother. "I thought you'd finally escaped." Four times she'd said that since I returned to my father's house. But she was dead, and it takes a while for the dead to learn anything new.

I pressed my cheek against the trophy case where my mother's locket was on display and thought patient thoughts. Ghosts couldn't help having trouble learning new facts—it's a side effect of having a mind but no brain, I think—but my mom was being even more stubborn than usual.

My father was out of the house for the morning. Without his presence to stifle us, I'd figured it was a great time to work on updating my mother and the other ghosts on my return home. I'd been hiding in my room whenever my father let me for days now, and the idea of doing something for myself had been exciting. At first. I missed my mom. Alive or dead, she'd always been awesome.

"I came back. I got into trouble and in the end, all I could do was come home." I tried to inject some brightness into my voice. "But it's not that bad. This way I can still see you." And it was true. Even as a ghost, my mother was the best thing about my father's house. Leaving her behind had been really hard.

The misty figure within the trophy case stretched out the hint of a hand and condensation formed on the glass to show me the delicate palm and short fingers I remembered. The picture within the tiny locket frame was a partially scorched photo of a smiling, brown-skinned, curly-haired woman not much older than I was now. Both of those visuals were stronger than my memories of my mother alive.

"I didn't want you to ever step foot in this house again," she said gently. Her voice was the hum of a half-remembered lullaby.

Well, I hadn't planned on coming back either, but sometimes life doesn't work out the way you want. I couldn't argue about this with her yet again, not with her, not with the woman who had taught me how hard it was to ever really escape. I put my hand against her imprint, feeling the chill of the glass.

"He's out with the pack," I said instead. "I thought I'd work on catching you up." My breath hitched, but I forced it out cleanly. "I *need* you to catch up. You've got to remember I'm back, that I'm not going away again."

My father had taken the pack out into the forest beyond the lodge where we lived, for a day of killing every furry thing they came across. I could smell the blood from the lodge's great hall, via the open veranda. It was one of those perfect Pacific Northwest October days, where the sky is intense blue and the leaves are orange and yellow and there's a rim of clouds all around the dome of the sky, promising rain.

Personally, while the clear autumn days were beautiful, I thought the rain couldn't come soon enough. The pack was always the most excitable in the fall, and this year it was going to take at least a week of drenching downpours to calm them down. The rain would wash away the smell of blood, too. I hated the smell of blood, because part of me loved it so very much. It was hard for me to pretend to be normal, even to myself, when the pack was slaughtering everything in the forest nearby.

"I don't want to catch up," said my mother, pulling back into the locket again. "I want this to be a bad dream."

"Mom!" I protested. "I'm really here. It's not a dream." I hesitated, then added, "It's just real life. The part where I left—think of that as the dream."

"How? How did he bring you back again? He promised. I heard his promise to the Lady in Red."

"I don't want to talk about it," I whispered. That was a new question, and exactly the one I'd hoped she'd never ask. I couldn't tell her the truth. She'd never forgive me.

"Oh, AT. My Annalise, my baby girl." The ghost sighed again. "I was dreaming of when you were just a tiny girl. Things were good then. Before *he* came back from the dead. Do you remember?"

"Of course I do. Best days of my life," I said automatically. It was an old conversation and I've always stretched the truth when she asks. If I told her that mostly I remembered her stories, not the actual good old days, she'd be devastated. I tried, really, I did. But Dad came back from the dead when I was only four and the most I could really remember from the time before was this sense of warmth and hope, and the smell of onions and cayenne pepper.

"We've lost so much, you and I. So much. It could have been so different."

"Mom, no! We haven't. You're still here, you remember, you tell me stories. Nothing's lost." I had to pause to scrub my eyes. My mom was awesome, but she was also a ghost. That came with baggage. It wasn't her fault.

She'd always been a fighter in her own way, my mom. Not like what my father had trained me to be, but after he found us and made us come live with him, she fought him the only way she could. She taught me things he didn't want me to learn, like how to be kind to those unluckier than me, and how to be careful around danger. And after she died, she'd whisper to me at night, telling me stories about herself when she was a little girl named Denise and stories about me when I was a baby. And sometimes when he didn't want me reading certain books, she'd do her best to tell me the stories herself, if she knew them. She could never read anything new, but she could remember. I learned about all sorts of classics that way, like Jane Eyre and Mansfield Park.

Her phantom sharpened, until it seemed almost like a living person knelt behind the glass of the trophy case. She wore the pale yellow dress that I remembered her in the most, and her face seemed so young. She'd been so pretty. "Listen, baby girl. Something dreadful is coming, to take away all the dreams and all the memories," she said. "I've felt the ripples. You go and see your friend, please."

Bewildered, I asked, "Where? What friend?" I didn't have any living friends left in Washington state. It was too dangerous for them.

"Out of this house." With the sudden edge of total exasperation, she added, "And this time, don't come back." The haziness emerging from the locket vanished. The chill became autumn warmth and the glass cleared. She was gone.

My chest hurt, and I had to rub my eyes again. She didn't have to leave so quickly, did she? For a moment, I felt like I was once more seven years old and I'd just learned she would never be able to hug me again.

Then the scent of blood washed over me and I heard the sounds of the pack returning. There were yips and laughter and the occasional howl and cry of pain as the wolves became men again. Not all of my father's pack could turn into wolves, but the mortal men had just as much fun hunting as the ones he'd remade, and they all dreamed of being granted the same gift.

That's what they called it, a gift. They gave up the most important part of being human to become slaves and they thought of it as a *gift*.

I held my breath, listening for my father's voice among the others. I didn't want him to see me with my eyes still red, and when I didn't hear him, I relaxed a little. Sometimes he stayed out longer, on business of his own. That usually made dealing with his pack easier. They liked to try to impress him by harassing me, but they were warier without him there. And I didn't have to worry whether I was pleasing him or displeasing him when I made them leave me alone.

I went out the front door and headed down the private road that was the lodge's driveway. I wanted to go to the Black Clearing and speak to its ghosts, but not while there was any chance my father would be there.

Most people can't see or hear ghosts, unless things are really bad. But most people aren't the child of a mortal woman and a fallen angel, either. That provides a body with a variety of abilities. And no, they're not gifts, not any more than what my father does to his pack. Sometimes they're practically curses. But seeing ghosts is okay. It gives me a steady supply of people to talk to, anyhow.

And it's not common even among the half-blood nephilim, which means it's a secret I've managed to keep from my father all these years. It probably helped that the first ghost I met was my mother and I knew that he didn't want me to talk to her. And I've always been good at picking up on things other people don't notice.

There are ghosts near almost every road, too. Most of them don't notice me, but I like to keep an eye on them. Some people watch birds; I watch ghosts. The ones that don't already belong to my father are pretty safe from him, and that's always a nice thought.

After looking around for the ghost I called Flower Picking Girl at the driveway's edge and not finding her, I ran all the way down to the two-lane blacktop that curved through the forest and led to the lights of civilization.

Everything always got really quiet when my father was in the forest. But as I ran, the forest slowly came back to life around me. Birds chirped and whistled and small things moved in the underbrush. A breeze sighed through the trees, making their green tips sway. And briefly I heard a snatch of music.

At first I thought it was just a car stereo blaring. But the music wasn't distant, and it didn't doppler like it would from a moving car. It began and ended mid-phrase, and it was barely musical, more like somebody having an argument with a violin.

I came to a halt, listening intently, but when I didn't hear it again, I finished my run to the county road. Once I was there, I slowed to a walk. I wasn't tired—my father's blood means I can run for hours before getting tired—but I was far enough away from the house that I felt like I didn't have to run alone.

I concentrated. There's a spot inside me that I can reach when I close my eyes, where I stop being me and I start becoming something else. I imagined opening a door, and then I whistled.

My dogs, all three of them, burst out of my shadow, tangling around my legs and licking my hands. I felt better right away. I'm always happier when my dogs are around. They're the only real friends I have that my father can't take away.

I laughed and crouched down, running my hands over their fur and behind their ears. Grim, Nod, and Heart. I had no idea how it worked, but I knew they were mine, and that they lived inside me when it wasn't okay for them to run beside me. Without them, my life would have been a disaster instead of just hard sometimes. A ghost mom can give you good advice, but with dogs running beside you, you feel like you can do anything.

They bounced around me for another moment, and then Heart and Grim broke off to go investigate the trees beside the road. There were some jack o' lanterns there, carved by the pack, with some especially interesting scents. But Nod stood on his hind legs and put his black paws on my shoulders. His tongue darted out, once, twice, a third time, licking each of my eyes to catch the remnants of the unshed tears before licking my nose. Then, with a grumbling woof, he trotted after Heart.

I grinned after him and wiped the dog slobber off my face. I felt so much better having them out. They'd mostly been stuck in my shadow since I got back home again, since my father does *not* approve of them. He can't make me get rid of them, but he can be nasty in so many other ways that it's safest to only bring them out occasionally to snuggle with as I slept. But they weren't just stuffed animals, and they deserved a real chance to run and play sometimes.

Once they'd sniffed around a bit, I continued my run to town. There were other ghosts there I'd known before I ran away. They probably hadn't even noticed I'd left, but that just meant I wouldn't have to have any unpleasant conversations.

Okay, so the "updating the ghosts" plan was mostly just an excuse to get out of the house. Which was kind of funny, really, because I was the only person who expected an excuse. My father's been trying to get me out of my room and active again for days, ever since the injuries I came home with healed. Because *he* wanted that, *I* didn't. But as soon as my father's pack hit the forest, I couldn't stand being closed into my room anymore. I wanted somebody to talk to, even if they weren't going to be great conversationalists.

It took about an hour to get to Issaquah Commons, with a few squirrel-chasing diversions along the way. It was mid-afternoon and there were a lot of other people out enjoying what was probably the last sunshine of the year.

Issaquah Commons was completely tricked out for Halloween, with pumpkins and black crepe streamers and the annual costume store that spontaneously appeared in any empty building. The town had plenty of ghosts, too, although since they were real, nobody else could appreciate them.

The shopping center wasn't particularly old, but some of the ghosts were. One of my favorites was a young man who sat on a bench outside a boutique in worn overalls, holding a push-broom. I think he was over a hundred years old. I don't really know why he was there; he never talked to me. I just assumed ghosts liked window-shopping and people-watching as much as living folks.

As I got closer to the shopping center, I sent Heart and Grim back into my shadow again, and put a collar and leash around Nod's neck. Having a dog out was crucial when I wanted to talk to ghosts in a public place, so I didn't look like I was high or something. But I'd found that most people were uneasy about a girl like me with two leashed large dogs and occasionally called the cops when I had all three with me, even if they were on their best behavior.

Nod was the best behaved of my dogs, most of the time. Grim was too bouncy and energetic to walk nicely today, while Heart was shy and sometimes she got nervous. She has gorgeous red fur that everybody wants to touch and she's not okay with that.

Nod, on the other hand, walked at my heel and waited quietly on the sidewalk when I ducked into the Overalls Ghost's boutique to check out some cute jeans. He and the ghost were looking at each other when I came out, but as soon as I unlooped Nod's leash, the ghost's gaze went away again. That was fine. I didn't mind at all. Sometimes a dog was all the people a person could handle.

When I went into the coffee shop across the street, Nod rested under the table we'd staked out, relaxed enough to attract and tolerate the attention of a nearby toddler. I was so proud of him; he'd come such a long way from the savage feral I'd saved years ago.

I set my coffee and pastries down on the table and smiled at the little girl and her mother as they went back to their shopping trip. I liked little kids, although I didn't get a chance to play with them much. When I was in California, I'd gotten to know two adorable little girls—but I didn't like to think about what had happened with them. I'd heard they were safe and happy now, and that was good enough.

The radio playing over the coffee shop's speakers finished up a metal ballad and switched to a song that had only really hit the airwaves a couple of weeks ago. I'd heard it a few times before, a touchy-feely song about calling back what was lost. It was catchy, one of those songs you like even when you think the lyrics aren't your style, and I hummed along as I sipped my coffee.

Another ghost I recognized passed by, a woman in a business suit with wild hair and about a hundred plastic shopping bags. She was more contemporary than the others, I was pretty sure, and sometimes she talked to me about what she was hoping to fill her bags with. "Baby powder, just the right sort, to help me sleep. Hyacinth soap to keep away nightmares." She spent a lot of time outside Bath and Body Works, but she never seemed to have anything in her bags.

Today she only nodded at me absently and hurried past. I thought of the missing Flower Picking Ghost near my driveway and my gaze flicked back to the Overalls Ghost at the boutique down the street.

He was sitting up straight, looking at a man walking down the sidewalk toward him. The man wore a black cowboy hat and proper cowboy boots peeked out from worn navy denims. He wore a dark pinstriped suit jacket, too, and a black tie against a black shirt; I wondered if that was what passed for businesswear in Texas or something.

To my surprise, he bent down to say something to the Overalls Ghost. I wondered if he was a human initiate into supernatural matters, or a nephil half-breed like me, or something like my father. I was just about to activate my magical sight to find out when the Overalls Ghost shot to his feet and started stumbling down the sidewalk in my direction. He looked almost as solid as the living, but he passed through them without any of them noticing.

The cowboy had a faint smile on his face as he tapped the fingers of one hand against the palm of another. He was counting, I realized. And the Overalls Ghost was running.

Nod growled and crawled out from under the table and I stood up without quite knowing why. Ghosts could be frightened, but they couldn't really be hurt unless they allowed it, and they couldn't be destroyed at all. But still—why frighten a ghost? And how? If I were better with my magical sight, I could just flick it on and learn more about him—but if I did that, the chaos of the Geometry would make it hard for me to watch anything else, and I wanted to see what happened when the cowboy finished his count.

He counted to five four times, then started moving after the Overalls Ghost. He didn't walk; he sauntered, weaving around the other people on the sidewalk. There was no way he should have been able to catch up with the ghost, but the Overalls Ghost seemed like he was stumbling through deep snow and after less time than it took to count to twenty, the cowboy reached him.

He smiled dreadfully and stretched out his hand to catch the ghost's arm, like somebody playing tag in slow motion. It had just that air of a game being played. But when he touched the ghost, the ghost screamed.

It wasn't like any mortal scream I'd heard before. It wasn't a noise. It was a blow, straight down the spine. It raised Nod's fur and the hair on the back of my neck, and every mortal in earshot paused and looked around. The expression on the ghost's face was terror and agony. And then the ghost just... disintegrated into wind, and his scream was the last thing to go.

The cowboy looked at me, actually at *me*, through the space where the ghost had been and grinned widely. Horribly. Then he pointed a finger gun at me, winked, and vanished into thin air just as the song playing over the coffee shop speakers ended.

-two-

Hey, kid, are you all right?"

I was huddled on a bench somewhere—where? The bus stop outside the high school—with my dogs around me. The ghost's scream—the ghost's *expression*—consumed my mind's eye, and I couldn't stop remembering my mother saying she wouldn't be around for long.

But a boy a little older than me had stopped beside my bench to check on me. I couldn't concentrate on him very well, just enough to pick up that he was Korean, wearing big sunglasses, and he smelled of tea and cedar and basil. I shook my head, muttered that I was fine, and tried to wish him away. Instead he patted Grim, who was curled up beside me on the bench, and looked at me for a long moment. Then, finally, he kept on walking, and I was glad that I didn't have to come up with an excuse for my distraction.

I didn't know what to think. I didn't think that cowboy, whatever he was, could get past my father to do *that* to my mother. She was *his*, by her choice, and it was awful but it was a fact that my father didn't let anybody take what was his. Especially now, especially after the shift in fallen angel politics that had come along with the lake monsters and the other changes. He'd had to make concessions and there was no way he'd make more willingly.

A car door slammed and a familiar figure stalked toward me. I hadn't seen her in months, ever since I'd come home again. For a moment, I panicked that she'd found me, before I remembered the incoherent call I'd made right after the cowboy destroyed the Overalls Ghost. I was here to meet her. She wanted to talk.

Thinking that didn't actually make the panic go away. I wasn't ready to face her again. I didn't know if I ever would be. But here she was, her cold shadow falling over my bench, because I didn't have anybody else to ask.

Picking up my mood, or the woman's scent, Grim leapt off the bench and hid underneath. The demon I only knew as "Tia" took his place beside me gracefully. She was gorgeous, with deeply tanned olive skin and dark hair pulled back into a chignon. She wore designer sunglasses and a sleek cream suit, and she smelled like fire and sunshine and peaches and wrath. My mother called her the Lady in Red, but I'd never seen her in that color. Just like my father, she was one of the Fallen, although the demons had scruples my father and his kin laughed at.

Nod licked his chops, then yawned hugely, showing off his teeth in a totally-not-growling way. I put my hand on his head, studying his ears as I tried to manage my own desire to get up and run away.

Finally, Tia said, "Well, AT?" Her lovely voice was calm but cool.

"I wanted to ask you about something I saw today," I mumbled. "But first—"

"First?"

"I'm sorry," I blurted out and stole a glance up. She was looking at me over her sunglasses with yellow-green eyes. "I know you worked hard on helping me get away from him and I really *do* appreciate it. It just didn't work out. I'm not—"

"I don't want to hear about what you're not." Tia's tone was as crisp as an autumn leaf. "Ask what you want to ask. I have a client waiting on me."

"Client" was how Tia referred to the person she was currently assisting. I'd been her client once upon a time. I thought we'd been friends, too. But now, with the scent of her suppressed anger filling my nose, I had to face the fact that I'd probably ruined that. She'd worked so hard to coerce a promise from my father that he wouldn't chase me down when I left, and then I'd ruined it by pretty much coming back on my own.

"I saw a man destroy a ghost today," I began, then added anxiously, "But that's not possible, is it? Ghosts are souls and souls go on forever. I mean, I've *always* heard human souls can't be destroyed by anything they don't consent to."

Tia wasn't surprised by my story at all, so I kept talking in case she didn't understand. "I mean, I know they can be tricked, but this... man... didn't do any trickery. He scared the ghost into running, and then he chased him down, and then the ghost was just gone. He screamed..." I trailed off as Tia held up a hand.

"That was probably Ion, First Huntsman of the Wild Hunt. It isn't even Halloween yet, but he's been slipping out in advance of the big day," she said flatly. "Usually when that Gravity's Angels song plays. He isn't a faerie, but he's bound by some of the same restrictions."

Huntsman. My father went by Hunter. He really embraced the name, all the way down to how he decorated his lodge. And I remembered how the cowboy had looked directly at me, as if he knew me. There were other things Tia had said that I knew I should pay attention to, but I couldn't yet. "Huntsman. Is he connected to...?"

"Your parent?" Tia's gaze went far away. "No. Nor are any of the others who ride with him. They are both more and less than he."

"Hah," I muttered and stared down at my hands, trying to calm my racing heart. My father tried to trick me sometimes. For a moment I'd thought—but Tia was honest. And my father was the one who'd first taught me about the immortality of souls. I didn't know why the cowboy had winked at me, but it didn't matter if he wasn't part of my father's game.

Tia ignored me and went on. "Your father wasn't born a Hunter; once, he was something other than he is now. But the Wild Hunt was created precisely to hunt down and destroy souls."

My hands went cold. "Why? How? Who would do such a thing?"

Tia blew a tendril of hair away from her face. "They were created in response to certain other things going wrong, back in the early days. We'd learned that the very inviolability of souls could become a threat, if they became badly corrupted and destructive. We needed a way to stop the damage from spreading when that happened. Six of my extended kindred gave up something of themselves to a celestial artifact, and the Wild Hunt was born."

"But the ghost this Ion destroyed wasn't corrupted or destructive.

All he ever did was sit there and look at people!" I was almost wailing, but I didn't know how to cope with this. Heart whined and put her head in my lap.

"I'm sure you're right," Tia said, with a flat calm. "What we created was just as flawed as what we tried to fix. The Wild Hunt became too enthusiastic, too concerned with its own pleasures. It was unable to discriminate between appropriate targets and inappropriate ones. So when the faeries were locked away outside the world, so was the Wild Hunt."

"But—" I began, and then said, "Oh." Something had happened recently. I didn't know the details, because it made my father angry to talk about it, but the door between the faerie prison and the rest of the world wasn't stuck as tight as it used to be.

"Yes." Tia clasped her hands over a knee. "Once, they could only be summoned through a very involved ritual one day a year. Now they can escape occasionally, momentarily freed as the faeries are. But because we needed them sometimes, they were not bound entirely as the faeries were. And so, when their summoning day comes, they will completely slip their leash."

"Just for that day, right?" I asked, anxious for a bright side.

Tia kicked her foot a little before saying gently, "No. There will be no ritual to draw them back again. On the first of November, when Halloween ends, they will be free to ride over the world, hunting down any wandering soul. We don't know if they'll respect the marks of celestials on claimed souls, either. I think not, myself."

I demanded, "Is somebody doing something about this? You can't just let it happen!"

With a cool, almost unfriendly look, Tia said, "Somebody *is* trying to do something about it. It's not going to work, though." She pulled out her phone and began to play with it.

"Why not?" I threaded my fingers through my curls and stood up, dumping Heart's head off my lap. "Why are you so *casual* about this?"

"Because having a tantrum about it helps nobody." Tia shot me a glance over her sunglasses. "If you're going to help out, you're going to have to stop behaving like a baby."

I took a step back. "Me, help? How can *I* help?" Various faces passed across my mind's eye and I shook my head. "I can't help anybody."

Tia's delicate eyebrows arched. "Really? And here I thought that was where this was going." She stomped one foot lightly and said mockingly, "You can't just let it happen."

I flushed, my ears burning. "That's different."

"Of course," said Tia sweetly, standing up. "I have to go. When you called me, I thought we had a chance, but..." She shook her head. "Oh well. Go make your excuses to your ghostly friends. And your mother—" She smiled, as if it was twisted out of her. "Maybe your father can protect her. Probably not, though."

"This isn't fair," I said. I knew it was stupid but I couldn't help it. I felt like the shadow of my father was just behind me. He wouldn't like me talking to Tia again, let alone helping her. But my mother—

Tia tucked her phone back into her handbag. "Of course not." Her gaze went to somebody across the street and she said briskly, "See you around, AT."

She started to cross the street, then turned in the middle to call back, "Back in LA, you could have called almost anybody for help, you know." The gentleness in her voice was worse than the scent of her anger.

My throat hurt. "Yeah. I've thought about that. But I didn't. I called for him."

It seemed like her eyes were burning through the sunglasses for a moment. Then she turned and walked away, leaving me alone except for my dogs.

The Black Clearing wasn't actually black, not in the physical mundane world. It was a tiny clearing in the forest on my father's land, draped in the greenery of the pines. There was a little firepit in the middle and the ground around it was scuffed up. There were old needles everywhere, with odd patterns drawn in them. There was the smell of old beer, too, but not a single abandoned can to be found. You could just see a bit of the sky if you looked up from the center. It always felt like a cage to me. I was pretty sure my first best friend had been eaten there.

I didn't know if she'd died there, or somewhere else. I wasn't even sure if her ghost lingered in the Black Clearing. Sometimes I saw the chains of a haunt, a ghost's dream forming, but the dream never pulled me in. But even if Emily hadn't lingered, other victims of my father did. They didn't belong to my father the way my mother did, but they'd been caught by him all the same, unable to move past the memory of my father's torment.

The Black Clearing wasn't actually black, but it wasn't entire mundane either. Viewed through the magical Geometry vision, the land itself glowed with the pain of its many-layered ghosts. The trees cringed away from the firepit in the center and a stain sank into the stones.

"Hi," I said, kneeling down and shoving my hands into the dirt for a moment. They ached just being here. After Emily had vanished, I'd reported the Black Clearing to the police as an anonymous tip. My father hadn't liked that at all.

"I brought you some things." I dug some scented candles out of my jacket pocket, along with a few pieces of candy and some ribbon I'd scavenged. Carefully, I laid out the candles along Geometry lines that made sense, then lit them with my firelighting charm. The candy I scattered in the dirt and the ribbons I tied to the trees. All the while, I could feel ghostly attention on me.

It wasn't friendly. It never was, not here. That was okay. I was the daughter of their tormentor and all the candy in the world wasn't going to make up for that. But it was important to me that they knew they weren't forgotten.

I pulled my knees to my chest and hugged them, staring at the whorls in the bark in the tree across from me without really seeing them. My dogs were back in my shadow again; we were too close to home and I was afraid of my father remembering they existed.

My own memories opened up and I let them: memories I normally tried not to remember, but were here impossible to forget.

Emily's smile the last time I'd seen her was innocent and cheerful. She and her mother dropped me off at home after a sleepover, and we were going to talk later that day about a school project. It was one of those moments of normality I cherished so much. We hugged each other, and I hugged her mom, too. It was real and wonderful.

My father smirked when he asked me why Emily hadn't called me. Panic infused Emily's mother's voice when she *did* call me, begging me to tell her Emily was with me. When I looked at my father, he smiled and winked, like we'd enjoyed a secret. I ran through the forest until I reached the Black Clearing, where the smells told me everything I didn't want to know.

I scrubbed my face and clawed that memory away. I wanted to remember her alive as well as dead. I wanted Emily to be more than just a victim. But instead, a different memory swallowed me down, something much more recent and just as awful.

A woman, a mortal woman, came to my father's house to do business with him. He made her stay the night, then used me as bait to lure her into breaking his rules. She'd wanted to be my friend. She'd wanted to help me out. She screamed as he broke her arm, and he laughed as he talked with his pack about what he was going to do to her next. And then—no.

No.

I buried my face against my knees and dragged in deep breaths until the terror and shame receded. Remembering was the sacrifice I offered the dead, but it wasn't the only reason I'd come. I couldn't go so deep into the memories that I started screaming, too.

"I saw a thing today," I told the hidden ghosts. "A man who could destroy ghosts with a touch. Apparently he'll be doing that a lot soon. Unless somebody stops him."

Wisps of ghost-stuff appeared around the ribbons I'd tied to branches. Something was listening.

"I don't know what I can do to help," I added irritably. "She wouldn't even tell me. I did ask, too."

The ghost-stuff around the ribbons and the smoke from the candles wavered and formed into a young woman, similar in age to my mother's locket picture. It wasn't Emily. It wasn't anybody I'd ever seen before. But she looked at me like she knew me well, and she didn't say anything at all.

After waiting a long moment for her to berate me, scold me, attack me, I tried to fill the silence. "Why do you stay here? Why don't you just go on to where the unbound ghosts go? Why waste eternity *here*? You're dead. You could get away from him if you really wanted to."

The ghost spread her hands and her words emerged from the top of the silence like coffins bobbing to the surface of a lake. "There's no justice. There's just us." And for a moment, I had a dizzying sense of something growing underneath the turf and clay of the Black Clearing, something dark and glittering and charged with hatred.

Then the ghost spoke again. "All you have to do is find them."

I glared at her. "I know where he is. He's easy to find. He's always there."

She stared at me for another long moment, her eyes like the shadowed moon. Something was wrong. I'd misunderstood something.

"You mean the Wild Hunt," I said reluctantly.

"They live in a hidden fold of the other world. She who would fight them for us cannot find them. We heard her looking."

I shifted uncomfortably, pushing my fingers into the dirt again. I was good at finding things. I was even good at finding things that crossed the boundaries between worlds. Or, rather, my dogs were. They had all sorts of interesting talents.

"Who is she?"

A ghostly shoulder shrugged; she gave no other answer. A cloud seemed to drift over her eyes.

"I want to help," I admitted. "I want to help you. You're my friends."

"No," said the ghost. "We're not."

I curled around the turmoil in my stomach. "I know," I whispered. Then I forced myself to my feet, dousing the candles and snatching at the ribbons. "I have to go. I'll... I'll think about it. I'll do what I can."

My father was home already, and he and the pack were grilling dinner on the back deck. Beef, it smelled like. Beef steaks from the grocery. I guess they hadn't found anything large enough out in the woods to bring home. I smelled marinated tomatoes and sizzling potato skins, too. And beer, of course. My stomach rumbled at the scents. The pastries at the coffee shop had been hours ago.

My father heard me arrive and slid open the door to bellow cheerfully, "Hey, kiddo. You're just in time for grub. Grab a plate." His rugged face glowed with good humor.

I stood just inside the front door, almost nauseous with a mix of hunger and fear and nerves and loneliness. Sometimes he could be so generous and so supportive. If he wanted, he could convince any stranger he was the best of fathers. I'd seen him do it. But he was pretending. He'd always been pretending, since the beginning.

He saw me hesitate and his yellow eyes darkened. Something about the set of his mouth made me remember the sound of breaking bones, and I lowered my head and hid my hands behind my back. "I'll be right there."

And after putting my jacket back in my room, I dutifully returned, slipping out the back door as unobtrusively as possible. But as soon as I'd settled on the edge of a planter full of purple monkshood, Dad brought me a plate and the eyes of the pack turned to me.

"Where's she been?" said one of them. It was Scott, who'd shown up while I was in LA. He was loud and smug and hateful, with a lot more confidence than his status in the pack warranted.

"She went out for a run," said my father. "Getting herself back into shape." He watched me eat approvingly. It was good food, but I ate too quickly to really enjoy it, both because I was starving and because I wanted everybody to stop looking at me.

Scott sounded displeased as he said, "Alone? What if she runs off again?"

"Her? Nah," said Hunter, as I swallowed the last bite of steak. "She came back, remember? She'll always come back. She knows this is the only place she belongs. Don't you, Annalise?" He took my empty plate from my hand.

I knew, but I didn't want to talk about it, so I didn't answer. Another time he might have been annoyed by that, but tonight he only laughed and ruffled my hair before turning back to the grill.

But Scott didn't drop the issue. "Look at her, sitting like a scared rabbit. She ain't ever going to be one of the pack, boss. I don't get why you've been coddling her, either. It'll go to her head."

"She's been recovering. But no fear, she'll serve one way or another, my cub. Even the Lost Boys needed a mother, eh?" Hunter grinned as the pack laughed, but there was an old familiar glint in his eye as he watched Scott.

Scott didn't see it, or didn't know what it meant. He didn't know somebody was being tested. I knew, but I couldn't tell if it was me or Scott under scrutiny.

Scott drifted closer, his nostrils flaring as he looked me up and down. He wasn't as big as my father, but he had plenty of muscle and a cold, narrow-eyed handsomeness. "A bit young," he said doubtfully, reaching for me.

I leaned back out of his way, sniffing as I did. I was looking for a nuance in his scent, and I found it: a note of genuine animal musk that hadn't been there before. He was one of my father's wolves now. Hunter had probably turned him this morning as part of the day's entertainment.

That meant we were *both* being tested. It also meant my father had no intention of ever giving me to him, since his wolves couldn't breed. I relaxed, just a little.

Scott scowled as silence spread over the patio, the few pack members who hadn't been paying attention turning to see what was going on. "I'm not going to hurt you, girl. I just want to see what you've got under that awful sweatshirt you slop around in." This time, he grabbed at me with both hands.

I stood up and broke his arm. I didn't have my father's gift of *fracturing*, but I was very strong and Hunter had trained me well. It really didn't take very much at all to make Scott's arm bend the wrong way.

As he howled in agony and danced away from me, I sat myself back on the planter again and folded my hands in my lap, watching my father to see what he'd do.

He roared with laughter. "She's older than she looks, and she's got way more than you can handle, cub."

Clutching his arm, Scott threw Hunter a look filled with fear and hate as he backed away from the pack.

My father's eyes half-shuttered in amusement and he said, "Ah, Scotty, you missed the chance for that to interest me. Come on over and I'll fix that arm right up, though."

I muttered, "Yes, now coddle *him*," and the words carried. The whole pack exploded with laughter and Scott looked around wildly, as if calm waters had suddenly sprouted fins. Then, instead of obeying, he jumped awkwardly off the deck and ran into the forest behind the lodge.

Hunter, less amused now, growled under his breath. There was a short, high scream from the forest as he did something to his new wolf remotely, which I didn't even bother imagining. Once the men became wolves, I generally stopped thinking about them as individuals. They were all subject to my father's will, and he could make and unmake them as easily as I summoned my dogs.

Then Hunter's shadow fell over me again. I flinched as I looked up at him, but all he said was, "You were a little slow. You got soft with the half-breeds. We'll have to work on that." The way he bared his teeth was not a smile, and I knew the period of my recovery, where he'd insisted on my company but not my activity, had come to an end.

-three-

Halloween *is tomorrow.* I woke up with the thought echoing in my head. The clouds I'd seen on the horizon rolled in overnight, but by the time I woke at dawn, the rain was still just a promise. The sky was low and dark and lightning flickered from cloud to cloud. That was unusual; we don't get thunderstorms much in the Pacific Northwest. The rising sun flamed red behind the storm cloak. It was beautiful, and a bit ominous.

Halloween is tomorrow. It had snuck up on me. Traditionally, my father held a big party on Halloween, which I did my best to avoid. This year I'd managed to miss most of the planning meetings, but when I went downstairs, one was in full swing in the kitchen.

I paused to eavesdrop, lingering by the trophy case. I looked at my mother's locket and thought about how ridiculous it was that I was counting on my father to protect her. She was the only one who did any protecting; she'd protected me my whole life. And now I was just going to trust to my father's power to save somebody I cared about.

Again.

"Annalise!" my father barked from the kitchen. I jumped. "Get in here." I slipped into the kitchen, then purposefully headed past the group of men to the fridge. It always helped to walk with purpose.

My father watched me. "If you're going running again today, go into town and pick up some candles for the party. Good ones, mind. Don't be lazy."

"Yes, sir," I said.

He scowled at me before returning his attention to his pack and the discussion of such sundries as playlists, grilling rotas, bedroom time-shares, and haunted forest walks. I found myself some leftovers from the barbecue the night before and leaned against the counter to eat.

Scott still wasn't back, I noticed, and I was pleased to see it. It felt a little like victory, and I savored it because I knew it wouldn't last long.

Then, as soon as I'd polished off the leftover steak and potatoes, I left before my father could assign me any more chores. Fetching candles was typical of what he'd demanded I do since I came back. Serving drinks and sitting pretty. Bait for the prey. If I didn't stay out of the way, he'd make me act as guide for his "haunted forest," which I really didn't want to do.

But I would, if he told me to. In the end, I would. I couldn't even imagine refusing anymore. Even if he didn't always win when we fought, I always lost.

I brought out Grim and Nod and Heart, all three, and kept them with me all the way to the home decor store in Issaquah Commons, in order to banish the bad thoughts. I even considered bringing them into the store with me, but Nod stopped himself at the entrance, then snapped at Grim when he tried to follow me in. Heart looked between them, then curled up beside the doorway.

"Fine," I told them. "I'll be fast." And I was, dashing through the store and cutting in line with my stack of economy-sized boxes of black and orange and white candles. When I was back outside again, I slung the big plastic bag over my shoulder and, without meaning to, looked over at the spot where Overalls Ghost had once sat.

With a catch in my breath, I looked away, then back again. Then I walked over and sat in the same place. It was, I told myself, no different than what I and every other part-celestial nephil faced. Our bodies were sustained indefinitely by our celestial heritage, but we had no souls; we left no ghosts.

It was the same, in a way. But it wasn't right.

Heart trotted down the sidewalk and started sniffing around the ground where the cowboy had touched the Overalls Ghost. Her ears perked up and she looked back at us. Grim galloped over to her and vanished, crossing the boundary between worlds in that instant way they had.

"Hey, come back," I called to Grim and walked toward Heart, Nod trailing behind me.

I rumpled Heart's ears as Grim squeezed back out beside me. "We should get out of here before somebody notices magical vanishing dogs."

Heart took that as permission and started following the trail she'd picked up, across the street, between two buildings, across the parking lot, and toward the lake.

And I went with her, because, well, we were good at it. I followed them all the way down to the bottom of Lake Issaquah, until I realized that the trail wasn't heading to the lake; it was headed to Seattle.

I crouched on the roadside and gathered the dogs to me. "I'm pretty sure the Wild Hunt doesn't live in the city, guys. Dad would have mentioned it, if nothing else." I concentrated, looking inside their minds.

Heat and Grim had each caught a different element of the Huntsman's trail. Grim had wanted to take the direct route, the same route the Huntsman had taken, but when he'd investigated, it was impassable for mortals and part-mortals like me. Heart was tracking his movements in the other world on this side of the Curtain, like following a waterborne scent along the bank. Eventually we'd have to cross over, but until we did, it was easier and safer to travel here.

I stared at the gently moving water, thinking about my mother and the representative of the Black Clearing, and the flower-picking ghost who usually lingered beside my driveway but was now gone, perhaps for good.

My father was expecting me home again with a load of candles. I couldn't just run away. I didn't like it there, but it didn't change the fact that it was where I clearly belonged.

I tossed a water-smoothed rock and watched it sink into the grey lake.

Half an hour later, the candles were on the lodge's kitchen table, holding a note in place: "I've gone into the city to get a Halloween costume. Back later," and I was getting on a bus to Seattle.

And it was true, too. I'd pick up a costume, and I'd be back. I'd just wander around the city awhile first. I'd find the quickest path to the Huntsman's home, call Tia, and be home before the party. No problem.

It took two bus transfers to get into Seattle. As the final bus rolled over the bridge that floated on the lake between Seattle and its Eastside suburbs, I saw the flash of a fishtail the size of a minivan slapping the lake's surface. It was only visible for a moment before it slipped out of view, but I wasn't the only one who had seen it. A full third of the bus moved and rustled in response to the splash, and more than a dozen people trained their cellphones on the lake in case the owner of the tail appeared. Traffic on the already crowded bridge slowed to a crawl.

I traded seats with the woman leaning over me. I'd grown up in the shadow of my father's magic; I had magic of my own. Most people didn't have my experience. They lived and worked and loved, oblivious of the shadow world of fallen angels and wizards and monsters that I could never escape.

But the seals keeping some of the most dramatic magics out of the world had been weakened recently and strange things were popping up all over, including on the news. It was one of my father's favorite topics of conversation, although it varied whether it irritated or amused him. He wouldn't tell me exactly what happened, but he *did* like to talk about the consequences of the event, oh yes. I knew he was thinking about how it would impact his own activities, his own plans.

The lake itself was brighter, I realized. Despite the overcast sky, it glittered like it hadn't realized summer was over. It looked almost inviting, as if a cool dip would be the very thing to shake off the last of a morning drowse. A couple behind me whispered about taking their kayak out later to see if they could get a better look at the "lake monster" and I hoped whatever had moved in was playful rather than dangerous.

Then the bus rolled off the bridge and the lake vanished behind a hill. As we entered downtown Seattle, the bus passengers settled down again. By the time the bus got to my stop, nobody seemed to be thinking about the possible lake monster anymore.

As I stepped off the bus, I looked around, getting my bearings since I hadn't visited Seattle for almost a year. And I was no longer surprised the lake monster had been only a passing attraction, no more exciting than a deer in the road. The new magic had touched Seattle proper at least as much as it had touched the lake. The music playing over the speakers was louder; the sounds of traffic were muffled. The smell of shattered ozone was strong even here, right next to the street.

There was a bright new mural of a ring of dancers on the wall across from the bus station and dozens of tourists stood underneath gaping up at it. The headline of a discarded inner section of the *Seattle Times* warned people to BEWARE STRANGERS, as if the city was populated entirely by five-year-olds.

It was also clear Halloween was only a day away. Black and orange crepe streamers festooned shop windows and mannequins posed with pumpkins and animal masks. One of them turned to watch me as I passed, which I told myself was probably only electronics just so I wouldn't be creeped out. It's one thing for magic to be running around causing mischief for others and something else entirely to be stared at by a mannequin.

A temporary costume shop was doing brisk business out of what had once been a stationary shop and I could tell via my nose that some of the costumes coming out of the store were less "costume" and more "genuine" than others. I also noticed cops on almost every street corner, looking harassed. One of them argued with a nearly nude pink-haired woman with large pixie wings "glued" to her back. As I waited at the street crossing, I had to suppress a gurgle of laughter as the cop tried to herd the giant pixie back to the costume shop and the pixie glumly tried sprinkling sparkling dust in response.

I ducked inside the bookstore down the street and stood in front of the magazine rack as I checked in with my dogs. I'd left Grim and Heart following the trail, keeping Nod in my shadow so I wasn't utterly alone. They could move really fast when they set their minds to it and they didn't have any trouble keeping Ion's trail, even when it went skimming across Lake Washington.

More than half the news magazine covers featured photographs of some of the strange stuff that the faeries were doing now that they'd been partially freed. *Time* had a collage. I wondered if anybody would notice a pair of dogs galloping across the lake's surface. I winced, thinking about it, and hoped if they did, it wouldn't make it into any magazine my father glanced at.

The hair on the back of my neck prickled. Somebody was watching me. I glanced up and saw a man standing outside the bookstore window, looking at me over the Halloween window display. He wore a weirdly cut suit the color of oxblood, with the jacket unbuttoned over a rumpled shirt. His light brown hair was messy, too, like he'd just gotten off a long day at work. Since it was the start of most people's workday, he stood out. He caught my eye and smiled as if he recognized me.

He waved, then came into the store. "I know you," he said, still grinning.

"We've never met," I told him warily.

"No? Maybe you're right. But you're Hunter's little girl. And Tia's little protégé." I took a step back, narrowing my eyes. Anybody might know Hunter, might have heard him talk about me. He liked to do that sometimes. But nobody ordinary knew about Hunter *and* Tia.

"Who are you?" I asked as I activated my magical sight and waited for the wavering tangle of colored light to resolve into something meaningful. It usually took a while.

He chuckled, continuing on with his previous thought. "It's some trick juggling the two of them. Like oil and water, they are." He caught my narrowed eyes and added, "Oh, don't worry. I'm one of Tia's associates. Alastor. She ever mention me?"

Through the lens of the Sight, Alastor had a glow around his head and feet, but not the seven structural nodes that came with human blood. The radiance around his head flickered like a crown of fire, while the light at his feet shimmered like cracking ice. I relaxed marginally. "No, she hasn't."

His grin became a smirk. "Ah, well. I'll have to try harder to impress her. So what are you doing in Seattle today, Miss—Annalise, isn't it?"

I shrugged. "I'm getting a costume for Halloween. How about yourself?" I mentally told the dogs to meet me at a park nearby where the trail seemed likely to pass and wondered how to get rid of Tia's friend without offending him. Demons weren't as awful as my father's brethren, but if you annoyed them enough, they'd kill you with the consequences of your own desires.

Nod, pressed against the edges of my shadow, indicated his willingness to get out and cause a ruckus in the store; that'd be sure to send him off. I resisted the temptation.

"Oh, I'm keeping tabs on some of the consequences of the return of the exiles. You know how it is," he said, with a grimace that was meant to be good-natured and wasn't. He may have been Tia's "associate," but he had exactly the same kind of good old boy charm my father exuded like sweat. And I'd seen too many times how that particular kind of geniality could bend to include punishment.

"I know how it is, yeah." Backtalk earned a backhand with a tsk and a smile. No thanks. I snagged a copy of a teen magazine promising an interview with the explosively successful Keenan Cortice, as well as "30 costume ideas to make for under $20!" "Well, I have to get going. Nice meeting you."

His eyes tracked my hand. "Sure, yeah. Hey, can I give you a ride anywhere?"

"Uh, no. Thanks." I couldn't help rolling my eyes a little at his offer.

He noticed and chuckled again. "Just trying to be useful. Well, have a good day." And he kept watching me, the entire time it took me to buy the magazine and leave the store. It was just like being at home, and I was so happy to finally vanish into the crowds of pedestrians and escape his gaze.

I went to the park and sat down to flip through the magazine until the dogs arrived. I couldn't manage to summon up any interest in Keenan Cortice, though, despite his attractive smile and incredible hair. And I had only a little bit of interest in the Halloween costumes in the magazine. I had to find something, and ideally it would be something that pleased me and didn't annoy my father, which was a thin line to walk. Sometimes it was like part of me craved annoying him. But that never worked out so well. I could never stand up to him when push came to shove.

Instead, I watched the people wandering through the park. A lot of them were in costume, as if one day of Halloween wasn't enough. Most of them were older than me, college-aged or more. There were a few ghosts wandering around, too, although in cities, most ghosts preferred to come out at night. I'd never learned exactly why that was so, but it was true anyhow.

Rain spattered down and the living rapidly cleared out of the little park. Soon, it was just me and the ghosts. I watched a little old lady ghost trying and failing to pick up litter. She was spry now, and she didn't seem to notice her failure. Another ghost, a little boy, kicked an invisible ball, and I wanted to cry for both what he'd lost and what I'd never had.

Then Heart barked a greeting and I stood up and turned to my dogs. I might not have a soul, but I had them.

I brought Nod out of my shadow and he ran to meet Heart and Grim, then raced away and hid behind me as the other two jumped on me. The sprinkling rain stopped, but I was soaked anyhow, because Heart and Grim had brought half the lake with them. They could run on water, but they'd never figured out the trick of not getting wet. Or maybe they'd just never wanted to. And the mud from their paws never vanished when they did.

When they were done lavishing me with attention and dampness, I shucked water out of my clothes as best I could and ran my fingers through my hair. Then we went along the edge of the park and down the street. The Wild Huntsman Ion had passed this way, in the other world. We started climbing the hilltop neighborhood of Queen Anne. Heart thought his trail was getting stronger, which was exciting. Maybe he hadn't gone that far. Maybe he'd come back out of the Backworld again. Maybe, I thought hopefully, I could just deal with this right now.

We walked down an alley and turned left to follow a row of fences: the yards of some townhouses. The noise of the street faded to a dull roar as I strolled down the narrow pavement. Grim gamboled ahead of us, teasing some dogs in the fenced yards, while Heart had her nose to the ground and Nod flanked me.

As I was speculating on how exactly one dealt with the Wild Hunt, I heard a single footstep behind me. Just one, and it was odd because the dogs didn't seem to notice—

"Aw, Annalise," said Alastor, falling into step on my other side. "You said you were going shopping."

Startled, all three dogs burst into a cacophony of barking. Nod leapt forward and growled, low and deep. I stopped dead and Alastor took another few steps, then looked over his shoulder at me, his eyebrows raised inquisitively.

"You shouldn't startle my dogs," I told him mildly. "They don't like it." I should have known better than to expect anybody who knew my father's true nature to just want to chat with me.

He smiled. "You *should* have gone shopping. Instead you're heading into trouble. I can't let you do that." Turning, he braced his feet shoulder-width apart, waved a hand, and did *something*. A pulse of energy spread out through the ground. I could feel it tingling in my feet and the dogs whined and backed away. He looked down at both his hands and nodded. "All right. Expensive, but for the best. I can't say 'be a good girl' because you *are* your father's daughter, but do try to stay out of what doesn't concern you." Then, with a smug little smile at me, he vanished through the Curtain into the Backworld.

I frowned and instinctively set Nod to capture Alastor's trail on the other side of the Curtain. But he could find nothing. It was as if Alastor didn't have a scent, even a supernatural one that supernatural dogs could follow.

No.

Nothing had a scent, except me and the dogs. Slowly, achingly, the scent of the path and the yards nearby drifted close enough to pick up. But whatever Alastor had done had utterly destroyed the trail we were following. No matter how we ranged around, we couldn't find it. It was just *gone*.

-four-

I **retreated** to a coffee shop, fuming. Once I had my chai latte and my croissant and a chocolate doughnut for good measure, I slouched against a wall in the crowded courtyard while the dogs nosed around for crumbs. A table emptied out precipitously after Grim zeroed in on a timid dog-hater and I couldn't feel even a little guilt as I moved in to replace the previous tenant. There was no room for guilt; my irritation filled every nook and cranny.

I tried to sip my latte and calm down, but it just wouldn't do. So instead I called Tia to complain.

I got her voicemail, which made me snort rudely into the phone, and I complained anyhow. "Hi, Tia. I thought I'd help out like you asked, and I was tracking this guy we talked about when *wham*, your 'colleague' Alastor showed up and ruined the trail. That was great, I really appreciated it. So if you could let me know what you expect me to do now, that'd be good. Otherwise I might as well just go back home." I finished by telling her where I was, then, feeling a bit better, ate my croissant.

But I couldn't stop thinking about what Alastor had done. Why had he destroyed the trail? Had I offended him somehow? Was he working with my father directly?

Thinking of my father made me remember my excuse for coming to the city, and I realized I still needed to come up with a good costume. Luckily, I'd picked up a magazine full of ideas earlier. I spent a while flipping through it, but nothing jumped out at me as perfect.

Plenty of stuff that would amuse my father and please the pack—it's *easy* to dress to please them—but I hardly wanted to do that. I had to find something I'd enjoy wearing, even if only in secret. I spent some time toying with a Little Red Riding Hood With Secret Axe plan, but I couldn't figure out how to make the secret axe work, and without it I'd just be asking for trouble.

I was still hungry after finishing both of my snacks, so I went back to the counter for a ham and provolone sandwich. As I was settling back into my seat, Grim raised his head, his ears pricked forward, and I looked toward the courtyard entrance to see who he'd recognized.

The Korean boy who'd stopped to make sure I was okay the day before moved through the arch and stood to one side, scanning the seating area. He still wore the same big sunglasses, along with expensive clothes still so new they were stiff. He twiddled a big coin between the fingers of his left hand absently, and I knew when he'd seen me because he froze. Then he walked over and made as if to sit at my table all uninvited.

Heart, curled up in the chair he wanted to take, grumbled under her breath and threw me a look to determine if I was on board with this heinous speciesism. I indicated she could stay while I considered the boy. Even with the sunglasses, I could tell he was attractive, with a strong jaw and shoulders perfectly set off by his brown jacket.

Attractive men who tried to sit down without being invited were not my friends, especially not with the encounter with Alastor so fresh.

"My god, it's full of dogs," he said. When I didn't say anything—it didn't seem to need a response—he sighed. "Yeah, so I've got a couple of messages for you."

"From who?" I asked warily, stirring the dregs of my drink.

He ignored my question. "Message the first: Alastor is not trustworthy."

"No shit!" I snapped involuntarily.

The boy's mouth quirked up on one side. He was definitely pretty. "I'm not done. This guy Alastor, he's not trustworthy. Don't trust him. Also, he's an asshole and working for the other side. In conclusion: guy calls himself Alastor? Bad guy."

I gave the boy a flat, dubious look. "Right. And who sent you?"

"Lady by the name of Tia Zelaya. Possessed of a kind of peculiar sense of humor. She had another message, too."

I sighed, wondering why Tia couldn't have just called me. "Let's have it." And she had a second name? She'd never told me her second name.

His quirked mouth became a full-on grin. "Trust me."

I was already on edge, and that didn't help. Nod, under the table, came slinking out, his ears flat and only one curled lip away from a snarl. This guy smelled human, but... "Why? What are you?" I demanded.

His smile faded. "Come on, you're supposed to say, 'What's your name?' But since you ask, I'm a Scorpio. What are *you*?'"

"This isn't some kind of audition, pretty boy," I snapped, and turned on my Geometry sight to figure out what he was.

A moment later, I recoiled so hard that I knocked my chair over and fell backwards. "What *are* you?" I repeated, gaping from my sprawl on the ground. I knew how humans looked, and how demons looked, and how nephil halfbloods like me looked. Humans, ordinary humans, had seven magical nodes along their spine. Demons and other Fallen like my father had no nodes, but did have auras at their heads and feet. And halfbreeds, nephilim, like me, had both.

But I had *no idea* what this boy was. Far more than seven nodes clustered within his form and more bubbled off like foam in an overshaken soda. It was horrifyingly different than anything I'd seen before.

Others in the coffee shop courtyard stood up in concern as the boy flushed. "I'm Yejun. And Tia sent me to help you find what you told her you lost. I'm going to go wait outside while you get your shit together." And he did, vaulting the low fence around the courtyard and vanishing around the corner.

Somebody tried to help me to my feet, but Nod, already feeling protective, lunged between me and my potential assistant, growling. That put an end to that. Nobody likes the idea that they might be bitten for trying to help out.

"Thanks," I said, and, "Sorry," and I kept my head down so I didn't have to see how the friendly concern turned to distaste on the stranger's face. I tossed my trash and went out through the store entrance, stopping just outside to pull out my phone and glare at it. Without much hope of an answer, I dialed Tia again.

This time, she picked up. "What is the problem *now*, AT?"

"Hey," I said, injured, "I'm trying to help. Don't be like that."

"You have absolutely no concept of the scale of what's about to happen. I'm very invested in not wasting my time, so yes, thank you for your willingness to help, *what is the problem now*, AT?"

Stung—more than stung, really hurt—by the reference to wasting her time, I mumbled, "Did you send a really weird boy as a messenger?"

"Didn't he say?"

"Well... yes, although Alastor told me *he* was your friend, so you can see why I'm not sure about trusting *this* guy. Tia, what *is* he?"

"Why exactly is that important at this moment?"

"He's *weird*. And I looked at him magically and I've never seen anything like him."

I could practically hear her eyes roll. "Heaven save me from the fears of infants. AT, it doesn't matter in the slightest, but he is human. And I did send him and he will help you. Please go carry on the good work, because time is running short. I'll be seeing you soon."

And before I could say anything else, she hung up on me.

Grim peeked around the wall to where the boy lounged. His tail wagged slowly, and then he sidled around the corner to go make friends. "Hey!" I called after him, but he ignored me. Heart licked my hand encouragingly instead, and then Nod butted me from behind.

I stood there for a moment, thinking about those bubbling nodes. I understood seven. I had seven. Everybody I knew except my father and Tia had seven. This Yejun had so many more, and they moved and changed and it *bothered* me. It scared me. I didn't know how to deal with it.

On the other hand, before I'd looked at him magically, he'd just seemed like a young man. Annoying, too attractive, but not anything I wasn't capable of facing. Maybe I could just... not think about those bubbles. And never, ever activate the Geometry sight around him.

It wasn't like I used it all the time anyhow. Between the dogs and my own nose, I could get almost as much information from a scent.

That settled, I went around the corner to where Yejun was crouched down near the wall making friends with Grim. Without looking up at me, he asked, "What's his name?"

"Grim," I said. Grim lolled his tongue out at his name, looking very smug.

Yejun scratched behind his ears and looked up in my direction as if surprised. "Grim? He doesn't look very grim. He looks like a big puppy."

I shrugged. "When I was little, I thought 'grim' meant grey. It's a grim, grey day, that sort of thing. So... you said you could help me?"

He didn't answer, concentrating on the itchy spot between Grim's shoulder blades, and I wondered uneasily if he was offended by my earlier reaction. But if he was mad at me, why was he petting my dog?

I shifted my weight uncomfortably and waited. After a moment, Yejun seemed to come to some sort of decision. He gave Grim one final pat and stood up. "Come on," he said, and started walking up the sidewalk, heading for less trafficked streets.

I caught up with him and the dogs trailed behind. "Where are we going?"

"The hotel we used to be staying at."

"We? Who are you?"

His head turned toward me. I already hated his sunglasses and the way they hid half of his expression as he said, "You're big on asking questions that I've already answered, aren't you?"

I wanted to kick him in the shin. "Who's the 'we' that stayed at this hotel?"

"Sen and Jen and Cat and me." He said the list of names sing-song, like he was reciting a nursery rhyme.

"Okay..." I said, encouraging him to go on.

"What, you want more? Sen was a nephil wizard. Jen was her assistant. I don't know what Cat is. And I'm their brown-eyed problem child." He slid his hands in his pockets as he walked.

I thought for a moment. "Is Sen the person who is working on solving the Wild Hunt problem? Tia and the ghosts said there was somebody."

"She was, yup. She had a big plan to reboot the Hunt and sort everything out." His voice was bright, almost chipper.

"Are we going to see her?"

"In a manner of speaking. Left here."

I peeked at him from the side, wondered if I should stop talking, and couldn't. "Are they your family?"

He laughed unpleasantly. "That would have been cool. But no. Not at all." Changing the subject, he asked, "So how did you end up with all these dogs?"

I didn't want to talk about that to a stranger, so I only said, "They started out as strays," then let the silence draw itself out for a while.

He came to a halt. "Here we are." We stood in front of a convenience store, but across the street was a burnt-out motel. Half of it was cinders and fallen struts and the other half was blackened and stinking from both the fire and the stuff they used to put the fire out. Tape and cones warned people away, but a couple of homeless men were picking through the ruins anyhow. One of them held a smudged pillow and wore a singed, smoke-stained bathrobe. "Tia seems to think this is all you'll need to get back to work." He didn't sound like he believed her.

I frowned. "Did it burn down while you were staying here?"

"Oh yeah," he assured me, and there was an acrid note in his voice.

I put two and two together. "What was Sen doing when she died?"

He lowered his sunglasses to look at me, his eyebrows high with surprise and his brown eyes glittering. "She was summoning a demon called Alastor. She thought he might be helpful with her big spell. He wasn't. Sen died. Jen barely survived."

That hit me like a blow. "Really a bad guy," I whispered, then flinched in anticipation of him mocking me again.

But he only nodded and pushed his sunglasses back up. "I wonder why he didn't set you on fire, too, if you're doing the same chore."

"Probably because my father wouldn't have liked that at all," I muttered, reaching out to pull my dogs close. They crowded around my legs, no more eager than I was to go poke around in the burned-out hulk.

Yejun didn't bother trying to hide the sneer in his voice when he said, "Daddy's little princess, huh? That's cool. Too bad Sen didn't have anything like that."

Shame squeezed my chest and stole my breath away. I hunched my shoulders forward and fought against the desire to run away. "Sorry," I managed, then rushed on, looking for any change of subject. "What are you guys doing now?"

He shrugged. "Cat's taking care of Jen. I'm thinking about moving on, myself. Sen was going to teach me, but that plan kind of got barbecued."

How could he be so cold? "Why don't you do that, then?" If there was hostility in my voice, it came from the same place as the shame.

He shrugged and said, "They're good people," missing my point entirely. "Haven't quite decided yet."

I shook my head and walked across the street. Nod and Heart came with me, but Grim lingered at Yejun's side until I turned back to look at him sternly. Yejun scratched his ears absently, frowning after me.

I snapped my fingers at Grim and he wagged his tail slowly in my direction without lifting one paw to join me.

"Grim!" I called. I didn't look at Yejun. I did my best to pretend he'd already left. After a few seconds, he lifted his hand from Grim's ears.

"Oh," he said, as he understood what I'd meant. Then he said, "Fine. Good luck finding what you're looking for," like he wished no such thing. Grim's ears flattened. Finally, as Yejun turned and walked back the way we came, Grim joined me on the other side of the street.

I watched Yejun walk away. He was insensitive and weird and disturbing, so I wasn't sure why. I found myself wishing he'd been nicer so I hadn't gotten upset and told him to go away. It had been a long time since I'd had that much of a conversation with somebody who was both around my own age and reasonably clued in about the secret powers of the world.

It was for the best, I told myself sternly. Hanging around me being nice wasn't a position with good benefits. The health care in particular was downright backward. And I thought of Emily and cringed at myself, and at my ridiculous desire that Yejun had stayed. I wish I'd been able to see his eyes more than that brief glimpse over his sunglasses.

Grim licked my hand and I pulled myself together. Heart and Nod were already nosing around the ruins. The ragged men picking through the wreckage watched me warily. Or, rather, they watched the dogs warily. I liked having all three dogs with me when I was in places like this. Even one dog discouraged uninvited attention, while three told everybody that I was a downright troublesome target. Not harassing me was always better for everybody. But I made a point of showing the scavengers I was ignoring them because, hell, more power to them for taking what they needed before it was all carted away to a dump.

The scent of the fire was completely overpowering, even after a few days. If the trail I'd lost really was to be recovered here somehow—and I was a little confused about that, to be honest—the dogs would need my help. So I perched on a fallen beam and called Nod to curl up at my feet as Grim and Heart spread out to investigate.

With Nod close enough to keep an eye on things, I closed my eyes and let my awareness merge with Heart's. It was simple enough, but it always made me slow and inattentive and weak. If somebody walked up to me, I might not notice. But Nod would.

Heart sniffed around the ashes, distinguishing between the ashes of wool and wood, avoiding pools of plastic slag and stepping delicately around broken concrete and metal pipes. Those were all mundane smells, not what we were looking for. She could smell people: the various firefighters and fire inspectors and the hotel guests and when we really concentrated, she could smell the fear and frustration of the hotel staff. Stuff like that lingered, especially when you were as sensitive to emotions as Heart was.

She followed the scents to the place where the fire began, where there was nothing left but cinders and cracked, pitted concrete, and there we paused. Another nephil had died there. Someone like me. And nothing was left behind but ashes and somebody else's memories. And Yejun's bad jokes.

Heart could smell helplessness, desperation, frustration. Hope. The scents painted an emotional portrait of a woman reaching out for something that betrayed her, destroyed her, and of a last furious burst of magic as the nephil woman died. And nearby, from somebody else: fear, pain, horror, guilt. That didn't seem like the emotional profile of a hunter, even with the guilt.

But she couldn't find anything else. With a whine, she curled up where the nephil wizard had died, and I switched my focus to Grim. He licked Heart's nose, then moved away from her to stick his nose through the Curtain between worlds. The stink of the demon Alastor was much easier for him to pick up. As for anybody else supernatural—

Nod chuffed a warning and Heart turned her head to look toward me. I released my focus on Grim and started paying attention to my immediate vicinity again.

The scavengers were gone, and it was easy to see why. Tia stood at the edge of the lot, her hands on her hips, and she was angry enough to frighten anyone.

-five-

I **stared** at Tia warily, wondering what she was mad about now. That was so distracting that it took me a minute before I realized she wasn't alone. A girl who looked about thirteen stood beside her. She wore knee-length canvas shorts and a Gravity's Angels band t-shirt, with a hefty camera bag slung over one shoulder. Light brown hair bobbed around her elfin face and she held onto Tia's short jacket with one hand. Her eyes were bright with wonder.

She looked around as if she couldn't believe what she was seeing. "That was far out!"

"Where's Yejun?" Tia inquired, then held out her hand, palm up, as Nod came over to greet her.

"He left," I said, because if a demon asked you a question with an obvious answer, it wasn't wise to just ignore it. "I'm not sure what I'm supposed to—hey!" I changed verbal direction suddenly as I got close enough to notice the change in Tia's scent. "What happened to you?"

Tia pulled her hand back from Nod instinctively, then returned to petting his ears. "What do you mean?" Jealous, Heart and Grim gave up investigating the possible trails and came over to try and crowd Nod out of the way.

I sniffed. "You smell different. Is that a new body?"

"Whoa, what?" demanded the new girl. She eyed the three dogs jockeying for Tia's attention as if she wasn't quite sure about them.

Tia glanced at the girl, then said carefully, "This is a resource-intensive project. Resources get consumed."

I bit my lip. "Are you all right?"

"Must we discuss this now? I think there's enough on the table already." She stopped petting Nod and waved her hand at the other dogs dismissively. I could feel the faint tingle of energy she sent at them to encourage them to go back to work.

I shrugged. Of course she was all right. She was a demon. "Fine. As I was saying, I'm not sure what I'm supposed to do here. Even if I can track down the Huntsman's scent, this is a few days old. It'll just end up going to where your not-a-friend blew up the trail. I'm not going to find him this way."

"Oh no. You're not trying to find *him*," Tia said. "Do your best to never encounter him. I want you to find where he came from. In the home of the Wild Hunt, there's a horn. It holds the heart of the Hunt. That's what we need. Didn't I say?"

I narrowed my eyes at her. "No. You didn't. You didn't tell me anything. I had to get my instructions from a ghost."

"Ghosts have a unique perspective," Tia said calmly. "They're certainly better at persuading you."

Sighing, I said, "You want me to follow an aging trail *backwards*? And through the other world?"

She tilted her head and raised one eyebrow at me. "Are you going to tell me you can't?"

I thought about it. "I guess not. It'll be hard work, though." I realized that the girl Tia had brought was staring at me, her wide-eyed wonder faded away. "Who's this?" I asked.

Tia put her hand on the girl's back and gave her a gentle shove forward. "This is Brynn. She'll be going with you on your trip."

"What?" I demanded.

With a faint smile, Tia said, "It's dangerous to go alone. I'd hoped you'd have the sense to keep Yejun, but—" She opened her hand as if releasing a fading dream. "And now I must go have another chat with Alastor. Work fast, children. Halloween is coming and the Wild Hunt rides after."

Then, while I sputtered for an argument, she stepped backward through the Curtain and vanished.

I almost went after her to start the argument, but something about the way Brynn stared at me made me stop. It was definitely wrong to abandon a kid in the middle of a city without at least making sure she had the resources to take care of herself.

"Are you from around here?" I asked, silently summoning all three of my dogs to me. The girl had a light, fresh, and definitely human scent.

Brynn looked around. "Uh, no. I don't think so. Ms. Zalaya said you—said we were going to Seattle? I'm from LA. She took me through this hole in the world and into this room full of mirrors and then we stepped out here."

Ms. Zelaya, I thought. "How do you know her?"

"Oh, she's my substitute teacher sometimes," Brynn said airily. "She needed a helper and I volunteered."

I gazed at the other girl in consternation, then switched on my magical sight to try and understand *why* Tia had thought this was a good idea. And... I couldn't tell. The girl had all seven nodes filled with complex charms, but I would have been more shocked if anybody hanging out with Tia hadn't had that basic magical grounding. But she definitely wasn't a nephil, and she wasn't some kind of prodigy human wizard—you can spot wizards by the eighth and ninth nodes on the palms—and she wasn't a freak like Yejun. She was just an ordinary human girl, who Tia had dragged from LA to Seattle and deposited on me.

"What does she want you to do?" I asked at last.

Brynn shrugged. "Help out." She dropped her camera bag on the ground and started rummaging through it. "Shoot, we left in such a hurry that I forgot my cellphone. Do you have one I can borrow? I ought to make sure my family won't worry while I'm here."

My hand went to my pocket where my phone was, but I didn't give it to her right away. "She wants you to help me find the Huntsman?"

"The Huntsman's horn," Brynn corrected. "No phone? I can find a prepaid somewhere, I guess." She gave me a friendly smile and rose to her feet again.

"How old are you?" I demanded. Brynn's smile made me feel irrational and a little panicky. She was being friendly. Emily had been friendly, too, and about the same age. "Do you know you're standing in the place where somebody was killed for trying to find this damn horn? This is a dangerous situation. Your family *should* worry." *You should go back to them.*

Brynn looked down at her feet, but I could smell her mood shifting from excitement to nervousness. "Creepy. And I'm fourteen. How old are *you*?"

"Seventeen," I said, which was close enough to true.

"No way! Really?" She was more bothered by this revelation than by the idea that she stood in a woman's ashes, which I thought was particularly unfair. "You look like you're my age. Barely."

"I'm not. Look," I said irritably. "You're too young to be involved in this. It really is dangerous, honest. Your family would be upset if something happened to you. You don't want to do that to them."

She blinked at me owlishly. "Would yours?"

I stared at her. "Why would you ask a question like that?"

"It seems fair." She looked around, then held out her fingers to Nod like Tia had done before her. Grim lolled out his tongue, then darted forward to lick her hand. "Nah, I think I'll stay for now. This magic Tia has been telling me about sounds pretty rad and you look like you could use some company."

"I have plenty of company," I protested, waving my hands at my dogs.

"Human company," Brynn clarified patiently. She patted Grim cautiously on the head, like somebody without a lot of experience with dogs.

"Hah," I said. "That's exactly what I don't need." Then, realizing I'd said that aloud and hoping to avoid questions, I rushed on. "So did Tia say exactly how you were supposed to help me? Because I'm not even really sure I need help, honestly."

Brynn shrugged. "She put some magic on me, but I'm not quite sure what it does. She said I'd figure it out when it was ready."

"Hmm," I said. I wasn't convinced. But I turned away and went to where Heart and Grim had tracked down the scent of Alastor—and, much more faintly under it, the scent of the Huntsman. I concentrated until it filled my nose and I had a sense of the direction both entities had come from.

"You can really smell magic? That's so cool." Brynn stood right beside me. I hadn't noticed her coming over and my dogs had decided they liked her, obnoxious beasts. She smiled at me when I met her gaze and held out her hand. "That wasn't really an introduction earlier. I'm Brynn."

"I'm AT," I said. I didn't take her hand, though. It wasn't her. I didn't like to have people touch my hands. It brought up bad memories.

Brynn noticed, but she misunderstood. A flash of hurt sparkled in her eyes, but she only sighed and brought forth another smile, this one wry. "So where do we go from here?"

I thought about that for a minute. I knew where I had to go, but where *she* had to go seemed like a very different matter. She was going to be a liability in the Backworld, and if my father found out she'd been trying to befriend me—

Just the thought made my insides curl with dread. But getting rid of her wasn't as easy as just stepping into the Backworld and leaving her behind. That was irresponsible and would make Tia even angrier with me. But she clearly wouldn't take a hint, like Yejun had. I missed his belated good sense already.

Yejun had said the people he was staying with were good people, those who had survived Alastor's arson. And this Wild Hunt thing had originated with them. Possibly they were still involved. Maybe it was time to introduce myself.

Responding to my thought, Grim darted across the street and found Yejun's scent. "This way," I said, and followed him.

A moment later, Brynn caught up with me. "We're not going to the magic world?" She sounded disappointed.

"Uh, no, not yet." I wondered what Tia had told her. But before I could figure out how to ask, the wind gusted and I caught another scent, one that made my fists clench.

Animal musk, grocery store body spray, cinnamon breath mints. Not too close, but coming up behind us. Scott, my father's newest wolf.

I swore under my breath. I'd really hoped my father had unmade him after last night's game, but I should have known better. I had no idea if he was tracking me on his own or as assigned by my father, but it didn't matter. Anything he saw would eventually make its way back to his master.

"Let's walk faster," I suggested to Brynn. "Really fast."

"What's wrong?" she said, but she broke into a skipping sort of jog alongside me.

"There's somebody I don't want to meet behind us. If he notices us—" *you*— "there could be trouble."

Nod dropped back on his own and I realized he was going to decoy Scott away from our trail. I wasn't really excited about that, either, but Nod was sometimes hard to stop when he got an idea into his head. This was one of those times and all I could do was silently insist that Nod only let Scott glimpse him, that Nod was not to confront my father's wolf. And if that didn't work—well, there was more we could do.

"Let's try to lose him," I told Brynn, dragging her by her shirt inside a bath products store. Grim and Heart kept following Yejun's trail. They'd find him and I'd find them. It would all work out. And splitting up like this would make Scott even less likely to notice Brynn's scent, I hoped.

I pulled Brynn over to a samples display full of body sprays and miniature bath bombs beside little bowls of water. "Ooh," she said as I started spraying her liberally with everything I could get my hands on. That sort of thing wouldn't stop me and my dogs, but my father's wolves weren't nearly as talented—especially somebody who had been a mortal man until the day before yesterday.

Brynn held out a wrist for something green and said, "Is this hiding out or just fun?"

"I don't want him to smell you," I said. "He's good with his nose like me, and he's not my friend. Yesterday I had to break his arm."

"Whoa," said Brynn, her eyes widening.

My phone rang, the special tone I'd set for calls from my father. I froze, then fumbled the phone out and stared at it.

I didn't want to answer it, but I knew I should, or I'd be in trouble later. But if I did, he'd ask what I was doing, who I was with. He'd order me to come home. My hand trembled.

"Hey, you *do* have a cellphone," accused Brynn, and my paralysis broke.

I dropped the still-ringing phone into one of the bowls of water, then dropped one of the tiny bath bombs in after it. The phone halfrang one more time, a drowned sound that ended with a fizz as the bath bomb bubbled over.

I looked up and met Brynn's shocked gaze. "It's broken," I said, as calmly as I could.

Hesitantly, she said, "Sometimes... you can... dry them out?"

I unscrewed the lid of a bath oil tester and poured the whole thing into the phone's watery grave. "Maybe," I agreed. I swished around the mixture with my fingers. It mostly smelled like lavender.

A store employee came over. "Hey, what are you doing?"

"Just had a little accident," I said, snatching my phone out of the bowl. "My bad. Come on, let's go." I rushed past the annoyed employee and out the other door of the store. It opened onto a shopping arcade decorated for Halloween, with orange pumpkins and straw-stuffed scarecrows dressed in flannel. Another costume store was across the way, and I told myself I really had to make sure to come home with something good. Maybe I could offset my father's anger about my phone that way. In fact, I knew exactly what I could pick to please him, and I found myself scoping out the display to see if I could find the right costume now.

"So what was that about?" said Brynn. Her voice was light, but I could tell she was bothered again.

I shook myself out of my costume thoughts. "I didn't want to answer it. And it would have been dangerous for you to use it." I was acting like a crazy person, I knew. The sooner I got rid of her, the sooner I could get back to pretending I was normal.

"I have to check on something," I added, and leaned against a concrete column. When I reached out for Nod, I found him a few blocks away. He and Scott had made eye contact, but Scott hadn't taken the bait. On the other hand, he hadn't yet entered the bath store, either. And Grim and Heart had found Yejun's new lodgings.

I opened my eyes to see Brynn regarding me worriedly. "It's okay," I told her, more out of hope than certainty.

"I don't really understand what's going on," she confessed, while still looking at me as if she expected me to fall over suddenly.

"Of course you don't. You're just—" I caught myself and shook my head. "Let's get moving. I don't really understand what's going on either. There's this Wild Hunt and they're dangerous to ghosts—I saw that myself. And these people we're going to see can maybe do something about that, but I have no idea why Tia brought an ordinary human into this mess."

Brynn frowned and stopped. "People? I thought we were going to find a horn. Ms. Zelaya said you were supposed to find a horn." She gave me a suspicious look. "You know, you haven't tried to convince me to leave you alone for fifteen minutes at least. Are you trying to trick me or something?" I kept walking and she ran to catch up after a minute. "Well?"

I shrugged. "I'm not very good at tricks, obviously. And I *am* going to find the horn, as soon as I make sure you're safe."

"I didn't come out here to be safe," she said angrily. "Ms. Zelaya *did* warn me it was going to be dangerous, even if she didn't mention walking in the ashes of burnt-up people. And I'm not going to just stroll along with you while you take me to some kind of witchy babysitter."

"If you want to split up now, that'd probably be good, too," I suggested. "There's a cellphone kiosk right there."

She ran her fingers through her hair. "Oh my god, you are so infuriating. Tia was *right*."

That stung, but I just kept walking. And she just kept following me, which I didn't mind as much as I thought I should. It was better, I told myself, to leave her someplace safe. Surely wherever Yejun's friends were staying now would be safe. Safer.

We went down the arcade and out onto a busy street in the middle of downtown. Skyscrapers towered around us. Two blocks away, Heart sat outside the main entrance of the Four Seasons hotel while Grim cadged snacks from a bellhop nearby. As we approached, Nod trotted up from the other direction, his head down and his ears flat with irritation. If I'd given him free rein, he would have bitten Scott, just to make him angry. As it was, we'd both lost track of Scott when Nod had left him slowly circling the shopping arcade.

I looked at the hotel for a moment. It was an expensive-looking place, a far cry from the motel that had burned down. It seemed like the kind of place likely to not notice the dogs of a guest but make a fuss over mine. So I called all three of them to me and sent them to pace me just on the other side of the Curtain. They were still close enough to appear at a moment's notice and I wouldn't even have to summon them if something went wrong. And Grim still had Yejun's trail.

"Wow," said Brynn. "Where did they go?"

"They're around," I said vaguely. "Come on."

She hung back reluctantly until I went through the glass doors into the lobby. Then she caught up with me. "So we're here to get some information about our quest?" She sounded too innocent.

"Sure." I glanced at her.

"But not to leave me with a witchy babysitter."

I shrugged. After looking around the lobby for a moment, I headed to the bank of elevators.

"I'm too old for a babysitter," Brynn pointed out. "And I'll just track you down again. Somehow. Ms. Zelaya wanted me to help you."

"Well, hush," I said mildly as we found an open elevator. "I need to concentrate to figure out what room this guy is staying in." And I stared at the bank of elevator buttons, trying to transform Grim's tracking input into a floor.

But before I could decide on a button to push, the elevator doors slid closed and it started moving. At first I thought somebody had called it from a higher floor and decided to just go with it. Then I realized that Brynn was staring at the row of numbers above the door, her face pale. With a start, I realized that no call lights were lit up. Then I noticed the tendrils of magic wrapped around the elevator. I had no idea where the elevator was going, but it wasn't going there naturally.

-six-

The elevator traveled smoothly; without the floor display working, I couldn't tell how high we were going, but the trip was long enough that I assumed it was all the way to the top. I had just started to worry about what to do if it got to the top and then plummeted down again when the elevator slowed, then halted. The door slid open.

Yejun stood on the other side, without his sunglasses. His hair was rumpled and his face looked drawn. He was angry, I realized, and I remembered too late that I'd driven him off before. I hadn't wanted him around, and now I'd chased him down.

My face grew warm and I wondered if I should start with an apology. But before I could say anything, he demanded, "What do you want?"

A witchy babysitter, I almost said, and bit my lip instead.

Brynn, though, stepped out of the elevator. "That was really weird. I think that elevator's broken," she told Yejun. "You should probably wait for a different one."

Yejun glanced at Brynn, then did a double-take, his eyes narrowing as he looked her up and down. Then he said, "Both of you might as well come meet Cat and Jen," and started walking down the hall.

"Oh," said Brynn. "Is he who we came to see? I was expecting somebody older."

Mutely, I shrugged and followed him.

We walked all the way to the corner of the hotel, where Yejun opened the door into a sumptuous suite. A fortyish woman with silver-streaked black hair sat on a plush couch, her legs tucked beneath her and her gaze focused on the middle distance. Nearby, sitting at a table covered in old books, was a gorgeous young man about Yejun's age, with long golden-blond hair and small round glasses. The woman didn't respond to our entrance, but the man glanced up and offered a faint, welcoming smile.

"Tia's other friends, I take it?" He had a beautiful voice, too, honed like he'd spent time in a drama club. There was something familiar about it, but I couldn't identify what it was.

Yejun threw himself into an armchair the size of a loveseat and jammed his hands into his pockets. "I guess so."

Brynn scowled at both Cat and Yejun while pressing close to my side, as if she thought they were going to haul her physically away from me. I hoped it wouldn't come to that, but first things first. I cleared my throat. "I'm supposed to be tracking down the horn of the Wild Hunt, but I thought I'd stop by and introduce myself first. Among other things." The woman on the couch turned her head toward me, although her gaze remained focused on something far away.

"Actually, it's just introductions," said Brynn. "I'm Brynn, AT's helper. Who are you guys?"

Cat arched one perfect eyebrow. "I'm Cat. This is Jennifer Cole, and Yejun you've met already. We're what's left of Ascensción Flores's mission to solve the ghost hunter problem."

I looked around. "Are you safe here? This isn't the sort of place I expected to find you after looking at what was left of your previous digs."

"As safe as we'd be anywhere," said Yejun darkly.

Cat's mouth thinned into a grim line. "The one who slew Sen isn't the sort to waste energy on trifles, not these days. As far as he knows, our ability to interfere with the Wild Hunt has been nullified, so there's no reason for him to bother us and no reason for us to hide."

"And I was tired of shitty motels," Yejun added. He fidgeted with the pocket zipper on his black cargo pants.

I fidgeted with my hands behind my back myself. It wasn't comfortable in that room. There was something off about silent, dreamy-eyed Jennifer Cole, and Brynn looked like she wanted to punch everybody and run away, and Yejun kept glaring at me, and Cat in his round glasses was far, far too beautiful. I really, *really* wished I hadn't come. Brynn wasn't that much trouble, was she? "Is he right? About your ability to, uh, interfere?"

"Yes," said Yejun, at the same time that Cat said, "Not as right as he'd like to be."

They looked at each other, then Cat went on. "I think we can still do something. Actually, I think we *have* to do something. But it's become a great deal more complicated."

"What's up with her?" asked Brynn, pointing with her chin at Jennifer. "Is she sick?"

Once again, the two boys glanced at each other. Then Cat said, "That's one of the complications."

"Hah," snorted Yejun, sinking back into the armchair so deeply it seemed like he was trying to vanish.

She must have realized we were talking about her, because Jennifer slowly focused on me. "It's you. Our promised tracker. May I see your dogs?"

Without speaking, I waved my hand to draw them through the Curtain. They burst through barking and dancing around—well, mostly that was Grim, but he more than made up for the better manners of the other two. No matter how you look at it, three supernatural dogs really add to a room's atmosphere.

Heart went to Jennifer immediately, while Grim frisked over to Yejun and Nod pressed against my leg. Jennifer put her hand out and Heart sniffed it politely before sitting down to gaze up at the strange human wizard.

Cat, who had risen to his feet when the dogs tumbled through the Curtain, came around his table and knelt down. He scrutinized each dog, his eyes soft behind his wire-rimmed glasses. "Amazing," he said. "A manifestation of your intrinsic magic?"

"Kind of." I shrugged, self-conscious, then did a double-take as I actually thought about what he'd asked. He looked barely older than Yejun, but he was far more assured, and he seemed to know a whole bunch more about nephil magic. He didn't *smell* like a nephil, or even like a wizard, but both of those traces can be disguised. I wanted to look at him with the Geometry vision—it mattered to me whether he was a really old nephil or a young but clever human—but I didn't dare while Yejun was around. His massive network of nodes would be all I'd be able to see.

"Amazing," Cat said again. "I wouldn't have expected it in—in your father's daughter." He waved his fingers at Nod, who ignored him. My poor feral puppy was still irritated about how the encounter with Scott had failed to play out and he wasn't interested in meeting new people at the moment.

I summed this up for Cat with, "He's shy."

Cat nodded and stood up again. "I think they can do it, Jennifer. It's not over." She didn't respond, staring down into Heart's brown eyes. Cat grimaced and said, in a different, more cajoling tone, "Sen's dream can still be realized."

That got her attention. She ran her hands down the front of her jeans, then twisted her hands together. "I need to do that. It was her last wish. If we can get the horn and use your knife, then I can—" She stared down at her hands, then glanced up at me. Her eyes were a vivid, intense blue, shadowed with a grief I recognized. "I never thought I'd outlive her, you know. It seems... wrong. She should have still been vibrant when I was only bones." She sighed and stood up. "I'm sorry, AT. I used to be more focused, but my mind seems far away these days. She taught me everything I know..." She focused on Brynn. "And who's this? Tia mentioned you and your dogs, but—"

"I'm Brynn," my companion said, then rushed on, establishing her credentials early. "Ms. Zelaya—uh, Tia?—she brought me up here to help AT out."

Yejun, scratching behind Grim's ears with both hands, snorted. "Babies, both of you. We're doomed."

"She's older than she looks," Brynn told Yejun archly.

Cat gave him a look of mild disapproval. "Children they may be, but we can't give up."

"Things are a bit weird with Jen, but—" began Yejun, half-rising from his chair.

"Jen can't give up. And neither can I," countered Cat calmly, crossing his arms. "So these kids—"

"Yo, maybe I'm wrong, but it looks to me like the only adult present is this lady," interjected Brynn. "Maybe instead of having this manly men argument over the girlchildren's heads, you could actually talk to us."

I gaped at Brynn for a moment before catching myself and snapping my jaw closed. Yejun and Cat were staring at her, too, so I added, "Yeah. What she said."

"Actually, wait. Carry on your chest-beating while I make a call," Brynn said. "If I don't tell my family *something*, there will be new problems." She looked around, then added, "Somebody give me a phone."

Silently, Yejun pulled his phone out of his pocket and tossed it to her before sinking back into his chair again. She caught it, said, "Thanks," and went to stand by the window on the other side of the room.

Jennifer's gaze followed Brynn as she said, "I *miss* Sen. She would have—" She stopped and shook her head. "Is there some way we can help you with your task?"

I bit my lip, then moved closer to Cat and Jen and lowered my voice. "I don't know why Tia wants her to come with me. It's not safe for her to be around me, and it's not safe in the other world, either, and that's where this trail leads." I felt Brynn's eyes on me from across the room, accusing, but I ignored them. She had a family that loved her. And she was human. "Maybe she could stay here? If you guys think you're even a little bit safe right now, that'd be better than where I'm going."

Cat's gaze went from Jennifer to Yejun, then he said, "Does she want to stay here?"

"No!" called Brynn, then returned to her conversation.

Cat shrugged. "We're not equipped to keep her against her will." His gaze went to Yejun again and I knew that he wasn't entirely telling me the truth.

"It's not really safe," said Jennifer quietly. "I'm—"

Nod started to growl. "Hold on," I said, grabbing hold of his ruff and reaching out to discover whatever was bothering him. It wasn't hard to determine: Scott had tracked us down. Nod could sense him at the base of the building, chatting with the bellhop as he smoked a cigarette.

"Shh," I told Nod. "We have to learn to ignore him." I glanced up and realized how tense the residents of the suite were. "Just a pest," I told them reassuringly. "Nod is still sensitized to him. It's nobody you have to worry about."

Cat's fingers, white-knuckled on the chair back he was holding, slowly relaxed. Jennifer's gaze had gone faraway again, while Yejun was leaning forward in his chair, staring at me like I was a strange beast.

"Somebody *you* have to worry about, though?" Cat saw a little too much.

I shook my head firmly. "Nope. Although it's one of the reasons I wish Brynn would stay here."

As if in response, Brynn finished her call and came back to the group, toying with Yejun's phone. "All right, I think I've got a couple of days before my sister manages to get up here. I hope we're done by then or all hell will break loose."

"In more ways than an irate big sister," Yejun muttered.

Obliviously, Brynn went on, her voice higher-pitched than usual. "I'm trying to decide if I should text my girlfriend, too, so she doesn't worry. The thing is, she's going to be so jealous. She's such a ghost freak." She slid a sidelong glance at me, her cheeks pink.

Cat said, "*You* have a *girlfriend?*"

Brynn gave him a scornful look. "Yes. You have a problem with that?"

Raising both hands, Cat stepped backward. "No, no. I was just surprised. You're so—" Wisely, he shut his mouth.

"Hah," scoffed Brynn, then started working Yejun's phone with a vengeance. "I'm probably the only one here with a girlfriend, too."

"Actually," said Yejun, looking uncomfortable. "About that—" And he looked at Jennifer, who had tears in her eyes, and smelled of such terrible grief.

"Be quiet, Yejun," said Cat sharply.

"It doesn't matter," said Jennifer, and there was something odd about her voice, as if it came from a deep well.

Cat went over to her and touched her hair with the back of his hand before moving to gather her in his arms. She pushed at him blindly. "No, stay away from me—it was you. If I hadn't been thinking about you—" Her hair floated in a wind I didn't feel and red and black lights twinkled on her limbs. She pushed Cat hard, hard enough that he staggered backward.

The dogs started whining. I could smell smoke, and fire, and the crisping of flesh. Blackness crept out from the shadows of the room.

Yejun said, "Oh, hell, not again," but he stared at Jennifer like he was watching a replay of his world ending.

Cat straightened and stood quietly, watching Jennifer's form shift subtly. "As you can see, it's not safe here, either. Yejun, get them out of here. Help them. Once she calms down, we'll be in touch."

All at once, I knew what was happening to Jennifer. I didn't know how it was possible; she smelled alive, but she was manifesting a haunt, where the dreams and delusions of a ghost became real and dangerous.

"What if *he* shows up again?" demanded Yejun. "He shows up when she's like this and you're alone, it's all over."

"Just go!" For the first time since we'd arrived, I saw a crack in Cat's calm façade.

Yejun shook his head, glanced at me, and headed out the door. Brynn ran after him. I watched, my skin prickling, as Cat calmed himself. Then, as red apples glimmered on the black trees tracing out cracks in the finely wallpapered walls, I sent my dogs back into my shadow and backed out of the room, leaving Cat and Jennifer to whatever awaited them.

-seven-

The elevator stayed open at the far end of the hall, waiting for me. As soon as I stepped inside, the doors slid closed. Yejun slouched against the opposite wall, wearing his sunglasses again. Brynn stood in the corner of the elevator, so stiff she was practically trembling.

"Relax a little," I told her as the elevator descended. "I guess I'm taking you with me." I could, I thought, set the dogs to look after her. And if anything too catastrophic happened to me—well, it probably wasn't good for her in the long term no matter what I did.

Not a comforting thought, really.

"Of course you are," she burst out. "But what in the world was happening back there? I didn't mean anything—I was just teasing—" she faltered to a stop, looking between Yejun and me.

The elevator stopped, but the door didn't open. Yejun tapped his fingers together. "Jen's still coming to terms with what happened."

"Which was, surprise! *Dying*?" I asked sharply. "I know ghosts. My *mother* is a ghost. She was manifesting a haunt."

Yejun shrugged. "She look dead to you?"

I thought of her faraway gaze. "Sometimes. But she definitely had a physical body. How is that possible?"

The elevator started moving down again. "How should I know? Nobody ever bothered teaching me anything." The elevator sped up and then stopped so abruptly Brynn stumbled into me. I caught and righted her as the doors slid open onto the hotel lobby. As Yejun passed through them, he said over his shoulder, "Cat says that Sen did something with her celestial magic that's keeping Jen going for now."

I went after him, then stopped as he flopped onto one of the lobby couches, leaning his head back on the cushion like he was planning on taking a nap. Brynn went past me and stood halfway between us. "So, she's like... undead? A zombie?"

Yejun put his feet up on the coffee table. "She doesn't crave brains or anything. Though hers doesn't work right anymore. She can't read now."

"Ghosts can't," I said quietly. "It's hard for them to learn anything new without a body. They *can* if it's repeated enough, but—" I thought of trying to teach my mother that I was back again and shook my head.

Everybody was quiet. Then Brynn hugged herself and changed tracks. "So what was up with the elevator?"

Yejun looked toward her for a long moment, then said, "I was just playing around with it."

This, Brynn took without a blink. "I wondered." She slapped her hands together. "All right! I guess that poor Jen is probably target number one for this Huntsman guy if he's after ghosts, huh?" She gave me a sidelong look. "Are you coming with us?"

Despite her look, it didn't occur to me at first that she was talking to me like *I* was the tagalong. As she stared at me expectantly, realization dawned. "What? Yes! I mean—"

"Good!" she said, running over my words. "Let's do this."

A hint of a laugh in his voice, Yejun said, "You know where we're going, Miss Thing?"

Brynn gestured grandiosely at me. "I'll let AT lead the way."

I shook my head and walked out the hotel doors.

It was only luck—definitely not wisdom—that prevented me from walking straight into Scott. He still held a cigarette as he leaned against a brick pillar exactly twenty-five feet from the front entrance. He was positioned so he could watch the comings and goings and he happened to be looking down the street as I emerged. The arm I'd broken was in a sling, which surprised me. Even without my father's direct assistance, his wolves healed fast.

I backpedaled so quickly that I crashed into the doorframe. He looked over and met my eyes. A nasty grin spread across his face.

"Hey there, girlie," he called, pushing himself away from the pillar to move toward me.

My head hurt from backing into the door and I wanted to rub it. Instead, I clenched my aching hands. "What do you want?"

Scott held his hands up in a conciliatory way. "Aw, let's be friends again. I hear you're out doing some shopping. I can carry your packages for you. I know sometimes you have trouble with your hands." His grin became sly. "We both know what it's like when your daddy loses his temper, eh?"

I shook my head. "Go away before I break your other arm." And I desperately wished he'd listen before it got worse.

It got worse. Yejun came up beside me—Brynn apparently remembered enough of what I'd said before to hang back—and looked at Scott over his sunglasses. "Who's that?"

Scott's horrid grin changed as his face filled with angry delight. "Coming out of a hotel with your boyfriend. Oh, girlie, and you were so shy last night. Wait until your daddy finds out!"

"Shut up!" I said, taking a few quick steps toward him. He stepped back again, to the pillar he'd been loitering at before. A few people near the entrance were starting to watch us curiously.

"How do you think you can convince me to do that?" Scott asked suggestively. "All I want to do is be friends again."

My fingernails bit into my palms. I couldn't kill him. That would just kill his body; his mind would go flying back to my father all the faster. I couldn't even stop my father from reaching into his mind right now and taking what he knew. I couldn't do *anything* to him except avoid him and I'd failed miserably at doing that.

Instead, I turned to Yejun, pushing him away from me. "What are you doing out here?" Then I grabbed him by the sleeve and pulled him back toward me again. "We have to get out of here. We have to go do this thing if we're going to do it."

Brynn slipped out from inside the hotel and attached herself unobtrusively to my other sleeve. Scott laughed, an awful jeering sound. "Where are you going now, girlie? You know you can't escape him again."

Breathing hard, I started walking, hauling Yejun after me. He tried to untangle himself from my grasp, putting his hand over mine, and I said, "Don't! Just—don't. Just come. Or go. But if you go, I'm sorry."

"I just want my sleeve back," he said mildly.

I let him go. "I need my dogs," I said. "Hold on." I concentrated and released them from my shadow. Nod stalked out, but Heart sidled and Grim slunk, his belly brushing the ground. Scott laughed again behind us, a disbelieving crow, but I told myself I didn't care. I had my dogs. I wasn't alone. No matter what happened to me, I wasn't alone.

Yejun and Brynn both looked at me. It was clear they still didn't understand anything: what Scott was, what he represented. It was too late to keep my father ignorant about my contact with them. All I could do was figure out a way to convince him he was better off keeping them alive instead of killing them.

I didn't have a clue how to do that.

If I didn't get away from Scott's stench, I was going to kill him, which would just make everything that much worse, that much faster.

"Come on," I said. "Let's go. Now." I started walking fast, the dogs ranging ahead of me, and Brynn had to run to keep up. Yejun didn't bother at first, and I tried to be glad of it. Then, all of a sudden, he appeared at my side, strolling alongside my powerwalk with his hands in his pocket.

"Your friend is following us," he told me.

"Not my friend. I hate him," I answered. "No good way to stop him, though. He can track us just like I'm tracking our guy."

"That got screwed up before, yeah?"

I shrugged. "I have no idea how he did it. Demon magic, I assume."

"Hmm," said Yejun. He took his sunglasses off and fell silent. We moved fast and Scott didn't, which meant he fell out of sight eventually. I didn't let Nod circle around to "deal with him," no matter how expressively he conveyed his interest in doing so.

Then Yejun did something that made my stomach churn. I barely knew how to describe it. It was like rays of distortion stretched out from his back and swapped pieces of the world around. But nothing actually moved, and nothing actually changed, and the only way I knew for sure something had happened was the way all three dogs whirled around, ears flattening, and how Brynn said, "Whoa, what was that?"

Yejun said, with smugness hiding under overplayed boredom, "Oh, I just scattered our trail."

I realized that the rays of distortion I'd seen had been his crazy array of nodes moving around. Just imagining it made my insides twist up again.

Yejun didn't notice. Calmly, with just a trace of interest, he asked, "Was that what the demon did?"

"No!" I snapped. "No. Nobody does stuff like that. I don't understand how you even exist."

His faint, pleased smile faded. "Yeah, that's what they all say," he said, and put his sunglasses back on. "Oh, no, no point in teaching him about the tangle. That'll just make it more dangerous when he inevitably explodes." He pulled his sunglasses down just enough to look at me over them. "But I haven't exploded yet."

I stared at him for a minute, my anger fading with my nausea. Slowly, something else replaced it. I remembered my father talking about other nephilim, and I felt nasty and dirty. "I'm sorry," I muttered. "It made my stomach hurt. I didn't know what was going on. I shouldn't have said that."

Yejun shrugged and walked on ahead. I looked after him, miserable, hating myself. When Brynn touched my arm questioningly, I pulled away and crouched down. All I could think of doing was hiding. I was already so messed up and it was only going to get worse. I wanted to be a good person, wanted to be somebody my mother would be proud of, but everything my father did or said seemed to get stuck inside my head. Sometimes he seemed to fill the whole world.

"Hey," said Brynn, kneeling down so she could look at my face. "It's okay. It was a really weird feeling."

I jerked away and scrambled to my feet again. "We have to keep going."

I concentrated on what I could smell, what Grim and Heart were still tracking. Alastor and the Huntsman had both entered the world through the same loosely woven spot in the Curtain. The trail led us across four intersections and I kept my head down at each one, following the crowds of pedestrians but not looking at them. I didn't want to think about Halloween. It made me think of my father and that made me hate myself.

Grim finally sat down outside another tall building. Looking up, I thought I recognized it from the skyline, but I'd never bothered finding out what it was called. Now, thanks to a large sign next to the main entrance, I knew: McAllister Law.

Brynn looked the building up and down and said apprehensively, "Do we have to go inside? This place doesn't look as friendly as the hotel."

I thought about the information I was getting from Grim and Heart. "The soft spot they've been traveling through is up. So it's best if we go up, too. We have to do some more traveling once we're on the other side of the Curtain and if we start from the wrong place, it could take a lot longer."

Brynn sighed and hauled one of the big doors open. "After you."

I sent Nod and Heart away again and pulled a leash from my pocket. Grim sat down patiently to let me attach it, then bounded to his feet again and immediately started pulling at the leash.

"Cut that out," I said sharply. "Walk properly."

Grim's tail came down and he gave me a pained look, but came back to sit primly by my side. "Okay," I said, and led him through the door Brynn was still holding open.

The first floor of the building was an open space, with a couple of restaurants and a coffee shop and a lot of random seating. A security desk stood near a bank of elevators. Yejun was peering at a large digital building directory. "Pretty big law firm. There's a few other tenants, too. Do you know what floor we're going to? Or do we get to go joyriding in the elevators?" He looked speculatively around the lobby. "They have a lot, they wouldn't miss one."

I stared at the display, chewing on my lip. "It's not here."

"Whoa, what do you mean, it's not here? You said it was here." Yejun took off his sunglasses to scrutinize me.

"I don't know," I admitted. "It's in the building, but nothing on the map matches the sense I've picked up from Grim."

"Maybe ol' Grimwhiskers here is just messing with you?" Yejun suggested, lightly twisting one of my dog's ears around.

I gave him a flat look. "Grimwhiskers."

"He's too cute to be Grim. You can't say he's not cute. He's your dog and you're a girl."

"You're not renaming my dog," I warned him.

"It's a nickname." Yejun grinned at me.

"Some buildings have hidden floors," said Brynn loudly, bumping me with her hip. "Maybe we could figure it out if we focused."

Too loudly, it turned out. A slim man with silver hair and a fine-boned face stopped leaning on the security desk and approached us. I eyed him warily, but Yejun actually scowled and stepped backward, closing ranks with us.

"Hello," the man said politely. He had a polished, beautiful voice, and his eyes were inhumanly luminous. And he smelled like vanilla natively, which was enough for me to realize he wasn't human. Faerie or faerie's spawn—they called them changelings—but either way, not good news. A badge around his neck said, "Winterwhen Special Security" and "My name is Jake."

Probably a changeling, I decided. I couldn't imagine a celestial, even a faerie celestial, going by "Jake."

"Do you have an appointment with somebody in the building?" Jake inquired.

"Yes," said Brynn, at the same time that I said, "No."

Brynn dug her elbow into my side and went on. "Not an appointment, exactly, but we need to return this dog to its owner."

The faerie held out his hand. "I would be pleased to assist you. Just tell me to whom he belongs and I'll take him up." He paused, and when I didn't hand over the leash and Brynn didn't say anything at all, he smiled, all flashing white teeth. "Or you could simply leave." Lowering his voice, he added, "You look like nice kids. You don't want to get into trouble."

"No. We just want to go to the hidden floor," said Brynn, meek as a kitten.

"There's nothing interesting on the mechanical floor," he assured Brynn kindly. "And it's not a safe place for younglings. Even younglings of your friends' capacities. Do run along and play somewhere else." And he gave us a meltingly sweet smile.

I backed away. "Let's go." Then I all but ran from the building, hurrying Grim alongside me.

"Why did you run away?" demanded Brynn a moment later when she emerged with Yejun. "I could have talked him into it."

"You couldn't have. He was using some kind of magic," I said. "I'd have to fight him. I didn't want to fight him."

Yejun frowned. "He didn't look like he was using magic to me. I mean, nobody ever bothered to train me, what do I know, right? But the ol' tangle wasn't moving at all like it does when even Tia does something shimmery."

I shuddered. "He was a spawn. Faerie spawn. Changeling." I stumbled over my words. "They're *built*. Everything they *are* is magic. If they're ever nice, it's because their master wants something."

Yejun crossed his arms and leaned against the wall beside me. His shoulders were noticeably broader than mine. "Do you think he's specifically there to stop us from getting to this mechanical floor?"

"He must be," said Brynn.

But I shook my head. "I don't know. Maybe." I thought of his nametag. "Maybe not. A law firm must have an awful lot of secrets. Maybe he's just there to protect them from people like himself."

"People like us," said Yejun deliberately, looking up at the tower looming over us as if waking up to the possibilities

"It doesn't matter," I decided. "We'll go in down here." I pushed away from the wall and went around the corner, looking around until I found a Dumpster. Brynn followed me like she was on the leash, not Grim, but Yejun didn't, not right away.

"Here," I said. "I'll open a tear in the Curtain. It's not the right spot, but it's close. And on the other side we should have more freedom to do what we need to do."

"This is to make a door to the other world?" Brynn swallowed and adjusted her camera bag on her shoulder. "I'm ready."

I eyed her but resisted suggesting once again that she stay where it was safe. Scott was still out there. The only way I'd know she was safe was if she was with me.

Yejun appeared around the corner of the Dumpster. "You know, I cracked an ATM so we wouldn't have to spend any more time in dumps."

Brynn goggled at him, but I just concentrated on releasing Nod and Heart from my shadow. Then I unleashed Grim. It was best when traveling to the other world to be ready for anything.

The dogs prowled around me, picking up on my tension. It occurred to me that I ought to explain a little. "So what I'm going to do isn't what other people do. Wizards and all. They have spells and

stuff. This is just part of my magic. It's going to look like a window."
I looked at my companions and realized they had no idea what I was
talking about. Neither of them had been in the Backworld before.

I hurriedly went through what else they absolutely needed to
know. "Right, um. Until we've figured out where we are on the other
side, we need to hold onto each other. Sometimes it's just sort of a
white featureless hallway. If we end up there, we need to keep in contact or you'll maybe fall out. I don't know for sure, but that would
probably be bad."

Brynn and Yejun each grabbed one of my hands. I heard a crunch
and blackness passed across my vision. When it was gone, my hands
were tucked under my armpits, just fine, and I was leaning against
the wall again, panting. "No! Did I scream? No... Give me a minute.
I need to just... get ready." Brynn gave Yejun the stink-eye while he
watched me with genuine concern in his eyes.

I'd taken some friends through the corridors of the Backworld
once before and I'd held their hands without losing it. But I'd been
living in LA for months then, away from my father. I'd even occasionally forgotten about him. But—now, I just couldn't.

"One of you hold onto my wrist, then hold onto the other. That will
work fine." I untucked my hands and held out my left one, fist clenched.

Yejun gestured Brynn ahead of him with a sardonic grace. Brynn
gently wrapped her fingers around my wrist and held out her hand for
Yejun like a queen.

"All right," I said, and opened the window to the other world.

Or I tried, anyhow. But, as usual for today, something went horribly wrong. It was like digging into a sandbank, and as I dug, the sand
teetered over our heads. And then, as I tried to withdraw and recon-
sider, the sand collapsed on us and, like Alice in the rabbit hole, we
fell through the world.

-eight-

The tunnel to Hades is guarded by a three-headed dog.
What?
I was falling.
I was dreaming.
I jerked away, and fell again.

I always hated that story. What her mother wanted was meaningless. She belonged to her father and the man he gave her to. And they manipulated her so she paid forever for a moment of compassion.

The walls of the blackness flashed with light, like pictures from a silent film. I couldn't understand what they were supposed to be. I looked down.

I was falling, like Alice, like Persephone. I'd pay forever.

Alastor, with wings like a black eagle, looked into a pool and called to the Hunt. They emerged, many in one. The horses and the hunters, bound to the same howling horn. Horses and hunters, but no hounds.

The demon spoke to them.

Ion, the First Huntsman, looked up.

He saw me. He knew me. And he raised his hand and his Hunt stopped its restless shifting to look at him.

He pointed at me. The horn blew and my dogs burst out of me.

The horn became music, a fall of burning notes, not a horn, but strings.

I woke up.

The alley with the Dumpster had become a night forest. A full moon (and that was wrong, *wrong*) shone down between the branches of the tree above me. I lay on packed dirt and knobbly roots, and except for the *wrong* moon, I might have thought I'd fallen asleep in the forest near my father's house.

Heart licked my cheek and I sat up with a start. Music, real music, still danced in the air. I looked around wildly. Behind me, Yejun and Brynn were shaking their heads, but most of my attention was grabbed by the tall violinist playing on the other side of the clearing. He wore a long coat the color of a distant star, he had wild storm-shot hair over Chinese features, and his violin shone like water in moonlight. The song he played was eerie and aggressive, but also familiar in that can't-place-it way. Nod and Grim sat in front of him, heads cocked identically to one side as they listened to the song.

I rose to my feet and tried to look around again without letting the musician out of my sight. All he was doing was playing, but here? Now? After so much had already gone wrong? This was bad.

We were in a clearing and right away I saw the first problem. Brambles filled the space between the tall trees; the only path out of the glade went through the musician. Of course. He stood there with his legs braced, swaying a little with his eyes closed as his fingers danced over the neck of the black violin. The bow seemed to be strung with lightning.

The music he made wanted to get inside my head. It wasn't just familiar, it was catchy. But there was something discordant about it, too, as if once it got inside my head, it would leave scars behind.

Brynn had her head tilted to one side as she stared at the musician and I figured she felt the same way. I glanced at Yejun, then went over to him. "Are you all right?"

He was looking around wildly, his sunglasses in one hand. "I... I don't know. This place is weird. It's not real. It's like... a movie. Even that guy." He scowled in the direction of the musician.

Doubtfully, I said, "Backworld places are different from the normal world, especially in the realms. I don't know about him. Is he a faerie?"

"You mean like the security guy in the building? No way. That guy was real. This guy is a... projection of some sort." Yejun shook his head and pressed his fingers against his eyes. "I feel like I've gone blind."

The musician stopped playing mid-phrase, lowering his bow and opening his eyes to give us a cool, unfriendly look. "Please be quiet. I'm trying to catch a song and you're distracting the queries." He looked Chinese but he had an accent I couldn't identify, and his voice made me think of honey, thick and golden. "Why did you come if you were just going to talk over the music?" His violin hummed along with his voice.

"This isn't where we're supposed to be," I said uncertainly. "Grim, Heart?" Grim leapt to his feet guiltily and started nosing around, but Heart stayed near me, watching the musician warily. "Something pulled us here."

Grim couldn't find the trail nearby, which didn't surprise me; we hadn't crossed over where the Huntsman had crossed and the connections between the Backworld and the mortal world aren't linear. But still, that shouldn't have put us so far off course. I was pretty sure that we should have either been in empty white corridors, or in something resembling a dream of Seattle. That was what *usually* happened when I stepped between worlds. This forest was something out of a fairy tale. It wasn't even a Seattle forest of long ago, despite what I'd thought when I'd first woken up. The pale-barked trees were uniform and deciduous, their leaves autumn-bright against the night sky above.

I wondered uneasily about the night. Had we lost time in the descent? It had seemed endless. Was it night already? Was it Halloween? Was it too late? I reached out to open a window back to Seattle. We could go back and try again, and leave this strange musician to his song-catching, whatever that was.

Except I couldn't find the latch, so to speak. I'd always been able to catch hold of space and tear a hole into it, but now I was just flailing at the air. "Why isn't it working?" I demanded of nobody in particular, and commanded Nod to step between worlds himself.

He chased his tail instead, then flattened his ears when he realized what he was doing and gave me an accusatory look. He could no more go through than I could, and he wasn't very pleased I'd made him look foolish.

Yejun watched me, then said, "Let me try."

"Don't," said the musician. His cool expression had become one of mild, detached interest. "I'm afraid I've changed the local properties enough that you'll only create problems."

"Problems for you?" said Yejun. "I just bet." He raised his hand and plucked at something over his head.

Lightning flashed all around us, with a horrible twanging clash of notes. When it faded, Brynn was kneeling down, her face buried in Heart's fur, her entire body quivering. I grabbed Yejun's other hand before he could make things worse. "Stop!"

Yejun's hand turned until it was palm to palm with mine. Then he pulled away and stalked over to stand in front of the musician, who hadn't lost his look of vague interest. "What did you do?"

The musician winced, his detached interest turning rueful. "I didn't *mean* to do anything. I'm just trying to find a song. You must understand about unintended consequences here, yes? The lines are so simple, but even so, all it takes is changing the tension and everything is different."

Yejun bristled, then all of a sudden, the aggression drained out of him. He gave the musician a wry smile. "I know all about unintended consequences, yeah." He held out his hand. "My name's Yejun. Who're you?"

The musician clasped Yejun's hand, and Yejun visibly started. "I am called the Fiddler. This is Arabet the Howler, my companion." He tilted the violin he was holding so that we could see it better. It was black, polished, and without a visible grain. After staring for a moment, I realized that it was made of stone.

Yejun must have realized the same thing, because he said, "Real rock music, I see."

"Real enough," said the Fiddler blithely. His gaze went past Yejun to Brynn and then to me. "I wonder, do any of you know much about music?"

I shook my head and sank down to my knees, holding out a hand for Grim. He came over to me and pressed his head against mine long enough to understand my nerves and unhappiness. Then he licked my temple and darted out of the clearing, past the Fiddler.

Brynn said, "I had music lessons for a few years." There was a quaver in her voice and she kept one hand knotted in Heart's ruff. "Are we going to go find this horn or what?"

"Grim's looking for a way out of this forest." The ground was damp beneath me, but I leaned back anyhow to look at the sky and the worrying, unnatural full moon. I remembered falling, and dreaming of Hades. I kept landing with a thump on hard ground and jerking awake to the sound of music. I had to concentrate on what to do next, but I couldn't seem to make my mind work right. My thoughts ran in circles, as if chasing something only visible peripherally.

"I'm afraid the radius of my distortion is rather large," said the Fiddler, apologetically. "I hadn't intended to stay, but when I discovered what had happened as a result of my last visit—"

Abruptly, I realized what the problem was and I sat up. "It's that song you were playing earlier. Finish it."

An impish smile flashed across the Fiddler's face. "Is Arabet bothering you?"

"Please?" I asked. "I keep trying to finish the song—"

"Me too," sighed the Fiddler. He raised Arabet the Howler and started to play where he'd left off before. The music danced through the air and I closed my eyes to listen. It painted strange pictures behind my eyes: of stars swooping around and singing to each other, of a comet spiraling through a nebula, inviting each of the stars to a dance, and leaving them all atitter behind him. Nonsensical thoughts, and once the song ended, they faded away like a dream.

I opened my eyes. My head felt clear, but I was curled up on the ground, my cheek on my hands. I stretched out and my body felt stiff. Brynn was similarly curled up an arm's length away, while Yejun sat with his arms around his legs and his chin sunk between his knees. His hair fell across his face, but Heart could feel how distant and sad he was. She rested between us, head on her paws, while Nod stood, alert and irritated, watching the Fiddler with his ears flattened. The Fiddler himself stood easily, his instrument at his side as he gazed back at Nod.

We'd lost time. How much, I wasn't sure. Dogs aren't the best judge of time when the light doesn't change, and the wrong moon hadn't moved. Grim stood behind the Fiddler. Hiding, I realized. He hadn't found the trail. He hadn't found a way out, either. He'd trotted away from our glade and ended up right back where he started, like we were on the inside of a bubble.

"Did you find your song?" Brynn asked as she unfolded herself.

"Did I fall asleep?"

"Yes," said Yejun, dully.

At the same time, the Fiddler shook his head. "No. It is elusive."

I stood up. "So is this trail we're trying to follow." I glared at the Fiddler. "Your music stole time from us. We didn't have a lot to start with. You need to leave and take your little bubble of forest with you."

"Oh, I can't leave now. That would be dreadfully irresponsible," said the Fiddler firmly. "But what are you chasing?"

"We're following a trail back to its source," I explained, short-tempered. "Made by a demon sort of thing. Or maybe a faerie. A celestial, anyhow. One of you."

The Fiddler smiled faintly. "Not one of me. This nook of the cosmos isn't my usual haunt. That's why I thought it would be safe to leave this troublesome song here. But come, describe your trail to me and perhaps I can help you find it."

I stared at him, baffled. How did you describe a trail? And even if I could, how would describing it in words be helpful at all? "It smells like acid and greed and tears and musk and—and this is stupid." I scowled at the Fiddler, irritated by his expression of bland, almost blank interest.

Yejun raised his head. "Maybe I can... if you..." and he trailed off, frowning. "I don't know." He knuckled his forehead. "I wish..." But he didn't finish whatever he wished, staring fixedly at the ground instead.

"I know," said Brynn. She cleared her throat and started singing.

After a moment, I realized it was that new song that had played when the Huntsman appeared. The song from the band called Gravity's Angels, and she was wearing the band's shirt.

I barely had a chance to wonder at Tia's games before Yejun lunged for Brynn. "No! Don't—"

Heart interposed herself in a flash, barking furiously, foam flying from her mouth as she warned Yejun away. Yejun recoiled, right back into me. As soon as I put my hand on Yejun's arm, Heart quieted with a final snort. She gave Yejun a scornful look, then turned to lick Brynn's sleeve. Brynn, her song frozen on her lips, patted her warily.

"Why is she trying to summon him?" Yejun demanded. "Why is the dog letting her?"

"It's okay, I think. There's no ghosts here, right?" I looked at the

Fiddler dubiously. "Maybe it will give him the trail."

Brynn shifted uncomfortably. "The faeries come when that song is played. Ms. Zelaya said the Wild Hunt does, too. I thought it might *be* the trail, for a musician. My dad's always following music around." She studied her fingernails. "It was just an idea."

"I know a version of this song," offered the Fiddler. "It's why I returned to this world. It wasn't what I hoped it was, but it did give me the chance to see the mess I'd made last time I was here."

"Oh," said Brynn, disappointed.

He raised a finger. "I know *a* version, but not *your* version. Will you continue singing? Language is a little hard for me sometimes. Music is easier."

Yejun's arm was as hard as a rock under my fingers and he was breathing hard, but he didn't move. I realized that he'd been ready for that song, or for the Huntsman to appear, for a while. Maybe since Alastor had attacked his mentors. "You okay?" I asked him. I loosened my fingers, but didn't stop touching him. Sometimes touch helped.

"Yeah," he said slowly. "Jen's not here. But if this asshole *does* appear, I'm going to do whatever I can to him, no matter what Tia says."

Brynn swallowed and started singing again. Her voice cracked at first, but when nobody interrupted her, she grew in confidence. She knew the song perfectly and any other time, I would have enjoyed her performance. But I was too busy looking around for the Huntsman or something else to appear, and too aware of the warmth of Yejun's arm under my fingers. But as the song went into the final verse, I found I was humming along—it *was* catchy—and since nothing had appeared by then, I joined in for the chorus, thinking about the Huntsman as he'd pointed at me.

After our last notes faded away, the Fiddler closed his eyes for a long moment. Slowly, I released Yejun's arm, realizing as I did that my hold had slowly tightened into a deathgrip while Brynn sang. He flexed his fingers and gave me a sideways glance under lowered lids.

When the Fiddler opened his eyes again, they gleamed like molten gold. "Ah. Yes. I think I can help you." The violin hummed with the sound of his voice again. He raised it into position and brushed the lightning-strung bow across the strings.

What came out was not music, but a storm.

-nine-

For the third time in an hour, I lost track of where I was. It was a horrible thing. Wind howled out of the violin, sweeping up leaves and twigs and dust into a storm of debris. Clouds rolled in behind the wrong moon and rain blew sideways into my face and lightning chased thunder backwards across the sky. I could no longer see the clearing. I could no longer see my friends. I could barely see my hands. I staggered toward Heart, who was closest to me, and when I touched her ruff, I felt the ground again beneath my feet. I reached out my other hand and found Nod, and my bewilderment was replaced by anger. When Grim touched the back of my knee, I had had enough. I spread out my awareness through all three of the dogs and found my friends. Friends? Were they friends? Had I used that word?

Whatever they were, they were my responsibility. Mine to care for, mine to guard, mine to play with.

You have to understand, I wasn't really feeling like myself just then. I was angry and I was lost and I was afraid. And I was all of us.

I shouted my frustration at the storm. It laughed back at me and, with a thump, it deposited us on the ground again and raced out across the forest.

We were still in the clearing, or maybe back in the clearing again: Brynn and Yejun and the dogs and me. The Fiddler was gone. Almost everything else was the same, but the only other difference was a major one. The scent trail of the Huntsman and the demon Alastor roiled around us fresh as the moment it was laid, rising from the soil and dripping from the leaves. It was too good to be real, but I didn't know how not to trust our noses. Somehow—I couldn't even imagine how—the Fiddler had found the trail and transferred it through the distortion that hid it. It was like a road now, broad and sweet and open. And it was pungent, too. I could barely smell anything else.

I sprang forward, eager to make up lost time. Then I remembered my companions (*companions*, that was a better word, a safer word) and I turned back to them. Heart had the edge of Brynn's baggy shorts clenched between her teeth while Grim held Yejun's shirt.

"Hey," said Yejun foggily. "Don't tear it. It's a good shirt." Grim rolled his eyes at me before releasing the shirt delicately and standing on his hind legs to lick Yejun's face.

"Did it work? What happened?" asked Brynn, setting her camera bag on the ground and checking its contents.

"A trail so wide even Nod can follow it," I said tersely. Nod, sitting by the edge of the clearing, gave me a dirty look.

Brynn flashed me a proud, triumphant smile. "Great! See, I *am* helpful." She looked around. "Where did the Fiddler go?"

I shrugged. "Maybe he had to leave so we'd pick up the trail. Or maybe he's still here, in another layer of the Backworld. It doesn't matter as long as we have the trail."

Yejun looked around, then shook off his confusion and Grim's paws on his shoulders. "You know that song awfully well. It's a dangerous song. You should know it less well."

Brynn's pleasure vanished abruptly as a wall went up around her. "It's catchy. Gets stuck in your head," she said, her gaze fixed determinedly on her bag as she dug through it.

"I've noticed," said Yejun darkly. "It's a trap. But you're a fan of the band, I see."

"Yeah, I am," Brynn said defensively. "They're just people. What happens with the song isn't their fault. They were—" She snapped her mouth shut, shook her head, and zipped her bag shut.

I demanded, "Did you find what you're looking for? Can you two bicker while you walk? I don't want the trail to vanish again." And I took a few steps backwards, toward Nod and the edge of the clearing, trying to lure them along.

Suddenly all cheerful again, Brynn stood up, slung the bag over her shoulder, and brandished what she'd found. "Yup. Got my little camera. Next time some weirdness carries us off, I'm totally getting pictures."

"Right." I set out at a brisk walk, my dogs *(my only friends)* ranging around me. My head still wasn't quite straight from the storm that had rushed over us, but movement always fixed that.

The brambles surrounding the clearing turned out to be raspberries twined 'round with morning glories. Berries were just visible in the wrong moonlight. Brynn stopped to investigate and I said, "*Please* don't eat strange berries you find in a magical forest we shouldn't even be in."

"I know," she said mildly, taking a picture of the bramble. The flash was too bright, just as out of place as the moon, and Brynn said, "Oops. I always forget to turn that off."

"It's night," observed Yejun. "You don't have a tripod. What else are you going to do?"

"I *do* have a tripod, though I guess I can't set it up now," countered Brynn, "Also, it's not really night. It's just dark."

"It's definitely not nighttime," I agreed. "This is just... an illusion. That moon is totally wrong." I glared up at it. "The full moon isn't for days yet. And the clouds go behind it. I really hope this trail leads us to someplace more normal." But I knew that was a vain hope; the trail led deeper into the wilds of the Backworld, where things would only get stranger.

Yejun squinted up at the moon and Brynn looked at her camera. Neither of them paid the slightest attention to where they were walking, although they did at least walk. Exasperated, the dogs and I guided them past the brambles. On the other side of the thicket, the forest opened up a bit. The ground was covered in an unusually thick carpet of the same crisp leaves that clung to the pale trees. Only the occasional slender white mushroom poked above the detritus. We could have walked in any direction easily, and every direction looked the same. Sometimes the trees were closer together, and sometimes they were farther apart. Sometimes there was a broad trunk with a hollow in the roots. Nod was wary, but Grim wanted to go play in the leaves and scent out the animal trails he was sure would be there. Rabbits! Foxes! Deer! Mice! He was very excited about the mice.

I wasn't as sure. The hollow we passed was empty, unlived in, and if anything mundane lived in the forest, surely it wouldn't pass up a den like that?

Unless it was too big to fit.

That was a nasty idea. But it made me look around a little more. Eventually I noticed long furrows on some of the trees, as if something very large had been sharpening its claws, or marking territory.

I wasn't really concerned for myself—it takes my father or something out of a nightmare to make me worry about my own skin. But my charges, my tagalongs—what would they do if a giant creature started chasing us through the wood?

Even if it seemed empty, the forest wasn't really quiet. The air thrummed with the sound of occasional birds flapping, but I never saw one in the dim light. The trees creaked and rustled even when there wasn't a wind. It wasn't a dead forest, even if it wasn't normal. And once, in the distance, just at the edge of hearing, there was a roar. It didn't seem like the others heard it, which was for the best.

Grim started ranging further and further from the main pack, which irritated Nod more and more. Finally, when Grim was off sniffing at a cluster of slender saplings growing in the ruins of an ancient trunk, Nod dashed after him, growling. About fifteen yards away, he skidded to a halt and looked around with an almost comical look of horror. I reached out to figure out what was wrong, then stopped dead.

"Nobody leave the trail," I commanded. "It stops existing about where Nod is."

Yejun turned to look back at me. "Isn't that how trails work?"

"No," I snapped. "It's a scent. They fade away. This one turns off like there's a switch. If we go exploring all over this wood, the only way we'll find it again is if we get really lucky. Hell, it might stop *existing* if we all leave it. I don't trust that Fiddler guy one bit." I whistled for Grim and Nod to come back again and ran to catch up with Heart, who was still faithfully following the trail with her nose low to the ground. Grim flashed past, turned back to give me a guilty look, then fell in alongside Heart.

Brynn fell into step beside me. "What if the whole trail is fake?"

"I can't think about that," I said shortly. "It's the only trail we have."

She grinned. "True that. This forest is pretty amazing, isn't it? But you don't like it. Where were we supposed to end up?"

"I thought we'd cross over and be in the corridors, honestly." I gave her a sideways look. "Big empty spaces. And we'd go from there to... well... somewhere like this forest, actually. Except more regionally appropriate."

Radiating puzzlement, Brynn asked, "Why big empty spaces? Corridors? Like... hallways?"

I shrugged. "My father says that the Backworld is like maintenance tunnels for Creation. Or it was, before the faeries colonized it. Normally when I cross over, I cross into that, unless something's been built exactly where I'm crossing."

"Your father..." said Brynn thoughtfully, which was not the conversational hook I wanted her to pursue.

Quickly, I said, "I have to concentrate on the tracking. Maybe you can find out from Yejun if he knows what we're supposed to do once we find this horn." And I did concentrate, trying hard to shut out everything but the track. It wasn't an appealing scent, but it was nuanced and very clear, and it took focus to follow it back to its origin instead of forward to where we shouldn't be. If I had to do it alone, I'd be totally oblivious to everything else around us.

A few moments later, the ground vibrated with the distant sound of many hoofbeats and Brynn froze, listening as the sound rose, then faded away again. "What was that?"

"Just a trick of the forest," I told her. "There's been a lot of weird noises. Distant animals and stuff. It's a forest."

"It sounded like horses," she insisted.

I shrugged. "Maybe. Hooves, anyhow. That could mean a lot of things in a place like this."

Brynn shivered and looked around. "A horse stepped on me once. I'm not a fan of horses."

Yejun lowered his head as if to look at her over the rim of the sunglasses he wasn't wearing. "You're a junior high girl. You love horses."

"I loved horses when I was eleven," Brynn corrected. "Then I went to horse camp and Chili the pinto mare tried to trample me to death. Horses are *big*. I do not like them."

"Do you like them in a house? With a mouse?" quoted Yejun.

"Shut up," Brynn said, but without any rancor. "And I'm in ninth grade, thank you very much."

I turned around, walking backward for a moment. "Come on. If a herd of wild horses appears, the dogs will chase them off."

"Right," said Brynn, hurrying after me. But Yejun took her place beside me before she could catch up. He didn't bother me with distracting questions, though, and for a while we just hiked through the forest. The ground, once level, began to rise and fall in hills so gentle they were really more like waves. The trees grew more densely together, too. They were older here, although the ground was still carpeted with the debris of an endless autumn. It was uneven, slippery footing and it kept annoying me that the trail we were following had left no sign on the ground.

Until, eventually, it did. I could only make out a few signs of it, because it was dark and I never actually studied sight-tracking much, but I could tell somebody else had traveled over the composting forest floor before us. Maybe more than one somebody, but all I could smell was the trail that the Fiddler had magically summoned up. Which was *also* pretty annoying. If I ever saw the Fiddler again, I was going to have some choice suggestions for him about how to share a trail.

But at least we'd left the region of the clawed-up trees. That had to be good.

Brynn started humming behind us. Then she said, "What's that humming?" and I realized it wasn't her. Somebody else, somebody with a light girl's voice, was singing in the forest. It was hardly a song at all, really, especially compared to the sublime music of the Fiddler. It was just some sing-song gibberish. Still, I stopped to listen to it for a moment. Music worried me. It had demonstrated risks that couldn't be bitten through. And it was hard to run from because it got inside your head.

"La la lala la, lala lala lala la," went the girl's voice, sweet and floating.

"Somebody needs to update their repertoire a bit from the sixteenth century," said Yejun.

"I don't know, it's kind of catchy," said Brynn, her gaze faraway. "Are we going to meet whoever it is?"

I listened to it from my dogs' perspectives for a moment. "It keeps moving around. I hope not. It's bound to just be another distraction. I bet the home of the Wild Hunt has defenses and this is one of them."

I kept walking, and the singing followed us. I wondered if it even attached to a person. Maybe it was a disembodied voice. Maybe it was a ghost. But it seemed really unlikely that there'd be a ghost on the way to the home of the ultimate ghost slayers.

After a while, the song stopped, but the sense of presence that had come with it remained. I wished whatever it was would come out of the darkness and face us directly. I wished we'd reach the end of the forest soon, too. My stomach was grumbling hungrily.

When the singing started again, I called irritably, "Come on, cut it out." Everything went silent, even the rustling of the trees. There was nothing except the sound of our footsteps. Slowly, the ambient noise crept back in again. And the third time the song started up, it was different: faster, with more variations between "la" and "la la" and even "da." And it was moving away. Good.

My stomach grumbled again, and I suddenly wondered if Brynn had packed any snacks in her giant camera bag. "Any food in that thing, Brynn?" I asked.

There was no answer.

My heart in my throat, my limbs filling with leaden fear, I turned around. Yejun, a little behind me, cursed softly in what sounded like Korean. And Brynn—well, Brynn was gone. She was just... *gone*.

"Did she wander off?" asked Yejun.

"I tried hard enough to convince her to wander off before and it didn't work," I responded. "Something took her. And we didn't even notice."

It was the trail. The overwhelmingly strong magical trail. We were hardly able to smell anything else. As soon as I realized that, Heart jerked herself away from the trail and started running back the way we came, almost stumbling over her paws in her urgency to find out what had happened. I followed behind more slowly, staring at the ground fixedly, my jaw clenched tight.

I hadn't smelled anything, I hadn't heard anything. The trail explained the scent, but what explained the silence? Brynn's footsteps had dropped away and I hadn't noticed. I probably hadn't wanted to notice. She was in the way, after all. Hadn't I said that, believed it? If she wandered off and something happened, that wasn't my fault, was it?

Heart found Brynn's bag, dropped on the ground on its side. She pawed at it anxiously, then looked up at me as I approached. I made her sit down, then studied the ground around the bag. After a moment of peering at the moonlit ground until my eyes hurt, I fumbled around in Brynn's bag until I found—aha—a flashlight. That made it a lot easier to figure out where she'd left the trail.

"Go find her scent," I commanded Heart and Nod, gesturing in the direction Brynn had gone. Grim started to go too, but I called him back. Yejun stood behind me, watching with veiled eyes. "Yejun, you and Grim stay here. We can't all leave the trail or it might vanish. Can you take care of yourself? I have to go get her back."

Yejun nodded, but his hand closed on my arm like I'd once held his. "I don't need Grim to stay with me."

I pulled away. "I do." Then I was running after Heart and Nod.

They hadn't stopped when I pulled Grim back, and once they made it off the broad swath of magically generated trail, they'd found the scent of Brynn's kidnapper easily. They shared it with me: the half-human, half-not scent I associated with monster spawn. Not one of my father's wolves, but still the servant of some other monster. She was moving fast, almost as fast as my dogs; I wasn't going to catch up unless they caught her and slowed her down.

Well, she was only *almost* as fast. And Brynn wasn't bleeding yet. Maybe we could save her.

Then a cloud went in front of the wrong moon and the dim night became nearly black. I had Brynn's flashlight but I still had to slow down. My dogs didn't bother, until Heart ran straight into a tree. Her yelp echoed back, bouncing off other trees and lasting longer than any echo really should. Nod stayed beside her until she snapped at him. Then he picked up the trail again, moving slow enough to avoid running into any trees the kidnapper might have climbed.

Heart waited for me, whimpering. I crouched down beside her and inspected the gash on her nose. Then I pulled a bit of my shadow out and rubbed it into the injury, holding her by the scruff of her neck as she tried to squirm away. Once the injury had sealed up and the scar had faded away, I stood back up again.

While I had been concentrating on Heart, the cloud that covered the moon had descended to earth. Cautiously, I started walking after Nod. The flashlight was nearly useless in the thick fog, which made me angry and afraid. My father could summon and banish fog, but I hadn't inherited that gift. Every year he used it on his Halloween forest walk, when he identified victims for the coming year. The trees were different, but I had too many ugly memories swimming to the surface all the same. Walking through a mist-filled forest with a flash-light, nervous, giggling people behind me.

But there was nobody behind me this time.

Was there?

I stopped and listened, then whirled around. But there was noth-ing. Heart cocked her head at me, ears lifted quizzically. Then she trotted ahead, focusing on Brynn. She wasn't worried about memories in the mist. There were plenty of things to worry about right now.

A whisper of sound echoed through the forest, just as Heart's yelp had. It sounded like a voice, but I couldn't make any details out.

Nod could, though. I closed my eyes, concentrated, and listened through his ears.

-ten-

The trees had changed again. The trunks were thick and rough, and the leaves on the ground were yellowed rather than crimson. Gnarled roots rose from the packed soil and a dry streambed meandered into a clearing. Nod wriggled his way behind a particularly large root and listened as two women spoke.

"—what you asked for," said the first voice. It was the singer, and she sounded eager and puppyish.

"Hmm," said the second woman. Her voice was older: rich and mellow. "So you have, sweetling. Let me see her. Ah, yes. Let me just—" and there was a percussive cracking sound. Not the sound of cracking bone. Nod knew the sound of cracking bone.

"Thank you," said the rich voice. "But be honest with Auntie Tala. You stole this prize, didn't you?"

"So? What if I did?" said the singer defiantly.

"Those you stole it from no doubt wish it back. They trample through the forest. They hunt you down," the rich voice said sweetly. "You can hardly be a hunter if you yourself are hunted."

"Hey! You said if I—" and now the singer was petulant.

Auntie Tala had no patience for petulance. "Amber, my sweetling, I said if you brought me the demoness's weapon, I would help you to join the Hunt. Go now and become the hunter rather than the hunted and I will help you further."

"I hunt all the time," the singer called Amber said sulkily.

"You scavenge from the shadows. A hunter chases down her prey.

She is not chased."

"That's such a waste of energy," complained Amber.

"I really have no interest in convincing you, child. You may either hunt, or you may be hunted." Tala paused significantly. "I will take this prize to the others now. Once you have made your decision, you are welcome to come boast of it."

Nod buried his nose under the rotting tree trunk to suppress a whine. Tala was picking up Brynn and leaving with her! He backed away from the tree and tried to circle around the clearing. He wanted very much to bite the thief, but rescue was more important than punishment.

The thief, the singer, the one called Amber, she disagreed with his priorities. Even though Nod moved like a shadow through the mist, she saw him and darted up a tree, then dropped down in front of him. She glared and Nod growled. She smelled like blood and celestial musk and talcum powder, and her shadow was the thin shadow of those who had given up their souls in exchange for a lease on immortality.

I pulled out of Nod's head and started stumbling through the forest again. I didn't understand any of what I'd overheard, but that didn't matter. I didn't want Nod fighting a monster spawn alone.

She was fast. Even distant from Nod's mind, I could tell she was fast. She had reflexes like a cat, and she wouldn't let Nod go around her. I tried to hold him back from attacking her—he was mine, he shared my power, and so he could be very strong. But it was better not to fight alone, especially the spawn-daughter of an unknown monster.

Heart slid into the shadows until only a crimson glint could be seen in the darkness. I ran as fast as I could, given the darkness and the mist. Nod and the singer moved as if in a dance, as Nod tried to feint around her. Every so often she hummed, then stopped mid-note, as if she hadn't meant to do that.

I arrived in the clearing but the dance had moved to one side without Nod quite realizing it. I swept the flashlight around the open space. Shards of stone were scattered around an ancient paved pool. It looked like a statue had stood there, then utterly shattered. The back legs of a horse statue jutted up beside the shards and a large shape moved inside the pool.

My breath quick, I darted forward. The rest of the horse statue lay at the bottom of the pool. It wasn't moving after all, except for the vines drifting in the water. The broken legs of the statue weren't bleeding. It was just water that splashed from the pool. It was just the mist and the distortion of the water that made the granite flanks seem to heave. It wasn't a tortured animal, just a statue. Just a statue.

A cacophony of growls and barking yanked my attention away from the pool and its broken stone. Heart had joined Nod and they were trying a joint maneuver to distract the singer. Heart silently urged me to go around, go after Brynn, even as she barked and snapped and dodged around Amber.

But the wannabe huntress had seen my flashlight. "Oh, to hell with this," she cried, and sped back to the clearing with the pool. Nod tried to trip her but she leapt lightly over him, caught a tree branch, and used it to fling herself into the glade with the grace of an acrobat.

Seeing her with my own eyes, my lip curled. She had pale skin and light eyes and a sheet of blond hair that didn't seem the least bit tangled by all the running and dodging and jumping she'd done. And she wasn't dressed like any hunter I'd ever imagined, except maybe a bargain hunter, with a blue top that at least showed some signs of wear, a swirly black skirt, and high-fashion combat boots with laces, buckles, *and* zippers.

I'd been a little afraid of her when I first scented her: afraid of what her presence meant, afraid of what she'd do to Brynn. But as soon as I saw her, I hated her. She was beautiful, in a magazine-movie-star way. "Were you born looking like that, or is this what you traded your soul for?" I demanded.

She slowly rose from the crouch she'd landed in. "What?"

Furiously, I threw the flashlight at her, then lunged after it, catching her by her tree-torn blue top a heartbeat after she caught the flashlight. She was a good six inches taller than me. "Were you born all pale skin and blond hair, all beautiful as the damned sun, or did you give up your soul to whoever the hell remade you so you could be so perfect?"

"What?" she said again, clearly bewildered. "I've always... the only thing that changed... he didn't change me on the *outside*," she said sullenly, and tried to pry my hands off her clothes.

She was strong, but I was stronger. I could have torn her apart. The dogs ranged behind me were *waiting* to help me tear her apart. Instead, I shook her like a rag doll. Her answer wasn't what I expected, but I shook her anyhow. I was trembling with fury and I didn't even know why. It wasn't Brynn. It was something about what she was, and what she wasn't. I remembered wishing once when I was in middle school that I was pale and blond and magazine-beautiful. I'd wished I had a soul since my mother died.

I pushed her hard away from me. "You stole my friend and I'd really like to kill you for that, but since it would only be a damned return to sender, I'm not going to waste my energy. Get the hell out of our way and stay there."

She caught her balance and lifted her chin. "You can't. I can't let you. But if you run away, I won't chase you." And she was serious. She actually believed she was offering me something I might care about.

I shook my head. "You? Are a wind-up doll. I'm the real article."

"Go to hell!" she blazed savagely, her teeth flashing. "You're not going anywhere else." Her canine teeth were quite the little fangs. I was not impressed.

I planted my feet shoulder-width apart, then launched myself sideways, into the shadows. I was leaving the flashlight behind, but I didn't care. It wouldn't help, not now.

I think that on a clear day, and an open track, we might have gotten away from her cleanly. She was fast and she had the reflexes of a cat, but I was my father's daughter and I had a lot of power to channel into how my body moved. But right now, either her night vision was amazing or she knew the forest like the back of her hand. I could have drawn the dogs back into my shadow for more power—but no. No. I didn't want to be alone.

So she caught me, grabbed my arm, and I flung her off. And she caught me again. She couldn't really stop me, but she wasn't letting me catch up to Auntie Tala, either. Then she landed on my back and caught at my face and hissed into my ear and I gave up and turned on her.

She was easy to see, even in the mist. Her golden hair and white skin gleamed like a phantom. She leapt backwards as I surged toward her, then scrambled up into a tree. Among the branches, peering down at me, she started to sing under her breath. It was the same "la la" number she'd sung before. I climbed up after her and she jumped down. Nod lunged toward her and she swarmed up another tree, still singing to herself.

I clambered out on the branches of my tree, toward her tree. I really regretted not tearing her apart before, when I'd surprised her. She'd seemed like a person when she answered me. But a person had some sense of self-preservation, right?

Her singing was starting to get on my nerves. I maneuvered toward a position where I could jump to her tree and said, "So what particular brand of monster are you, anyhow?" just in case that shut her up.

Amber's eyes narrowed. "None of your business." She shifted in the tree, then climbed higher. "Keep running after your friend so I can drag you down," she suggested.

"That was a bad call," I admitted. "But I wish it had worked. I really don't have time for this." I edged out along a narrow branch. For once I was glad that I was small and lightweight compared to most of the things I fought.

Something odd passed across her face. "You're better off running away. You can't hope to get her back. This way you're still alive."

That hurt, that brought up bad thoughts I had to work to push away, and I froze, balancing perilously on the swaying branch. "Was that woman your master? Why are you doing this?"

Her delicate face twisted up. "Her? Hardly. But you wouldn't understand. You're the real article, remember?"

I didn't look behind her, to where Heart was edging up the tree. My dogs could get up smooth walls with a bit of effort, so trees weren't exactly a problem. They just didn't like them. "Yeah. That means I never had what you gave up."

"I just made a mistake, okay?" The force of Amber's cry made her tree sway gently.

"You—what?" I stared at her, so astonished that Heart and Nod both stilled to watch me. A monster spawn claiming that her transformation was a mistake? I'd never heard anything so unreal. "You must have a very strange master," I said uncertainly. "Is he playing some kind of game?"

Instead of answering, Amber started humming again. She looked down at the ground, saw only Nod, then turned to see Heart peering over a pair of crossed branches. She scowled. "Tala and the Wild Hunt are going to help me escape. I thought she'd do it when I freed her from the stone, but—" and she went back to humming again.

I hesitated, intrigued despite myself. "You know, I'd love to talk to you more about this, but I really have to get Brynn back before your Tala does something awful to her. But—from what I overheard, that woman isn't so different from my father. I bet serving her isn't trading up."

I glimpsed her startled look as I dropped from the tree. I was running as I hit the ground, leaving Nod and Heart to slow Amber down. She didn't jump from the tree right away, which was all I needed. I wove through the forest, following Brynn's trail alone. As the terrain around me grew rockier, I realized distantly that Amber hadn't left the tree at all. She'd curled up into a ball. Heart left her, coming after me, while Nod stayed behind to watch her. It was a tiny ray of sunshine that I wouldn't be entirely alone while getting Brynn back.

I had no idea how I was going to do that, though. Barge in and demand her? Steal her? Fight? If Tala was one of the Wild Hunt, she was probably going to be a pretty tough fight. I felt sick thinking of it and slowed to a walk. I'd been in a pretty tough fight while trying to rescue somebody once before. I'd lost, and the only thing that had saved me had been calling on my father for help.

Doing that here would be the ultimate weakness: choosing my own life over Brynn's. At least before I'd been trying to save others and the person who had actually helped me had been somebody doing my father a favor, not *him*.

Besides, maybe he wouldn't even hear me from here.

That was comfort enough. I started jogging again. Brynn's scent was mingled with the scent of a human-shaped predator: hunger and flesh and leather and steel, and it cut straight through the forest. At one point, it crossed the trail of another predator, this one an animal. It smelled furry and almost bear-like, and just as hungry as the huntress Tala. I wondered what it ate; I had seen so little sign of prey in the wood.

But hopefully that wouldn't be my concern. After looking around where the trails crossed and remembering the roaring and the clawed trees, I kept going, dodging around the large stones that now protruded from the earth in equal measure with the trees.

Eventually I heard conversation. Because I hadn't been moving particularly quietly, the conversation was about me, or at least my noise.

"Hark at the vermin scurrying around," said a dry male voice. "We've allowed them too much freedom here." I froze and dropped to the ground, desperately aware I still didn't have a plan.

The woman called Tala said, "Soon they can have the Wood. Unless I decide to burn it down before we leave." I smelled a spark, then burning wood. A curl of smoke lifted over the trees ahead of me.

"What, no fondness for your shelter in exile? I should have thought you'd enjoyed your time in stone. The view must have been spectacular."

I listened until my ears ached, trying to decide if Tala was lighting a forest fire or a campfire. It made a big difference to the plan I didn't have yet. The dry, detached voice of the male speaker made me think it was a campfire; he didn't think it was worth remarking on. But it was clear I needed to actually see what was happening.

The ground was rocky, with pebbled soil and old squared-off blocks of stone protruding from the ground. I crawled behind a large one and waved Heart, just now catching up, to another. Then we listened together. There was a bonfire in the center of a stone-lined clearing and two figures stood nearby. Nobody was near my stone and the fire wasn't casting much light yet, so I risked glancing around it.

Tala and her companion were huge. I won't say giants—"giant" is a word with as many meanings as "monster" and nearly useless as a real description—but they both had to be close to eight feet tall. And they didn't have the rolled-out look of the very tall. They were fit. Muscular, like professional athletes. Or at least Tala was. It was easier to tell with her. She had golden hair and bronzed skin and she wore a sleeveless white tunic over buckskin trousers.

Her companion was the same size she was and wore a long brown tunic with full baggy sleeves that covered his hands. Several belts wrapped around his waist, hung with knives and other implements. He also wore a horned helmet with cheek pieces that hid his face, but his enormous nose protruded like a beak. His bare legs under the tunic seemed scrawny, but scrawny on an eight-foot-tall man was as thick around as my entire body.

He kept talking. "What is this prize you have here, that you try to assemble us all?" He looked down, and I realized that Brynn was curled on her side next to the fire. He pushed her with his foot and she rolled over. Her eyes were closed and her hands had been bound behind her back. A surge of adrenaline and fear almost sent me out from behind the rock, but I kept control of myself and watched until I was sure she was breathing. Tala was talking about her plan to regain status she'd apparently lost in the organization of the Hunt, but I couldn't pay too much attention. I had to figure out how to move between two near-mythical figures and steal back Brynn, all before Tala could do whatever she ultimately intended.

I circled the clearing, sniffing, looking for any kind of idea. And slowly a plan formed. Unfortunately, it was a plan for what to do once I'd freed Brynn and it depended on her being able to run away. I wondered if I could just walk in, introduce myself as my father's daughter, claim that I was his emissary—

My stomach churned at the thought, but if that's what it took…

Nod came up behind me, settling down at my side, and only then did I realize that he and Grim had been getting closer and closer for a while. And they weren't alone. I could smell Amber, and Yejun too. Somehow Amber had convinced Nod to let her pursue me; somehow Yejun had convinced Grim to leave the magic scent trail. I didn't have time to dip into the dogs' memories to find out how. They'd be here in a few moments and I was on the opposite side of the clearing from them. If I didn't get over there, they'd stumble right in and ruin everything.

-eleven-

Hoofbeats thudded toward me as I pushed my way through the underbrush. I ducked behind a rock again, my fingers clutching at my curls in frustration. A magnificent silver stallion, with neither bridle nor saddle, practically flew past me into the clearing. He stopped on a dime, turning and flinging dust into the fire. Then he reared dramatically in front of Tala, sniffed at the fire she'd kindled, and nudged her with his nose.

Tala smiled coldly at her companion as she raised a hand to the horse's neck, continuing a conversational thread I'd missed as I scrambled for a plan "My *only* mount. We are bound together like the red tassels on the Horn. I stole him from a gutless boy when this wood was but saplings. Ion can claim many things, but what is mine he cannot have, or else he will unmake all we have worked for. He must be content with this, Ipa. Alastor will make him see if I cannot."

I could see Tala's companion's wrinkled face from this angle and he looked amused. "You will have to do more than—but look, your prize stirs."

I changed my angle, craning my head and peering under a branch and between several leaves to see Brynn. She'd rolled over again, toward me and the horse, and her eyes were open. They seemed to glow in the firelight. Even though her hands were bound, she levered herself first to her knees and then lurched to her feet. Then she staggered toward the horse.

"Do you like my horse, little mortal?" inquired Tala. "You must, to overcome the peace I laid on you."

Brynn laid her forehead against the horse's side. It was so unexpected that I could only gawk.

"I knew she secretly loved horses," hissed a voice beside me and I startled so badly that the brush rustled all around us. It was Yejun, grinning at me.

And then Amber popped up on my other side. "I do kind of want to talk to you more. Your boyfriend is a jerk, though."

I goggled at both of them, then rested my head against the tree branch and tried to figure out how to convince them to just go away. At least they weren't currently prisoners of Tala as well.

"The vermin multiply," observed Ipa.

Right. This wasn't the place to argue. So all I whispered was, "We need to get her out of there somehow."

"You need a distraction," Amber said. "You owe me for this," she added, then stood up and walked into the clearing.

"Didn't she steal the kid in the first place?" asked Yejun. "She told me she'd made another mistake, whatever that meant."

"Shh," I hissed. I was trembling with nerves. Yejun looked at me, then shifted so he was closer to me, his leg touching mine. I could feel his warmth, and for a moment I wished I could squeeze his hand. Instead, I found Nod and buried my other hand in his fur.

"Little Amber. You return?" Tala sounded surprised.

"Of course," said Amber casually. "That's a pretty fancy horse you have there. Do I get one?"

"What is this?" asked Ipa. He inspected her up and down. "She has a surprising amount of vivacity. Her maker wrought well."

"A gift, I think," said Tala, talking over Amber's head. "Sent by one of Alastor's allies." Amber, meanwhile, circled the horse, then ran into Brynn.

"Oh, you still have this? I would have dealt with her by now myself," said Amber airily.

Brynn didn't react the way I would have expected. She didn't move at all from her position with her head pressed against the horse's side.

"You didn't turn the hunters into prey," said Tala, almost gently. "You must prepare yourself to run, sweetling."

"What, them? Of course I did. The girl even squeaked when I

jumped on her. It was, uh, satisfying." Amber met Tala's gaze with a brazen fearlessness that I couldn't even imagine.

Tala's gaze darkened, despite the firelight. Mythological figures don't much like being lied to. I mean, nobody does, but some of the celestial-born are really good at knowing lies from truth.

"This is not enough of a distraction," I muttered. "She's going to get killed and we're still not going to have Brynn back."

"All right," Yejun said, with a lightness that made me pull away. "My turn. I figured I'd do this later, but—" He shrugged.

"What?" I whispered. "Do what?"

"Try to hold onto your stomach," he whispered back. "Remember when you said the moon was wrong? You were right. It's not the moon at all."

Then he reached up and pulled the moon out of the sky. The night came with it, trailing from Yejun's hand like a veil, leaving behind a brilliant blue sky and the afternoon sun where the moon once was.

Everybody reacted. Amber screamed and the two Huntsmen cursed and I gagged as my stomach tried to follow the moon. I met Yejun's eyes and then I stumbled away, into the clearing. The horse reared again, and Brynn had fallen onto her backside. But her hands were free, and she was scooting away from the horse and toward the fire.

Amber had her arms over her head as if she expected the sky to fall. Tala grabbed her. "What is—" and then all three of my dogs and I were in the middle of them, adding to the chaos. I caught Brynn from behind, then leapt over the fire. The dogs barked, jumped up, and snapped at whatever was handy. Brynn fought me, struggling.

"Why didn't you fight Amber or Tala?" I demanded, exasperated. "I can just leave you here if you really want to stay..."

She went limp. "AT. I thought—" Then she raised her head. "More horses."

"Hey!" shouted Yejun. "Better move! Guy with the chicken legs is trying to start something in the tangle."

Then another horse burst out of the shrubbery directly ahead of us. This one had a rider. Brynn froze, but I lunged forward, dragging her with me. The horse stomped, then reared, because apparently that's part of the job requirements for Wild Hunt horses. While the horse was busy showing off, we went around him. As we did, I glanced up and saw Ion, First Huntsman of the Wild Hunt, looking down at me with the same amusement he'd shown the first time I'd seen him. He could have reached down and grabbed me or Brynn. He might have ended up with a broken hand for his trouble, but he could have done it.

He didn't. He didn't even turn his horse to pursue us when we were past him. And I wasn't at all surprised. Catching us then would have ruined all the fun.

"Come on," I said to Brynn as we put a tree between us and him. The daylight forest was alabaster and crimson and gold, interrupted by all the jutting grey rocks. It would have been beautiful if I had a moment to appreciate it. Instead, all I could do was hope that maybe the horses would break a leg on one of the stones.

"What about Yejun?" asked Brynn, pulling against the way I yanked her after me.

"He showed up on his own. I assume he can escape on his own."

"AT!" she said reproachfully.

I sighed. "The dogs are with them. We'll meet up soon. But we have to move fast because pretty soon those people with the horses going to start chasing us."

Brynn's mouth opened, then closed again. Then she followed me, docile as a chastened puppy.

I headed back the way we'd come, casting about every so often for the trail of the giant predator I'd crossed before. It was odd, though. The only way I could tell we were going back the way we came was the ghost of my own scent. The land didn't lose the rocks that had sprung up as I pursued Brynn and Amber. If anything, it became rockier. The crimson leaves that covered the ground thinned out and the trees thickened, their branches tangling up. Twice I stopped to carefully move around, to make sure there really was a trail, and not something wrong with my nose. It was always tricky following my own trail, since my own scent was always with me. I could detect faint traces of Heart's scent, just enough to *think* we were going the right way. But it was weird. When we reached the predator's trail, I almost didn't notice.

I stopped absently and Brynn jiggled my arm. "We have to keep going," she said urgently. "All three of them have horses now."

"Let's wait—ah."

Heart appeared around a tree, a moment before Grim bounded over a fallen log and Yejun climbed after him. Grim pranced over to me and sat down, wagging his tail, clearly expecting praise for being a good dog. I gave him an unfriendly look.

"You were supposed to stay on the trail." He licked my hand and wagged his tail more, his ears pricked hopefully. I blew out my breath and scratched his head.

Yejun said, "Where's that blond chick? Amber? She seemed pretty upset when I brought back the sun." He reached into his shirt and pulled out his sunglasses.

"She's running. Nod is with her." I frowned, skimming the surface of Nod's perceptions. "She doesn't like the sun. How the hell did you do that?"

"You don't like it either?" He gave me a crooked grin.

"I love it. But let's be clear, you also picked the damned moon out of the sky." My stomach churned just remembering it.

"Well, it wasn't the real moon," he said, as if that excused matters. He looked down at something glinting in his hand. "Kind of like a lens filter, really. Maybe somebody left it behind."

"Are we waiting for the singing girl, too?" asked Brynn nervously. "She cut my hands free back there. I don't know why. I saw her on the trail, and then... " She shook her head instead of finishing.

"I was—" I started to say. Then a horn blew nearby. It was a long, sweet sound, as if all the terror and death it heralded was simply the shadow cast by the beauty of the horn's voice. A tremor went down my spine. "Please tell me that's not the horn we need?"

Yejun frowned. "I don't know. I can find out, if we're not about to be—"

"We are," said Brynn and I together. I turned away, to the predator's trail. It meandered around a large tree and vanished into the forest depths. "Come on."

"Yo, this is the wrong way," said Yejun, like he knew what direction we should be going.

"I know. It's got a distraction at the other end, though."

"They're coming," said Brynn tersely.

"Let's run," I suggested.

We ran. It was a lot easier to avoid tripping in the daylight, but the ground was still uneven and rocky and slippery with old red leaves. Once Brynn tripped, and when she rose to her feet there was more crimson on the rock than when she'd fallen. That was bad, I thought. On the bright side, the ones pursuing us didn't seem to have any hounds. Instead there was the horn, and the thunder of hooves and the bell-like laughter of Tala against the chanting song of Ipa.

It seemed like we ran for hours, though I didn't think the humans had the endurance to run that long. The predator's trail I followed just went on and on, without us ever catching up. Brynn was the first to tire and Heart and Grim ran beside her to lend her their strength. But as the sun slipped toward the horizon and the light streaming through the trees turned scarlet, Yejun too flagged. When he stumbled, I turned back to him.

He pushed himself to his feet and rubbed sweat away from his face, still wearing those sunglasses. I said, "I'm going to try the Curtain again. See if the two of you can get out of here."

Yejun only glanced over, then looked past me, as if what I said was irrelevant to him. Brynn was so tired she didn't even have the breath to argue. But it didn't matter. I reached out and the Curtain was still as hard and slippery as a soap-slicked shower door.

"There's a hill ahead," said Yejun. "We can do something there. Well, I can, anyhow."

I turned and peered against the glare of the setting sun. Squinting, I could just see the rising roundness of a stony knob of land. Excitement flickered against my growing weariness. "I think that's where we're going." And I plunged ahead again.

It was as if our hunters knew. Brynn yelped and sprinted ahead of me a moment before the hoofbeats made the ground shake. The forest opened up on the approach to the hill, giving both the riders and us a chance to stretch out. Silently I urged the dogs to look for a cave, and they dashed ahead to do so. I slackened my pace so that both Yejun and Brynn overtook me. Then I turned for just a moment to look at the three riders approaching us.

It wasn't three riders anymore, though. It was four, and the spectral forms of two more paced them as they surged toward us like something out of a dream of shining death. Ion was in the lead, on his black and crimson steed, and once again, he pointed at me and grinned.

Then the dogs found what they were looking for, and they found what I was looking for, too. At their furious barking, I turned and dashed after my friends. As I passed them, I panted, "This way. And be ready to get out of the way. Throw yourselves down if you have to."

Something roared inside the hill. Heard from a distance, it had just been a noise—the sort of roar you barely notice when you live in or near a city. There's always engines somewhere, after all.

This wasn't an engine. This was an enormous, furious animal, and it was far too close to my friends. *I could fight it*, I thought hazily, instinctively.

The memory of my father's voice in the back of my head said, *Yes*, and I remembered the taste of flesh in a horrible flash.

But I hadn't come to fight it. Not myself. The dogs, still barking furiously, hurtled out from a cave back in a gully amid scattered, rounded stones and broken trees. The animal they'd annoyed emerged after them and roared again. It was a giant bear, rank and red-furred, standing at least as tall on all fours as Tala the Huntress. It was rangier than the bears in the Pacific Northwest, as if it hadn't eaten in a while, and its face was more like a raccoon. And did I mention it was huge? It was huge. I'd never seen a natural predator so large. There were swords shorter than its claws.

"Oh my god," said Yejun, and his hands twitched.

A loose rock rolled across the ground, and my stomach rolled over, too. I grabbed his arm. "No! This is what I was looking for. Just... get out of his way."

Grim and Heart turned back to the bear and took turns darting in to snap at the big guy. Brynn and Yejun and I circled around them, trying to be inconspicuous. But it *knew* human shapes and after roaring in fury at the dogs, the bear turned to glare balefully at us.

The hunting horn of the Wild Hunt sounded again, just beyond the screen of trees. I gave Brynn and Yejun a shove forward, toward the bear. "Straight to the cave, guys!"

The Huntsmen burst from beyond the trees, their horses screaming in excitement. The great bear looked between the three of us

charging him, toward the dogs teasing him, and finally at the Huntsmen on their prancing hoses. He stood up on his hind legs and roared
so loud that I felt it through the stone underfoot. Then he dropped to
all fours and loped around the hill, away from the Huntsmen.

As the bear fled, we scrambled over the lip to his den and pressed
ourselves against the inner wall. The dogs dashed in after us and, at
my command, flattened themselves on the ground.

Yejun whispered, "This is a terrible hiding spot. They saw us run
in here."

"Go further back," I suggested. "Their horses won't like it back
there. They won't, either. But it doesn't matter. Look."

The horses of the Wild Hunt danced with an excitement their
riders shared. I could see the discussion, what there was of it, happening just through their body language. They were delighted to find
the bear, eager to pursue and finish him, all but the one called Ipa. He
pointed at our cave and argued, but he was the only one. I watched
the horses backing up and adjusting their position as a fifth hunter arrived. Then they turned and cantered around the hill, after the
bear. Ion held out his hand to the cave as they went, in a gesture that
seemed to indicate approval or possibly amusement.

"We're not hiding," I said as the thunder of hooves softened. "Not
exactly. We're just putting off on the inevitable. And getting out of
sight to make the decision easier for them. That bear looks a lot more
fun to fight than three kids will be. Taking his claws will be a serious
trophy. Posting our heads on the wall of their castle or whatever isn't
going to impress the locals nearly as much. Whoever the locals are."
Yejun and Brynn both stared at me and I shrugged. "So we have some
time now."

I looked around the cave. It was dim, because the setting sun was
on the other side of the hill, but it was still brighter than the wrong
night had been. There were drifts of hair and small bones, and a lot of
chewed branches. There were glints under some of the debris I didn't
want to investigate. It was an *old* cave and it looked like something
had been living there a long, long time. It wasn't shallow, either; the
cave narrowed at the back, becoming a passage to deeper inside the
hill. It was much, much darker back there.

Brynn sagged against the wall, then slid down it. "Okay. Some time. That's great, because I'm bushed." She put her head against her knees, then lifted it again. "What happened to me? Wait, no, more important question: where's my camera bag?"

Yejun sat down against the other wall. "I left it on the trail so we could find our way back."

"Great," sighed Brynn, and put her head down again.

"Why did you decide to come after me?" I asked Yejun, and I tried not to snap. Without help, I didn't know that I would have gotten Brynn away. That was more important than losing the trail.

He stretched out on the floor of the cave and took his sunglasses off. "Talked to Cat and Jen. Jen said you'd need help, and we weren't getting anywhere without you."

"Oh." I thought about that for a moment. "Wait, what? How did you talk to them? Cellphones don't work in the Backworld. I've tried."

Without a word, Yejun flopped his arms out to the sides and opened his palms. With only a tiny twist of my stomach, two lifesize images shimmered into existence, one near each hand. Cat sat at a table that faded out of sight, while Jen paced in place. Both of them looked down at Yejun when they appeared, then around the cave.

"AT," said Jen, a smile flickering across her face. "I'm glad you're together again."

-twelve-

I ran my hands through my hair as I looked between the image of Cat, the image of Jen, and Yejun lying between them like he was taking a nap. There'd been a lot of weird today. This wasn't the weirdest thing. I just needed a minute to readjust. Clearly the three of them had worked out some magic to manage communications through the Curtain. That was excellent. Great news. An innovation I'm sure everybody would want to copy. But Geometry magic wasn't my gig. All I had to do was accept that it worked.

"I wanted to apologize for what happened before," Jen added. "Sometimes I get so tired now. When that happens, I can't stop thinking about bad things. And after Sen... saved me... my bad thoughts can take over everything around me." She said "saved me" like she didn't think it was the right phrase at all.

I waved her apology off. "It happens. Even if you're not—"I stopped.

"Undead?" Jen laughed, but it wasn't a happy laugh. "Thank you. Was Yejun helpful?"

"He stole the moon," I said, and I couldn't help the note of accusation in my voice.

"Really?" asked Cat, looking down at Yejun.

"It wasn't a big deal," Yejun said without opening his eyes. "Really, it wasn't. I saw how to do it, and I did. It wasn't the real moon, just some old tangle of magic. If I'd known it was going to upset her so much I would have done something else."

Jen looked between me and Yejun, then shook her head. "Where are you now?"

"Resting in a cave," I told her. "I don't know if we can get back to the trail. The Wild Hunt is riding through the forest." I remembered the uncertainty I'd had about the horn they were blowing and added, "It may not matter. They had a horn."

Cat and Jen exchanged a look that went on too long. Then Jen hugged herself as she said, "The Wild Hunt only chases loose souls."

"I think maybe they've changed the rules some. These guys had the Chief Huntsman leading them around and they were chasing *us*," I said. "Maybe since we're in their territory we're their legal prey now. How should I know? But they were definitely hunting us and now they're after this prehistoric bear I found for them."

I thought Brynn was asleep, but she lifted her head suddenly, listening to something I couldn't hear. Then she stood up. "Can we go back further into the cave? I don't want to be here when they come back looking for us."

Even tapping into Nod's senses as he moved through the forest with Amber, I couldn't hear anything. But I remembered how she'd always heard the horses before I did when we were running. "Good idea." I looked down at Yejun. "Do you, uh, have to lie down like that to summon them?"

Yejun's eyes slitted open, then he rolled to his feet, fished something out of his pocket, and headed deeper into the cave. The images moved with him. Grim darted ahead, because he always had to be in the lead, while Heart stayed back with Brynn and me.

Whatever Yejun held glowed with a soft, silvery light. He'd come more prepared for this adventure than I'd expected, given how quickly we'd run into it. We walked behind him for a few minutes, the images of his teachers drifting along silently. The cave narrowed into a claustrophobic neck, something barely tall enough for Yejun. The Huntsmen would have trouble squeezing back here after us. And if they changed their size, even for a short time, they'd be easier to fight.

And then the stone neck opened up again, into a rounded cave with three more irregular passages leading off, and a sort of natural chimney rising up to a stone shelf that opened to the outside. There was an old stack of firewood against one wall, and the blackened remains of an ancient fire.

"Did a bear make that?" asked Brynn uncertainly.

"They don't *usually* make fires, but I admit the bears here could be special." I cocked my head, listening. Somebody was walking down one of the other passages. But it was a familiar tread, and even Grim didn't think it was worth barking about. He was far too interested in nosing about the woodpile, eventually discovering what looked to be the rotted remains of a rough leather satchel.

"You can rest here," Yejun told Brynn. He put his glowing rock or whatever it was into the firepit, then touched the curving wall near the woodpile with both hands. Cat and Jen flickered onto the wall as Yejun went on. "At least until we decide where we're going next."

He shot me an inscrutable look. I wanted to shout at him, because I'd know exactly where we were going if he and Grim hadn't left the trail.

"Thanks," Brynn said tiredly, collapsing onto the ground. Then she sprang to her feet again, looking around wildly. "Somebody's coming."

"It's Tia," I assured her. Brynn stared at me, then at the passage.

A moment later, Tia emerged from the middle passage, the one that tended downward. She wore stylish running shoes and crisp new jeans under a button-down blouse. It was the most casual outfit I'd ever seen the demon wearing. And while her hair was rumpled and her scent disordered, she had the same calm expression she'd had the day she promised me that if I wanted to, I could be free.

Even though she was wrong, I still loved her for trying. Even if she was angry at me, she was still the closest thing I had to a friend who would last. I was so very glad to see her.

Crossing her arms, she said, "All present, I see." She glanced up at the chimney shelf, as if she, too, could sense Nod and Amber closing in. "I mustn't stay, but I'm pleased to see you all together."

"Tia," I began, stopped, then started again. "Tia, it's all going wrong. I didn't even want to bring us here. I'm sorry."

Jen said quietly, "The children say they were chased by the Wild Hunt, but I'd thought the hunt was scattered until Halloween ended. Sen didn't predict this. If the Horn has already pulled them together, I don't know what we can do."

Tia looked between Jen and me. "The Hunt must be pulled together to manifest the true Horn. If you're being chased by the

Wild Hunt, you're on the right path. What is it you think you're doing wrong?"

I shook my head. "This place is wrong. We met somebody who said he was distorting the Backworld and everything's been wrong since then. This forest isn't where we're supposed to be. And if we pulled the Wild Hunt here somehow, that makes it even harder to get to where we're supposed to be. Do you know who the guy with the violin is? Is he one of Alastor's friends? Or yours?"

She gazed at me a little too long, then said, "There is always some wildness in the Wild Hunt. The nature of their unique power lends an element that is not just unpredictable, but alien."

"That's not an answer," I said reproachfully.

"Ms. Zelaya likes us to figure out answers for ourselves," Brynn told me hurriedly.

"If she's been telling the truth, there's an awful lot riding on this for riddles and guessing games," I pointed out.

"Once upon a time," said Tia, sitting down on the ground, "Six celestials gathered to solve a problem. They had with them a shard of power beyond their ken, which they believed they could use to do the impossible. They thought it was a receptacle they could fill. And they were right. The shard took something from each of them. One gave her shadow, one gave his name. One gave his blood, one gave his will, one gave his body, and one gave her life. But the receptacle wasn't empty to start with, and what was there merged with what they'd put in. The power of the Horn radiates out and when it bounces off objects it cannot pass through, echoes and reflections are created. The power passes through almost everything, but the stranger you met, it does not pass through. I don't know why that is, and later I would very much like to find out."

"Ah!" said Jen, like she understood everything. "This forest is one of those reflections, then."

Tia nodded once. "And the true Horn is at the heart of their power, not in this forest. What Ion carries now is just another shadow, a link to the source of their strength."

"But who's the stranger?" I demanded.

"Somebody smart enough to know when he's causing trouble and considerate enough to try to offset that." Tia gave me a sweeping glance, then turned her hands palm up. "Otherwise, I do not know."

I frowned. "What about the monster spawn girl? What's *she* doing here?"

Tia clicked her tongue. "AT, I'm not going to be your window to the world. You'll have to talk to people yourself eventually."

Jen said quietly, "Yejun, can you tell me more about the stranger? Sen was researching where the Horn came from when—when she realized the current threat."

I stopped paying attention to instead gnaw on my lip and think about what Tia had said. She clearly knew something about Amber, and just as clearly wanted me to find out for myself.

I muttered, "Be right back," and went to the stone chimney. It sloped very slightly. Most of the time I couldn't walk up truly vertical walls like my dogs, but this wasn't much of a challenge. I gauged the height of the shelf above, put a booted foot on the chimney wall, and pushed off into a jump. My fingertips just caught the lip above and I hung for a moment before hauling myself up.

The chimney flattened out, rising gradually to the rocky hillside opening. Amber was curled on her side near the chimney's exit. Nod rested nestled under a shrub nearby. He was only visible by the starlight reflected in his eyes.

Amber's eyes didn't just glint, they glowed. Not brightly; I wouldn't be using any Amber booklights anytime soon. But I felt strongly that you oughtn't be able to tell somebody's eye color on a dark night and yet I could see that Amber's eyes were blue. And her teeth were white, and her face was... strange in the darkness. She had her head on her curled arm, and she didn't move as I crawled out of the hole in the ground.

Jennifer and Tia murmured below about horns and strangers and Machines and the sources of Wild magic. Brynn asked Yejun something and he responded in his low voice. Cat said something, his voice still beautiful, and Jen responded sharply. I looked back at the dim light radiating from the cave like it had swallowed the moon. With the meaning of their words blurred by stone, I could hear the emotion there and I wondered again what was between Cat and Jen.

"Do you want your dog back?" Amber's voice was soft. "He wouldn't leave me alone after that bastard brought the sun back. I stopped minding after a while."

"It seemed ungrateful to just abandon you," I said apologetically. "I hoped he'd help you get away."

"It figures," she said, sighing. Then she sat up, stretched her back, and rubbed her hands over her face. "Ugh. I hate it when I get hungry. I know it isn't real, but even if I sing myself into resisting, it shows up here." Her fingers drifted over her mouth, and then she looked down and away from me.

I looked away, too. "So what are you doing here? Why did you steal Brynn and then change your mind? I mean—" I snuck a glance at her. She was looking steadily at Nod as he regally surveyed the hillside. "I mean, um, I grew up around people like you. They don't usually help me out."

"People like me?" she inquired, distantly. "Funny way of putting it."

"Well... people who were human once but who gave that humanity up for... I've never really understood why, to be honest. For a little bit of power? For a kind of immortality?"

"For love," Amber said, her voice still cool and calm and faraway.

Cat and Brynn were talking over each other below us. In the far distance, I heard the sweet cry of the Horn's shadow and a rumbling, enraged roar. The wind rustled the shrubbery around us. Amber leaned over and plucked a tiny blue flower that grew from under a stone.

Blankly, I said, "For love? Who do you love?"

"It doesn't matter anymore." She began to methodically destroy the flower. "I'm sorry I took your friend. You have her back again."

"She's not my friend," I said. "She's just... a tagalong. A helper, she calls herself. But I'm responsible for her now."

Amber's eyebrows went up but she didn't look away from the tiny flower petals she was arranging on top of the rock. "What are you doing here? So many of you, and Tia Zelaya, too."

Even she knew Tia's second name, dammit. I cleared my throat and answered her. "We're trying to stop the Wild Hunt from getting free and wiping out all the unbound human souls."

"Hmm." The petals and leaves and stem were all lined up, like an anatomical diagram without labels. "How will you do that?"

"I don't know," I admitted. "My job is just to find their home and get their Horn. Which isn't the horn we just heard, as far as I can tell,"

I added grumpily. "Then other people will use it to reboot the Hunt somehow."

"This wasn't always a forest," Amber said. "When I came here, it was something else. Then, day by day, the forest grew up around me. What lived here adapted so quickly, maybe it's happened before. The Hunt destroys ghosts? I think that's a little hypocritical of them, given that they're all ghosts themselves." She began disassembling another flower.

I shrugged. "People are hypocrites, news at eleven." I paused, thinking about what she'd said. "How long have you been here?"

"I don't know. Sometimes it feels like years. But it doesn't look like fashions have changed much since I came here, if so. So maybe a month? I talked to the Fiddler once, before you arrived. He was looking for you."

I had been planning on asking about her master again because I didn't know how to stop worrying about him, but that did the job of distracting me just fine.

"What? He had no idea who we were." I frowned at her. "You're just making things up. I don't trust you at all."

She shrugged again and swept the dissected flowers off the rock. The breeze picked up the petals and spun them around her. "That's probably a good idea. You just came to take your dog back, after all." She paused. "I'm Amber, by the way. What's your name?"

"AT. I never—" I stopped, flustered. She hadn't really told me anything since I'd climbed up here. She'd evaded all my questions and told me untrue things instead. But she seemed so lonely. "What are you going to do now?"

"Probably follow you and your friends around until I find another way to get what I'm looking for."

"They're not my friends," I corrected automatically.

She looked at me through her long, silvery lashes, the moon-like light from the hole below catching the pale curve of her cheek. "I'll trade you, then."

"What?" I blinked at her, bewildered.

"I'll trade you. I'll take the surprisingly heavy little girl and the sarcastic moon-stealing bastard, and you can follow along behind in the shadows." She paused, waiting as I groped for words. "No?" Standing up, she added, "I wonder what they have to do for you to consider them friends."

"You're right," I muttered, staring into the darkness beyond her, seeing nothing. "I should trade. I should."

She leaned forward, peering at me. Her blue eyes were hypnotic. "What's that? No, don't be silly." And she smiled lightly as she added, "You didn't choose this life, after all."

Now I *knew* she didn't know nearly as much as she thought. But I didn't want to talk to her anymore. I didn't want to talk to anybody, and I thought longingly of just leaving them all behind in their cozy cave and setting out on my own... to where? Maybe I could pick up Ion's new trail and follow it back to where he came from? But the whole "reflection" thing confused me. Technical magic wasn't my specialty and I'd probably just make things worse if I tried to find the Horn by myself.

Then again, I hadn't done so well with the others, either.

"AT?" called Brynn from below, as if she knew what I was thinking. "Tell me you're still up there?"

Besides, Heart and Grim were still below. If they left, everybody would realize. Tia probably wouldn't approve, and I'd disappointed her enough.

"I'm here. I'll come back down." Without looking at Amber, I clicked my tongue at Nod and sent him down ahead of me. Then I wriggled into the hole and slid down to the cave, leaving Amber alone in the darkness on the hillside.

-thirteen-

I **landed** on my feet in the cave and brushed myself off before looking around. Everybody was looking at me as if they'd been talking about me. I shifted uncomfortably. "What?"

"You owe me five bucks," said Yejun to Brynn, turning away to hold his hand out to her.

But Brynn was grinning at me as she waved him away. "I thought maybe you ditched us."

"Naw," said Yejun. "Amber's awful company. Like some *Idol* wannabe who never got over her missed audition."

"Is that who you were talking to up there?" Brynn asked me, coming over and patting Nod.

I said shortly, "Yes. So what are we doing now? Does Tia have a new trail for us?" I glanced at Tia, who regarded me liquidly. "Something other than our own scent to follow would be great."

Brynn shuddered. "What does she want? That girl up there, I mean. Why did she grab me? Is her singing magic?"

"I don't know. Her name's Amber. I don't know and probably. Was that everything? It wasn't exactly a productive conversation." I glanced at Brynn's worried expression and softened. "I don't think she's going to grab you again if she can help it. She's weird, but I don't think she wants to be bad."

"She'll fit right in, then," muttered Yejun, rubbing his forehead with the palm of his hand.

Cat cleared his throat loudly and pushed his glasses up his nose.

For a moment, he looked familiar, but I couldn't figure out where I might have seen him before. Then he said, "Jen and I have put together a spell for Yejun that will let him find his way back to the camera bag he left on the original trail. I think you need to be very careful of this Fiddler, though. We don't have time for mischief."

Jen glanced at Cat, then looked away again, as if she wanted to argue with him, while Yejun looked between them with a furrowed brow.

Amber's voice drifted down from above. "Hey, get out of here! Shoo!" I caught a snatch of humming and then there was a piercing cry, like the scream of an eagle. A moment later, Amber tumbled out of the chimney.

Brynn darted behind me and Yejun rolled his eyes. "Uh, hi," I said, as Amber stood up and brushed herself off.

"Hi," she said breathlessly, her eyes still glowing faintly. There was a distant thump and the walls around us quivered. "Um, there's a giant bird out there. I think maybe he's looking for one of you? He seems kind of intense."

"Ah, yes," said Tia. "I did say I didn't have much time. Go carefully, children. And try not to fight too much amongst yourselves." And before anybody could respond, she blurred out the passage we'd arrived by.

Yejun said, "Demons. *So* helpful. So secretive, too."

"She tries," I told him sharply. "Just because we don't know everything she's doing doesn't mean she isn't being helpful."

There was another quiver of the walls and then a long hoot, like the deepest note on an oboe. Then... silence.

Yejun gave me a dark look, his eyebrows pulled together. "Of course you'd say that. What have you lost to them? You practically *are* them." And that was such a horrible thought that all my words fled and I stood there, fists clenched behind my back, as my dogs pressed up against me. Distantly, I heard them continue talking.

"Yejun," said Cat, with a tone of gentle reproof. "Don't—"

"You know what, Cat? Shut up." And Yejun flicked one hand and the image of Cat vanished.

Jen's image remained. She took a quick step toward Yejun, her hand outstretched. Quietly, he told her, "I'm sorry you're stuck with him. You should have sent him along here instead of me."

Her face clouding, Jen dropped her hand and looked down. "It's not his fault."

"You hate him," pointed out Yejun.

But Jen shook her head. "I don't. I didn't." She glanced up, and there was a painful half-smile on her face. "That's the problem, really." Then she moved her hand, and her image vanished, too.

A pool of silence spread out. Yejun stared off into the shadows while I tried to bring myself back from where his accusation had sent me. It was like my mind had gone numb. Every time I tried to get on with things, I thought, *How could he think that?* And froze up again.

Then, at the same time, Brynn said brightly, "So we're off, then?" and Amber said, "Well, that was awkward." They glanced at each other.

"Sorry, kid," said Amber. "I thought maybe I could trade you in. Sort of a 'get in with the cool kids' voucher. I was dumb." She sighed and flipped blond hair away from her face. "That happens a lot."

"Uh, okay. Apology accepted, I guess." Brynn shifted her weight. "Hey, Yejun? You ought to apologize to AT, too. You've got no idea what she has or hasn't lost."

"Hush, brat. This isn't kindergarten," Yejun said, still staring at the shadows. "Or go back to making small talk with Blondie. I'm trying to find your camera bag."

The idea of Brynn defending me broke my paralysis. "It's fine," I said. My voice was so rusty I didn't recognize it, and I cleared my throat. "It's fine."

Despite his supposed distraction, Yejun shot me a look under his lowered brows and I had the sudden, dizzying idea that he'd wanted me to say something different. He'd wanted me to *argue*. But what would that accomplish, other depressing anybody who cared and boring anybody who didn't?

Better to move forward. "Anyhow, I'll send Nod out to scout around the front of the hill. Make sure nobody's around."

"No point," said Yejun. "We're going that way." He waved his hand at the passage that Tia hadn't passed through arriving or leaving.

I frowned. "That's totally the wrong way. How do you know?"

He waggled his fingers. "Magic. A wizard did it."

"I didn't feel anything," I said suspiciously.

"That's probably because Cat designed it. It doesn't have my precocious flair. Do you doubt?"

I gave him a disgusted look and went with Grim to investigate the narrowing of the cave where he indicated. "It smells like dry leaves and bones. Like nobody's walked this way in ages."

"Maybe it's a shortcut. But I miss my flashlight," said Brynn, taking hold of my arm.

Amber said diffidently, "Probably nobody ever *has* walked that way. Not in a way that would leave a scent."

Yejun picked up his glowing stone from the old firepit and shouldered his way past me. "And yet, this is the way we go to get to the camera bag and the crazy Fiddler's magic trail."

Moving forward was better than staying still, even if it was the wrong direction. So I went after him, dragging Brynn along with me since she was clinging like a lamprey. Grim trotted up to pace Yejun while Nod dropped back beside Amber, who trailed along in the far rear. She'd warned me she would, I remembered.

Our feet crunched down the tunnel. It was pitch black beyond Yejun, which made me uneasy. Our noses told us there was nothing living ahead of us for thousands of yards. On the other hand, the tunnel went on for thousands of yards, and so much could change here in that distance.

Brynn's fingers dug into my arm. "Do you think this tunnel is haunted?"

I glanced at her and noticed how pale and tense she was. Reassuringly, I said, "I don't think so. This doesn't feel like a haunt. They're not usually subtle."

"And you know about haunts, right? You said your mother was a ghost?"

Had I? I vaguely remembered saying something like that when talking about Jen and wished I hadn't. But not answering wouldn't reassure Brynn at all. "Yeah. When she has bad dreams, my father's pack knows it right away. They have nightmares, too, waking ones. Everything turns against them." My father'd eventually locked her locket in the trophy case when I was around thirteen, because nothing else would stop the haunts. I'd really *enjoyed* how they pretended nothing was going on.

After a moment of silence, Brynn asked, "What happened to your mother? How did she die?"

"She had a bad heart," I lied, with the ease of long habit.

"Really?" asked Brynn, her voice odd. I snuck another glance at her. "My dad died when I was a baby. He had a heart attack while he was driving home. Do you think he's around as a ghost, too?"

"Uh." I flailed for an answer that somebody as removed from the supernatural world as Brynn would be able to follow. "Well, it depends. Most people don't stick around as ghosts. They go on to Heaven or whatever. Some of them stay on Earth because they've accepted an offer from somebody like Tia. And sometimes they linger because they're not ready to move on. Because they've got unfinished business, or they're afraid, or they just like it here." I realized this wasn't much of a reassuring answer and added, "If your dad was religious, or even just raised religious, he probably didn't stick around."

"I don't think we've had any haunts," Brynn said thoughtfully. "There was the fae—um, there was something once, but it turned out there was another explanation."

"Oh, haunts only happen if they're unhappy about something," I said quickly. "There are plenty of ghosts who just like to stick around and watch their descendants."

That seemed to satisfy Brynn, and after a minute, she found her courage or something, because she let go of my arm and dropped back with Heart. I couldn't help myself: as soon as she let me, I moved up to pace beside Yejun. Grim, trotting between us, looked first at him and then at me before giving a whole-body wiggle of delight. He really liked it when I walked beside Yejun, because he was ludicrously optimistic.

Yejun scratched Grim's ears, but he didn't look at me at all. The disc he held glowed with a peculiar radiance, lighting up the passage ahead and behind without being blinding. He had his sunglasses off again.

"I want to know more about Cat," I said after a moment of his silence. "Why did you apologize to Jen about him?"

Yejun's gaze slid toward me before returning to the path, but he didn't say anything.

Brynn muttered behind us, complaining about how endless the passage seemed. Heart chuffed companionably in response. Amber was far enough behind us that I couldn't hear her, and only my connection with Nod told me she was still there.

"Because," I explained to Yejun patiently, "He's really cute, but I kind of want to tear him apart right now. I know not to trust nice-looking men, I really *do know*, but he seemed different. He seemed... kind." I gnawed on my lip. "Is he hurting her somehow? Because if so, we have to do something."

Yejun stopped and looked at me, his expression inscrutable even when Brynn bumped into him and complained loudly. After a second or two, he caught up with me.

"Sen was the wizard and Jen was her assistant, but they were also together. You know?" Yejun kicked a pebble down the passage. Brynn shut up abruptly. "I was only with them a few weeks before the demon inferno, and they'd picked up Cat around the same time. And it was cool at first. Sen talked about spending years teaching me after this Wild Hunt thing was over." He laughed humorlessly. "I think she wanted to adopt me, like I was some little street urchin."

I paced along beside him, bouncing on the balls of my feet. He'd never said so much at once before and I was afraid of where the story was going.

"It was different with Cat. He looks like he's my age, but he's... not, somehow." He glanced at me again. "Maybe he's like you, older than he looks. He moves kind of like you. But I don't know. There was a... a thing between the three of them. I didn't really want to know details. None of my business. As long as he didn't mess up what I had going for me, I didn't care. And Sen..." He shook his head. "She *promised* me it would be fine. That no matter what happened, she'd keep me with her. You don't trust cute guys? I *should* know better than to trust anything that looks like it could be good. Anyhow, since Sen died, Jen has been even weirder about Cat. She's told him Sen would be alive if he'd never showed up. She's told him they'd both be dead, too. Like she wishes that was true." He fell silent.

After a moment, I prompted, "And what does Cat do when she says this stuff?"

"What? Oh. He listens, he puts up with it. He loves her, I think." Yejun shrugged, as if this was normal, as if what he'd said hadn't hit me like a hammer.

I blinked rapidly. I wanted to run away suddenly, wanted the story to be over. I liked my love stories light and frothy, not full of blood and fire and grief. But I'd asked and now I had to listen.

Yejun went on. "He told me right after the fire that Sen contacted him as she was working her final magic. Told him to save Jen. I don't know if that's true or not."

I frowned, trying to work through this. "I don't understand. How does she feel about him?" The corridor curved ahead of us and the sound of our footsteps changed subtly.

He sighed and closed his hand loosely over the light he cupped. His fingers made bars of shadow on the walls. "She's not happy with him around, but when she gets all spooky, he's the only one who can get through to her."

"Yeah, but why did you tell him off?" I persisted.

Yejun turned and looked at me again, his eyes glinting. "You're something else, you know that? I hung up on him because he's not in any position to treat me like a little kid who's pushing on the playground. Especially when the person I'm pushing is you."

I stopped, staring at him. The light made the planes of his face stand out so that he looked not quite human. Except for his eyes, his face was impassive, like once again he wanted something from me. I swallowed and said, "Okay. Thanks for the answer."

His eyes narrowed. "Don't you ever defend yourself?"

"Sometimes I break peoples' arms," I said distantly. "Wouldn't help here. It's okay. Let's keep going."

"Guys," Brynn ventured cautiously. "We're not in a cave anymore. Why is that?"

I looked around. The walls of the passage were smoother and more angular than they'd been before. The few protrusions were regular, rectangular.

"Bricks," said Brynn, touching one with a single finger. "They're walls. Concrete walls."

Yejun closed his fingers more tightly over his glowing disc. I immediately noticed Amber's luminous eyes behind us, which I still didn't like. Then I realized that there was a very dim light spilling around a corner ahead of us.

I went toward it.

"AT?" said Yejun in the dark.

"What?" I said, stopping.

"You owe me a better answer sometime." He brushed past me, the back of his hand touching the back of mine. The dim light faded until he went around the corner.

Brynn put her hand in mind and I instinctively pulled away. "Dammit," she muttered. "Sorry. You don't owe him anything, though."

"I do," I whispered. "He answered me." Something about his response made me think he didn't just want me to argue with him, he wanted me to win. But that was crazy. Nobody wanted to lose a fight. Nobody wanted to be wrong. Did they?

Behind us, Amber inquired, "Are we waiting to hear if he screams? Because I'm okay with that. He probably deserves to scream a bit."

I shook my head and went around the corner, too. Yejun waited on the other side, looking down what was very clearly a corridor, poorly illuminated by a very distant hanging light.

"We're still on the trail of the camera," he observed.

"Did somebody move it?" I was bewildered.

"I don't think so," said Yejun slowly. "Send one of the dogs back the way we came, will you?"

Grim volunteered before I could ask, galloping back down the passage behind us. He ran for a solid minute, but the concrete walls did not become an earthen cave. Eventually, he came to a corner, dimly lit from the other side. When he peeked around the corner, in the distance, he saw a hanging light we'd never passed. It was enough to make even the happiest of my dogs whine and put his tail between his legs.

"The cave is gone," I told Yejun flatly, and called Grim back to me. I was used to Backworld terrain being strange, but I'd never been trapped by it before. You were supposed to be able to get back to where you came by going backwards, right? But apparently not anymore.

"That's what I figured," he said. "It's like we're traveling through depth as well as breadth. Although I didn't really expect a concrete hall to be on the far side of a forest."

"The more fool you," said Amber glumly.

Yejun frowned at Amber, then said to nobody in particular, "Why exactly is she with us? Do we need an annoying tagalong blond—"

It was Brynn who cut him off. "Because she knows Tia too.

Right?" She shot a look at Amber.

Amber crossed her arms and leaned her hip against the wall. "Sure." She made a show of studying her nails.

Brynn scowled at Amber, but only said, "See?"

Yejun squinted at Brynn. "How do you know? That wasn't very convincing."

Now it was Brynn's turn to look uncomfortable. "She recognized Tia earlier. And Tia knew about her."

"Tia seems to know a lot more about everybody than we know about her. It's not really inspiring double the trust here." Yejun turned and walked away down the corridor.

Grim stayed with me. All three dogs clustered close enough to trip me if I wasn't careful. There was something wrong with the concrete hallway, something that worried Nod and Heart. It actually frightened Grim, who didn't hesitate to fill my head with his anxiety. He thought the light from the fixture was the reversed shadow of something alive. He worried that it would make us sick somehow. He was afraid that it would devour us and what came out the other side would just be flesh on bones.

I might have laughed at him another time, but the image he shared of me walking around post-light was too disturbing. Me, as I looked in the mirror, just me. Except the image was imbued with the horrifying awareness that really, I was just raw meat clinging to bones, that any semblance of life was a dream, and the true me had been devoured by the secret behind the light.

My breath caught in my throat. Heart growled at Grim, then licked me. Whatever Grim sensed, she and Nod didn't think it was *that* bad. Or that his vision was particularly likely.

After a minute, as if giving me a less than honest reassurance bothered him, Nod admitted Grim's vision was basically *already* true. But Nod always thought like that. It was probably why he liked Amber so much.

"What's wrong?" asked Brynn, looking at me curiously.

"She can probably sense where we're going," said Amber darkly.

"And where's that?" Brynn demanded, looking between Amber and me.

"You'll see." Dramatic music failed to crash with Amber's words, but the hairs on the back of my neck prickled all the same.

"Hey, come on! I don't want to walk around this corner and strand you all in endless back hallway hell." Yejun stood directly under the hanging fixture, looking back at us. I hurried after him and he started walking again as soon as we caught up.

We went around the corner.

Another long hallway stretched ahead of us, lit dimly by a distant, hanging fixture. The walls were bare concrete blocks, jutting out a handswidth here and there. As we walked down the hallway this time, Brynn counted her steps under her breath.

We went around the corner.

Another long hallway stretched ahead of us, lit dimly by a distant, hanging fixture. It looked exactly the same as the two hallways before.

My skin creeping, I stopped dead. Brynn brushed past me with her jaw set in an oddly familiar way. I wanted to catch her arm and draw her back before she got hurt, but I didn't know why. Instead I walked close behind her, looking at the walls and the floor and smelling the dry and dusty scent of the concrete. The floor was poured cement with no cracks, no slab lines except at the corner itself.

We went around the corner, into more of the same hallway. Brynn stopped. "They're the same length. We're walking in circles."

Yejun shook his head slowly. "I don't think it's circles. Spirals through this screwed-up place, maybe."

"Evidence?" Brynn demanded. "Because I counted. You can count, too. You walk eighty-seven steps, turn right, walk eighty-seven steps, turn right, eventually you end up exactly where you started. Basic geometry."

"Funny you should say 'geometry'," I muttered, but she was too busy glaring at Yejun to hear me.

Yejun looked annoyed. "The spell I cast says your camera bag is ahead of us. If I turn the other way, it's behind me. If we were going in true circles, that wouldn't be true. It's just a trick, like the night was before."

This time Amber walked past the rest of us, to a point halfway down the hall. She fished in her cleavage and pulled out a tube of lipstick. Opening it, she displayed it to us, announced, "Sinner Red," and then carefully drew a smiley face on the wall. "Well? Come on."

We went around the corner. Another long hallway stretched

ahead of us, lit dimly by a distant, hanging fixture.

Yejun said, "See?" The wall Amber had drawn on looked unblemished.

"Let me see," said Brynn and ran down the hall. "Hah," she said, and the look she threw back at us burned. "Hah!"

We caught up with her and looked at the wall. The smiley face was gone, but in its place was a faint red smear, as if somebody had imperfectly cleaned up the graffiti.

"Hah what?" said Yejun. "It's not the same. It's exactly what I would have expected. Unless you think somebody is running ahead of us with a roll of paper towels."

Brynn opened her mouth, hesitated, then turned toward Amber and held out her hand. "Sinner Red, please."

Amber said, "Nuh-uh. You're too young. What do you want to do?"

"Mark how many times we pass by." Brynn drew a line with her finger beside the faded red smear. Amber shrugged and copied her with the lipstick, except she drew a stick figure instead.

"Now we keep going?" I encouraged, my fingers curled tight in Nod's fur.

We went around the corner. Another long hallway stretched ahead of us, lit dimly by a distant, hanging fixture. The fixture was swaying gently, making the light move and twist. It had a texture that I could no more describe than I could describe a scent. I couldn't remember if normal light had a texture, too. I'd never thought to look.

Acidly, Yejun said, "Maybe the fiend with the paper towel roll hit the light on his way through."

As we watched, the swaying stopped. Only when it had stopped did we walk forward to inspect the Sinner Red smear. The second mark Amber had made was smeared now, too. This smear reached toward the first smear.

Humming under her breath, Amber made a third mark: a happy face with a question mark for a mouth. Then we kept walking.

Once again, the light fixture was swaying when we went around the corner. Nobody except me waited until it stopped swaying this time, setting out into the writhing light like they were unaware of the danger.

"What?" said Yejun, turning to look back at me. The light moved behind him like the bubbling of his tree of nodes and I averted my eyes.

"Nothing," I lied, and moved forward. If the light attacked us, maybe that would at least be something to fight.

The third mark was a faded smear as well now, and the two previous smears had changed shape, crimson inkblots crawling across the
wall toward each other. Amber pursed her mouth, turned the base of
her lipstick to push up more color, and drew an EXIT sign. "Because
why not?"

We went around the corner. The light fixture swayed as if somebody had just bumped it, and we ignored it. The EXIT drawing was
just a smear, reaching toward where the other smears had merged into
a single writhing bloodstain.

"Oh well," said Amber. She drew a 5. We went around the corner.
The quivering light. The smear. 6. The walk. I stared at the ce-
ment floor and listened to each of our footsteps. Amber, Yejun, Brynn,
Heart, Nod, Grim, me. Was there somebody else walking with us?
Behind us?

The corner. The trembling light. The smear. Brynn caught Amber's
hand as she went to draw a 7 and said in a sick voice, "Don't. Stop
feeding it."

All but the previous smear had merged into one now, and it was a
different shape. There was a hint of a hand, a hint of a mouth.

"If we keep going, we're going to get somewhere eventually,
right?" I asked.

"Yes," said Yejun flatly. "Brynn's camera bag."

"Okay," I said. "Can we run?"

"Good idea," Yejun said.

We ran. The stain on the wall animated, frame by frame, each
time we passed it: the bloody hand, the screaming mouth, the shape
of knees and feet, the stains left behind by somebody first standing,
then crawling along beside us. And the mouth got larger and larger,
and the light started spinning clockwise, just like us.

Brynn's breath grew labored and Yejun panted and Amber
hummed as she darted lightly along. But we didn't reach a camera bag
and the hallway didn't end, and I was almost certain somebody was
running beside us. When Brynn stumbled and fell, I spun to catch her
and held her while she caught her breath.

"You've trapped us here," I told Yejun as he leaned against the
wall opposite the stain and wiped sweat away from his face.

He gave me a sharp, angry look. "We had to run forever in the forest, too."

"We weren't trapped in an endless hallway where a stain on the wall was about to turn into a monster and eat us. I don't understand how you're doing magic to track down a bag anyhow. I don't understand why people would or wouldn't teach you and I don't understand how you stole the damned moon. Are you sure your magic is reliable?"

Yejun glared, his eyes bright with anger. "Go to hell," he said, then walked over to the stain and put his hands against the bleeding eyes that had appeared. He pushed, hard, until the stain widened under his hand and blood started dripping down the wall. Was it his? Was it the walls?

Then a brick fell out of the wall and gashed Yejun's forehead open. "No," he said furiously. "Get out of the way."

I couldn't tell if he was talking to me or the hallway. I didn't have a chance to find out, either, because the building then collapsed around us.

-fourteen-

I dreamt. It was the kind of dream where your subconscious punishes you for avoiding its calls by making your memories more intense and vivid than reality ever was.

The sun beat down on the rooftop, cutting through the haze of smoke from hillside fires. It glinted off the twisted metal form of an insectoid monstrosity looming over me. My blood dripped from its claws. I'd fought it for what seemed like hours, but I couldn't beat it. I wouldn't be able to save my new friends. Because that's who it wanted. Every time it knocked me back, it turned away, turned toward the children who had brought it to life.

They'd wanted to make somebody who frightened them go away, and they had. But it's tricky with little kids and lots of magic and terror. Monsters under the bed are scary enough without the power to bring them out of your imagination and into the real world. When you're still learning to do things like control your bladder and hop on one foot, managing the unbound power of a fallen angel can be especially rough. Sometimes, it tries to kill you.

I should have been able to save them. They were powerful but unfocused. I was powerful and I was *trained* to fight. I wasn't good for anything else. I should have been able to take their bad dream apart and put it back to bed.

But I couldn't and I didn't understand why. It flung me across the rooftop and I somersaulted to land on my feet. My shadow stretched out beside me, all the power I'd called to me distorting it into the shape of a wolf. My dogs were gone. My shadow and I lunged, grabbing the monster by one of too many spindly legs. It turned away from the children yet again, brought one of its claws whistling down on me. As the metal sliced through my arm, I gritted my teeth and hefted the monster away from the children. I'd tried throwing it off the building, but it had too many legs; it could cling and climb and return again and again to try to destroy its creators.

I knew what I had to do. But I was as afraid as the kids were. I didn't want to give up the freedom I'd won. But if I couldn't save them, it was a fake freedom. It was a lie, and I'd have to live with how I failed them to hold onto a lie forever.

I didn't know everything my father was capable of. He had powers I'd barely guessed at. I knew distantly that the celestials were all cut off from their largest workings by the Hush, but I'd never really internalized it. Love died and the sun set at my father's hand. He'd be able to deal with this metal nightmare. All I had to do was ask for his help. All I had to do was admit that I needed him, just like he'd always said.

There was no time left. My blood was everywhere and my muscles ached and I could feel the broken bones screaming in my right foot and my vision blurred. I needed help. I couldn't do it alone. I was a failure without him.

I screamed for him to save me.

The dream changed, went backwards.

"Catch me, Daddy," I commanded and flung myself off the swing. And he caught me, and smiled past me at my mother. He told me I was his beautiful baby girl. But I wondered why his smile was warm for me and so very cold toward Mommy. Later, I'd overhear—

No.

No.

I wasn't going to have this dream. I wasn't going to let my brain punish me by showing me again and again and again how young and stupid and sweet I'd been. I was never going to be what my mother thought I should have been, not since I was conceived. I was his daughter, and her daughter, and that combination only made something brittle and nearly useless. A fighter who refused to defend herself. A monster who cowered like a puppy.

I woke up, clawing my way out of the confusion and self-loathing of my dreaming thoughts.

I wasn't buried under tons of rubble, to my bleary surprise. I was curled on my side on a hard surface, my head tucked against my chest and my hands dug into Nod's fur. Grim lay nose to tail at my feet, while Heart nestled against my back. I could feel the open air above me and smell the stink of nearby asphalt. The wind moaned and my stomach growled.

I lifted my head and opened my eyes. Yejun sat across from me, legs crossed, watching me impassively. We were both on concrete and a strange, high light streamed from somewhere above. He had a long cut across his forehead that nobody had cleaned, and the backs of both his hands were slashed and gory. Brynn was curled up and asleep nearby, while Amber was nowhere to be seen. I didn't like not seeing her any more than I liked her glowing eyes. She was monster spawn, after all, no matter how much she seemed like a human.

My gaze was drawn back to Yejun. He was backlit by the stormy sky behind his head, and it shadowed his eyes. I thought the storm-light made everything but him seem a little unreal. Even Brynn looked more like a painting than a real girl.

He slowly raised his eyebrows at me. "Welcome back."

I stared at him a moment more, marveling at the way the light made him look like something out of a movie. Then I realized I'd been silent and staring too long and blurted, "What happened?"

"This is the final layer of the onion," said Yejun. "I tore through all the others. Since you were so sure I'd led you into a dead end."

I flushed. "I was afraid." He still looked super-real, like everything else could wash away and he'd remain. I concentrated on Nod's fur in an attempt to make my eyes adjust to wherever we were. Nod pressed close to me in response. None of the dogs liked it here, and they all had bad memories of the magic that had torn down the layers of Backworld.

Sardonically, he said, "Are you less afraid now?"

I automatically looked around. It occurred to me that maybe the unreality was the place we were in now. We were in a city, which at least matched the previous concrete hallway motif. But my first impression was that it was a dead city. We sat on a cracked sidewalk with an empty four-lane road to one side and an abandoned five-story building to the other. The bottom floor was a storefront with empty windows. Similar buildings lined the street on both sides, varying in height or façade or windows, but they were all of them empty. There was no graffiti. The pavement was cracked, but no grass poked up through the fractures. No trash blew along the gutters.

After looking around for another minute, I revised my opinion: dead implied previous life, and it didn't look like this city had ever been alive. It didn't smell like it, either. It wasn't new and shiny like a model city in advertisements. It wasn't worn down enough to be a ruin. It was... strange. Strange was better than the fear I'd felt in the endless hallway, I told myself. But I shivered as I said, "I like the open air. There's lots of directions to run. Is Brynn okay?"

Yejun said, "She fell asleep while waiting for you to wake up."

I glanced at him, then looked away from his too-vivid dark eyes and scooted over to check on Brynn. She seemed fine except for a couple of big bruises on her hands and arms. She shook her head and mumbled as I prodded her, but refused to wake up. Then Heart nosed her way in and started licking Brynn's face. I left her to finish the job and turned back to stare at the pavement near Yejun.

"Where's Amber?"

"Wherever Ambers go, I suppose," said Yejun. When I gave him a confused look, he explained, "She went racing away across the roof-tops once the scenery settled down."

"That's a little worrying," I said. "Um, so not everybody passed out?"

Yejun shrugged, his eyes never leaving me. "Just you."

I shifted my weight uneasily, listening to Brynn struggle against her furry alarm clock. "Your magic is so weird. You do these incred-ible, strange things I've never even imagined and you say you don't even know magic."

"I said nobody would teach me," he corrected and paused.

I didn't say anything as I stared at the pavement. I didn't know what he wanted me to say.

After a moment, he went on anyhow. "Nobody wanted to show me anything. But every wizard who came to gawk at me had charms. I gawked back. I didn't know how to do what they did, though, so I had to try things out on my own." He paused again, waiting through the long moment until I looked at him. His mouth twisted into a sneer as I did. "You're the only person I've ever met who gets sick from my magic. Most people barely notice. But you're special."

"I'm sorry," I muttered, my face hot and my hands cold. Nod licked me. The wind picked up, blowing the strange concrete and plastic scents of an unpeopled city into my face.

He sighed, as if I'd annoyed him. Quickly, I pushed the subject back to him. "But why wouldn't they teach you? You've got some amazing gifts. Weird, but amazing."

Yejun shoved himself to his feet. His shirt was torn across his ribcage, letting me see a flash of skin as he stretched. "Waste of time. They thought I'd die before I grew up. They thought if I knew magic, I might do some damage on my way out."

Appalled, I said, "They told you that? How old were you?"

"Nah, they told my parents when they started showing up when I was five or so. But my family already—" and he cut himself off. "Never mind. It doesn't matter. I'm not going back. It's over."

I looked down at the pavement again. One of the cracks looked like the letter Y.

I wanted to talk with him more, I wanted to understand him better, but somehow we kept running into walls. And I just couldn't push him on his family. Do unto others and all, and I certainly didn't want to talk about *my* family. If he felt like he could get away for good, that was great. I was sure he had what it took to make it on his own.

Brynn made a small noise that told us she was finally awake, for which I was profoundly grateful. Then she said, her voice rusty, "I was dreaming about your friend. Jen. What happens to her if we pull this off? Does she stay undead?"

"I have no damn idea," said Yejun. "Cat must think so, because if she's going to vanish when this is over, I think he'd be a little more upset."

"Oh," said Brynn, digesting this. "So where are we, did you figure it out?" She pushed Heart away and stood up, rubbing her cheek where her arm had indented the skin. Then she subjected me to minute inspection before flashing a bright smile.

Yejun shook his head. "Just that we're at the heart of the onion. I can't contact Jen or Cat. It just doesn't connect. Or it does, but there's nobody on the other end."

"Maybe we're too far away?" Brynn gave me an inquisitive look, as if I could answer the question.

"Maybe," said Yejun, but doubtfully. He didn't look at me at all.

I searched my memory. "I don't think charms that connect two people—if that's what you even have, no clue—are limited by distance. But they can be blocked."

Brynn's eyes sparkled. "Not limited by distance? Not at all? Instant communication? My brother is going to love that."

I hedged uncomfortably. "Well, all charms use some kind of power. They might require a lot more power across long distances."

Brynn didn't seem fazed by this warning, but Yejun frowned. "Jen and Sen mostly used these little battery-like power sources. I have a couple for the charms they gave me, but it's not how I work on my own. I wonder..." He fished a couple of what looked like D-cell batteries from his pockets. I recognized them from my time in California.

"What are those, M-cells?" Brynn asked. "Get it? M-cells? For magic?" She snickered.

"Why don't you go back to sleep, kid?" Yejun told her. "What do you do, AT? You have some charms. How are they powered?"

I startled a little, remembering. "Oh, yeah, I guess I do. I don't really use them much. They're very small, not the sort that can really hurt me if they use my personal energy, especially since I'm a nephil."

Yejun's eyes narrowed. "What does that mean?"

"Uh, well. It means I'm faster and stronger than you, and the same energy that makes me faster and stronger feeds the charms." I wondered how he'd react to me stating the truth so baldly. My father's pack always hated the idea.

"That's what I thought," he said, looking satisfied. "Mind if I borrow some?"

I blinked at him. "What?"

He gave me a teasing smile, shocking in how unexpected it was. "Can I borrow a cup of nephil magic? I'd really like to check in with Jen, and if we simply don't have enough power to make it work, I bet you can help."

I shook my head in confusion. "Can you do that? I mean... just do it?" Something nagged at my memory. Something somebody had told me once about powering strong Geometry magic with intrinsic nephil magic. It was okay with weak charms, but strong charms... But Yejun was grinning at me and that made it hard to concentrate. I kept feeling like I'd done something right, or I was about to.

"Give me a minute.... Yeah, yeah, pretty sure I can. I just need to—well, can I?" He held out a hand to me.

I hesitated, glancing at my dogs, then asked, "Can you limit it to just a cup?"

"Absolutely," he said, his eyes fixed on mine. "This would be a lot smaller and gentler than what I did before."

"Um," began Brynn, then fell silent, sighing and sitting down again.

I should have looked around. I should have weighed the benefit of getting Jen's advice about the creepy city versus the risk of ending up flattened by exhaustion. I should have made the decision rationally, set up safeguards, explained about my dogs, worried about being sick. But instead I just thought about how much I treacherously, dangerously, wanted him to like me. That smile was so brilliant, and his eyes were dark enough to drown in.

I reached out and took his hand. His was bigger than mine, and warm. His fingers were very gentle as they laced with mine. "Does your hand hurt?" he asked softly.

My muscles twanging like a taut wire all the way from my neck to my toes, I shook my head. "It's all up here, anyhow." I touched above my ear.

"Yeah," he said. "I know." Then his gaze went far away and his free hand moved through the air in a complicated dance.

At first it didn't seem like anything was happening. I wondered if he saw magic the same way I did. Most people had the Sight as a charm, but he didn't, I was sure. I could look and see, I realized. I'd avoided the Sight since meeting him, because I didn't want to be distracted or sickened—but if I was just standing here, letting him do his thing, shouldn't I watch and learn? Maybe I could understand.

But then I started to feel what he was doing. I closed my eyes against the growing nausea, the twinge of a headache. For a heartbeat, I felt like he was moving things around me in quadruplicate. Four points of view on the same thing, and none of them were the same. How could I not be sick? Then he caught at my intrinsic magic, at the power I'd inherited from my father. He started drawing on it as he sent out the seeking aspect of his communication charm. And I remembered, too late, what I'd heard about powering charms directly from intrinsic magic.

-fifteen-

I have no idea what my father was before he became what he is now. They say that the celestials were the caretakers of the world, each one devoted to nurturing some aspect of Creation. I can't even imagine some nurturing thing he could have done, because what my father does now is break things. Bodies. Hearts. Minds. Relationships. Ideologies. All of those at once, if he can. He's the wolf in Grandma's bed and the patron saint of turning on those who love you.

I don't know what he used to be, but sometimes I wonder if his power is as twisted as he is. He's taught me how to break things, but it's not my core, magically speaking. Maybe it would have been, if, at the age of five, I hadn't found a dying puppy and saved his life by mingling my magic with his soul. I don't really know. But ever since then, I've had a connection to dogs. I can feel what they feel. I can empower them, then do what they do. My own dogs are special, of course, but I can get along supernaturally well with any dog. In a very real, life-changing kind of way, I'm part canine.

And my father, the wolf in the bed, only minded the veneer of domestication. He only liked dogs when he could teach them to bite the hand that fed them. A daughter who was a wolf inside was just his style. After all, there's a word for a person who is part wolf and part human, especially when all they know how to do is destroy things.

Yejun's charm to borrow a cup of power activated and it pulled my magic forward, from the back of my mind where it was normally under my conscious control. The rush of power wrapped around me, turning on me, taking over my mind.

My body was wrong. I was pretending to be human, fully human. I was trying so hard, but why lie? I could be different. I could be better. I was so limited by trying to be only one thing. Imagine how much better I could be if I just let go.

Yes, the memory of my father whispered. *Stop cowering. If you hate me, stand up and fight.*

We fought him, we killed him, and he just came back again, my mother whispered in quiet horror. *Don't make our mistake, baby.*

I gasped and tried to resist the magic sweeping over me. My free hand found Grim, my first dog, the puppy who never really grew up, and I clung to him. I didn't think to let go of Yejun. How could I? I was helping, wasn't I? I clung to that, too.

Brynn wrenched our hands apart, panting, her eyes blazing as she shouted, "She's crying, you idiot."

I scrubbed at my face and reached after Yejun. "What? No, I wasn't," and added hastily, "Did you get anything?"

Yejun glanced at Brynn, then at me. "She was changing," he said, stepping back out of my reach.

My heart sank. I bit my lip. I didn't want to talk about *that* even enough to deny it. "Did you contact Jen?"

Slowly, he shook his head. "I thought I did, at first. There was a link. It was like something opened. It still feels kind of open."

Brynn looked up in the sky. "Yeah, about that."

The storm-lit clouds were lower and darker than they had been when Yejun took my hand. They moved rapidly, tendrils curling across the sky like the hair of an angry sky goddess. The buildings near us weren't tall, only two or three stories, but beyond them loomed skyscrapers and a huge clocktower. All of them were dim and dingy, except for one, which had three glowing windows at the top.

I frowned and rubbed my eyes. "Has that always been there?"

"I don't think so." Yejun pulled out his sunglasses and looked at them, then shook his head and put them away again. "I want to get a closer look, but the path to the camera bag is that way." He pointed in a line perpendicular to the illuminated skyscraper.

I took a deep breath, steadying myself. I could feel my magic settling back into the back of my mind. My dogs were still with me. I hadn't actually turned into a monstrosity. And Yejun still had a trail to follow. So what if some mysterious tower glowed like a lighthouse? So what if Amber had left us? We'd find the Wild Hunt's home and get the Horn and save the day and then I'd go back to my father's house again and I wouldn't have to worry anymore what the likes of Yejun and Brynn thought of me. I'd have my dogs. That would be enough.

"Okay," I said. "We don't have time to explore and I don't trust this city. That light makes me think of an anglerfish, anyhow. So let's just follow your trail to the Horn's trail and get this done."

Instantly, Brynn said, "All right."

But Yejun was slower in agreeing. He looked at me carefully and I wondered if, having been so close to my magic, he was now wary of traveling beside me.

"I'm sorry," I told him. "But for now we have to work together. Even if the scent trail I was originally following is in this city, it would take me too long to find it on my own."

"Of course," he said, his voice touched with snow. Then he added, "You are the strangest girl I've ever had the luck to meet. Don't apologize, it's annoying." And without giving me a chance to respond, he snapped his fingers in an invitation to Grim and set out in the direction he'd pointed.

Grim gave me a cheerful look and an encouraging wag of his tail, then galloped after Yejun. I told myself that I only cared so much because Grim was so fond of him. Grim thought he was *great*. Hilarious, friendly, fun.

But Grim didn't notice his smile like I did.

"You don't have to just put up with it if somebody's bothering you," Brynn told me. "You certainly don't have to apologize. My sister would flip—" and she cut herself off and shook her head.

"I fight back sometimes," I offered, moving after Yejun and silently instructing Nod to keep a nose out for Amber.

"That's not actually reassuring." Brynn frowned at the bruises on her hands and caught up with me. "I mean, what do all the people you're not willing to fight back against, even just with words, have in common?"

I wondered uneasily what she knew, what Tia had told her about me. My steps slowed down until she passed me and turned back inquisitively. But I didn't want to walk with her anymore. I desperately wished I was alone, that Tia hadn't saddled me with a companion, that I didn't need Yejun's help getting back to the trail we'd left behind.

I shrugged and looked away while Heart went and nudged Brynn to keep her moving. Disappointment in her voice, Brynn said, "Well, y'know, think about it?" She patted Heart on the head and caught up with Yejun instead.

That was good. The two of them could be friends. They were both human. This adventure wasn't an act of charity for them; it was ultimately self-preservation. And I was going back to my father's house after this. It was the only home I had. And going home again without any lingering relationships was going to be the best thing I could do. My father didn't want me to have any friends who were girls, but he was all too eager to see me interested in a boy. He'd destroy either of them, one way or another.

I looked around, trying to chase away my thoughts. At an intersection, we passed a tall pole with twisted metal struts at the top. It was the only thing I'd seen so far that looked like it had been purposefully damaged, as if a street sign had been torn away. There were other signs over the storefronts, faded and illegible. Nod went to sniff around an ornate, unlit streetlight. No dogs, although he did detect the faded scent of some kind of engine. I tried to concentrate on that, on whether or not it was interesting. But a sheet of light raced across the sky and made the reflections of the streetlight writhe in the dark-glassed windows of the empty buildings.

I remembered the moving stain in the hallway. But I knew it was the lightning, just a reflection. I *hoped* it was just a reflection. Out of the corner of my eye, I kept seeing my father, like he was watching me from the other side of the glass. I could hear him complaining about how I made him sick with my moping. I made *myself* sick. I didn't want to be here, feeling things I didn't dare feel, but I didn't know where I'd rather be. Sometimes, I didn't want to be anywhere. Other times, it was worse than that. There were times when I *wanted* to be at my father's house, where things were awful but at least I understood them. And there were times when I wanted to just tear things apart.

It was so easy to get angry, especially when I was alone.

Lightning flashed again, crawling through the sky to wreath one of the skyscrapers in a net of light. There was no thunder. There was never any thunder, not since I'd woken up here. No thunder, no rain.

But I did hear a violin. It started me out of my horrible thoughts. With an effort, I dragged the mental manhole cover over the oubliette of my hopes. Then I cursed. "Do you hear that?"

Brynn and Yejun both stopped. "What?" asked Brynn.

"Music. Violin music."

"Oh. Oh, no," said Yejun. He started walking again, a whole lot faster. Brynn had to skip every few steps to keep up, and I jogged ahead of them. The sidewalk was in better repair here and the buildings were less dingy. Apparently even weird cities on the far side of the Backworld had slums. The windows of the buildings flashed like black holes.

"I hear horses," said Brynn, her voice shrill.

"I don't. I hear engines," Yejun said grimly.

"Yes, those. Behind us," said Brynn.

I felt a twist in my stomach as Yejun did something.

"Don't!" I said sharply. "Don't, I can't take it right now."

He stopped whatever he was doing without saying anything, and his silence was another kind of pressure. I could hear the engines behind us, too. Motorcycle engines, distant. Moving perpendicular to us, I thought. They weren't coming up behind us, which was the important part.

Then Nod growled and darted into an alley. His growl became a snapping snarl and Amber yelped. "What? No! Stop it, you pest!"

I stopped. Yejun did, too, leaning against another streetlight and closing his eyes. Brynn tried to join me and I went toward the alley instead. "Amber?"

A moment later, she backed out, herded by Nod and his deep snarl. His head was lowered and his ears flattened, and I thought it was pretty clear even to somebody not in his head that he was really, really angry at her for running away.

"Please at least tell me you did something about Ye's bleeding," she said weakly, glancing between me and Nod.

I looked back at Yejun, and the untreated cut on his forehead and the gore on the back of his hands. "Uh, nope."

"Oh god, I hate you all," she moaned. She started to hum, then covered her face with her hands and looked away.

"It's not like we have a first aid kit. Or even clean water," I pointed out.

"I have a kit in my camera bag," offered Brynn. "If we ever find it."

Amber tried to get past Nod back into her alley, but not hard enough to actually succeed. "Can't your dogs lick him clean or something? Shoo, Nod."

"Ew," said Yejun. "These scabs are wholesome and healing. I don't want a dog developing a taste for my blood."

"You'd rather I did?" Amber turned a flat stare on Yejun, like a snake watching prey.

"I thought you already had one," said Yejun as he yawned. "Why don't you let her run away again?" he added to me. "Don't we have enough to worry about?"

Amber made a pathetic effort to dodge around Nod. He lunged and tore her skirt. She wailed, "I'm *hungry.*"

As in response, my stomach growled emptily. Yejun gave me a frosty look, as if I'd done it on purpose. "I know I smell delicious, but I am not for eating."

"Ugh," I said, wrinkling my nose. "I wouldn't dream of it. No matter what my—no matter what. I'd starve first."

He looked taken aback. "Oh. Well, I *am* delicious. But if Blondie goes for me, I'm going to tie her in a knot. She's more trouble than we need right now."

I listened to the faint music coming from one direction, and the roaring elsewhere in the city, thinking about where else Amber could be. A single engine sounds different in a vast empty city. The urban jungle needs the roar of engines, lots of engines, like a green jungle needs birdsong. You learn to tune out the endless roar of highways so that you can't even imagine the lack of noise unless you're far from roads. That solitary distant roar meant trouble.

I wondered for a moment if it was the thunder the silent lightning was missing, escaped to rumble around the city independently. My skin tingled in the unceasing flashes of lightning and I wished it would rain. Rain would solve a lot of problems right now. I looked back at Amber again, at the way she scowled at the ground and crushed her skirt between her fingers.

"Yeah," I said to Yejun slowly. "But..." I didn't say that I couldn't help wondering about her. About what it was like to be her. About whether she'd eventually lose her veneer of humanity and start lashing out. I wanted to see that when it happened, although I couldn't tell if it would satisfy me or make me cry.

Yejun shook his head, disgusted. "She followed you home once and now you feel like you have to keep her."

"It's a popular strategy," I admitted, tilting my head toward Brynn in acknowledgment of her own efforts in that field. "But not home. She'd be toast at my house." I frowned. "You know something about this city, Amber. And it wasn't friendly to take your secrets and run away. Spill."

"See how friendly *you* are when you know you're just one angry thought away from being nothing more than a picture in a yearbook." Amber pushed her blond hair behind an ear and kept her gaze on Nod. "This city is creepy. Especially if you go into the buildings. Don't go into the buildings. And you know how there's signs written in a different language everywhere? Well, it's an alien language no matter what language you read."

I sighed. "I could have guessed all that myself." I looked her over. Her hair was still perfect, even though her clothing was torn and she looked gaunt and feral. "Who likes the idea of her behind us thinking about how hungry she is? Not me. But maybe we can do something. Nod, keep an eye on her. Bring her in when I say."

"Bring me in? Bring me in?!" demanded Amber, her voice rising in pitch. "What am I, the Hamburger Bandit?"

"Constable Nod is just going to mosey down to the bar," Yejun told her brightly. "But don't get any ideas, Wild Amber."

I shifted uncomfortably and started walking away, down the sidewalk. The light banter reminded me of the kids I knew in junior high, the ones who would spend half their time bickering, but you never saw them apart. I didn't know how to do that.

"Hey, wait up," called Brynn as she realized I was prepared to leave her behind. Yejun fell into step beside me, slowing his long stride.

"Where are you going?" he inquired casually.

I stopped, confused. "Toward the music, I guess. Which direction should I be going?"

"Oh, you were going the right way. I just didn't know if you knew. Toward the music, eh?" He tilted his head. "I think I hear it. Y'know, I always kind of liked strings. My little brother is in the school orchestra. This is spookier than the stuff he plays, though."

"Well, it *is* Halloween," Brynn told him as she fell in on my other side, walking so fast that she was almost jogging.

I sped up again. I didn't want to walk with them. I didn't want to feel like I was part of their crowd at school. I liked them too much.

I turned a corner, at a tall building with a sequence of unreadable signs running down the side. It looked like a shop for invisible ghosts, buying invisible things. The street sign here was unmutilated, with ornate and unreadable calligraphy.

The new street went a few blocks, then widened out into a plaza paved with pearl-grey stone. It was large enough for eight lanes of traffic, but there'd never been any motor traffic here. No pedestrians, either. The stone was rough, with a tooth that Heart and Grim could feel on the pads of their feet. A central column of multi-colored stone rose ten feet into the air and spilled water out of several holes into a huge basin set into the paving, bordered by rose-tinted marble. A large and unreadable stone sign declared the fountain to be whatever it was, and another sign, made of metal, requested or warned of something else. And beside the fountain, one booted foot on the basin's edge, stood the Fiddler.

Once again, he played with his eyes closed, and once again my dogs went to be his audience. But I wasn't in the mood to listen, or even be polite. "Oh god, it's him again."

The Fiddler ignored me. Maybe he couldn't hear me. Maybe to his ears, he was still in the forest where we'd arrived. Counting my blessings, I circled around him to approach the fountain from the opposite direction.

Yejun moved past me. "It's here!" On the other side of the fountain was Brynn's camera bag.

Brynn dashed past both of us to scoop up her bag. Or at least she tried to. When she pulled on it, it didn't budge, which was so unexpected that she lost her balance and sprawled on the ground.

"What the heck?" she complained.

"My bad, sorry." Yejun waggled his fingers and my stomach quivered. Only a quiver, not a lurch. The bag came away from the ground with a click. Then he asked, "So is the trail still here?"

I rolled my eyes toward the Fiddler, then sat on the ground and closed my eyes. The dogs spread out at my request, and together we explored the area around the bag. "Yes. It's different. Not nearly as broad or strong. But it's there." I opened my eyes again.

"Great," said Yejun, and flipped Brynn something glittering. "You might as well take that. It looks kind of like a lens."

Brynn caught and examined the glittering thing. "What is it?"

"The moon," said Yejun, a little too casually as he looked at me from the corner of his eye. I looked down, because I didn't know what he expected me to say.

"I wonder what it does to pictures," mumbled Brynn. "Oh, here!"

A metal box inscribed with a red cross skidded across the paving stones to bump up against my foot. I stared down at it.

"You know, I kind of expected we'd make it back to the forest again when we found the bag. But this isn't a forest," said Yejun, looking around. "I mean, even if you really stretch the definition. I wonder, if the forest was just some kind of dream, what those red leaves meant."

"Blood," said Amber sharply, stalking out from between two buildings on the edge of the plaza. "Clean him up now, or tell your dog to stop bothering me." Nod slunk along behind her, still growling under his breath.

As I picked up the first aid kit, the Fiddler's song finished in a burst of angry noise. I froze warily. Then I moved to peer around the curve of the fountain, ignoring Amber's little whimper of frustration.

The Fiddler sat on the fountain wall, his head in his hands, the very picture of dejection. Grim and Heart *both* darted past me to go comfort him, because they had no sense of perspective.

Faced with two canine heads shoved into his lap, the Fiddler brought his hands down on their ears and looked up at me. "Oh, it's you. Am I causing you problems again?"

I hesitated. Earlier I wanted to tear into him for the crazy way he'd presented the trail he'd unearthed. But at least he'd tried. "Not really. I didn't expect to see you again, though. Uh, have you moved from where we met before?"

"AT," whined Amber behind me. "No, leave me alone, dog,"

The Fiddler looked around. "Yes, I think so?" He seemed puzzled by my question and I dropped it.

"I take it you didn't find the song you were looking for?"

He sighed, running his hands through his hair. "I did, but there's been a difficulty—" He stopped and looked past me, his eyes lighting on each of my companions and lingering a moment longer on Yejun.

In a faraway voice I immediately distrusted, he said, "I know what I need."

"Oh no. No, no, no." I backed away, silently calling my dogs away.

"I have had enough of this," announced Amber, the whine replaced by new resolution. Nod backed up, confused, and she stalked past him, past me, and flung out a hand at the Fiddler.

"You. Stop, you. Don't distract AT with scary things until she's cleaned him up. She distracts easily. So please, shut up until nobody is bleeding all over the place." Her hand trembled.

The Fiddler blinked at her, then bowed. "Of course."

"It's hardly all over the place," said Yejun, looking at his hands. "You really need to relax."

"Look, once you're not bleeding, I can try to explain what it's like to be around you. All the gnashing of teeth and the longing to knock you down and tear your throat out—" She shook her head and kept her hand up as if she could push the thoughts away.

"That isn't how you feel when I'm *not* bleeding? Wow, I must be losing my touch," said Yejun. He settled on the edge of the fountain and looked at me. Then he plunged both of his hands into the water, wincing.

"What if that sign says, "Contaminated water?" asked Brynn sweetly.

"It's fine," I said crisply, pulling what I needed from the first aid kit and advancing on Yejun. Maybe the Fiddler would wander off while I worked. "It smells like it came straight out of a filtered spring. Do you want to dunk your head, too?"

He looked up at me, his black hair catching on the scab. "Ah. I'd rather not. Dunkings aren't really my thing." His dark eyes didn't change, but I recognized the tension that ran through his frame. I felt the same way when somebody wanted to take me by the hand.

"Okay," I said, letting it go. "This may hurt more, then." I positioned myself in front of him and started swiping at the cut with one of the antiseptic wipes I'd pulled from the kit. It was slow, delicate work, made distracting by just how close he was. He kept his gaze on my collarbone, but there was something disturbingly intimate in the way he looked at the curve of my clavicle, like any minute he was going to trace it with a finger.

I bit my lip and pulled trapped hair and grime away from the cut. It was long and wide and shallow, left by the brick that had fallen as he'd torn apart the layers between the endless hallway and the city. Somehow, he'd managed to make sure nobody else got hurt. As I finished cleaning away the nastiness, a drop of blood trickled from the cut.

Amber hissed and Nod growled, body-blocking her. I ignored them as I fumbled a bandage open and used it to hide the cut. "You'll probably have a scar for a while," I told Yejun. "I'm not stitching you up, though."

He gave me a lazy smile that made me feel warm all over. "Doctor AT," he murmured. Hastily, I looked down at his hands, taking one to examine the injury there. His fingers curled under mine, then held still.

The wounds were odd. There was a raw spot on both the palm and the back of each hand, but the hands themselves seemed fine. "It's like a pair of burns. Does this hurt a lot?"

"Not right now," he admitted quietly. "Some, when I'm not so distracted."

I froze, and he twisted his head so he could see my face under my mop of hair. I shook my head and bent to get some gauze. "I don't understand you."

"Well, when a boy and a girl of a certain age—" he began lightly.

I began wrapping gauze around his left hand, without much gentleness. "I get it. I get that. And believe me, I appreciate that you're not treating me like I'm twelve. But I don't know why sometimes you seem like you hate me and sometimes you're—" I stopped and tucked the gauze under itself, staring down at the white cotton against the gold of his skin.

He pulled his hand out of my grip and gave me his other one. "You were nasty first," he pointed out. "Who likes being treated like something disgusting left under the couch?"

I raised my eyes to his face, trying to guess what was behind his dark eyes. "Is that really why?"

He met my gaze and shrugged. "Not really. I'm used to it, at least from everybody interesting."

He'd said something important, something worth thinking about, but I couldn't concentrate on it. I looked down and started wrapping the next hand. "It's not like you need an excuse. I'm sorry I asked."

He did touch my collarbone then, poking me with a single finger. "Cut it out."

"Cut what out?" I shivered.

"Pushing everybody away."

"I don't want to talk about this now," I said stiffly. "You wouldn't understand."

"All right," he said calmly. "What are you doing after we get done with this place?"

Focusing hard on his hand, I said, "Going back to my father's house, where I belong."

"You're right," he whispered. "I don't understand. Tell me more."

I glanced up involuntarily. The compassion in his expression hurt. "I—"

"Come on, come on, come on," Amber called loudly. "Did you run out of gauze? Tuck that scrap in if that's all you've got, it'll do."

"Shhh, dreamchild," said the Fiddler. "This is exactly what I'm looking for. This connection. This bridge."

"Hey, Amber?" Yejun raised his voice and pulled his hand out of mine, finishing the wrapping on his own. "What would happen to you if I pulled the sun out from behind the clouds?"

"You can't do that," she said scornfully. "Not the real sun."

"Whatever passes for the sun here was enough to send you into hiding yesterday, eh? Just something to think about."

I stuffed the remaining supplies back into the kit and snapped the lid shut before rounding on the Fiddler. My face burned and my hands were cold and I didn't want to look at any of my companions.

"Who the hell are you? Why are you messing things up? What do you want?" I sounded angry. Maybe I was, a little. I couldn't tell, my emotions were in such a turmoil.

"I thought I told you when we met before?" The Fiddler peered closely at me. "I'm sure it was you. I am the Fiddler and I'm looking for something that I must reclaim. A song. It's turned out to be more complicated than I thought. But I've figured it out. You can help."

"We're a little busy right now," I told him icily.

Yejun's fingers brushed my arm and I jumped away from him, moving to the far side of the group. Being close to him made it so hard to *think*. It made me want to give up responsibility and do whatever I felt like.

Brynn asked, "How can we help, sir? If we can, we will."

The Fiddler bestowed a dazzling smile on her. "Each of you is a note." He played a jerky, discordant series of notes on his violin. "If I can tune you properly, you will be exactly what I need."

Amber stared at him. "That's gibberish. And creepy, too."

Brynn held up a hand toward Amber, frowning. "It's wrong, at least. You don't tune notes, you tune instruments."

"Oh?" The Fiddler's smile became vague. "It's hard to use this language, it's true. Frankly, I'm not even used to talking. And translating from the music to your words perhaps requires more of an education in your language than I've had. But let me see." He tapped his bow against his chin, and the violin he called Arabet played a little trill of notes on her own. "The connections between your group may allow me to unpin the song I seek from the world. The mortal-born have a gift for ending things that is sympathetic and remarkable, but I can't use it unless it's been, yes, tuned to understand value." He gave Brynn an apologetic look.

I shook my head furiously. "We have to find the Horn of the Wild Hunt. Unless that's what you're looking for, you're going to have to—"

"Not looking for it, exactly," he interrupted. "I know where it is. And I know now you are seeking it. My challenge is to reach it and detach its song from the world."

My mouth snapped shut. For a moment, all of us gazed at him in silence.

Then Brynn said, "But it has a role. I mean, from what Tia said, even if the Wild Hunt is corrupted, we still need something in that position. If you take the Horn, that'd be destroying the Wild Hunt, not just rebooting them, right?"

The Fiddler frowned. "I don't... I believe you refer to the way the world itself has grown to depend on the artifact? Yes. That is why the song is so hard to reclaim. The weight of a world is quite an anchor. The Horn was never meant for such work.. Though, because of the song it carries, it has adapted and grown under the load." He grinned wryly. "I should have expected that even here, the power of song would be contagious. But you see how you can help."

"Not a clue, man," said Yejun. "Sorry. You're still talking crazy."

"Reclaim?" asked Brynn, talking over him. "It was yours originally? You brought it here? How come?"

This is exactly what I'm looking for, he'd said, as I'd stood so close to Yejun. Loudly, I said, "If you know where the Horn is, Tia doesn't need me after all. That's great."

Brynn's head whipped around toward me. "What are you talking about?"

"Look, you guys stay here and talk to the crazy Fiddler. I'm going to go scout around. I'll leave Heart here for now to keep an eye on things." I backed away, babbling nonsense in my hurry to get away. He wanted me close to Yejun for entirely his own reasons; he'd reacted too much like my father would have. I couldn't stay.

Yejun looked away, up at the sky, as if he didn't care. It was Amber who caught Brynn by the arm, who met my eyes like she understood and said, just loud enough for her voice to reach me, "Don't go too far. Being alone isn't going to help."

I shrugged. "I've got Nod and Grim." Then I darted away around a corner. I'd go as far as I had to, far enough that I stopped wishing for things I just couldn't have.

-sixteen-

hat I want you to do, my father said, *is go out there and be one of them. You're cute. You can use that. They'll never know what hit 'em.*

I was the guide at Halloween. I was the bait in the junior high. I was the sweet face of treachery. And the Fiddler, whatever he was, wanted me to get closer to others, too. My whole world reeled as I jogged, then ran, away from the plaza. I had no place to go. I just had to get *away*. And if the Fiddler came after me, like my father eventually would, I'd fight him. I would. He wasn't my father, after all. He was just a weird guy with a stone violin. He couldn't know what he was getting into with me.

I wasn't thinking very clearly. I ran as fast as I could, Grim and Nod beside me. I was distantly aware of Heart's anxiety, a pale shadow of my own. I'd left her behind so the others wouldn't stop me from leaving. I could call her to me whenever I needed to. And I would, once I—

Once I what?

I had no idea. Was I giving up, running until I escaped this horrible empty city? Was I scouting, like I'd said?

I slowed down. Scouting didn't work at high speed.

Was I trying to find the Horn on my own, to prove that I could do it without them?

But I was going the wrong way. Again.

I wished I could find Tia and talk to her. Maybe she'd scold me or maybe she'd stroke my hair, but she'd help somehow. She'd tell me if I was being selfish, or just stupid. And even if I didn't take her advice, she'd *be there*, untouchable, and I wouldn't be so lonely.

The distant roar of the motorcycle circling the city came closer.

That was a way I could help without being near my companions. I'd led the Hunt to more interesting prey before. If they were looking for us now, on steel horses, I could distract them and lead them away. And if the roar was something else, well, that was information, too.

I moved toward the sound. The tall, soulless buildings became smaller. Some of them looked very much like houses, although each one was a shade of burnt roses. My stomach gnawed at me, reminding me I hadn't eaten for hours. Was there invisible food for invisible ghosts? Would that be better than nothing? I could go a long time without food, but I hated the feeling. My father had tried a lot of things to take my dogs away.

The temptation to search for food in one of the buildings was almost overwhelming. I was *really* hungry, and I remembered Amber's warning against going inside. It enticed rather than frightened me.

But then I went around a corner, past a picket fence painted damask, and the roaring of the motorcycle was much louder. That gave me something else to think about.

Just one. I could handle just one, no matter what it was. When it rolled around the corner, I stood in the middle of the road with my legs braced, Nod and Grim sitting alertly beside me.

The bike, blood red with black trim, fought like it had a mind of its own as the rider brought it to a halt. But he stroked it once and whatever spirit it had died away. I found myself stroking Grim's ears in sympathy. He pressed against my leg.

Then the rider leaned back and raised the visor on his helmet. It was Ion, the First Hunstman. For a long moment we looked at each other. His dark eyes were cruel and proud, and his mouth was curved like the grin of a shark.

"Found you," he said.

"I wasn't hiding," I pointed out.

"You ran very well before," he observed.

"I had people to protect then."

"Ah, yes. The humans. We'll get to them later," he said, and a trickle of cold fear twisted in my stomach.

"You're only supposed to hunt down corruptive souls," I said sharply. "What happened?"

He shrugged, his riding gear creaking. "Who is to judge whether a soul is corrupting Creation?" He paused, then added, "Me, that's who. There are certain signs, you know, in every soul. Besides, the Horn hungers, and once it has been fed sufficiently, all will be pure once again. And we will be free of the shackles of Creation." The motorcycle growled and again he stilled it.

I gaped at him, then said, "Right, so you're just evil." I sighed. "Well, I know the type."

"You don't need to worry," he assured me. "You have a different destiny."

"Oh, right, yes, tell me more." I wondered if I could just take him out right now. It'd hurt, it might even kill me, but it'd be a service to the world.

He just comes back again, my mother whispered in my memory. She was talking about my father, but it was probably true here, too. A short-term solution, then. A solution to the problem of me.

"You've done it once already." Ion gestured at me, his fingers spread. "You led us to our prey, sent it running before you. Your dogs are marvelous. They belong with us."

The cold trickle of fear became an icicle of terror slamming down my spine. "No," I managed. "I'm not working for you and you can't take them. This is stupid, really—"

"Can't I?" he murmured. "But each of the Hunt was once part of another. Blood and name and shadow, all ripped away in service of the Horn."

I backed away a step, then turned and fled, driving my dogs ahead of me.

As I pounded down the pavement, past the odd houses, the motorcycle roared to life again behind me, angry and full of bile. I ran from him, casting around as we fled for anything I could lead him to, any way to buy time, distract him from what he'd said. *Anything.*

But I was a stranger in the city and it offered no assistance. If anybody wandered there other than my friends, they hid away when the Hunt rode. Or maybe it really was empty. I tried to make my way into twisty little streets where I'd have a size advantage at hiding and escaping. But the problem with twisty little streets is that so often they go nowhere. I turned into a dead end, where six tall linked houses crowded a cul de sac, and the Huntsman followed behind.

Don't go inside the buildings, Amber had said, but I was desperate. I ran to the center building and tried to open the locked door. Then I threw myself at the door, trying to break it down.

The doors of the other houses opened, and the other Huntsmen stepped out. They walked down the stairs, synchronized reflections of each other. Ion dismounted his bike and grabbed my collar. I turned on him and Nod and Grim and I fought him. We *fought* and Heart came running to join in and we did our best to kill him. He had flesh like any man, and when we tore it, he bled. He had power like a celestial to knit himself together again, but we were many and quick and savage and *desperate.*

But when he fell beneath our teeth and claws, the other members of the Hunt were still there. Three of them caught me, held me so I couldn't move. Once again dismounting his bike, Ion came toward me. I knew I'd killed him, I remembered his throat in my teeth. But his body was gone and there he was, opening his arms wide.

The door behind me opened and Alastor stepped out. He clicked his tongue. "I did try to keep you away, Annalise. Still, I think your father will be pleased." He moved to one side, straightened his sleeves, and started picking something out of his teeth.

Somewhere else in the city a horn blew, *the* Horn blew. The clarion sound rolled out across the city, swelling, getting louder. It reached fingers inside my heart. And I could do *nothing* as my dogs at first became confused, then terrified. Heart howled and snapped at her own flanks, while Nod dug frantically at the concrete, leaving bloody smears from his torn feet. Grim whined, his tail between his legs, licking Heart until she bit him, then rolling on his back and waiting to be kicked.

Ion brought his fists together slowly. One by one, my dogs slunk over to cower at his feet, and one by one, I felt the power I'd invested in them return to me. I couldn't look away, couldn't stop calling on them as they changed. Heart's scarlet fur became the color of blood and Nod's teeth lengthened and Grim's soft brown eyes became savage. He looked at me and looked away again, as if he didn't recognize me.

He looked up at Ion and growled, and I felt a tiny flicker of savage, violent hope. But Ion's hand settled onto his head and, like the motorcycle, he stilled.

"What shall we do with her?' asked the Huntsman called Ipa. He was standing at Ion's shoulder.

"She rejected us," said Ion. He grinned again. "Kill her."

Alastor cleared his throat, but before he could say anything, somebody else did.

"So stupid, Ion. That's your solution to any rejection," Tala cut in sharply. She was holding my arms behind my head.

Silkily, Ion said, "You survived." He dropped his other hand onto Heart's head and twisted at her soft ears.

Tala said coldly, "Despite rather than because of what passes for wisdom in your mind. Do think, bright star. Three dogs are hardly a pack. Let her live and she will eventually make more spirit dogs for us."

"Indeed, it is wisdom to not slay the golden goose," said a Huntsman I didn't know except that his hands on my legs were very cold.

Ion looked at me dismissively. "She will refuse."

Tala held both my wrists in one hand and twisted her fingers in my curly hair. "She won't be able to help herself, in the end. She is so very lonely. Look at how her heart aches," she crooned.

Ion looked disgusted. "You will never get over the taint of your sex, Tala—"

"That's you," she flashed.

But he ignored her, kept going: "But so be it. Release her."

"This way, it's a gift that her sire will repay," observed Alastor. "That may be valuable."

With a sneer, Ion said, "More valuable than your service, I'm sure." Both of them moved away, their voices fading under my distracted pain.

The hands on my legs and torso went away, until it was only Tala holding me. She leaned forward and whispered in my ear, "Don't disappoint me, precious." Then she gave my head such a savage jerk that red darkness exploded across my vision.

By the time it faded, they were gone. I was alone. *Really* alone. Alone in a way I hadn't been since I was five years old, and at least then I'd had my mother. I felt cut off from everything, even my own body. I couldn't believe they were actually gone, but I felt so *strange*. Even when they'd been in my shadow, part of my power had been theirs. And the Wild Hunt had pulled my dogs away and returned the power. I hated it. I wasn't hungry anymore. My stomach felt full of bile and churning, destructive energy.

I rose to my feet and stumbled out of the dead end where they'd caught me. I wanted to find them, throw myself at them until they *did* kill me. The Wild Hunt had done what my father had never been able to do. And oh, he'd tried. He would have paid a high price to strip me of my dogs, my triune soul. Only silence my mother and steal my dogs, and I would have been exactly what he wanted to mold me into. How could I have resisted, with nobody to cling to but him?

I fell onto the paved street and crawled forward a few feet before pushing myself to stand on two legs again. My magic wanted to change me and only habit led me to resist. I knew, fuzzily, that I was human, or at least I wanted to look like one, pass as one. But what was I? Was lying to the world any good at all?

My *father* lied to the world all the time.

I was so alone, and so confused. The city loomed around me, full of shadows that moved like they were independent. I kept seeing my dogs and my father both, just from the corner of my eye. A clocktower hidden behind other buildings played a carillion of bells and I jumped and hid against the wall, afraid it was the sound of the Horn again.

I tried to summon Heart from within my shadow. Maybe it had all been a bad dream. Maybe this aching emptiness inside was just a trick of the sandman. But nothing happened, because it wasn't a bad dream. It hadn't been a bad dream when Hunter killed my mother and my friend, and it wasn't a bad dream when the Huntsman stole my dogs.

I really wanted to wake up.

I ran into the corner of a building, the sharp edges of the bricks slicing into my forehead. The building had moved. It was breathing. Suddenly, I was sure the city itself was alive. Alive, and waiting. I fell back, staring at the building. Maybe I wasn't as alone as I thought.

Maybe being alone would be better? I could barely imagine what my senses were now screaming.

Maybe I should have been terrified. I didn't know. I couldn't think about it.

Blood ran into my eye and I wiped it away. Maybe I'd have a scar to match Yejun's.

Yejun. The name made me feel hot and angry. I wanted to find him and make him understand how I felt. I wanted to find the others, too, and stop repressing everything. I wanted them to *know*.

The street wavered ahead of me. The road widened while the buildings neatened themselves, becoming smaller and more polite and connected together. The city glared at me balefully and the locks on every door rattled.

I was *afraid* of being alone. But I was also afraid of being with my friends. *Oh, my friends.* I wasn't afraid for them because of my father anymore. I was afraid for them because of *me*. My father had known what he was about when he'd tried, over and over again, to tear my dogs away from me, to force me to reject them. He'd guessed how they kept me from being the daughter he wanted. But now, nearly blind with rage and despair, I wanted more than anything not to feel helpless. I was willing to take what I could get.

I thought of the imaginary enemy I was constructing in the city itself—*anything* to not be alone, right?—and I tried to find self-control. In the distance I saw the glowing tower that had appeared after Yejun had borrowed my power. That had been there before. It was probably real, and distinct from whatever I sensed in the city. It was far from the plaza where my friends waited, too, as much as distance meant anything in this surreal place. If there were lights, then there were probably people. Maybe it was even the Wild Hunt's stronghold. I could find where my dogs were kenneled, crawl in with them. Maybe they'd bite me, but they'd bitten me before. Maybe they'd kill me, but then they'd eat me and I'd be with them again.

I was on my knees again, staring at the cornerstone of an ashes-of-roses building, when something moved in the air over me. I looked up, slowly.

A large brown owl had settled on the edge of the roof. It peered down at me, then hooted softly.

My lower lip trembled and my eyes filled with tears. I stretched out a hand to the owl, imploringly, hoping against hope it would come to me. I didn't know where it had come from in this horrible city, but I didn't much care. It didn't hate me and that was all that was important.

But a winged shadow passed overhead and the owl glanced up at the giant eagle circling. The owl mantled, and I saw the flash of injuries under its soft feathers. One of the feathers slipped loose, and then the owl flapped into the air again, darting low between the buildings as the giant eagle looking for it soared overhead.

The brown and white feather drifted down until it landed in my outstretched hand. I wrapped my fingers around it.

Instantly, I remembered Tia: remembered her saucy wink and her laughing smile as she promised me she could talk my father into letting me go. I remembered her hand tousling my curls as she waited with me at the airport for the Senyaza representative who was going to give me a place to stay. I remembered her hug goodbye, her perfume a tickle in my nose. She wasn't human, she was a demon, but she'd been arms around me and that had meant so much.

Heart and Grim bayed somewhere in the city. Nod never barked like that; it was either a snarl or a howl with him. They were together, as I was alone, and they were hunting something. Maybe they were hunting my friends.

It was weak and shameful, but I couldn't stand the thought of my dogs against my friends. If that's what was going on, I couldn't be there for it, not now. Whatever I did would be wrong. Whatever I tried would fail. I held the owl's feather close to my face, then ran the other way, to the tower with the glowing windows.

It was a tall building, a skyscraper. And while the top glowed brightest, it shimmered all over. In this strange semi-real city, there was a truly dreamlike element to the tower, like it was a painting on the walls of a soap bubble. I touched one wall hesitantly, but the cool, smooth steel didn't vanish away.

It was also different from the other city structures because it didn't have a closed door. Instead of an ordinary entrance, an elevator stood open and waiting. Warm light shed by a small chandelier spilled over the threshold invitingly, and the walls of the elevator were upholstered in burgundy leather. Faint chamber music drifted out.

I stumbled into the elevator. There was a panel with a single button, already lit. The doors closed as I leaned against the soft corner and the elevator began to rise.

It was a slow, steady ride. I sank into a haze, letting the gentle vibration carry me away from the horror of the streets below. After a while, I realized I wasn't alone. A translucent figure stood in the other corner, facing the doors, ignoring me. I could hardly make out details on the ghost, but it only took a moment of staring to realize that it was Emily. Emily, who had befriended me in junior high, and died for it. Emily, whose ghost had never once spoken to me.

She had nothing to say now, either. She didn't even seem to be aware I was there. She just stood in the corner, waiting for the elevator to finish its journey. Maybe I was imagining her just like I'd been imagining the city was alive. She was a lot more translucent than most ghosts.

"I'm so sorry," I told her. I'd apologized so many times before, and just like all the other times, there was no response. I was sorry for befriending her, sorry for failing her. Sometimes I was even sorry I'd never tried to avenge her. It was a fairy tale concept, vengeance, and I wasn't sure she would have cared. But she was also dead. That made a difference in priorities.

I edged over to her, felt the chill radiating from the space she occupied. It was very comforting. It took the edge off the hot pain in my heart. I thought that if I could just get her to occupy the same space I did, then I wouldn't feel any pain at all. But I couldn't bring myself to step into her space, to invade her like that. I just took what little numbness I could from her company. I was grateful for that small gift.

The elevator came to a halt so smoothly I didn't realize it until the doors slid open. Emily stayed behind me like my shadow as I crept out from the elevator just enough to see where I'd ended up.

I recognized the penthouse suite that Jen and Cat occupied, although it seemed no more real than Emily. It wasn't exactly translucent the way Emily was. Instead, everything was rimmed with light, Cat and Jen included.

They didn't seem to realize I was there. Maybe it was a projection, something like what Yejun had done in the cave. Maybe I was hidden behind a wall. Or maybe Emily's close company had made me into a ghost, too.

I rather liked that idea.

Cat sat at the table, looking at a beautiful knife placed there. It had a long, thin, shining blade made of folded metals, and a wooden hilt burnished to a glowing chestnut. Cat leaned his chin on one fist as he tapped the blade thoughtfully. After a moment, he transferred his gaze to Jen.

Jennifer sat on the couch where she'd been sitting when I first met her. This time she had a book. She stared at it like she could still read, but her eyes didn't move across the page. She never looked up at Cat, but her entire posture showed that she was aware of him.

A portable alarm clock on the table buzzed. He stood up and said, "You should eat. I'll reheat some leftover Chinese."

She shook her head at the book. "I'm not hungry. And it would be rude to our guest."

To my numb half-surprise, Cat looked directly at me with an eyebrow raised. "Would it?"

-seventeen-

Emily vanished, taking away all the numbness I'd been borrowing from her. I gasped at the rush of loneliness. It made me stumble further into the room before I caught myself. Cat held out an arm as if to steady me, but his fingers passed through my skin like he was shadow.

"What are you doing here?" I whispered.

Jen closed her book on one finger and looked at me. "I think something unexpected happened the last time Yejun tried to call us. We're not really where you are, you understand. Our windows look out on the Far City, but the door leads to the hotel. You drifted through a wall a while ago."

"The Far City? You know this place?" I sank down to the floor, then wished I hadn't. I sat on the floor to be with my dogs, and my dogs were gone. Instead, I held the owl's feather to my cheek.

"I've read about it in books," Jen said. She held up the book she'd been looking at. "It's a strange place."

Hesitantly I asked, "Can you read now? Yejun said…" and I trailed off, afraid of upsetting her.

"No," she replied calmly. "The letters don't mean anything anymore. But I can remember very well when I focus, and the habit of holding a book focuses me."

"Will you be all right if Jen eats something?" asked Cat patiently. "She's trying to use you as an excuse."

I put a hand on my empty stomach. "I'll be fine."

"I don't want to eat, Cat," Jennifer said gently, still looking at me.

"That's too bad," said Cat, just as pleasantly. He went to the fridge and started scooping some noodles onto a plate.

I looked between them, puzzled. Jennifer looked wan and thin, like she hadn't eaten well in days. I would have given her a good meal, too. But I didn't like Cat insisting Jen eat the food he gave her. It was too much like my father handing me a plate. And that comparison made me want to head back down to the streets. I wasn't ready to go home yet, even though I knew I would eventually.

"Why...?" I began, then wasn't sure where to go.

"She wants to die," said Cat, matter of factly.

Jen looked away, embarrassed. "Let's be accurate. I want to *finish* dying. It's not going to happen very quickly no matter what I do. Sen's magic is strong."

"I bet the Huntsman's magic is stronger," I said bitterly.

They both looked at me intently. Jen admitted, "Yes. That would be fast. And also a failure. A final betrayal of Sen."

"You keep using that word," said Cat lightly. "I do not think it means what you think it means." He put the plate into the suite microwave and started it whirring. I stared as flashes of light burst silently out of the microwave, but the other two either didn't notice or didn't think it was unusual.

I thought about the exchange between Cat and Jen, decided it was more than I could think about right now, and tried to change the subject. "We did try to call you. Yejun borrowed some of my power. I guess that might have messed things up."

"Ah," said Jen, and picked up another book. "Where is he?"

Oops. I'd picked the wrong topic for casual chat. But maybe nothing would be easy to talk about again. "I left him with the Fiddler."

Jen looked up from her book at me, compassion in her eyes. She touched the seat beside her, but I couldn't. It took everything I had not to dissolve in tears, and moving would have broken that focus. Being so close and so far would have made it even worse.

"I had to get away," I said brokenly. "I probably would have gone back. I'm not very good at doing the right thing. But the Hunt found me—" I stopped and shook my head. How could I explain what I'd lost?

Cat glanced at me over his round glasses, then brought the steaming plate to Jen. It didn't smell like anything. The entire suite smelled like wind and cinders and lightning, not like a place where people lived. But that made sense. They were just an illusion of something far away.

She handed him the book and accepted the plate, like they'd done the exact same thing a dozen times before. Like she just had to argue so she wouldn't be betraying herself. It didn't *feel* like when I didn't fight my father. It didn't feel like she was afraid of him.

After watching Jen long enough to make sure she was eating, Cat went over to his knife. He picked it up and purposefully pricked his palm. As blood welled up and dripped down his hand, the light shining off the blade flickered and moved like the overhead fixture had changed position. Cat didn't seem to notice as he put the blade down and turned to me. I stared up at him dully, unable to really process what was going on until he'd wrapped his bleeding hand around my arm and pulled me to my feet.

His hand was warm, and his grip gentle. The smell of the blood was almost overpowering, though. It simultaneously turned my stomach and reminded me of the hunger my grief had hidden. My hands spasmed and the owl's feather drifted down to my feet. It wasn't that I wanted to eat *him*, not really. It was just... the essence of living warmth. I was a meat eater. And apparently I was also a comfort carnivore.

"Sorry for the mess," said Cat, his intense blue eyes glinting behind his lenses. He really was beautiful, and hauntingly familiar. "It was the only way for me to borrow a little bit of essence from the knife. So I could reach you. You looked like you needed a hand." He guided me over to the couch beside Jen and I sank down beside her, still staring up at Cat.

"Is... is it a Machine blade?" I asked, wondering blearily if he could use the blade to make a steak real for me. Sometimes celestials and nephilim had little bits of heavenly Machinery they could use as tools and weapons.

"No." His tone wasn't unfriendly, exactly, but it didn't invite more questions.

Jen touched my hair and I started. She wasn't bleeding, wasn't borrowing the essence of the knife, whatever that meant. She gave me a sad little smile in response. "Halfway between the worlds, they say." She tucked a curl behind my ear. "You've had a rough time of it, haven't you?"

The sympathy frightened me. My reaction to the sympathy frightened me more. I wanted to put my head into her lap and sob. But that would be such a waste. Instead I tried to pull away, my muscles trembling with the effort, and she let me.

"I'm alive," I said. It was supposed to be light and cheerful, but my voice hitched, which made it sound more like a confession of my ultimate woe.

"It happens," she said and sighed, not taking her eyes off me. Jen's eyes were blue, too, lighter than Cat's, but with a dark rim around the iris that made her direct gaze feel like falling into a crystal tunnel. At the end of the tunnel was only a black despair. She understood, I realized. She'd had the center of her life torn away from her, beyond retrieval or repair, and all she could do was try to tidy up loose ends before releasing herself to the darkness.

I don't know what she saw in my eyes, but she looked down at her food, took a few more bites, then put it on the end table and took a deep breath. "So. Now you've had a direct encounter with the Wild Hunt. I've been trying to work out the answer to a question. Maybe you can help?"

She didn't look at me as she asked. I thought about the Wild Hunt, about Ion's hateful voice and Tala's whisper in my ear. My dogs were bound to them now, all hunters together. It hurt, but there wasn't any escaping the hurt. "I don't know how I could help. But maybe."

"Sen—" her own voice hitched. "Sen collected a lot of stories about how the Wild Hunt was created. But there wasn't much to find about what made them go *wrong*. If we reboot the Hunt, I'm afraid they'll just go bad again. Everything—*everything*—will have been wasted."

I knew she was hoping I would give her some kind of answer, or at least some kind of encouragement. Some kind of reassurance. But what reassurance was there?

If the Fiddler and Yejun and Jennifer all managed to reboot the Wild Hunt, what would happen to my dogs?

The question arrested me. Would they go away? Would they return to what they'd been before? Not mine, but at least themselves again?

Grim's savage eyes were seared into my memory. Could I erase them?

I caught my breath, a feverish energy surging through me. I could suddenly see paths forward. All of them ended in the blackness beyond Jennifer's eyes, but anything was better than lying on the ground waiting to be kicked again.

Jen touched my hand and I yanked it away, unthinking. "Not wasted," I muttered. "Maybe different, but not wasted. How do we reboot them once we find the Horn?"

"Cat," Jennifer said. "Cat and Yejun. We've been writing it all down. There's a ritual. Yejun will hold it down—he's possibly the only person who can—and Cat will use his knife—" She paused, looking at me.

I stared past her at nothing at all, thinking about my dogs, thinking about Grim as a drowned puppy, about Heart dying in an alley beside her stillborn babies, about Nod, diseased and maddened. Thinking about how to release them a final time. After a little bit, I was vaguely aware of Jennifer standing up and passing into the suite's bedroom. As the door clicked closed behind her, I forced myself out of my reverie.

"I'm sorry. I was... remembering," I mumbled, and ran my hands over my face.

Cat put a chair directly in front of the couch and sat down in it, his long legs sprawling out very near my own. "Remembering your dogs?"

I pulled my knees up to my chin. "They're not gone, not like your friend is. Maybe it's worse, what happened to them, because they're not gone."

"Do you think they're suffering?" he inquired, almost casually, like he was wondering if I thought it would rain soon.

I shivered. "I don't know. I never tried to make them something they weren't. Not—not with my power. I never wanted them to be anything other than *there*."

He picked up the knife and started playing with it. Sometimes one of the human members of my father's pack played with a knife. They were usually new, and always showing off, trying to find a way to match the fangs of the wolves. This wasn't the same. Cat wasn't trying to impress anybody. I thought he'd just spent so much time with the blade that touching it was second nature to him. I remembered reaching out to stroke Grim, then cringed away from the memory.

"I'm something of an expert on the magic used in making constructs," he said after a moment. "In a way. I've thought about it a lot more than, say, Amber probably has."

I frowned, ran back through the conversation in the cave. "You know Amber? I mean, personally?"

He shifted his gaze from the blade to me. "I know *of* her. Tia recruited her when we were still coming up with a plan, and told us a little about her."

"What did Tia say?"

He shrugged. "Stuff I don't think I should repeat, not when you can ask Amber herself."

I bit my lip. "I don't know how much of a 'herself' there is, though she's really convincing. I feel so sorry for her, or for who she was, but she's like my father's wolves now. They're more like his shadows than real people."

Cat lowered his gaze to the knife. "Are your dogs only shadows of you?"

"It's not the same," I said, stung. "I'm not a celestial."

"You seem to have inherited that particular ability of theirs, though." His voice was calm and rational and implacable.

"It's not the same," I told him stubbornly.

He glanced at me. "As I said, I'm a little bit of an expert, and I think Amber and the Wild Hunt and your dogs and this knife all have something in common."

"Oh really." I leapt to my feet, went to the window, and stared down at the street far below. "What makes you such an expert, anyhow?"

"I've thought about it a lot," he repeated.

They had a great view of the Far City up here. I could trace the path I'd taken from the cul de sac where they'd stolen my dogs to the tower. And I thought I could see the plaza where I'd left my companions. "Why? Why do you care?"

"You're changing the subject," he pointed out mildly.

"You're avoiding the question," I shot back. As I turned to glare at him, I caught a flash of movement in the city below and looked back to identify it. At first, I couldn't see anything that might have moved on those desolate streets. Then, at the far range of my vision, something came into view.

It was a giant eagle, drifting low over the city, with vast brown-black wings that seemed broad enough to effortlessly keep the bird aloft all day. It twitched one wing and descended lazily. There was something below it, something moving fast.

As the eagle gained height again, I saw the brown and white owl that had given me a feather dart out from its shadow. It was flying steadily, close to the ground, weaving between the buildings that protected it from the giant eagle.

"Since you insist, it's a matter of—" Cat drawled, but I interrupted him.

"Wait. I think that's Tia over there."

Cat crossed to look out the window beside me. "Yes, I think it is. She's been keeping Alastor busy and away from the rest of you."

"Not far enough away," I said bitterly, remembering his presence at the cul de sac. "Why does he support the Wild Hunt?"

Slowly, Cat said, "He contributed one of the fragments that composed the Wild Hunt. That's why Sen summoned him, originally. But I remember the argument before the fire. He tried to convince Sen that everybody who lingered after death deserved to be, ah, *evicted*, I think was his euphemism.

"It's not eviction, though," I said "It's destruction. Jen's trying to figure out why they're broken? I think it's because they're destroying something that isn't meant to be destroyed. Once you think of the indestructible as something you can crush at will, where do you stop?"

"Angels aren't tuned toward destruction, generally." Cat sounded distant and academic again. "The ones who are have a very specific focus: destruction in service to growth, for example."

"My father destroys just fine," I said flatly. The owl dodged around a corner, then another corner. She was using the buildings to her advantage, but all the eagle had to do was gain a little height to see her from above.

Cat went on as if I hadn't said anything, his voice still faraway and thoughtful. "And they don't fear their own destruction, not naturally. Not like humans do. There is no *sympathy*."

Then I heard a howl. Nod's howl, followed by Grim and Heart baying, and the rumble of motorcycles. They came from nearly the same direction as the owl and the eagle, but they were closing in on her. The eagle wasn't trying to catch her, I realized. He was herding her, driving her toward the Hunt.

I put my hands on the cold glass as the little pack raced into sight. They looked wild, with tousled fur and scrapes along their bodies. They'd been fighting each other and hurt by the riders, I was sure. I wanted to reach across the distance and gather them close, hold them even as they turned on me.

Instead, Ion's hateful voice echoed, more imagined than heard, and they turned down the same street as the owl until they were racing beneath her. She put on a burst of speed and pulled ahead of both the pack and the eagle, then came in for a landing, *changing* as she did, until she was a woman in a business suit with feathers in her hair and owl wings that spanned the street flowing out of her back. She threw up a hand at the eagle and it flapped once to rise away. Then she turned back to where my dogs approached, and waited.

And they stopped. I couldn't tell what was happening, but I hoped—oh, I *hoped* they remembered her. I had a wild moment of joy when I thought she'd reclaim them for me. She'd saved us once before. She was going to do it again, however little I deserved it.

Then the Wild Hunt rolled around the corner. The figure in the lead gestured once, grandly, and my dogs surged forward. A white light flared out from Tia's outstretched hand, but my dogs, so talented, so special, barely noticed. It sank into their fur and Grim shook it off like rain while the other two just ran up it. How could mere light stop them? Nod leapt, teeth flashing, and—

Cat was beside me, his hand on my shoulder. He was trying to pull me away. He didn't want me to see what my dogs did to my oldest surviving friend. I don't know why. Even if I wasn't watching, I could feel it inside. The part of me that had been numb was burning now, raw wounds dipped in acid.

With a quick, habitual movement, I twisted away from his hand, grabbed his arm, and applied enough targeted pressure to snap the bone, all so he'd stop grabbing me. Then I tried to find a way to open the window. I could get out, go to them, stop them, save her, join her. But there was no latch, and I could break an arm, but the glass was slick and strong and hitting it only made my hands hurt.

"Do you really want out?" said an unexpected voice at my ear. "I can help. It might make your stomach hurt, though."

I whirled around. Standing just behind me was Yejun.

-eighteen-

Despite being disheveled and out of breath, Yejun looked as relaxed as I'd ever seen him. He had one hand under Cat's elbow. Cat, on the other hand, was pale, with a sheen of sweat on his forehead.

I didn't even think to ask what he was doing there. I didn't care. Nothing made sense anymore. I reached up to take hold of Yejun's shirt. "Tia. They attacked her, Yejun. My dogs. They weren't playing. I don't think..."

He ran one finger over the back of my hand, a light touch that penetrated my panicked haze without upsetting me, and looked over my head out the window. "Looks like they weren't," he agreed. Whatever he saw didn't ruffle his calm at all.

"But—Tia." My voice broke. I couldn't bear to look and see what he saw.

He tilted his head, looking down at me. "Demons are hard to really kill, though, aren't they? And they're hardly mortal souls."

I shook my head. "Tia went on and on about how the Wild Hunt had powers that nobody else did. I *felt* it. I don't know what it means, but they tore her apart."

He didn't ask about why my dogs would be attacking Tia, and I couldn't tell if he didn't really understand or just didn't care. "I'm sure she's fine."

"Like Sen was fine?" My voice cracked. "They're killing everybody who knows what we're supposed to be doing!"

"They must be worried, then." He was imperturbable. Glancing at Cat, he said, "Do you need help with that, man?"

"Little bit," Cat admitted. He was cradling one arm with the other. I remembered the snap under my hands as if somebody else had done it. I couldn't feel bad. All of my capacity for guilt and misery was eaten up by Tia, and my dogs, and the near-memory of tearing into her. It was so real: the biting, the ripping, the painful rage that drove it. It was too real to have just imagined it.

"Why didn't she run away?" I demanded. "Why did she just stand there? She should have run away."

"I don't think she had time," Cat said, as he moved to the table and carefully unzipped a case. "It happened very quickly." He sat down and looked at Yejun.

Yejun touched my hand again and I loosened my grip on his shirt. "Don't run away again. It wasn't exactly a walk in the park chasing you down."

I blinked in surprise, and then my eyes swam with sudden tears. Unwilling to give in, I turned back to the window and strained to see where Tia and the dogs had been. But there was nothing now: no sign of Tia, no sign of the dogs, no sound of the Hunt's motorcycles. The city had simply swallowed any remains. No matter what Cat said, I didn't understand. She'd turned around to face them, and the assault itself felt like it had gone on forever.

I didn't understand, and I was *angry* at Tia for letting my poor dogs do that to her. Didn't she understand that I needed her? Without her, I didn't have anybody left that I could really talk to. I didn't think it was possible to be more alone than I was after the Huntsman stole my dogs, but now I knew the truth.

I pressed my head against the glass hard. Cat made a soft, pained noise and I whirled on him. "You shouldn't have grabbed me!"

He and Yejun were in the process of doing something to his arm. They both paused and looked over at me. Then Yejun looked back at the splint he was working on, and Cat said gravely, "My mistake. I'm very sorry."

There wasn't any accusation or any mockery in his voice, and as quick as I'd flashed to anger, I was swept away by anguish.

"No, I'm sorry," I gasped, sinking down to the floor again. "I'm so sorry. There's no excuse. I couldn't do anything. I'm so *useless,* even to my father. All the worst bits. Oh, Tia." I covered my face. "I'm my father's daughter. My mom tried so hard to teach me to be good, but all she did was ruin me for what he wanted. I'm still... still what he put into me."

Lightly, without looking at me, Yejun said, "He put breaking arms into you?"

I held out one of my hands, flexed it, felt the ache. "I heal fast," I said bitterly, drunk on despair. "That made it easier."

Yejun finished tying a knot around Cat's splinted arm, then raised his eyes to mine. His brown eyes blazed with an unexpected fury that went through me like a bolt of lightning. "I'll kill him," he said softly. Then he was kneeling before me; he put his hands on my shoulders and held me tight. "Or I'll help you do it."

"No," I whispered. "You can't. He just comes back again. My mom and her friends killed him once, and he came back and he killed all the others and took us."

"A career project, then."

"No!" I scrambled backwards until my back hit the wall. "People don't come back to life again, only the monsters come back. *Please* don't. I don't want you to die. I've tried so hard to keep all of you from—" I shook my head frantically. "Don't even talk about it. He'll find out."

The bright, hard flames in Yejun's eyes deepened until they seemed almost black. Gracefully, he stood up. "We'll see about that. Get up."

I climbed to my feet warily. "Why?"

"We have to get back to the others. You can't hide here." The look he gave me was cool and insolent. "We have a horn to find. Tia's been keeping them away from us and whatever really happened to her, I bet she's not doing that now. How much time do you think we have?"

You don't need me, I almost said. But he'd said he'd come after me. And Tia, *Tia.* Tia wouldn't want me to hide up here. Tia would be *disappointed* in me again. It was a fact of life, but if she wasn't around anymore... I didn't want to think about it. I didn't want to cry.

I gnawed my lip as I glanced at Cat. "I'm really sorry."

"Are you going to do it again?" he inquired.

I shook my head. "No." Then I amended, "Well, not if you don't grab me when I'm really upset."

"Fair enough." Cat smiled so faintly I wasn't sure if I was actually seeing it. "Progress, Jen?"

Jen was back on the couch, I realized, and wondered how long she'd been there. "Maybe," she said. She looked at me seriously. "It's best if you go, AT. We're going to disconnect this place when you leave, in case the whole Hunt can get here the same way you did."

It was suddenly hard to speak around the lump in my throat, so I just nodded and walked over to the door. I reached out for my dogs as I did, calling them after me. The emptiness in response punched a hole right through me, and the grief poured in.

Shaking my head furiously, I ran to the corner of the elevator, then slid down the wall and pressed my face against my knees. Somewhere beyond the tidal wave of grief and loss, I heard Yejun step into the elevator and felt it begin its slow descent to ground level.

Yejun remained silent, although when I turned my head to one side, he was looking at me as he leaned against the elevator wall. I struggled to find something to say, something that would fill up the silence, distract away the pull of his eyes. But all I managed was, "How—how did you find me?"

"At first I tried to follow Heart when she ran away. She was a lot faster than I expected. I wandered around some. Then Jennifer contacted me. We reworked the communication charm so I could step directly to where she was."

"Why?" I asked, bewildered.

He shrugged. "She thought I could help you." The elevator dinged and slowed to a halt and he looked over at the door, then held down the Door Close button. I hadn't remembered a Door Close button. In fact, the panel had a whole lot more buttons than I remembered.

"This isn't the ground floor. I don't think I want to know who else is trying to hitch a ride on this elevator. Do you?" Yejun put his other hand, the bandage stained and sagging already, on the closed doors.

"Is it going to go down without opening first?" I stood up and rubbed my face and reached out habitually for my dogs, yet again. And again, the absence hurt, but I didn't have time to sob in a corner now. Instead I took a deep breath, gathering in my power. The lights were very even in the elevator, so I'm sure Yejun didn't see it, but I felt my shadow flicker and change.

Something banged hard on the door and Yejun called out, "Sorry, we're all full." Then he glanced up at the ceiling of the elevator. "It could. It might be very quickly. And it might bother you." He looked over at me, then did a double-take. I had no idea why. My shadow definitely wasn't showing.

"Do it," I told him. "I'll be fine. I want to get out of this building as soon as I can."

"All right," he said slowly. "Hold onto something."

He probably meant "the wall" or "a railing" or something like that, but that didn't occur to me until after I'd grabbed his arm and he'd given me a startled look. Then he lifted his hands away from the door and the button, did something, and the elevator plummeted down.

It wasn't quite freefall, but it was a lot faster than any elevator should ever go. I felt the magic, but it didn't make me sick. Maybe that was because my stomach was still above me somewhere. But at least I kept my feet and I helped Yejun stay up, too.

"Oops," said Yejun. "I hope—*jump!*"

We both jumped as the elevator jerked to a halt and landed a second later, hard. The doors crashed open and Yejun stumbled out of the tower, dragging me after him. Once we were clear away, he bent over to catch his breath and rub his legs. "Well," he said. "That didn't work."

I eyed him nervously, then glanced at the shining tower. The light above us started twinkling and bits of the tower had become transparent. "What didn't?"

"The jump," he explained, shaking his hands. "I always wondered if you could jump in a falling elevator to save your life."

"We're not dead," I pointed out.

"Yeah, but we weren't really falling, either, and I still landed pretty hard." He smiled at me.

"Is that why you said 'oops'?" More of the tower was vanishing away.

"Uh, no. That was because I messed up what I was disconnecting and the tower started vanishing around us." He looked irritated as he patted at his pockets. Then he said, "Ah!" and pulled out his sunglasses and started inspecting them for damage.

"Right. Maybe next time we should just see who wants into the elevator?"

"Sure," he said, as if it was already a topic he was bored by. "Probably just some kind of extraworldly monster. We don't have enough of those, after all." Then he looked me up and down again. "You look older than you did before you ran off. What happened?"

"Excuse me?" I had no idea what he was talking about, or why he was asking. I'd thought he'd understood what happened. I didn't want to talk about it again, either.

Yejun squinted at me. "When we first met, I thought you were around twelve. You know. An, uh, early bloomer, but twelve. Then I realized you were older and just super-Disney. Which made me feel better about... Uh, anyhow, you look like you're my age now. In your face, I mean. You're not as... cute."

"Do you *specialize* in sprinkling salt into open wounds?" I demanded.

He put his sunglasses on. "What, did you like being cute? You seemed kind of annoyed when I thought you were a kid before."

"I was!"

"Well?" He looked at the place where the shining tower had been. Now there was just a blocky four-story building, with empty display windows on the ground floor.

"We're not going to waste time talking about this," I said firmly.

"Good," he muttered. "Sorry I brought it up."

"Where is Brynn? And Amber? Why in the world did you come after me and leave them behind?"

He reached out to touch one of my curls. "I left them with the Fiddler. And really, did you think *I* was going to protect *them*? Amber's a lot tougher than I am. And Brynn told me to go after Heart. I'm an obedient man, miss."

"Hah," I snorted. "But—but you shouldn't have risked it. You don't need me now, anyhow. The Fiddler knows where to go."

He pulled gently on my lock of hair. "Walk and talk, please." When I took a step toward him, he grinned at me, stuck his hands in his pockets, and started walking backwards. We walked like that for a moment and he didn't stumble once, as if he walked backwards all the time. As we approached an intersection, he executed a right turn. "See," he confided, "You're not thinking too clearly right now. It's okay. You've had a hell of a day. But when you *are* thinking clearly, you're going to understand why I couldn't just let you run away. I hope."

"You know, talking down to me makes you kind of a jerk," I told him coldly.

"I can't help what I am." He pursed his lips thoughtfully, then said, "Nope. Can't do it. You'd just run away again. And right now we're all trying to save the world or whatever. No time for anything else. Let's talk after we're out of this dead city."

"No!" I said, frustrated. "You don't—"

An eagle cried over our heads and I reacted instantly, grabbing Yejun and dragging him under the eaves of the nearest building, a sprawling edifice that reminded me of the Seattle convention center.

A shadow passed over the street and I once again reached for my dogs, my extra senses, because I just couldn't learn. "Dammit," I muttered.

"Looking for us, you think?"

"I hope so," I said grimly. "Because if he's not looking for us, he's looking for the others." I listened as hard as I could, and in the distance, bouncing around buildings, I heard the cry of the horn and the howl of the hounds. "Hell. We need to get to the others as soon as we can."

"What's the rush?" Yejun asked mildly. "I thought you wanted to get away."

I let go of his arm, pushing him away in disgust. "I wanted to keep them safe." His eyebrows remained raised and I uneasily remembered that I'd actually fled because of something else, because of something the Fiddler had said, and because of a look in Yejun's eyes.

I turned away, looking up at the building we stood next to. "If we go through the streets, that horrible bird is going to see us. And... and I can't deal with my dogs yet."

Yejun pulled on one of the double doors. It clicked, then opened easily, and he looked over at me before vanishing inside. I darted after him, and ran into his back because he'd stopped just inside the room.

"What is it?" My eyes adjusted quickly. We were in an empty room, without dust or furnishings. The door behind us was still open, and when Yejun made as if to pull it closed, I caught his wrist. "Wait, don't. I don't want to be trapped here."

I remembered again what Amber had said, and how the doors had locked themselves before. Or had that been a dream? The long walk before I arrived at Jen's tower felt like a distant, frightening dream. Nothing had made sense then. Nothing made sense now, either, but now there was a visceral reality to the terror inspired by both the searching eagle and Yejun's smile.

"There are other doors," he pointed out. And there were, two more on other walls, and a big display window, too. But the thought of closing the door made me want to scream. It wasn't what they like to call a "proportional response" and I didn't know why.

"It's too crowded," I said, and shivered. It was like there wasn't enough of some vital resource, but I couldn't tell what it was.

His face went blank again and he released the door and stepped away from me. "Ah."

"It's the building," I told him, frowning and wondering what he was thinking. "It doesn't want us in here. It's pulling away. Can't you feel it? Did you unlock the door?"

An eagle screamed outside and in the distance, there was the call of a hunting horn. My head snapped around and I scrambled over to the window. The street beyond was still as empty as it had been, which wasn't any kind of reassurance. "This is bad on both sides."

I expected Yejun to say something, but there was only silence. When I looked over my shoulder, he'd vanished and the door on the far side of the interior was half-open.

I cursed, looking between the open door and the window. Once again I saw the shadow moving overhead. I could go out, get his attention, try to deal with him directly. Facing a full-blown demon alone in my current state was dumb. Going deeper into the building was terrifying.

Yejun had come for me when I thought I was most alone.

Slowly, I moved to the open door. The corridor beyond was pale and clean and as long as I'd come to expect. Other than a few closed doors, it was also empty until it reached a T-intersection.

My breath came hard and heavy. I didn't want to go back into that corridor again. Why had Yejun? Had it swallowed him up?

I wanted my dogs back so much. I couldn't face this alone. I'd fail. I didn't know how to succeed.

The crowding pressed against me and I could just catch Yejun's scent. I concentrated, then followed it to the T-intersection and turned left.

There were choices in this corridor. That was something different. Maybe it was just a corridor in a building. Maybe Amber had just been messing with my head. Maybe the Far City was running out of breathable air.

As I walked, the walls changed, becoming unfinished red brick and whitewashed cinderblocks. An open door led to an empty men's bathroom—a modern men's room, in this place? But that was another way it wasn't like the endless corridor from before and I'd never been so glad to see a urinal in my life.

Walking wasn't catching me up to Yejun, so I broke into a jog. Then I didn't want to wait to find him, and I ran. Only a moment later, I burst through a swinging door into an industrial kitchen.

Yejun stood in the center of the kitchen, near an empty steel table. "I know this place," he muttered, as I skidded to a halt. Then he looked over at me, as if surprised to see me here. "Where have you been?"

"We shouldn't split up." I darted over and took his elbow.

He yanked his arm away from me. "You know, I just don't know what to make of you. Half the time you grab me and then you say it's too crowded, so I thought, okay, maybe it's an indoors thing, we don't want that, I'll give her some space, try not to be a jerk, but goddamn you make it tricky sometimes—"

He was babbling, his eyes darting around the room. He didn't feel the crowding himself. He thought it was something about me. "It *is* crowded," I said, my voice going higher. I had to explain, somehow. "But we still shouldn't split up. I don't want to be alone in here. If we're going to deal with something nasty, it's better to be together." I glanced around anxiously, then let my breath out. The commercial kitchen touched on ancient memories. Before my father had found us and taken us away, my mother had done the books for a restaurant in New Orleans. I used to play under her desk.

"You know this place...?" I inquired quietly.

He shook his head. "My grandmother's restaurant." A muscle in his jaw twitched and his voice was flat and far away. "I hated it here."

Yejun looked up at the ceiling and I took the opportunity to hold onto his arm again. It wasn't anything like having a dog pressed against my leg or lazing in my shadow, but it had its own warm, muscular appeal.

"I think you're right," he added. "We should stick together."

I followed his gaze up. A pool of darkness blotted out the ceiling. Slowly, it started to overflow. I stared in horror as huge drops of shadow dripped from above and spread across the floor. Every surface they touched changed. Stainless steel blackened and aluminum corroded. The floor tiles beneath our feet cracked. Then, with a sizzle, every oven and range in the kitchen blazed with red heat.

-nineteen-

T*his,* I thought as the room around us transformed. *Was this what Amber had meant?* I really, really hoped so.

The huge knife rack on the table beside us hadn't been there before. One of the knives was out, lying carelessly on the table. The blade was the only shining thing in the room, gleaming bright save for the brown crust along its edge.

The heat from the blazing ovens hit me like a blow and I swayed backward. Yejun remained upright, as if he was used to it, but his face was pale and beads of sweat appeared on his brow. "Let's get out of here."

He didn't have to tell me twice. I headed over to the door, still holding his arm. It was awkward dragging him behind me like that and by the time we reached the door, he'd had enough. He shook me off and I gave him a hurt look. "We have to stay together," I insisted.

"Hand," he said, holding out his to me. I took a deep breath and put mine in his. He closed his fingers very lightly over mine, then lifted it to his mouth and pressed a kiss on my knuckles. He wasn't even looking at me as he did it, as if he did it without thought.

From the other side of the kitchen came a chopping sound, as if several knives were slicing onto wooden blocks. The knife on the blackened steel table had vanished, and so had three of the knives on the rack. The surfaces that had once shone silver now glittered scarlet under the patina of corruption.

Yejun glanced over his shoulder. "I don't want to know what that is." He kicked the door open and shoved me out ahead of him. As he stepped out himself, he flicked his hand backward and the knives remaining on the table scattered all over the floor.

As soon as he was through, the door slammed behind him and the lights overhead started to flicker wildly. Instead of the long tubelights, there was now a swaying incandescent chandelier, hanging from a rounded ceiling. The dripping corruption had not only been here, it'd had an even more dramatic effect. The floor was broken concrete and the walls were herringbone brick, with large gaping holes. Rusty hooks reached out from the walls like skeletal fingers and the far end of the hall was too dim to make out.

"No, no, no," I said, my stomach sinking. "I don't like this. All of the other doors are gone."

"That makes our choice easy, then," Yejun said. "Don't worry. This isn't like before." Something about his tone bothered me. His voice was strained under the light words.

Something hit the closed door behind us, so loud that I jumped five feet and hauled Yejun after me. Metal scraped down the door and an indistinct, high-pitched voice yammered something.

I stared at Yejun, my heart racing. His eyes were wide and shocked. I demanded, "Who's in there?"

"Nobody," he said, shaking his head. "You know what I said before about this not being like the other corridor?" He ran a hand through his hair. "This may be worse. I have a brilliant idea. Let's run."

We ran. We ran past the gaping holes in the brickwork, which led only to blackness. Blackness was better than what could have been there. Blackness was better than what the sounds emerging from the darkness *suggested* was there. Then the floor started developing holes, too, and we had to jump. I stopped before the second hole, a blackness two feet across. There were faint wet noises below us, and banging on the door far behind us. I tried to squash the queasiness brought on by fear and the sketchy dimness ahead of us.

"What?" asked Yejun.

"I don't trust the ground anymore. How can this be real? If this isn't real, are the holes real? Is the ground? I can't smell anything except death here." *Death, and Yejun.* "We're going to fall."

Then I flinched, anticipating mockery and impatience. But panic was going to sweep me off my feet soon and into my own darkness.

He didn't mock me, though. He slid his hand up to my arm, then took his hand away as he brought his other hand up to my head to tug on one of my curls. "It's real. As real as anything here. And the holes are real. I can tell. But I don't think we can jump them all while holding onto each other." Then he stepped away from me and jumped over the next hole.

Angry, I leapt after him. Hot, moist air wafted up from the blackness beneath me, sending unpleasant fingers under my clothes. "Don't do that. What if the darkness eats you?"

He shrugged and kept moving. "They all say it's bound to happen eventually. But I'd like to get this done first."

I chased him over two more holes. Then the floor was clear, and the distant pounding had faded into silence. I took his arm again and we hurried on. Maybe the worst was over.

That high-pitched voice screeched something I couldn't understand from only a few feet behind us. I looked back and saw a shadow stretching out of the last hole. It was almost human-shaped—and then Yejun yanked me forward as he stumbled ahead, almost tripping over his own feet in his eagerness to get away.

The far end of the hall turned abruptly. The light was very dim, and the red brick walls were apparently mortared with warm tar. The hall turned again, sharply to the right. After a few more strides it turned again, to the left. And then it turned again and again, until we could only hurry, not run.

"It's narrowing," I told Yejun urgently. I could touch both sides of the hall with my arms half out. "Can't you do something? If you can't, I'll try."

"What could you do?" he demanded, breathing raggedly.

"I'm stronger than I look," I told him.

"Strong enough to break these walls?" He stepped backward, bumping into a brick corner.

"I have no idea, but we have to do something!"

"Can you—" he swallowed. His face was very pale. "Can you deal with that?"

I turned around. The shadow thing was sliding around one of the walls.

My breath hissed between my teeth. I missed my dogs so much. They'd been my link to humanity before, my bridge back when I went too far. Now? I didn't know where I'd go, or if I'd want to come back.

"AT?" Yejun asked urgently.

"Yes. Yes, I can." I ran a hand through my hair, then held it out and looked at how my fuzzy shadow sharpened, grew claws. A red mist danced in front of my vision, but I tried to hold on. The longer I held on, the more focused I'd be later when I was cut free from identity.

Then I edged forward, using my shadow to catch at the one slipping towards us. It reared up, the elongated silhouette of a person, and started howling at me in an eerie voice that was barely human. There were words embedded in the noise, but not in any language I understood.

One of the creature's arms pulled away from the wall and tried to sweep me inside, but I dodged easily. The walls shivered around us as the silhouette's hand crashed overhead. The shadow held a bucket in one hand. Water sloshed out of it, an endless stream, and Yejun cursed in Korean. Something laughed, a deep, rumbling laugh that I didn't like at all.

It was so *crowded*. There wasn't enough space. The walls were closing in and the building hated us for invading it. Red-black fluid dripped from the grates overhead.

I looked up. And then the red mist took over, and all I had was scattered dreams of violence.

"Wake up," somebody said.

I didn't want to wake up. Last time I'd lost myself fighting, it had been my father who had woken me. I was afraid of what I'd see if I woke up this time. *Maybe*, I half-thought in that pre-awake way, *that was all a dream. Maybe I can stay asleep. Maybe it was a really bad nightmare.*

But that sent me digging through dream-memories, trying to figure out just how far back the nightmare went.

"Don't cry," said somebody, alarmed. "Hell. Come on, wake up.

We can't stay here."

And somebody picked me up. That was familiar, too, but this person smelled different. Scary, but not like somebody who would hurt me.

There was another difference, too. He was using magic to help pick me up. I could feel it, feel the rush of air under me and sense the movement of the lines. But my stomach didn't turn like it did when this *somebody* had used magic before.

This was the first thing that wasn't familiar or scary, and it was odd enough that I had to start waking up properly to think about it. There was something strange about how somebody's magic felt.

My dogs were gone. Still gone. There were no nightmares, just memories and waking up.

Yejun was carrying me, my head nestled against his shoulder. He felt me shift and said, "Good timing. I was just about to put you in a fireman carry."

"No!" I wriggled and pushed away. He let me. I regained my feet and stepped quickly backward. "I can walk. What happened?"

"You fought the building," he said dryly. "Eventually it pulled back to lick its wounds."

I looked around. We weren't in the same place we had been, but we were still inside a building that hated us and wanted to crowd us out of existence. It was huge and empty, with an open floorplan that went up several floors. Black catwalks, twisted and broken, crisscrossed overhead and a waterfall of red sparks cascaded down the far wall. Darkness pressed against the windows, with unidentifiable things moving in it.

"You were pretty cut up yourself," he added, overly casual. "But just like you said, you heal pretty quickly."

"Scrapes and stuff are okay. They don't hurt more when they heal fast," I said absently, staring hard at the darkened windows.

He was quiet a little too long, and then he said, "When you looked like you weren't going to bleed to death, I thought we should keep moving. This place is still pretty horrible."

"Yeah, let's find a door." I remembered what had pulled me out of my sleep. "Hey, did you use your magic to lift me?"

"A little bit," he said. "Not going to apologize if it helped wake you up because even a ninety-pound girl gets heavy after a while."

"I'm not that small," I grumbled, annoyed. "And it didn't make me sick. Are you doing something different?"

He gave me a thoughtful look. "No. I haven't changed a thing." Looking away, he said, "Hey, look. A door. Maybe you convinced the building that getting rid of us is better than eating us."

He pointed at a large double door some distance down the nearest wall.

Hopefully, I picked up my pace. Then a smoky cloud billowed in front of the exit. It was ashen at the edges and charcoal at its heart, and the charcoal writhed into a shape I recognized. But it was just a cloud, just my imagination. I couldn't admit anything else.

Making friends? my father whispered. *Is he a nice boy? Will you play with him? You know what I want.*

I stopped dead. "We can't go that way."

Yejun's voice was strained. "That's the way we have to go. Is that who I think it is?"

I bit my lip hard. "What are you talking about?"

He shook his head. "Don't, not now. The shadow is talking to you."

I could make out details in the charcoal, as if it was just barely veiling his figure. His eyes, his shoulders. He was real enough that I wanted to go limp and wait for it to be over. My father wouldn't just taunt me. No, after everything I'd done in the last day, eventually he'd get down to business. I tried to drag Yejun sideways and pleaded, "Let's just find another way out."

Can't you do anything right? Do I have to teach you another lesson? Give me your hand.

I clenched my fist, pulling away from Yejun when he resisted my tugging. He looked between the shadow blocking the door and me. Then he shook his head. "That's the door we have to use. Let's just run through the shadow. A little freakshow and we'll be out."

Remembered pain stabbed through my fingers. "I *can't*," I told him. The red sparks far above us began to move down the wall. I could smell scorched metal and burning hair and dirty machine oil.

Yejun dragged his hand through his hair, his eyebrows drawn low. Then he walked around behind me and pressed up against my back. "Sorry for crowding you," he said, not sounding sorry at all. He was taller than me, of course, and his lean torso was warm against me.

Confusion momentarily surpassed my paralyzing dread and I twisted to look back at him. "What are you doing?"

Without expression, he looked down at me, then started to move forward, pushing me ahead of him with his hands still at his sides. It was odd, and more than a little like when a dog leaned against the back of my legs. I sighed and braced myself just like I did with the dogs, and for a long moment we just leaned on each other.

Then, softly, Yejun said, "Your friends are just beyond that door. Just beyond that shadow. You want to get to them before the Wild Hunt does."

"I can't protect you from him," I whispered. "I don't—" I paused. I didn't want him to get hurt? I didn't want anybody to get hurt, not if I could stop it, but this was Yejun. He was creepy, too.

I brought up the Sight that I'd kept down since I first met him. The complex strands of the larger room were beyond me, but the dozens, hundreds of pulsing nodes that made up Yejun's Geometry presence were inescapable. It was like a tree growing from his spine, broad and old and ever-moving in a cosmic wind.

Yejun was creepy and he could clearly take care of himself.

I looked away, pulled away from him, and walked forward. I felt cold, almost frozen as I approached the shadow. My emotions had retreated to the place they went when I'd had to hide my dogs deep within my own shadow. When I was alone, and facing the endless shadow of my father.

I'd have to do that again soon, without even the hidden presence of my dogs.

I wanted to run away, but Yejun was behind me. I stepped into the darkness.

You came back, he crooned. *I let you go and you came back. That means you're mine forever.*

I froze, cringed. And then the strangest thing happened. My own memories of my father went up against the building's simulation.

Curling up like a weakling again? Even your mother was better than this.

One memory summoned another. *Baby, run!*

The child inside took over. I covered my ears and ran into the darkness, screaming for the light.

-twenty-

The darkness roared, became wet and clinging, like it was swallowing me. I couldn't stop, couldn't go back.

Then, all at once, I emerged into a storm-lit afternoon, on a plaza, in an empty city.

I blinked at the relative brightness and a door clanged behind me. I looked just enough to see that it was Yejun's node tree, then tucked the Sight away again.

He cracked open the door in the building behind us. Because that's what you do when you emerge from a building that tried to eat your soul. You open the door and look back inside again. At least, that's what you do if you're Yejun.

"It's a mall now," he reported, his voice very subdued. "Looks normal."

"Don't go back inside!" I scanned the plaza. A familiar fountain, but there was no fiddle music, no astonishingly tall Chinese man. Dizziness swept over me. Were we actually outside, or was this another vision? It looked just like the plaza I'd run away from, but that was awfully convenient and our companions were nowhere to be seen.

Before I could invent any really horrible theories, Brynn called, "AT! Yejun, you found her!" She and Amber appeared around the fountain.

"Where's the Fiddler?" asked Yejun, his fingers brushing my arm as he moved past me.

"He left," said Brynn, annoyed. "He said that we needed more time for the tuning and he'd have to make that happen. I *told* him you don't tune people but does he listen? You know, I thought I liked weird, but I'm really starting to *hate* this place."

Brynn wasn't quite as she'd been when I left her. The dark marks on her hands had sharpened. They no longer looked like bruises, but smudges of dirt. I stared hard at them, trying to figure out what they actually were. She noticed, and put them behind her back self-consciously.

"Where's Nod? And the others?" Amber asked quietly.

I took a deep breath. "Gone."

Brynn's self-consciousness flashed to alarm and her hands came out from behind her back again. "Gone? What do you mean, gone?"

How could I explain it? How could I explain it so we didn't have to talk about it? I didn't want to think about it. I didn't want to remember. But I'd never forget, even if I didn't ever talk about it again. And they'd known them. In the short time we'd spent together, my companions and my dogs had developed their own relationships.

This was like the shadow in front of the door, I realized. The only way out was through.

"The Hunt found me," I said quickly. "They wanted hounds. They ripped the dogs away from me, bound them to the Horn. And they changed. Ion, the first Huntsman, he controls them now. They're what he wants them to be."

Brynn shook her head as if a fly had landed on her nose and stared at me, her eyes widening. But Amber wasn't looking at me at all. She stared off into the distance, the whites of her eyes showing. Slowly she put her hands to her pale hair, her fingers digging into her scalp.

"Oh god," she said.

"There's more," I rushed on, before my voice could break. "I'm so very sorry. I wish—the Hunt went after Tia with the pack. They found her. They caught her." My voice failed.

Brynn gnawed on her finger. "So we have to rescue them all, don't we? That's what you're saying?"

That question was so sweet and so hopeful. I couldn't cope. I walked away, over to the fountain, then climbed the rim and splashed down into the cold water. It soaked my feet and crept up my pants and I rested my head against the stone block and let the waterfall course down over my head and back. It was gaspingly, painfully cold and I knew if I stood there long enough, I'd eventually go numb.

"What's your problem *now*, Amber?" Yejun sounded irritated rather than curious.

Then Amber splashed into the pool beside me.

"Your dogs were like me, right?" The intensity of her voice cut through the cold like a red-hot wire. She sounded *eager*.

I pulled away from the waterfall and shook my dripping hair from my face. "No." But I remembered what Cat had said and I didn't have the conviction I had before.

"They are," she whispered. Her eyes were dilated and hungry. "Tia was right. I could be free of him. Really free."

I stared at her, incredulous. I'd told her what happened to my dogs, to me, and how they'd changed. And all she could think of was how much she *wanted* it to happen to her?

"What the hell is wrong with you?" I pushed her hard enough to send her sprawling into the water.

She blinked up at me, then bounced to her feet. "Me? At least I *want* to be free. If my maker wakes up and realizes what I'm doing, I'll just *vanish.*"

That hurt a lot. I turned away, muttering, "You'll be a monster no matter what."

She grabbed me, spun me around to face her. "Yeah, well, you're not. But look at you, you're *going back* when this is over. So don't you dare judge me for wanting freedom."

"How can you know anything about me?" I demanded. "You're just this *spawn* I met yesterday." Out of the corner of my eye, I noticed Brynn looking down at her feet.

Amber sneered at me. "What's to know? You're a hot mess at the slightest provocation, you cringe and snap like a whipped dog, and you're *going back.*"

"You don't get it, though," I told her miserably. "You never actually escape."

"Sure you do," said Yejun, unexpectedly. "You just walk away from them. What goes with you is you. You just have to own it."

Darkness flickered across my vision for just a second and I stared at him, wishing desperately he hadn't said that.

Amber climbed out of the fountain. "Maybe that's true for you three, but not for me. I can't just walk away. I belong to him. If he dies, I die too."

"You *chose* that. You're exactly what you wanted to be and I don't understand why you're so miserable about it now." I raised my voice, but only because she was walking away. Honest.

You came back to me, and now you're mine forever, my father had whispered to me as he tended to my injuries.

She looked back at me and laughed bitterly. "It sounds so romantic, doesn't it?" Her voice became mocking. "Being with me forever would cost your soul, Amber. I love you, how could I do that to you?" She shook her head. "I thought he was so beautiful. So lonely. Misunderstood. And it was good at first, as long as I didn't make him angry. Until he started making me bring back others. Even then I tried to think of it as a game. Until it wasn't." She tugged on her hair as her eyes got that faraway look again. "I have to get out of here. You three stick together, okay? Enjoy having the ability to change your mind and change your choices, even if—" her eyes focused on me briefly, "—you don't always use it."

I shouted, "Go then! Nobody ever wanted you here anyhow."

Amber gave me a look full of pain and I knew that somehow I'd hurt her the same way she'd hurt me. But she only tossed her hair away from her face and ran out of the plaza.

I sat on the edge of the fountain and covered my face. Then I pulled my hands away and stood up. "We should get moving. We have to find the damn Horn before the Hunt finds us." I realized Brynn was standing very still, her arms wrapped tight around herself as she stared at the ground. "Are you hurt, Brynn?"

Slowly, Brynn shook her head. "I'm fine." She hesitated. "I've always been fine. My family's always taken care of me. They're nice. And I have a good school, too. Nobody's ever said anything awful to me there even though I like girls instead of boys. I worried sometimes about that but I never even thought—my family is really great!" Incongruously, her eyes were shimmering with tears. "All three of you have had such *horrible things* happen to you. It's not fair. You don't deserve it." She scrubbed at her face. "And I'm being so stupid. I have been this whole time. Can you believe I thought I could save you?"

"Wait, what?" Bewildered by her tears, I latched onto the most incomprehensible bit. "Save me?"

She shook her head. "My life has been so easy. I don't know how I thought I could save anybody."

"You've got those marks," Yejun pointed out cheerfully. "Whatever Tia did to you is still there. Maybe it's something really nasty."

"No, back up," I demanded. "What were you hoping to save me from?"

Brynn gave me a sad look but said nothing.

My life is fine, I started to say, then realized that was the selfish answer that pushed her away without convincing her to *stay* away.

"Look," I said, my heart thudding against my ribcage. "I had a friend in junior high. She was my best friend. We hung out together a lot. Her family was awesome. Then one day she vanished. There was an Amber Alert and everything. She was never found. But I knew what happened. My father mocked me when I was upset. He didn't want me having friends. I called the cops and told them where he'd gotten rid of her. They found some fragments, that's it. My father was angry at me. Later, I met this woman. She wanted to help me out. He shattered her arm just for talking to me. He would have done worse if somebody else hadn't saved her first." I never once looked away from Brynn's eyes. To my surprise, she never tried to look away from mine, though hers overflowed with tears.

"That's horrible. That's really horrible." She swallowed, then went on, her voice unsteady. "But you got out in between those horrible things. You got away. Tia helped you. I want to help you, too."

"There's no point. I came back," I said flatly.

Yejun, glancing between us, put in, "Why?"

"Because." I tore my gaze away from Brynn and glared at Yejun. "You wouldn't understand."

"Yo, my parents think I'm a witch." He crossed his arms. "They're hardcore religious, too. They tried hard to get the evil out, until the wizards turned up and told them I wasn't evil, just deformed. Then they fed me and gave me hand-me-downs and stuff, their own house charity, but they couldn't *wait* until I died. And every wizard who came by assured them I would. Any day. Not sure they're ever going to forgive me for *not* dying." A wry smile curved his mouth, drew down his eyes. "For my eighteenth birthday, I got Sen on my doorstep, offering to take me away from it all."

A wail burst out of Brynn, before she stuffed her hands in her mouth and curled around her sob.

"I'm sorry," I said quietly. "At least I always had my mother."

"Your mother the ghost?" Yejun said sharply. "You're sorry for *me* because you have a ghost to keep you company? That's not a family, that's a fantasy. "

The clocktower bells rang once, and I was glad of it, because I was running out of things to say. "We don't have time to talk about this. We don't have much time at all if we're going to do this before Halloween." I glanced back at Brynn, kneeling down with a tear-streaked face, and tried to put an optimistic spin on things. "Besides, I need to get my dogs back."

Brynn glanced up and wiped her eyes. "Do you think you can?"

"I have to do *something*," I said. "Get them back, release them, or go down trying. Something. I don't know what will happen to me if I go home without them. My father will be *so pleased*."

As I walked away, I let my inner wolf out just enough that my shadow changed. Immediately, the scents of the plaza overwhelmed my vision. I could smell my companions, and the Fiddler. I could easily detect the direction Amber went. And I could smell the mounts of the Hunt, faintly carried by the intermittent breeze: combustion engines mingled with the native scents of horses.

I thought about what we'd been following before: a magic trail created by the Fiddler that only I could follow. Why me? It wasn't really about scent, it couldn't be. It was more likely he was taking some other element and laying an illusion over it. But what?

I thought of how Yejun's magic almost always made me ill. It hadn't since my dogs had been taken. I was no longer feeling his magical manipulations from four directions at once. If the Fiddler's trail required that multiple perception, we were in serious trouble.

"Your shadow..." said Brynn, following behind me. "Is that your magic?"

"Yes," I said curtly.

"And you look older, too. The dogs made you look younger, somehow. I guess that makes sense. Dogs are cuter than wolves."

"Or I'm just more dangerous now." I looked at her out of the corner of my eye and my shadow twitched an ear. "What are you doing here, Brynn?" I asked, softly. I couldn't resist. It was always hard for me to let go when I got my jaws into something. And Yejun was walking behind us, hands in his pockets and sunglasses back on, so perhaps he wouldn't hear. "I'm not a victim. Before Emily, I was confused enough to bite when he said seek. And I *came back.*"

"But you need your dogs to cope," she said, just as softly. "That's not a good place to be."

I already regretted going back to the topic, she was that good. "Look, I wish things were different, I do. I wish I had friends like you and I appreciate your worry, but I have to do what's best for everybody. Besides, if I stay with my father, maybe I can stop him from being as bad as he would otherwise be." I had great hopes for that argument. It sounded like something a reasonable person would respect.

"Why did you go back?" she asked, as if she hadn't heard a word I'd said.

"Because I belong there."

"How do you *know*?" she persisted.

I sighed. "Because when I was losing a fight, I called on him to help me. I thought I'd rather die than do that, but I didn't even think of anybody else."

Yejun made a muffled sound behind us, like he was choking back something. I was grateful for his restraint. But relentless Brynn said, "But other people were depending on you, right? You had to do something."

"I—how do you *know*?" I stopped pacing around the edge of the plaza and stared at her.

"Tia knew," she said, too casual. She wasn't telling me something.

But if I pried more, she'd pry back.

I decided to drop it.

Besides, I'd come up with an idea. I'd inherited my magic from my father. The celestials were bound entirely to the world; they couldn't ever be separated from it, not really, no matter how you killed them. They'd always find some way back again. Not like humans, who vanished if nothing anchored them here. The Fiddler had talked about the Horn and its song like it was from outside the world, even beyond the far reaches of Heaven and the Backworld. It was an eerie idea, but maybe it was also the answer.

I inhaled deeply, like I was taking in as much of a scent as I could, and looked for the distortion in the world.

And there it was. It was the smell of an Outside far wilder than I'd ever experienced and it made a small part of me want to crawl away and hide. But the rest of me wanted to chase it.

"This is what we want," I announced, shivering with excitement. "We're almost there already." Unable to stop myself at first, I darted over to one of the plaza exits and started running down the street. But when Brynn cursed, I tangled my feet turning back and forced myself to wait. "This way," I urged.

Brynn nodded. Her skin was very pale under her black-marked hands and arms. Yejun trailed behind her, slow enough that I wondered if he'd changed his mind about coming along.

I remembered how he'd come for me in Jen's strange tower. I didn't understand him at all.

There was a thump on the roof of the building beside me and I recoiled, flinging my arms up to ward off a giant bird. Nothing appeared and I picked up Amber's scent. She liked traveling by jumping between heights, I remembered from the forest. It seemed about right: the four of us heading toward our goal, all as far apart as we could get, with mortal Brynn in the center.

The street was wide and well-paved at first. But as we hurried along, the pavement developed cracks, long black lines that radiated up and down the street, like something huge had crash-landed somewhere ahead of us. And the buildings—well, they'd always been just a little familiar before: a mortal city, just not one I knew. But as we traveled through the neighborhood around *chez* Wild Hunt, the buildings got weird. Exaggerated. Some of them were *very large*, and got bigger as they got taller. They loomed like something out of a cartoon. And between them were teeny-tiny buildings, buildings that would be cozy for a fox, or even a mouse.

Yejun's voice drifted forward. "They curve. The buildings and the tangle under them." And he was right. They curved out and then in again at the top, like the city was trying to hold something it hated.

I'd thought the city was the Wild Hunt's home territory, but it wasn't. The Wild Hunt was an invader here, just like we were. It was just an invader that the city couldn't frighten away or swallow—although not from lack of trying. The city cringed from the place ahead of us, metaphorical hands up to hold back the assault.

We passed doors that were ten feet tall, with matching windows. Then they were sixteen feet tall, twenty feet tall, and we were mice walking in a giant's playground, with shopfronts for crickets scattered between. There were no more intersections on the road now. What seemed to be a dead end ahead turned right instead, sending us parallel to the heart of the distortion. A single titan strip mall served as a final retaining wall.

I walked for a few minutes, until the clocktower chimed again. Then I turned to the supersized big-box stores and called, "We want to take it away. Come on, let us through."

Nothing happened, except that after a minute, Yejun came up beside me and said, "Who are you talking to?"

"The city," Brynn informed him, as if it was obvious. Maybe it was to her. I just wished the city had been as perceptive.

Something moved down the street: a flash of blond hair vanishing down an alley I hadn't noticed. Amber had found something. I ran after her and looked down the alley. It went through to an open space beyond, although it was half-hidden by a stinking giant metal bin locked closed.

"Good city," I said, and patted the nearest wall. The ground cracked underfoot in response, which was probably the equivalent of an unfriendly growl.

The space beyond the barrier of empty strip malls was paved with broken stone. Grass grew between the tumbled pavers, and small white flowers. Just the flowers made it far more *alive* than the rest of the city, and that was before I saw the Wild Hunt's home.

It was a red brick tower, squat and square, fronted by a pair of large black doors. A low, damaged stone fence added a decorative touch, always so welcome in situations like this. Inside the fence was a shack that reeked of horses, alongside a well and a trough. It looked medieval, and totally mundane.

It *also* looked like a seeping wound in the city, an open sore, a fleshy spike of pain made tangible. It was one of *those* kinds of things, both a vase and an old woman. The transubstantiation of the Wild Hunt.

A banner of blond hair once again drew my eye. I looked up just in time to see Amber pulling herself over the ramparts of the tower. It was bigger than its proportions indicated, or she'd shrunk. Without looking back, she vanished along the top of the wall, and I wondered uneasily if she was going to make things harder for us.

"Can we do that?" Brynn asked nervously.

"It depends," I muttered.

Then the Horn blew and engines roared. We scarcely had time to look at each other and pull back into the alley behind the redolent bin before the roaring of motorcycles rushed up to the strip mall and became the pounding of hooves. My poor lost dogs barked and leather creaked, as if the sounds of the Wild Hunt were all that actually existed. Then, with a crackle of lightning, the Wild Hunt manifested just beyond the fence.

The horses pranced and shied in a circle while the dogs raced around them in heartachingly familiar excitement. Beside me, Brynn caught her breath and squeezed my arm so hard it hurt.

I couldn't look at the dogs. The black one and the red one and the one that was brownish-grey. They had names when they'd been mine. I couldn't think about it, not until I was ready. I concentrated on the hunters instead. "They've got something," I whispered. "They've brought something back. Look."

The circle of horses and riders and hounds fell apart, revealing the Fiddler. He stood loosely, with his violin in one hand and his bow in the other. A golden rope wrapped around his torso, but he looked so unworried, so much like a mildly interested tourist that I half-expected him to burst into a flurry of attacks and escape.

Instead, Ion said, "And now—" and with no more warning than that, he thrust the spear he held at the Fiddler's chest.

-twenty-one-

As the First Huntsman stabbed the Fiddler, I stood frozen. Even if I'd had the courage to do something, Brynn was holding onto me so hard that it would have been impossible. She yelped, and I rallied enough to push her behind my back.

"Is he—?" she whispered.

"I saw it go in," I whispered back. "But—"

"I did say," said the Fiddler, his beautiful voice carrying. I stood on my tiptoes but couldn't quite make out what was going on.

Yejun pushed on my head lightly. "He's bleeding," he reported.

"So you did," said Ion angrily. "Now perhaps my companions will be content."

The one called Ipa said, "He *wants* to approach the Horn, Ion. The timing on this is dangerous." He held the golden rope wrapped around his wrist, which I thought was kind of stupid. He was tied to the Fiddler just as much as the Fiddler was tied to him.

"We do not let our prey defeat us in such a petty, ignoble manner," Ion said coldly. "The Horn will devour him. Can't you feel its hunger to do so?"

"His wound is healing up," muttered Yejun. "So is his shirt. That's a neat trick. *Your* clothes stay ripped up when you heal."

Not the time, not the time, but I felt a rush of warmth anyhow, including on the skin bared by my torn top. I hadn't even noticed until just now.

"You could let me go," said the Fiddler hopefully. "I really can't do anything right now. And I'd rather not be eaten by the Horn. That might be dangerous, now that I think about it."

Ion sneered and slid off his mount. The horse grunted and backed away, out of the crowd, until Ion reached back and grabbed its spiked bridle. "It is. The Horn is like nothing else in Creation. It will absolutely destroy you." He sounded so pleased by the notion that I realized that whatever he had been, he was something worse now. Something damaged, and *embracing* the damage.

With more than a little ire, Ipa said, "We are not taking this rabbit into the briar patch, Ion. Don't be a fool, not when we are so close."

Ion turned on Ipa, but before he could do more than glare, the Fiddler said with real puzzlement, "Rabbit? Is this the body of a rabbit? If so, that explains a few things..."

Ipa said harshly, "The trickster rabbit feigns fear of the place where he has the most power. I recognize the trickster in you, stranger."

"Ah!" said the Fiddler, enlightened. "In that case, please! Take me to the Horn! Whatever you do, don't turn me loose into the city again. I can't stand it out there."

Ion gave Ipa a smug look and yanked on the middle of the rope. "We take him in." Then he turned and looked at the closed black door. Just the force of his look seemed pressure enough to crack the doors, because they swung open. A moment later, the Fiddler and the whole Hunt, dogs and horses and huntsmen all, had passed through.

"Do you think that was a clever plan?" murmured Yejun in my ear.

"No, I don't," I said, stepping out of the alley. "I think if he had a clever plan, he wouldn't have been caught. Can you two stay hidden? I want to scout around the building. I *think* I can get both of you up to the top, but I'd be irritated if there was another, less dangerous way in."

"I could try to open the doors?" Yejun suggested, flexing his wounded hands.

I considered it for a moment, then shook my head regretfully. "I don't think blowing them off the hinges would be a good idea right now. We want to avoid getting their attention until we have to. Save it for the way out?"

He grinned at me. "All right."

I went to move away, but Brynn was still holding onto me with an iron grip. "Brynn, I'll be right back." I swallowed. "I need you guys. I don't work well alone."

She didn't respond, even to look toward me. She was staring at the door the Hunt had vanished through with a glassy expression. "Brynn?" I pried her fingers off my arm as gently as I could and she finally turned to look at me. "Brynn, what's wrong? I mean right this minute?"

"I feel so weird," she whispered. She looked down at her hands. The black marks swirled all the way up her arms, vanishing under her short sleeves. I remembered again what Tia had said when she'd pushed Brynn on me. *Take this. It's dangerous to go alone.* I thought it had been a joke. It had been *phrased* as a joke, especially attached to innocent Brynn. But maybe she hadn't meant Brynn herself. Maybe Brynn was just a carrier for the charms.

I felt a rush of unfair, irrational anger at Tia for using Brynn that way, immediately followed by a surge of grief. It wasn't fair and it wasn't right.

Then again, it almost never was.

"You'll be okay," I promised her, just in case this was one of those few times it was. Then I ran silently out of the alley. When I glanced back a few steps away, neither Yejun nor Brynn were anywhere to be seen. Even their scent was fading rapidly.

Wondering at how well the city hid them, wondering what else it hid, I approached the oversized red tower. The bricks were slabs of stained stone forming solid walls that ran at least ten feet up. Then there were narrow windows, almost more like arrow slits. They never widened, never became something somebody could look out of for pleasure. And it was the same on all four sides, and only one side had a door. Of course. It wasn't someplace anybody mortal lived. It didn't look like a place to *live* at all. It looked like a prison.

I was pretty sure I could get up the wall with Brynn and Yejun. It would be awkward, but it was something my dogs could have done, so as long as I was careful and used my power well, I could make it happen without them.

On my way back to the alley, wings beat the air overhead. I pressed myself against the side of the fortress and thought red brick thoughts as the black eagle descended from the sky. Just before claws hit the ground, the eagle's form glowed brightly. When it faded, the demon Alastor walked out of the light.

Peeking around the corner of the tower, I curled my nails against my palms as he put a hand on the door. He'd brought Tia down so that the Wild Hunt could catch her. I wanted to put him in the same position.

Alastor pulled hard and one of the two doors opened. Then he looked over at where I huddled at the corner of the building. "You can't get them back again, Annalise."

I stepped out from the wall, fists still clenched. "Maybe I want to join them after all."

He hesitated, then shook his head. "If you have any sense at all, you'll get out of here."

"You and the Hunt stole my sense," I said bitterly. "Why are you *doing* this? They destroy souls. I thought souls mattered to demons."

His eyebrows drew together in a slash as he frowned. "They are my children. Ion is my offspring just as those dogs are yours. And the souls *made a choice*." His voice was suddenly a lash. "Those souls could have faced their destiny beyond the sky, but they resisted. They allowed themselves to be drawn into bondage, or chose to linger where they no longer belong." He inhaled, exhaled, calming himself. "Every choice has a consequence. Tia and I agreed on this. Go home, Annalise. You have no soul. This doesn't concern you."

Even as I tensed to launch myself at him, he stepped through the open door and closed it behind him. I leapt after him, then kicked the door once, as hard as I could. It didn't even dent, and my toes hurt, too. Then I whirled around and loped back to where Brynn and Yejun were hiding.

Had been hiding. I looked at the empty space behind the stink container, then waved my hands through it and called, "Where did you guys go?" But there was no answer.

Uneasiness started climbing the first peak of the roller coaster of panic and I tried to think before it got to the top and went over. The Wild Hunt had gone inside. They weren't sneaky. None of them had come back out and taken my friends. Alastor *was* sneaky, but I'd been *talking* to him. The city was unfriendly but seemed to dislike the Wild Hunt a whole lot more than us.

Could Alastor have done something while I'd been talking to him?

Had that been a distraction? I thought about how he'd been standing there, turned toward me with the door half-open behind him.

I'd been the distraction, I realized. Somehow, Yejun and Brynn had snuck in behind Alastor's back.

Grinning, I went back to the red tower and put both my hands on the wall. The mortar between the slabs was a crusty dark brown that smelled faintly of insect carapaces. It was hard, but I scraped some away anyhow, because my nails were harder. Then I kicked off my shoes and started climbing.

Without having to haul anybody else around, with my intrinsic magic not invested in my dogs, it was a breeze. Halfway up, the texture of the wall changed subtly and I was reminded of my initial impression of the tower as a wound on the world. I'd never thought before about how similar scabs and stone felt.

When I pulled myself over the edge of the wall, I saw that the tower was actually a quadrangle, open to a courtyard in the center. The roof itself was bare of all the structures I was used to seeing on modern roofs: it was just a flat, open space behind some crenellations, with some deep scratches in the stone near a large slanted door.

Keeping low to the ground, I made my way over to the inner edge of the wall and peered down. Far below, on a stand exactly in the center of the courtyard, a large horn glittered with a slippery golden light. I knew right away that it was the real Horn, and that it hadn't left the confines of the tower while the Hunt chased down Tia. I would have noticed it in a Huntsman's hand, or hanging from the saddle. This slick golden instrument drew the eye like a warp in the world, and it stunk like shining corruption. It was what we'd come for, I could feel it with every fiber of my being.

But it wasn't the only thing I'd come for, and I dragged my attention away from the Horn to look around the rest of the quadrangle. The horses of the Hunt had been stabled along one wall, and I assumed my dogs were in there as well, because I couldn't see them. The Hunt milled around the Horn, all except Ion, who sat on a throne against one wall. He had one hand on his chin, as if he was considering something challenging.

There was no sign of either the Fiddler or my friends. That was, I told myself, a good thing.

I went over to the door. It was made of the same black wood as the front entrance, but this door had a dagger driven deep through a pair of leather jesses and into the wood. The dagger was plain metal and smelled of Ion, while the leather straps smelled of raptor. I stared at them for a minute, thinking of what Alastor had said earlier, and wondering which of them was really in charge. Then, just in case it was useful, I pulled the knife out of the wood and let the jesses fall to the floor.

The door opened easily and I cautiously descended a large staircase that went through several open floors, listening for any sound of my friends. The tower wasn't built for people, that was clear. The spaces I passed through were huge and echoing and strange, far too cold and unfriendly to be anybody's home. While the top floors were empty, the staircase ended on the ground floor in a room full of incomprehensible street signs from the city beyond. They'd been nailed onto the walls until there was no more room, and then leaned against the walls and piled in corners. Octagons, hexagons, circles on poles, triangles, glowing alien letters. It was the first clue I'd seen that any kind of *personality* inhabited the tower, and I wondered which of them collected the signs. The room itself smelled only of the city beyond, which was no help.

I stayed away from the quadrangle as I explored the rest of the ground floor, searching for the Fiddler and hoping I'd come across some trace of my friends. And the rooms I found were... odd. The structure underneath was straight-up fortress, built of wood and stone and designed to protect but not comfort an army. But the inhabitants were like hermit crabs, living in something that no longer fit them. The stolen street sign room was just the beginning. Another room had very carefully placed circles and spheres on the walls and floor. Streamers and ribbons drifted off of each night-scented sphere and I had the uncomfortable sense that I was walking through the model of somebody's mind. A third room was splashed with dozens of horrible, garish colors that made me think blindness was better than sight and a nose was better than both.

A fourth room had heads all over the walls. It was there I found the Fiddler sitting on the floor, still bound. The black stone violin and its bow sat on the floor beside him. Brynn stared at the walls while

Yejun knelt beside the Fiddler, inspecting his bindings. She turned when I scuffed a foot against the floor and stumbled over to me. The black marks, as vivid as fresh tattoos, stretched up under her sleeves and re-emerged on her neck: fillips and curlicues like the scrollwork on a frame. Her eyes looked wild and alien within an inky mask.

"You found us!" she said, and she sounded just like she always did. I relaxed, just a little. "I thought you would."

"No, you thought she'd run away," said Yejun distractedly. "*I* thought she would. She doesn't like to be alone and we're better than nothing."

I frowned, then stuck my tongue out in Yejun's general direction before looking around the room. "My father would approve," I said neutrally.

"I think some of them are mannequin heads," Brynn said nervously.

I thought I probably shouldn't correct her little self-deception. Then I looked closer and realized she was *right*. There were bear heads and lion heads and unicorn heads and a griffin head and, yes, people's heads (which don't really preserve well, to be honest) and several plastic mannequin heads and—

"Is that a car fender?" I asked incredulously.

Yejun glanced up. "I think there's a pair of tank guns down there."

"Yes, but mannequin heads?" demanded Brynn. "At least cars and tanks are dangerous. What did a mannequin ever do to anybody?"

"In this city?" Yejun asked.

Brynn opened, then closed her mouth. "Okay, point."

I ruffled her hair. "So what's going on? The assholes outside are all standing around looking at the Horn like they're expecting something to happen. But I thought we had a little more time than that?"

"My watch says we do," said Yejun. "Of course, it's telling the time in Toronto. Is the Wild Hunt on Eastern Standard Time?"

"That's a horribly worrying thing to say," I told him. "Don't ask things like that. Work on freeing the Fiddler instead."

"It's ingenious, really," remarked the Fiddler. "They can't hurt me, but I didn't make any kind of plan to deal with being restrained by a rope woven of their own essence. I can see next time, I'll have to plan better for an outing here." He shook his head.

Yejun tugged on the rope, which moved in his hands like an unfriendly snake. "I can just barely hold it, but I can't get a grip on it to untie the knots."

I moved around restlessly. "Maybe we should grab the Horn first? One of us can make a distraction, then somebody else snatches it, and we can..." I frowned. I'd been so focused on *finding* the thing that I hadn't really thought about what happened after we tracked it down.

"We have to take it to Jen," Yejun said. "And I don't think we should leave this guy here with the Hunt while we do. They might be a bit frustrated."

"I'm frustrated right now," I grumbled.

"Look at it this way. If we do free him, they'll probably know right away and come investigate. That'll be your distraction right there."

"Yeah, but how are you going to free him? You just said you couldn't get a grip on the rope," I pointed out.

Yejun reached out a finger to touch the violin's bow. The silvery hair flashed in the light. "I bet I can come up with something. There's always brute force."

"Excuse me," said the Fiddler politely. "That's a precisely crafted tool, not some sort of hacksaw. I made it from a tree I watered with the three songs of the last shadow-eater. I'd appreciate it if you wouldn't manhandle it. Somebody might end up bleeding."

None of us paid the Fiddler much attention. I looked around the room again, then peeked out the entrance, still not entirely resigned to this plan. "Have you seen any sign of Amber?"

"Nope," said Yejun. "If we're lucky, she won't stick her head in and screw things up at the worst time."

"She wants to help," said Brynn. "Why are you so mean about her?"

"If she wants to help, why did she run off?" asked Yejun, prodding at the Fiddler's rope-bound chest.

I coughed self-consciously. "I'll let her know what's up if I see her. If nothing happens soon—"

"Something will happen soon. One way or another." Yejun glanced up at me and gave me a little smile I didn't find reassuring at all. Thrilling, anxiety-inducing, nerve-wracking, in all the wrong ways. Ducking my head, I withdrew and went to go find a way to steal the Horn of the Wild Hunt.

-twenty-two-

Finding a place from which to keep an eye on the gathered Hunt turned out to be harder than I expected. There were four large arches leading to the wings of the tower. One was behind Ion on his throne, and it might have been perfect except that I couldn't stand the thought of being so close to him. Besides, I'd have to move past his throne to get to the Horn, and he had a stillness to him that made me think he'd be the last to respond to any distraction from Yejun and the Fiddler.

Two of the other archways offered a direct line of sight to the Horn, and to the Huntsmen standing around the Horn. All they had to do was lift their eyes to spot me. That was almost as bad as being caught by Ion. I was stealthy, but I didn't trust my skills against their very natures. Maybe Yejun should have come instead of me, because he'd snuck himself and Brynn in right under their noses.

And then there was the final archway, which led into the stable. It was, as I approached it, the one I'd hoped I'd have to use. I could hear the horses moving and making snuffling noises, just like real living horses, and I wondered why the Hunt seemed to prefer them in the form of machines. I didn't hear my dogs, but dogs were a lot quieter. And if they weren't in there, then they weren't anywhere in the fortress, because I'd looked on my way down.

As soon as I stepped into the dimness of the stable, I could smell them. Their scents hadn't changed at all, and my eyes flooded with tears I blinked away before they could spill.

"Heart?" I whispered. "Boys? I'm here..."

The horse in the stall nearest me whickered quietly, but I didn't even look at him. My eyes adjusted quickly to the darkness and I looked around eagerly. I could *feel* their presence. I knew it. I didn't know how. But I peeked around the edge of one stall and there they were, in an achingly familiar pile.

Nod turned his head toward me. His eyes glinted red and a white fang flashed as he pulled himself to his feet. I sank down on my haunches, whispering nonsense, the same nonsense I'd sung to him when he was feral and broken. Grim and Heart rose to their feet as well, spreading out in their stall. They smelled like my friends, but they didn't move like them. I tried to see if there was any kind of collar I'd missed before, something I could just unlatch and they'd return to me. But there was nothing, nothing that wasn't woven into their nature now.

The truth was that I'd collared them when I'd saved them, bound them to my shadow. I'd remade them out of my essence and our natures had mingled. And now that Ion had ripped them away from me, they were as much his as they'd ever been mine.

But there had to be a way to steal them back again. I couldn't just give up on them. Being the slave of something like Ion was horrible and painful. Nobody growled like Nod was growling for fun. You growled because you were angry, because you were hurt and frightened and driven beyond reason, or because somebody was driving spikes of misery into your mind, trying to force you into being a monster despite the better nature somebody who loved you said you had.

I had to rescue them, or I had to put them out of their pain.

Slowly, I extended both my hands to them. It'd only take one lunge from them and a misjudgment on my part, and they'd slash my arms open from hand to elbow. That would be kind of an inconvenience, but I was confident I could avoid that. I was fast, and I'd learned to avoid my father, after all. And I had to catch at least one of them by the scruff.

It was Nod I expected to lunge, but he hesitated so long that I wondered if he *did* remember me despite the spikes Ion was surely filling his mind with. Then, without warning, he raised his head and started barking at me: the furious, frightened bark of a dog who has spotted an intruder and doesn't quite know what to do about it. It was a bark to warn his master, to demand assistance against danger. Heart and Grim joined in, their voices blending almost musically with Nod's.

An icy chill replaced my moment of hope, and once again I felt a loneliness that could devour worlds as they bayed against me. But the response from the courtyard galvanized me. "They've caught a pest," said Ion laconically. "Fetch it out."

Panic made me tumble backwards and leap to my feet. I couldn't let them catch me again. I'd thought about it while making my way through the fortress, about giving myself up to them if everything else failed, just so I could be near my dogs again. But now that I could see it looming right ahead, the ship-sinking iceberg, I couldn't bear it—the thought of Ion looking at me and only seeing a tool. Of becoming a means of production because I'd failed to be anything else. I had that waiting for me at home, after all, and at least my father was familiar in his rages and his quirks.

One of the Huntsmen said something I didn't understand and the horses all started rearing and screaming as light blossomed near the roof. The figure that stood there was familiar: one of the ones who'd held me down before. The panic took over and I darted out of the stable, back into the tower main, as fast as I could run.

I left my dogs behind. I wasn't willing to fight for them. I was, as my father was so fond of pointing out, *weak*. Even my mother had been stronger; at least she'd been willing to kill him when she'd thought he was merely mortal.

Run, her memory urged me. *Don't fight. He only comes back and hurts you more.*

I stumbled through unlit rooms, always hearing the frantic barking of my dogs and the heavy footsteps behind me, until at last I found myself cowering in a corner, unable to run anymore. Panic is a bitch like that. It never leads you out of mazes.

I pressed myself against the wall and fought for control, fought for the will to fight, to escape sensibly. After a moment, I realized the thudding heavy footsteps were the sound of my own heart, and that if anybody was chasing me, they'd gotten lost in the maze of chambers.

Slowly I crept to the center of the room—just a room, wood-walled, unlit, barely more than a closet—and listened again.

Near me: only silence. So much silence that when Amber suddenly popped up behind me, I shrieked and leapt back to my corner again.

"Shh," she hissed, putting her finger to her lips. Her hair was wild and her eyes glittered oddly. "They're looking somewhere else right now. Thanks for distracting them."

"Amber," I gasped. "What have you done?"

"Oh, just stole the Horn." She had a sack in one hand. I came forward and she opened it enough that I could see brassy glints within.

I went cold with dread. *I* was supposed to steal it. Amber was a loose cannon; I still didn't know if she was on our side. "Now what will you do with it?"

"Now what? Now what? How should I know? You never told me what was supposed to happen *after* you stole it." She gave me an annoyed scowl. "Really, a little gratitude wouldn't be out of place."

Relief was overtaken by guilt, and both of them tripped over an enormous log of nervousness. "If I distracted them, how come you're here? Where are they?"

"Oh, something else distracted them after you pulled them away. Wasn't that your clever plan?" Her blue eyes regarded me artlessly.

That was when I realized the amount of power swirling above us. It cut through the walls of the tower like they didn't exist, a vast turbulent cloud of strange energy. I could actually see tiny lavender lightning bolts arcing to crawl over the walls.

I realized we were trying to hide from the Wild Hunt in the very heart of their home. This was the energy of the Wild Hunt itself, the energy that sustained them and the horses and my dogs, the energy provided by the Horn that Amber held.

Where the lavender lightning touched the walls, ghostly faces appeared, moaning. Ion had been feeding the Horn a lot lately, every time he was temporarily freed from prison by the magic song. When Halloween ended, he'd be free to let it gorge on all souls, and I couldn't even imagine where that ended.

"I don't think stealing it means anything until we get it to where it needs to be," I said. "We have to find the others and get out of here before they actually grab us."

"Okay," said Amber agreeably, pushing her hair from her face. "Do we meet the others now or later?"

Then, distantly, I heard violin music begin. It was even a song I recognized, although I didn't know the name of it. It was triumphant and a challenge and it made me want to dance.

"They freed him!" I grabbed Amber's arm and pulled her to the door. "The Fiddler!"

"That's good, right?" she asked.

"Yes—" I began. Then the music met the Wild Hunt's magic swirling above and pure chaos erupted around us.

Thunder shook the tower as the purple lighting leapt off the walls and started to dance—and by dance, I mean formal, structured movements. I think it was some kind of folk dance. White rain sheeted down from the high ceiling but it wasn't wet. It skittered down my skin, a hot and biting dryness. Fog boiled out of the floor, silver and black shot with lavender. The violin screamed above the thunder and the dry rain became sharp splinters of ice. I couldn't see my own feet and when I took a step, I stepped on something both slippery and crunchy.

I caught my balance, still hauling Amber after me, and fumbled for where the door had been. It was gone now, nothing but a drift of shattered wooden shards. Crimson flames wreathed the empty space where the door had stood, clinging to the frame without consuming it. I brought my hand close to one, felt the heat and pulled it back again.

But it wasn't spreading. The violin's triumphant song changed, became urgent. The wind howled in response and the flames became agonized faces.

Amber shrieked and stomped her feet. "Get away from me, you awful things." I didn't look back, just yanked her after me as I plunged through the doorway of burning souls. But the corridor beyond was no better. A hellish light illuminated the space beyond without providing any visibility through the ludicrous fog. I felt, rather than saw, the wall to my left collapse.

The Wild Hunt was laughing. It was the staccato beat under the thunder and the moan of the wind and the taunting of the violin. I wondered if this happened a lot. They *were* the Wild Hunt; maybe this was just their idea of applause for a great musical performance.

"How do we get out?" Amber shouted. "Can't see a thing."

I inhaled and closed my eyes. "I don't need to see."

It took a moment through the strange dry smell of the fog and the ozone tang of the storm and the really unexpected scent of apple pie. Maybe they were trying to cover up my friends' scents. But they were too close. No mere fog was going to keep me from them.

I led Amber through the broken wall and up a flight of stairs and down again. At one point I think we went back outside. I heard Amber's gasp, but I didn't want to open my eyes, see whatever she saw, and lose my concentration entirely. She didn't stop me, nothing stopped me, and we went back inside the tower again, and—

"AT!" Brynn called. "You found us. You have it? We have to go. This place is falling apart!"

I opened my eyes as Brynn appeared out of the fog, running over to me. Yejun loitered at the front door, hands in his pockets. The Fiddler was nowhere to be seen, but I could still hear his frenzied, distant music. It was no longer anything familiar, but it made me want to kick doors down and demand what was mine.

Instead, I said, "Is he going to be okay? If they catch him again, that's kind of a waste."

Yejun shrugged. "He didn't seem worried." His eyes widened as he looked over my shoulder. "What the hell did you bring with you? Never mind, let's get out of here." And he *did* kick the door open and hold it that way. "Out!"

Brynn ran past him and Amber followed her, still holding the bag with the Horn. I made the mistake of looking over my shoulder, though.

Ion stood behind us. The grin he'd had the first time I saw him was gone. He didn't even have the belligerence he'd shown when arguing with his fellow Huntsmen. He was calm, expressionless, and in his eyes, a hundred thousand souls screamed. A corona of crimson fire burned around him.

I could still hear the rest of the Wild Hunt laughing somewhere, amidst the thunder and the violin and the howling wind. My friends and I had been all but shouting to talk to each other. But Ion barely spoke above a whisper when he said, "What are you waiting for? Run."

I heard him. I saw the tendrils of crimson fire reach out skeletal fingers for me. And I ran, pushing Yejun out the door ahead of me. Then I hooked it closed and raced to the alley. Brynn huddled there, waiting for us.

"Where's Amber?" I demanded.

Brynn jerked her thumb upward and I looked up. There she was, half-hanging off the roof. "Look at it!" she exclaimed, laughing in delight. "The tower is actually falling apart. Do you think it's because I stole the Horn?"

"If it is, let's get it even farther away so it falls apart more. They're still in there, Blondie," snapped Yejun. "And they're going to come after us. That is what they *do*."

"Fine, fine," said Amber, and dropped down to land lightly on her feet.

"AT, any chance you can get us out of the Backworld the same way we got in?"

I hesitated, feeling the fabric of the world. "I don't think so." I tried anyhow, reaching out to tear the Curtain apart. Nothing happened. It was like trying to rip open a steel door with my bare hands.

Yejun shook his head. "Knew that would be too easy. Let's run instead. Maybe the Fiddler can make up for slowing us down by slowing them down as well."

"Why did he run off?" I demanded as I ran.

"So we could meet you and get the Horn out of here," Yejun panted.

"AT, didn't your mother ever tell you it's not nice to show off to the mortals?" Amber chided, jogging backward. "They don't talk and run very well."

I muttered and kept running. We quickly left the exaggerated region around the scar behind and emerged onto the nameless city streets. I didn't recognize where we were, but I could smell that we'd been here before, and that was good enough. If we kept moving, we could get through the city quickly, and then we'd end up—well, I wasn't quite sure. Right then, "not here" was good enough.

"That stupid bird is following us," announced Amber. I craned my head and saw the big dark shape of Alastor's bird form above us.

"It's pursuit. He's scouting for them," I growled.

"Inside again?" Yejun managed between long breaths.

I glanced at the buildings to each side. They were tall, thin townhouses, just like the ones that had clustered around when the Wild Hunt had stolen my dogs. "Not this time."

"He's gone now," Amber said. "Maybe he missed us."

I skidded to a halt. "I don't believe *that*." Changing direction, I scrambled up the side of one of the houses. "Keep running, I'll catch up!"

When I reached the roof of the townhouse, I rose to my knees and shaded my eyes. A storm still raged over the region we'd fled from, but the sky was otherwise empty. Alastor had vanished. Even more worrying was the utter lack of any pursuit. I glanced down. Yejun and Brynn were still moving away, but they'd dropped to a fast walk, Brynn holding a stitch in her side. Amber had stopped moving entirely. She held the bag with the Horn out in front of her, as if she was trying to get a good look at it.

A clap of thunder loud enough to shake my perch rolled across the city and something left the city. The stormclouds over the city's scar fuzzed into a mist of rain. At the same time, Amber screamed and thrust the sack containing the Horn away from her. The Horn tumbled out of the bag and as it landed on the pavement, it struck like a bell. A deep, sonorous note rang out, growing and echoing. The brassy surface of the Horn rippled.

Then Amber scooped it up again, muffling it against her chest. The long, low note faded away and the surface of the Horn stilled.

I skittered down the side of the building as fast as I could without simply jumping down four floors. "What just happened?"

"It bit me," said Amber angrily. "It's smug now. Look at it, can't you see how smug it is?"

And you know what? I could. The shine of the bronze was oily. The curve of the Horn's neck was like the smarmy grins of my father's pack. It was ridiculously, horrifyingly smug.

Brynn and Yejun jogged back to us. I said slowly, "It's not smug about biting you." I looked around, but I couldn't see the city's clocktower. I hadn't heard it chime, but I thought about how the Hunt had been waiting around the Horn, and about the lack of pursuit—

"Remember what you said about the Wild Hunt being on Toronto time, Yejun?"

"It was just a joke," he said quickly.

I shook my head, trying to come to terms with the awful realization. "It wasn't. You had a good point. Time zones are a thing. The Wild Hunt isn't a local magic."

"What are you babbling about?" snapped Amber, her eyes wide and glinting red as she stared at me.

I sigh and leaned back against the townhouse to close my eyes. "It's dawn on November First somewhere, even if it's not in Seattle or Toronto. We've failed. The Wild Hunt is free."

-twenty-three-

The silence that followed my explanation made the smugness of the Horn even worse. Then Amber said, "But I have the Horn right here. How can they—?"

"Stealing the Horn was only the first step," muttered Yejun. "Stealing the Horn was never enough to stop them from getting free. It does its thing, binding and powering them, no matter where it is."

Amber growled and smashed the Horn into the side of the building, hard enough that brick crumbled away. I opened my eyes, hopeful that maybe at least the Horn's oily finish had been marred. But it just shimmered even more. Little rainbows danced over the surface. I sympathized enormously with Amber's urge to smash it.

Brynn gave a tiny little gasp, and then another one, like she was hyperventilating. Her knees collapsed under her and she sat down between them, her eyes glazed over. Then her whole body jerked forward, like something invisible was yanking her around.

"Oh, hell," said Amber and pushed the Horn at me before sitting down next to Brynn and taking both her hands. "This happened before, while you two were off running through the city. That was when all these marks appeared." She squeezed Brynn's hands, then stroked her hair and tried to make her lie down. But her entire body was taut, too taut to unbend without hurting her.

I shoved the Horn back into its bag and went to Brynn's other side. "Is it a sickness?"

"How should I know? Do you want me to drink her blood and do

some kind of taste test?" Amber asked acidly, her voice at odds with the light touch of her hands on Brynn's shoulders.

"Catch them, catch them," Brynn muttered.

"Something's happening with the magic Tia gave her," Yejun said.

"Can you stop it?" I demanded.

He raised his gaze from Brynn to meet my own and spread his hands. "Maybe. It wouldn't be pretty, though. *Should* I stop it?"

I ground my teeth, but before I could make a decision, he shook his head. "Actually, I'm not going to. Tia was a professional, and I don't know a thing. I'd probably hurt her."

Frustrated, I shook my own head. As I did, something caught my eye. I swooped down and picked up Brynn's arm, turning her hand palm up. "What's this?"

The marks on her skin were spreading. Tiny, unfamiliar characters faded into sight across her inner arm near her elbow, filling in the space between the long dark curves previously present.

"It's like writing," said Amber, peering at it closely.

"It's okay," breathed Brynn. Her eyes in the mask of marks on her face were closed, but her body relaxed until she was crumpled in on herself. "It's okay."

"Brynn? What's going on?"

"Still figuring that out," she said, her voice barely a whisper. "Give me a few minutes."

"I don't know if we have the time," said Amber nervously, glancing up and down the street.

"Of course we do," I said bitterly. "We've failed. They're out there now." I sat down and hugged my legs tightly. "Maybe if you hadn't wasted time chasing me down, you would have made it."

Her voice strained, Amber said, "If you run off to sulk again, I swear by all that is holy I will hunt you down myself and kick your pathetic ass. Just... stay there for a minute while we think about this."

I pressed my face into my knees and waited for them to think about it. I wouldn't have imagined it was possible, but the whole city felt emptier now. I wondered what my father had planned for Halloween, and then I wondered if anybody else would try to stop the Wild Hunt. Somebody else had saved the people I'd failed to save before.

My mother was right. Fighting back just made it hurt more when you were beaten.

But even she hadn't been consistent there, had she? The stories she'd whispered to me as a ghost ran around my mind. Persephone, yes, but also Jane Eyre and Fanny Price, resisting all the pressures of love and scorn to maintain their integrity. My mother had died, but she'd done what she had to in order to stay with me. She hated him and she loved me, and she'd poured both of those into me.

"I'm feeling better," said Brynn. Her voice was still soft, but it was steadier. "I've been looking at the marks, and I think—"

"No," whispered Amber, and started humming. The song started out pulse-like, throbbing. As she scrambled to her feet, it became frantic. "I'm not here, love. Go back to sleep, darling."

Her eyes were wide and catlike, focused on something faraway, and she shook her head in tiny, insistent negations. "No, I'm sorry, please don't—"

My heart pounding, I looked around wildly. I knew what, who she was talking to, I knew he was probably far away, but if I could have found him, her nameless master, I would have thrown myself at him with teeth and claws. And I knew that even that wouldn't have helped, not at all.

"I'm sorry," said Amber again, her voice louder. I looked back and she was talking to us, her face twisted into a horrible wry grin. With a little shrug, she said, "I tried to fix what I screwed up. I wish I could have known you better."

I lunged forward, clutching her hand between both of mine, as if I could hold her together when her master pulled her apart. It was useless, I knew it was useless, fighting wouldn't do anything at all, but I had all this magic I'd inherited from my father and what was it good for? I wrapped my magic around her as I'd wrapped it around a dying dog, like I could save her like I'd saved them. But she wasn't free, she was just a memory pattern imprinted on somebody else's magic and even her sad farewell was just an illusion.

Right?

Brynn seized Amber's other hand, bringing it to her cheek, muttering something under her breath. The marks on her skin intensified. But how could it matter? What could we do?

Amber blinked at us rapidly, like her dry eyes stung, shook her head fondly as if we were being fools. Her long fingers curled around mine. There was a chill as her flesh faded and my fingers sank into her substance. She was thinning. It was much, much slower than how my father's wolves went when he took back what he'd given them, but fast or slow didn't matter. She'd be gone either way.

Then Yejun said, "Oh, hell," in a tone of utter disgust. He stepped between Brynn and me, elbowing us aside as he took Amber's head between his hands. Leaning in toward her, he looked down into her startled face. For a heartbeat I wondered if he was going to kiss her.

Instead, he pressed his head against hers and magic *exploded* off him, shoving Brynn and me backwards. I'd never felt anything like it before. It was closest to being in the center of an active ritual circle, but that was barely a point of comparison. Even without the Sight activated, I could sense massive strands of the Geometry twisting around Yejun and Amber, and it seemed like many, many nodes were being filled and emptied, all at once. More than Yejun stealing the moon in a fairy tale forest, more than him ripping through layers of the Backworld, this made me understand why the wizards who had seen him were so afraid of him. It was a titanic piece of magic, being worked spontaneously, without a circle, without components, without even the basic magical toolkit wizards carried in their palm nodes.

I waited, my heart in my throat, until Yejun's hands dropped away from Amber's head and his shoulders loosened up and Amber didn't vanish. Then I brought up my Sight and looked to see if I could discover what he'd done.

His tree of nodes had changed. Many of them—far more than seven—had stabilized, with long Geometric lines running from them to Amber's form. But even as I watched, one of the stable nodes disintegrated and the Geometric line it had held lashed around until a newly budded node caught it.

Amber's own form had changed as well. She had no nodes as humans and nephilim had them, but the Geometry lines that anchored in Yejun formed a sort of Amber-shaped cage around a single unattached node filled with a twilight glow.

"What was *that?*" asked Brynn incredulously. "Did you save her?" Amber sat down all of a sudden and put her face in her hands, and Brynn knelt beside her.

Yejun glanced at me from the corner of his eye. "I think so. For now. I thought that your dogs were kind of like she is, and the Wild Hunt stole your dogs. So I stole her." He transferred his gaze to Brynn. "What Tia did to you gave me some ideas, too."

Amber glanced up, met Yejun's eyes, then looked away, at the townhouse beside us. For a long moment she didn't say anything, although her throat moved convulsively. Then, with obvious effort, she said, "Thank you."

He shrugged and stuck his hands in his pockets again. "It's not going to last forever. But maybe Cat'll have some suggestions on how to really free you. I think he used to be like you, anyhow."

Amber shuddered, still looking at the wall. "That would be great. I'd rather not go on like this any longer than I have to."

Yejun's voice sharpened. "Hey, it's no treat for me, either, Blondie. You're heavy."

"I didn't mean—" She looked back at him, then narrowed her eyes. Standing up, she brushed herself off carefully. "We're agreed, then. This can't end too soon. But have you ever considered weightlifting?"

I boggled at the two of them. Yejun had given Amber a miracle, a miracle that was warping his entire Geometric frame, yet they were sniping at each other like Homecoming Queen rivals. "I can't believe—" I began. They turned to look at me together, the movement so synchronized that I stopped in confusion. I thought about how I used to be able to speak to my dogs without words, and wondered what the harsh words covered up, or if their new connection even stretched that far. "That was amazing," I finished, lamely.

"Why did your boyfriend try to hurt you?" asked Brynn urgently.

"Because he's an asshole," said Amber. "And I was an idiot. I wish—"

"No," interjected Brynn. "Why did he try to hurt you *now?*"

We all looked at Brynn. The tiny glyphs had spread over her entire right arm, down to her fingers, filling in the framing fillips that had appeared earlier. Her pale skin was barely visible under the dark markings.

Uncertainly, Amber said, "He woke up and reached for me. He discovered I was here?"

"Awfully big coincidence, him waking up right now, don't you think?" Brynn asked.

"I—" Amber stopped. "What do you mean?"

"I think that somebody woke him up. Somebody who wanted you out of the way."

"Alastor," I said grimly.

Brynn grinned at me with far more cheer than our situation really warranted. "Exactly."

"This isn't exactly something to be happy about," I told her.

"Sure it is," she said, rubbing the marks on one arm. "I heard the chief Huntsman tell Alastor to deal with us. And where is he? Not here. He went straight to the surest way he had of getting rid of Amber." She looked between us. "Don't you get it? Maybe they're out in the world, but we're still a threat. It isn't over unless we give up."

I glanced at Yejun and Amber to see how they were taking this wild idea. Both of them nodded. "Sure, makes sense," said Yejun. "It's not a pass/fail class."

"Exactly," said Brynn.

"What about all the souls they're destroying right now?" I demanded. "It's pass/fail for each of them!"

"Don't worry about them," said Brynn, so calmly that I goggled at her. It seemed so uncharacteristic of her to not care about the devoured souls. Maybe she didn't really understand—

"Um," said Amber, as if she shared my surprise.

Brynn looked at her, then back at me. Then she put her glyph-darkened hand on my arm. My skin tingled where her fingers touched me. "If they're really gone, they're gone, AT. We can't let caring about the lost get in the way of paying attention to what's happening to those still here. Including ourselves."

"I don't know how to do that," I said, troubled. "It's always been win or lose for me."

"So the game has just gone into overtime," said Yejun lightly. "One way or another, we have to get this Horn to Cat and Jen. Even if we've screwed up on dealing with the Wild Hunt, maybe they can use it to get Amber off my back."

I took a deep breath. It wasn't how I'd been brought up, but when I thought of it that way, the strangeness became a selling point. "All right. Let's get out of this city." And I caught myself, painfully, before I mentally called my dogs to me. I was learning.

We hurried down the street and turned in the direction of the red and white forest. I could smell it, I could feel it, but all I saw were more buildings.

"Hello!" said the Fiddler, stepping out from behind a building. He beamed at us like a proud teacher.

I recoiled. "You! What are you doing here? No wonder I can't get us out." I made a shooing motion at him.

Amber clutched the Horn close to her chest. "You can't have it. I need it more than ever now."

"Dear dreamchild," said the Fiddler, still smiling broadly. "I said I couldn't claim what I needed yet. There's an order to what must happen. That's why I need you four, and the two in the other tower."

"Jen and Cat," Yejun said glumly. "How are we supposed to get there if you're going to hang around gumming up the transit?"

He spread his hands, holding the bow in one and the violin in the other. "I'm afraid we're going to have to go the long way." He looked closely at Brynn, then told her, "You're filling up."

She raised her other hand, which was now covered with tiny characters. "I'm okay. They haven't even started on my outer forearms or legs yet." She peered at her arms. "I'm a bit curious about that, honestly."

"What happens when she fills up? What is happening to her, period?" I asked.

"I'm fairly sure when she fills up, she explodes and undoes all of the Lady in Red's efforts," said the Fiddler blandly. "Do you want me to spend the time explaining what I think the marks mean?"

I stared at him, then said flatly, "I hate you."

I started chasing down the scent of the forest again, moving as fast as the others could manage. We jogged past unfamiliar buildings and up long, spiraling hilltop roads. After searching for longer than I would have on my own, we paused at the top of a great hill to let Brynn and Yejun catch their breath. I took in the view from the hill, trying to decide if the city ever ended. There was a grey waste out in one direction, like a bay but composed entirely of drifting mist. I stared at it long and hard, then said, "That looks like Puget Sound from Queen Anne Hill."

"Sorry, forgive me for being city illiterate," said Amber acidly,

"But does that mean something?"

"Not... exactly." I stared at the vista some more. "Are you two ready to move again?"

"Yes," said Brynn, inspecting her legs. "I don't seem to feel tired at all anymore, so we don't need to stop for me."

"I'm pretty sure that's not good," noted Yejun. "Her nodes are swollen like you wouldn't believe."

I clapped my hands over my ears, then shook my head. "I think I have an idea how to get out of here now. Let's go."

Now that I knew what to look for, I could see other elements of the Far City that reminded me of Seattle. Had they always been there, or was the city reconfiguring itself in an attempt to get us out? I hoped it was the latter.

"That's a red tree," said Amber, pointing out a white-barked, red-leafed tree growing from the sidewalk.

"Great," I said, walking fast.

"They're all around us," said the Fiddler. He lifted his violin and played a light little air, and the ghostly shapes of the red forest appeared over the buildings near us.

"Don't take us there," I begged him. "I know where we are right now, but I'll have to start all over again in the forest."

"This is the best I can do, little wolfchild," he assured me. "I do wish I could do more without disrupting the path out, though."

Something about the way he said that made me turn to look at him directly. "Why?"

As if in answer, there was a distant roar.

"What's that?" Yejun asked uneasily.

"Crap," said Amber. "They noticed the Wild Hunt was gone."

"*Who* noticed?" I demanded.

Amber looked around, at everything but me. "You remember that bear you found for them? That wasn't the only thing they'd stocked the preserve with. There are things that have learned to hide in the forest and the city. I guess, uh, they're not hiding anymore?"

"We're talking about deer and stuff, right?" Brynn asked hopefully.

Amber shook her head. "Bigger. Meaner."

"Moose?" Brynn persevered, and now her hope was more like pleading.

"They like dangerous prey," said the Fiddler lightly.

"Yeah, but why should the stock care about us? And can we keep moving?" Yejun said.

"Anybody seen Alastor lately?" I asked, cocking an ear. I could hear the hunting cries of other creatures, mostly from behind us. Mostly. For the first time since I'd started this quest, I felt calm. Here and now, I knew exactly what to do.

-twenty-four-

Dozens of creatures that qualified as "dangerous prey" roared and screamed behind us, driven into a frenzy by freedom from their hunters. Maybe an insane demon was prodding them, too. I tilted my head, listening, then said, "Three blocks ahead, we turn left. Another five blocks after that and we reach the parallel to the McAllister building, where we came through before. There should be a scar on the Curtain there. I'll open it if I can, but if I'm busy, one of you will have to do it."

"Why would you be busy?" asked Brynn, bless her heart.

"Because those guys are faster than you guys." I pointed over my shoulder at the giant lion running down the pavement, and the flurry of dust with three oversized weasel heads just behind it. A bear's roar—I remembered it well—came from around the corner.

"Any tanks?" Brynn panted.

I remembered the cannons in the trophy room. "I think they got that one."

"Can we just get to this exit fast?"

And you know, I tried. I tried to get them there. Maybe I should have picked up Brynn. Maybe I could have done something else. But all I really wanted to do was stop running. I'd been waiting my *whole life* to stop running. So when the snarl of the cave lion carried the carrion stink of its breath to my nose, I stopped dead, spinning in place and ducking the beast's pan-sized paw.

I turned the duck into a roll that took me under the big cat's body.

I was so small it barely noticed. It noticed my shadow, though. My claws raked down its body and I caught its tail as it tried to leap after my friends. It was heavy, but I was able to change its direction enough that it yowled and turned back to try to shred me. But I wasn't there; I'd jumped over to the tangle of oversized mustelids, bared my teeth at them, and let myself sink into a pleasurable crimson haze. Yelping and blood and fur in my teeth and this isn't really the stuff one talks about in polite, human-shaped company, no matter what they do for a living. I retained just enough sense to see my friends clustered around the scar in the Curtain, and just enough foolishness to wonder if I should get away, and then the sabertoothed birds appeared, whistling like steamers, and I had to slow them down, too.

It was all going very well until I came up against the black eagle, perched on one of the phantasmal tree branches just at my eye level. Before I could charge him, his form flickered and Alastor sat there instead, one leg crossed over another. "Look at you," he said in distaste. "I suppose your father would be proud."

That stopped me cold, mid-rush. Before I could get my feet physically and mentally underneath me, a lizard the size of a bear pounced on me. It had six-inch teeth, and as I tried to roll away, I was able to count the double layer of them.

A single string vibrated and Amber's voice merged with it to produce a note so sharp that it made my ears ache. But it made the lizard about to eat me stiffen and then collapse on top of me, ears and eyes filled with blood.

"AT, you brat," screamed Amber. She sounded further away than I thought she could be, and I wondered if she'd arrive to get the dead weight of the lizard off of me.

When she didn't, and I didn't die from the crush despite my aches, I blew out my breath and exerted myself, lifting just enough of the lizard that I could slide out.

Alastor was gone, no big surprise there, and most of the other creatures were either unmoving or looking after their own wounds. I looked muzzily at the number of them—at least a dozen different varieties. I didn't take down that many, did I? No, they must have turned on each other as soon as I disrupted whatever was uniting them.

I wondered where Amber was, and turned around.

The road to the spike of an edifice that stood in for the McAllister building had been rent apart. A chasm at least twenty feet wide lay between me and the other side, where the Fiddler stood, playing a slow, gentle tune. Amber stood on a shimmering bridge that crossed one-third of the chasm, holding the Horn in one hand and her other hand outstretched toward me. "AT, you brat," she shouted again. "I can't get to you. When I try, the other side just gets farther away. The city doesn't want us back again. You have to jump over to me. I'll catch you."

I looked beyond her. Yejun and Brynn were nowhere to be seen, but I could see the tear in the Curtain they must have passed through. It shimmered like oil on water, like a return to everything I'd gained and everything I'd left behind. I *had* to get through.

But I hurt. I ached all over and I had scrapes and bites and any minute that cave lion, who was a really persistent kitty, was going to shake off the kick in the head I'd given him and come for another bout.

"Come on," called Amber. "Jump. I know you can do it."

I went to the edge of the chasm to gauge the distance. It was huge. Unpassable. I'd jump, and I'd fall, and wow, was the chasm deep. I couldn't even see how far down it went. "Um," I said, and looked over my shoulder. The cave lion was climbing to his feet.

My breath sped up. I watched the lion. I was no longer calm. I was *scared*. Not of the lion, but of something nameless. I didn't know what was going on. But I had to do something. I had to be with the others. Over here, I was all alone, except with a bunch of creatures that wanted to tear me apart.

I ran toward the lion, ignoring Amber's enraged cry. Then, just as the lion braced for my attack, I spun on one foot and raced toward the edge of the chasm. As I reached the edge, I pushed off, throwing myself into the void, my hands out for whatever I could catch.

My right hand slapped Amber's, and she hauled me backwards, dragging me across the shimmering bridgelet until we were both on cracked pavement. "Kill the music," she snapped, and the Fiddler cut off his tune in mid-phrase. I looked back in time to see the bridgelet vanish, just as the cave lion reached the apex of its own leap.

It was better at jumping than I was, but it wasn't a third again as good. Its paws scrabbled at the sides of the chasm and then it slid down, into the darkness. I hoped, briefly, that it landed on its feet. Then Amber wrapped me in a hug. "You tiny little idiot," she scolded. "You scared me to death."

I fought her off for a moment, then gave her a little squeeze. "We have to get to the others."

"Right," she said. "It's only been a few minutes. What could have gone wrong? Oh wait, it's us." And she ran through the portal.

I looked back at the Fiddler. "Do you need to go first?"

"Thank you," he said. "Perhaps we ought to go through together, in case I change things again. I tried to plan well, but I couldn't account for everything." He held out a hand to me, and without even thinking about it, I put my hand in his and we stepped through the shimmering tear.

Just as when we arrived, this was not a simple movement from one world to another. I fell through darkness, past the memory of my mother crying for murdered friends, past a vision of Cerberus slain outside the gates of Hell, past an older woman who looked like Amber looking out a window—

I reached out and found Amber's shoulder, and then we thudded into hard ground and stumbled forward onto the sunlit streets of Seattle.

"Never again—" I began. Then Amber squealed in agony and pulled away from me, pressing herself against the wall of the McAllister building and into the thin line of shade.

"I thought it was supposed to be night here!" she moaned, huddling away from the sunshine.

"Guess not. I'm not a world-time expert or anything." I peered at her to make sure she wasn't about to burst into flame. She looked haggard, and her eyes had gone into hungry-wild mode, and her skin seemed more pink than alabaster, but it didn't seem to be getting any worse.

"It's before noon," she muttered. "I'm really bad before noon."

She was right. It looked to be mid-morning, on a beautiful day. On Halloween day, specifically; I spotted a dozen adults in costumes and handfuls of costumed tiny children wandering up and down the sidewalk. Yejun and Brynn were waiting for us. The Fiddler stood a little further off, looking up and down the street like he'd never seen a living city before.

Yejun straightened up from where he'd been slouching against the wall. "What's wrong?"

"You didn't fix the stupid weakness *he* thought it was so cute to give me," Amber flared up at him.

Frowning, Yejun said, "Of course I didn't. I wasn't going to screw around with what made you *you*. I was only trying to save your life, you ungrateful hellion."

"I can't go out in this, I'll die," she sobbed.

Unsympathetically, Yejun said, "Then give AT the Horn and we'll leave you here."

"No way," Amber hissed, holding the Horn close. "This is *my* chance for freedom and you're not taking it away from me."

Brynn said, "Yejun—"

But once again, Yejun looked at me. I bit my lip. "Is there *anything* you can do? I mean... you stole the moon once."

Yejun gave me a startled look. "Oh. Right. Brynn, give me that lens I gave you before." After Brynn handed it to him, he pulled his sunglasses out of his pocket and stared down at them for a long moment. Then he gave a long-suffering sigh, shook his head, and said, "I can't believe I'm doing this." He popped one lens out of his sunglasses and inserted the lens Brynn had given him into the frame. Then he looked through them. "Perfect. Here, Blondie."

She stared at him incredulously. "How are sunglasses supposed to help me? Especially tacky ones like those?"

He shrugged and turned away, but she lunged out of the shadow and grabbed the sunglasses from him, whimpering in the morning light. Once back in the sliver of shadow, she slipped them on and recoiled so abruptly she almost dropped the Horn. "It's... a trick?"

"Come here and let's see," Yejun coaxed. He stepped away from the wall.

After a hesitant moment, Amber followed him. She didn't scream, or whimper, or even squeak.

"What did you do?" I asked, completely bewildered. "You said they were just sunglasses before."

"It's night," said Amber wonderingly. "Really night. I can feel it on my skin."

Yejun grinned. "Knew that so-called moon had to be good for something." He looked around. "We should get going, though, before—hey!" He ran after the Fiddler, who had walked into the middle of traffic and was inspecting one of the cars that honked at him. "Look, man, I don't know where you're from, but you can't just wander into the middle of the street."

"It didn't seem to matter in the other city," the Fiddler pointed out, but he let Yejun haul him back to the safety of the sidewalk. Then he stopped dead, looking up at the sky.

"Yes, yes, tall buildings," said Yejun. But I followed the Fiddler's gaze up, up, all the way up to the dark clouds tumbling into existence.

"They're coming here because the Horn is here," I realized out loud. "We need to move. We've got at least half a mile to go to get to Jen and Cat," I snapped, pushing Amber down the sidewalk. "Can you call them and have them meet us, Yejun?"

He shook his head, staring up at the sky. "Won't help. Not something we can do on the run." He turned and started walking in the direction of the hotel.

"Fine. Come on, Brynn!"

But Brynn stood in the middle of the sidewalk staring up at the sky. I pulled on her arm, but it was like tugging on a statue. I tugged harder, ready to pull her off her feet and carry her, but that statue comparison was really apt; she was *heavy* suddenly.

A single dog's howl, desolate and alone, echoed from the sky. Then horses screamed high above and I glanced up involuntarily to see the Wild Hunt emerge from a ring of lightning, pouring through the rip in space like a waterfall of mounted death. Traffic had barely started moving again after being halted by the Fiddler, but now it stopped once more, as everybody looked up in the sky. A silence fell at the screams of the horses and the roll of thunder, but the wave of sound that followed more than made up for the brief quiet. People started ducking inside buildings like they'd drilled for an event like this. They even abandoned their cars, except for a few who were approached and instructed to exit by cops. One of the police officers near me spoke calmly but rapidly into a headset while staring up at the sky.

"What are you going to do?" Brynn asked, her voice distant.

"You get on under cover, kids," said the cop. "We'll see what they're going to do and go from there."

"Will they hurt people, AT? Living people?"

I thought about it for only a moment. "They'll hurt us, so I'm going to go with 'yes.' Can we run now?"

"All right," said Brynn, but it wasn't about running. She pulled away from me and raised her palms to the Hunt.

"What are you *doing?*" I moaned and tried to pick her up again, throwing a helpless look at the cop. He was watching with far too much keen interest, I felt.

Brynn threw a dazzling grin over her shoulder at me. "I came on this adventure to save you. And I'm not really sure you need me, but *they* do. I can save *somebody*, and I can slow the Wild Hunt down, too."

I boggled at her. We really had to have a chat sometime about this idea she had of saving me, but I was too bewildered by everything else she'd said to do more than make a note of it. Besides, she was looking back at the sky again.

The Wild Hunt rode down the stormclouds, their mounts prancing and pulling under them and my dogs howling and barking alongside. They had new matching costumes in black and white, with lots of elegant froths of lace and neckcloths. Victorian gothic, I thought dizzily. Who knew? Two of the Huntsmen had swords that dripped ice, while Tala, notable even in the full regalia by her sheet of blond hair flapping in the wind, had a scarlet spear. Ion had his own spear in one hand, and his eyes were fixed beyond us. I knew instinctively he was focused exclusively on Amber, and the Horn. But the rest of the Hunt was ready to party, in their own particular annihilative fashion.

Brynn clicked her tongue three times, like she was calling something. I'd distantly felt the magic contained by her nodes working since she'd started picking up the little dots on her skin. It had purred along like a sports car, exerting a constant low draw on the Geometry around us. I had no idea what it was doing, but I felt it the same way I felt the Curtain between worlds. And now I felt the complex spell kick into overdrive. Everything blurred for a moment and I wasn't sure if it was just me or the whole world.

Brynn beckoned both her hands at the sky and the horses of the Wild Hunt went mad, bucking and rearing. The Huntsmen were expert riders, each of them, but they weren't prepared for this, and one by one, they were thrown off their mounts and out of the sky. They fell through the cloud road their horses stood on, vanishing into the city below. As each horse freed itself of its rider, it charged straight down at Brynn.

I stared, open-mouthed, as a black horse with a silver mane turned into a ball of silver-rimmed black light, and then, just as it slammed into Brynn's chest, it became an inkblot that passed through her shirt and rocked her back on her heels. Then I put my hand on her back, bracing her for the next impact, a champagne palamino-golden light-inkblot. And then the next, and the next.

At last, only Ion remained above us, fighting his horse with an astonishing dexterity. The horse bled from the mouth and wept tears of lightning, but it couldn't unseat him, no matter what it did. My dogs danced around the rearing horse's hooves, excited by its frenzy. I stared up at them, my heart in my throat. Could she steal them back, too?

Nod lunged, snapping at the stallion's flanks. The frenzy really was too much for them to resist, and Ion was far too distracted to exert control over them. Then all three of the dogs jumped on the horse at the same time, and it overbalanced and fell off the stormclouds.

Ion stayed on the horse even then, even as they were both falling, until Heart, swimming through the air, caught at his head and shoulders with her paws while Grim tried to nestle in his arms. That was too much; they knocked him from the saddle. I felt a warm rush of affection: even turned evil, they were still my puppies.

Screaming in rage, Ion and the dogs fell behind some buildings; I hoped nobody tried to play Good Samaritan with him. As soon as he was gone, the stallion righted himself and galloped to Brynn, turning into a blood-streaked inkblot right before he smacked into her torso. She gasped and clutched her chest, then shook herself all over. "That one hurt a little..."

She turned to me. Her outer arms and her neck, and probably her chest and back, too, had all been filled in with long, stylized tattoos of rearing horses. Dots appeared on her right cheek under the curling frame-like mask, and I realized that suddenly she had a whole lot less empty skin.

"Couldn't get the dogs," she told me apologetically. "I couldn't reach them the same way."

I shook my head. I couldn't even spare time to pay attention to my burning eyes; there were more important, more *current* things to worry about. "Didn't somebody say something terrible was going to happen to you when your skin filled up?"

"Uh, yeah," said Brynn.

"Hope saving those horses was worth it," I said, before dragging her along the sidewalk that Amber and Yejun had vanished down.

I made it to the first intersection before a voice from what seemed like a lifetime ago called, "Brynn McKenna Lennox! You stop right there!"

Brynn closed her eyes, paler and more frightened than I'd seen her yet. "Oh no," she whispered. "It's my sister."

-twenty-five-

I **looked** down the cross street to see two faces I hadn't ever expected to see again. I'd met Marley when I'd been in LA; she'd been the one I was trying to save when I called on my father's power. And I'd met Branwyn in my father's house. She'd wanted to save me and my father had broken her arm and thrown her into his dungeon as a result. I still didn't know quite how she'd escaped.

"Oh my god," I whispered. "Your *sister?* Oh, Brynn, no, tell me this is a joke."

"Sorry," she said glumly, watching the two young women advance. Marley was an ordinary-looking brunette, but Branwyn had green hair long enough to pull into a ponytail, and she was holding a hammer so large it was probably illegal without a permit. There was a smoky gem embedded in the handle. Marley was a half-blood nephil like me, while Branwyn was a uniquely determined mortal.

"Could we run? I don't think I can deal with this right now," I asked hopefully.

"They'll chase us," Brynn sighed. "They chased me all the way here, after all. The Wild Hunt's got nothing on my sister when it comes to persistence."

I gritted my teeth, then hauled Brynn toward them. As we got within non-shouting distance, Marley said brightly, "Hi, AT. You look like hell. Can I help?" She sounded so chipper and hopeful.

"No," I said. Then I thought about her particular intrinsic magic, which she used to protect people, especially troublesome children.

"Wait, can you do something about Brynn?" I presented Brynn by her shirt collar.

"Brynn, you are filthy," said Branwyn, putting her hands on her hips. "Why are you filthy? No, don't tell me yet. Tell me where that *demon* is so I can wring her neck." She said *demon* like it was a different five-letter word.

"I told you I was fine when I called," said Brynn, mustering some outrage. "You didn't have to—"

Branwyn cupped her ear. "I'm sorry, did you say 'fine' or 'fourteen'? And I certainly did have to, because if Mom came home and you weren't there, *none* of us would be 'fine.' Now, where is the demon?"

Brynn hesitated, then said uncertainly, "I think she's dead. Look, we don't really have time to—"

"Dead?" Branwyn frowned and looked at Marley, as if she could confirm. Marley just shrugged.

"I saw my dogs destroy her," I admitted.

Branwyn pursed her lips, looking between us. "Your dogs, huh. Well. You two are going somewhere. Let's talk and walk." She reached out and took Brynn's collar from me. With them side by side, I could not just see the family resemblance, but smell it, and I kicked myself for not realizing it long ago. Things would have been *different* if I had. I already owed too much to Branwyn to risk her sister this way.

"So you rescued my truant baby sister from Tia?" Branwyn inquired. "Thanks."

"No! No, no, it's... it's a lot more awful than that. Uh, did you see those guys in the sky a few minutes ago?"

Branwyn glanced upwards. "A bit. Are they a problem?"

"If we don't stop them, they're going to eat every dead spirit on Earth, and probably any living spirit that gets in their way," I said bluntly. "We're on our way to stop them. Our friends are ahead of us." There was a scream behind us and I flinched. "And we're in the bad guys' way."

"Well, pick up the pace, then. Lead on," Branwyn said briskly. She took a firm grip on Brynn's hand and started running.

Marley turned and looked speculatively back the way we'd come, then shook her head and shooed me along.

I dashed ahead of them, dodging other pedestrians moving just as quickly. When we got to the hotel, Amber and the Fiddler were standing quietly under the awning, watching Yejun face down a squadron of worried-looking bellhops and doormen.

"This is karma," Yejun grumbled, patting his pockets.

"What's wrong?" I asked, coming to a halt behind him.

"They're not letting anybody in unless they have a door key, at least until the 'crisis' is resolved. And Ye here apparently hasn't been bothering with keys," Amber informed me. Her eyes narrowed as she looked behind me and saw Branwyn and Marley flanking Brynn. "Who are they?"

"Helpers. I think. Actually, they're an object lesson in why you shouldn't be my friend, but we can talk about that later. Um." I looked over the hotel employees clustered around the door. A few of them had noticed Branwyn and her oversized hammer; this did not seem to be improving their mood. "Can't you... hum at them or something?"

"It's still before noon," Amber told me regretfully. "To them, anyhow." I looked at the Fiddler, saw the way he was staring at around with the amazed expression of a kitten just let outdoors, and wrote him off as useless.

I went up beside Yejun and leaned on him. "Want me to handle this?"

He stopped trying to sweet-talk the door guards and gave me a hassled look. "Be my guest."

"Isn't that the problem?" I gave him a tentative grin, happy to be able to solve a problem he couldn't for once. Then I turned to Marley. "Hey, Marley, can you keep this G-rated? These people seem like nice folks. I don't want to actually hurt them and I'm *sure* they don't want me to hurt them."

Marley gave me a startled glance, and then a pleased smile curved her mouth. "I think I can. Go ahead."

I gave the door guards my friendliest look, and I could tell they were just men, mortal men trying to be brave, by the way they barely looked at me. I was a short, dark-skinned girl. Yejun was scarier. Branwyn was *armed*. They barely looked at Marley, either, but Marley and I were the most dangerous combination there.

I remembered the monster that Marley's protective magic hadn't been able to protect me from, and my burst of amusement faded. "Yo, guys. Get out of the way so we can save your souls. If you don't, I have to move you."

They muttered, mumbled, refused. One of them, probably still in high school, managed to sneer and say, "You and what army?" Then one of his companions nudged him and made a little gesture at everybody gathered behind me.

I turned to look back at them. "Huh, I guess I do have an army. But that would be overkill." I took two quick steps and waded in and—well, I moved them aside. It felt like I'd imagined fighting would feel when I was very small. I could kick somebody aside and I knew they'd be fine, that Marley's shield would prevent them from actually being hurt. And they couldn't do a thing to me at all, though that didn't take Marley's help.

It only took a minute flat to create enough of a breech that my army could rush through. I waited until everybody was in, Marley giving me an amused wink, then waved at the door guards staggering to their feet as I backed into the building. "Sorry about that! We do have a room here!"

An elevator stood open and waiting for us, with several people inside frowning at its unresponsiveness. They saw us charging toward them and got out of the way fast. Once we'd all crowded inside the elevator, the doors slammed closed and the elevator jerked upward.

The ride up was just long enough for the adrenaline of the G-rated tussle to fade. I slumped against the wall. "That cost us more time than it should have."

Yejun tickled my wrist. "Sorry. I won't throw away my keycard next time."

I rolled an eye at him. "Next time? You want there to be a next time?"

"You guys are cute," said Branwyn brightly. "When do we find out more about what's going on? Any chance I can see Tia's body to make sure there's nothing I can do to leave my own mark?"

Brynn burst into tears.

Branwyn stared at her, utterly disconcerted, then pulled her close as the elevator came to a halt. The doors slid open. Cat stood there with a canvas bag over one shoulder.

"Jen's on the roof already. We need open air and more space for this," he said, joining us. "Take the elevator to the very top floor, Yejun, and then there's a staircase."

That was only a couple more floors, and then we piled out and thundered down the hall to a steel door that had been propped open. We went up the staircase like a herd of fabricated dinosaurs. This was not the kind of hotel that had a really nice garden with maybe a pool on the roof. No, it was a vast expanse of pebbly concrete with dozens of pipes and turbines sticking up. Also, there was Jen, who was drawing a diagram near the doorway with fat, colored chalk. Her hair kept tangling and blowing into her face until Cat walked over and handed her a clip from the bag he carried.

She beckoned the rest of us over and gave us a tired smile. "You got the Horn. That's good. And who are these people? Friends, I hope." She gave Brynn, who was wiping tears away, a concerned look.

"I hope so," said Marley, her voice sounding very strange. "Can we get some introductions, please?"

"Right," I said. "That's Jen, who is a half-dead wizard; Cat, who is her assistant and has a big knife; Yejun, who is a magical mutant freak; Amber, who desperately wants to be a real girl. You all know Brynn, but I bet you don't know she's got living tattoos of ponies up and down her arms. And, um, this is Branwyn, who makes things, and Marley, who does extreme babysitting."

"Cat, huh," said Marley, and she sounded unexpectedly hostile. I looked between the two of them in confusion.

Cat looked over at Marley, then took his round-framed glasses off. Once again the sense of familiarity swept over me. I knew him, but I didn't. I frowned as he said to Marley, "Ah. I take it you think you recognize me? But I promise you, I'm not who you think I am."

"Who are you, then?" challenged Marley. "There can't be that many not-quite-human blond prettyboys called 'Cat' wandering around."

He shook his head and considered Marley for a long moment before saying slowly, "I'm what was left behind when the, ah, previous owner vacated the premises."

Marley's eyebrows drew together. "What?"

Jen laid her fingers on Cat's arm and he startled, looking down at her. "Can we discuss this later? If you have a past history with Cat, that would be very interesting to discuss, given his nature, but we don't really have time now."

Marley hesitated, then nodded, and Jen went on: "And who is the man with the violin?"

I looked between Marley and Cat one more time before answering. "He's, uh... the man with the violin. You know, 'The Fiddler' isn't really a name," I told him, then looked at Jen. "He complicates everything, but he's on our side."

"Our goals align," the Fiddler told Jen quietly. "There's something I need to reclaim and I can't until you've done what you need to do. And you can't do what you need to do unless I'm here to help."

"Who are you? Sen never wrote anything about you." Jen gave him a look as if he'd offended her somehow.

The Fiddler looked around again. "I hid the Horn and its song here originally. I never expected it would be used the way it has been, or that it would... insinuate itself so deeply into the fabric of your world. I thought it would be safe. I thought it would be *simple*." He crooked that astonishingly charming grin at Jen.

She stared at him for a moment, then said gruffly, "Nothing is ever as simple as we think it is." Then she turned her back on all of us and busied herself with the magical diagram she was drawing.

Amber, still hugging the Horn, asked, "Now what?"

Cat gave the Fiddler a long, cool look, then said, "The Horn goes in Jen's circle. So do Yejun and I. The rest of you—"

There was a crash from far below and the entire building shuddered. Cat kept his balance perfectly and continued calmly, "The rest of you could help out by keeping the Wild Hunt away from us, however you can. This isn't a long ritual, but it's not instant, either."

I ran across the roof and peered over the edge. A figure stood at the corner of the building. As I watched, he drew his fist back, then punched again. Once again, the whole building shuddered. I eyed the drop, then shook my head and ran back to the roof entrance. Marley caught my arm and shook her head. "Don't go down there."

"Fighting on rooftops is bad, especially when they're willing to bring the whole building down."

Marley gave me a little smile. "I'll keep the building upright, at least for a little while."

I gaped at her, then said, "Right. You do that. That would be *great*." There was another crash below, but the building didn't even vibrate this time, and an angry roar rose from the base of the building.

Over at the circle, Amber was reluctantly giving up her burden. "Tia said—she told me there was a way I could—" she began, then fell silent, pushing the Horn into Yejun's arms. "Do what you have to. Make sure everybody else gets the chance I gave up."

Branwyn had an iron grip on both Brynn's hand and her hammer. I went over to them. "Brynn, quick, before we face off against demigods, can you please tell me what you meant about saving me?"

Brynn gave me a nervous look, which she then transferred to Branwyn, and then the sky. "Branwyn talked about you to Marley and I overheard. About how they needed to figure out a way to save you. Later, Tia told me about you, too. When I was interested, she told me I could save you myself, if I could just make friends with you. I thought it would be cool to... to be like a prince, rescuing a damsel in distress from a monster. I thought it was like a fairy tale, except I could be the hero."

I stared at Brynn, at this little fourteen-year-old girl, who thought she could rescue me from a monster just by being my friend, and then I thought about Tia, who had told her that. I couldn't decide whether I wanted to laugh or cry, hug Brynn or push her away.

Branwyn, however, facepalmed while still holding Brynn's hand. "I need to buy Mom and Grandma 'Thank You For Putting Up With Me When I Was Fourteen' cards," she muttered.

"And now things are all awkward," said Brynn earnestly. "I knew they would be. If you hate me now, I understand. I pretty much lied to you."

There was another roar from over the side of the building, but it was a lot closer and a lot louder.

"Brynn—"

Amber shouted, "Hey, AT? Could use your help over here."

"Brynn, you're kind of short for a knight in shining armor, but you make a pretty good friend." I reached out, squeezed her free hand. "Thanks. Gotta go."

As I turned away, Branwyn said, "Speaking of bad ideas, why exactly *are* you covered in tattoos of pretty, pretty ponies, Brynn?" But I didn't stay to hear her answer. When I skidded to a halt beside Amber, she was peering over the edge of the building with a grace and confidence I envied. "Three of them. Two over here, one on that side." She pointed.

"Okay," I said. "They reach the top, we kick them off. Easy peasy."

She gave me a dubious look, and then one of the Wild Huntsmen came over the edge. It was one of the ones I didn't know the name of, and he roared like a minotaur as he grabbed at Amber. She pulled her legs in as he yanked her toward him, then planted her feet on his chest and used the momentum to spin both of them around. Then she lunged toward him, all wide-hungry eyes and shining fangs and he recoiled, letting go of her. I stuck out my foot as he stumbled backward, and he tripped over it and vanished over the side.

"Easy peasy," I repeated, smiling at Amber as she glared over the edge.

"He didn't fall all the way down," she said flatly. "And now he's climbing up again. AT, they outnumber us, and they're not even all here."

I shrugged. Worrying about that was just going to slow me down and the next target was rising over the edge of the roof. I lunged at him, bringing my shadow claws around to bite into his groin. One of them got stuck in his formalwear. He jolted backward and I twisted, then kicked him hard enough that he teetered and fell off the building. "Keep an eye on them," I told Amber, as she peered over the edge. "I'll be right back."

Then I dashed to the next side of the roof, barreling into the figure pulling himself over the edge. It didn't work out; he was *big* and I was not. He caught me and went to throw *me* over the side, but I clung to him. Maybe we'd both fall. Probably neither of us would hit the ground.

But he staggered away instead. As the odds that I'd be able to throw him overboard decreased, I changed my plan. My shadow lengthened, pricked ears, bared teeth. I snapped my teeth at him as I clung to his arm and my shadow lunged, tearing open the flesh of his thighs.

He stopped staggering. "I will crush you," he whispered, and contorted so he held me close. My shadow and I snapped at him again, digging claws into his flesh. But his wounds closed up almost as fast as I could make them, and he was squeezing me so hard—

—I could change, I'd get bigger—

But there were too many people here, I didn't trust myself. I missed my dogs.

I couldn't breathe.

The red mist drifted in front of my eyes. Then, suddenly, the pressure vanished and he collapsed to his knees. Branwyn stood on the other side of him, her hammer in both hands. She'd hit him right in the center of his back. He flung his hand out and a blade dripping ice appeared in it, darting toward Branwyn. But my shadow and I were faster; we tore the muscle of that arm to the bone and his hand flopped sideways, the sword vanishing again. He goggled at it; then the pain set in and he contorted in agony from both the back hit and the wound.

"Take a minute, catch your breath," Branwyn suggested calmly, as if an ice blade hadn't almost struck her. "Then roll him off the edge before he gets up again." She nodded to me and went toward Amber, Brynn following at her heels.

I dragged in a single breath, enough time to notice Yejun standing in the circle with his hands spread wide while Cat crouched before the Horn with that strange knife in his hand. Jen stood to one side, her hands moving dance-like. Yejun shouted, "The Horn is fighting back, I'm not sure I can hold it."

Without thinking, I shouted back, "You stole the moon and saved Amber. You can do *anything*." Then I turned and started rolling the contorted Huntsman off the roof. As he dropped over the edge, his back arched and his hand lashed out. I jumped back just in time, and my shadow lunged forward to tear at him again, one bite more to slow him down.

The Fiddler started to play a quiet violin tune. It underlay the sound of the wind and the roar and crash of our enemies, as simple and omnipresent as breathing. Yejun cried, "All right, now!"

I held my breath, wondering if it was about to all be over. But whatever they were doing, it wasn't that fast. Amber shrieked in rage, and I had to look away from the ritual.

She backed away from the edge as the two Huntsmen both came over the side together. I ran toward her. But I'd only taken a few steps when something came over the third side of the building. It wasn't a

Huntsman this time. It was my dogs, red-eyed and raging. My dogs, coming for me.

-twenty-six-

Nod and Heart and Grim: my dogs, my best friends. Even red-eyed and snarling like hellhounds, I would always know them inside and out. I froze, then ran toward them, leaving Amber to deal with her two Huntsmen. She and Branwyn could handle them. I needed to deal with my dogs before they tore my people to pieces.

I placed myself squarely between them and the rest of the group. I whistled, clear and sharp, and it did the job of attracting their attention. I had to put them down, for everybody's sake. I had to kill them, or do whatever I could to hold them down until the ritual finished and ended them a different way.

But I thought of how Brynn had stolen the horses away and I couldn't resist trying one more time to reclaim my dogs, even as they surged toward me.

Behind me, Marley said, "This isn't right. Those are *her* dogs, why are they attacking her?"

My shadow flattened its ears and lunged forward, knocking Heart off her feet and back into the other two. I took a deep breath, trying to find the inner peace that I'd used when I'd saved the dogs in their mortal forms, long ago.

Jen said sharply, "Yejun, focus! You can't go to her or we'll lose everything!"

Nod leapt, clipping me on my shoulder, but I caught him on his ribcage and forced him back again. "Sit down," I bellowed. They didn't listen.

Brynn sobbed. "I can't reach them. They're wrong. I'm so sorry, AT."

Grim gathered himself, watching me with those crimson eyes. He'd been such a gentle, playful puppy. He'd grown up in my shadow. He was my baby, my twin, my first dog. He'd turned into a monster, just like my father wanted me to turn into a monster.

Baby, you aren't like him. You're my baby girl, sweet and good and kind. That's why you run away, okay? You run away and you live.

Tears stung my eyes. My mother had done her best to save me: because she loved me, and because I was hers. Her best hadn't been perfect, it had put me onto the hard road, but she loved me. I was still me. I wasn't crimson-eyed and maddened with hate, with nothing but spikes of pain in my mind. She'd built a wall around my self, with books and songs and love and the spikes came through the wall, oh yes, I had to contort myself to avoid them, but the very existence of the wall she'd built was itself salvation. Being me hurt, but I was me. Love mattered, sometimes.

But it didn't matter here.

"I wish I could have saved you," I whispered. Then my shadow spread out and around into a pool of darkling radiance. Fingers reached up to each of my poor dogs, wrapping around their throats. Leashing them, muzzling them. I knew them better than any monster could. I'd put my self into them and I knew how to take them apart again.

I was wrong. Love did matter here. It was the only way I had the strength to do what needed to be done.

The Fiddler's music stopped. "Wait!" he cried.

I held the dogs down, although they fought, while I looked around.

"There's something you should know," said a different voice, low but carrying. It was Alastor, rising up from below my eye level, in his grubby suit, with his hands in his pockets and one ankle crossed over the other as his great black eagle's wings flapped slowly.

I shook my head and looked over at the Fiddler. He was looking back at me, but as soon as our eyes met, he mouthed, "Wait," again, then started playing the same song as before.

Amber stood where she'd been knocking Huntsmen off the building, breathing hard. Branwyn stood beside her, but her eyes were on Brynn, who was right behind me.

Brynn wiped her face and said, "The elevator."

The door to the staircase opened. Ion and Ipa strolled out together, as if they were out for an airing. I ground my teeth; I could hold the dogs, but I couldn't do anything else while I was doing that. Were we just going to be outnumbered, as simple as that?

Ion passed a sardonic eye over our crew, then said, "We will kill everybody here if you finish the magic you're working. It won't destroy us, you understand. It will just unbind us. Just as the fellow with the knife does, we will have our own independent existences." He gave me a cruel smile. "Except for the dogs, of course. They are far too new yet to survive. But *we* will have plenty of time to enjoy killing you."

Ipa picked up the thread of the speech. "Yet there is an alternative. Surrender the Horn and we shall discuss limiting our activities to the most appropriate targets. My companion is less interested in this, but I can bring him to an agreement." While Ion leaned back against the staircase door, Ipa stood erect and attentive.

I looked frantically at the others, then at hovering Alastor. If he switched sides, gave up on his corrupted child, maybe we could survive. What had he wanted to tell me?

"Cat," said Jen urgently. "You've stopped. Why have you stopped?"

Cat didn't answer. He stood over the Horn, his knife held in both hands, a picture of hesitation. "I'm doing this so you'll live," he said softly.

"I don't care!" she said sharply. "I died when Sen did. I just want to do this and move on. Please, Cat."

Alastor sighed, clearly irritated, but the Fiddler's song changed, becoming something sweet and sad.

"Put the knife down," suggested Ion. Then he started whistling, a different tune than the Fiddler's. It was a jarring, horrible mash-up and the dogs surged against my shadow leashes. They wanted to fall on whatever they could: me, Ion, Cat, anybody, and tear us apart.

"Cat," whispered Jen.

He shook his head, as if rejecting something, and slid his knife along the edge of the Horn.

"Thank God," said Yejun explosively. He dropped his hands as if releasing dozens of leashes all at once. And then I stopped paying attention to anything else.

The dogs snapped free of the Horn. For a moment, they were

nothing more than unbound, barely structured information, ready to scatter in the sunlight into nothingness. But they weren't in the sunlight. They were in my shadow, bound by my power, and when the Horn's spiked chain shattered, I was holding them.

All three of them vanished, all at once, pulled back into my shadow, pulled back into their own minds again. I shouted in joy and hugged myself, holding them close, my Nod, my Heart, my Grim.

But there was something wrong. It was something odd. It felt *so strange* and it had something to do with my dogs. Something *tickled*. My shadow tickled. It felt *full*.

I didn't care, I had them back again. But it seemed like a good idea to bring them out as they were meant to be and let them recover in the open air. So I flung my arms wide and they burst out of my shadow, dogs rather than hellhounds, friends, companions, beloved.

They looked around, bewildered, wary, and then all at once, all three of them sneezed, and sneezed again. A mist sprayed out and coalesced into a ghostly form. It was a woman, with dark skin and wings the color of old roses wrapped around her body. Her wings unfolded and pale marks moved under her skin, the mirror of Brynn's dark marks.

"Well," said Tia. "That could have been more dignified." She gestured sharply and the tiny dark marks on Brynn shot off of her, leaving only the framing lines and the stylized horses. Each of the tiny marks unfolded dozens of times into the silhouette of a person: big and small, male and female, child and adult, until the roof thronged with barely visible ghosts. The chill was incredible and my dogs huddled around me, just as they always had before. As one, the ghosts turned to where Ion and Ipa stood.

"We save who we can, as we can," said Tia lightly, and then, to the ghosts, "My friends. They can't hurt you now. But can you hurt them?"

The door slammed open as neither Huntsman stuck around to find out if the ghosts could damage them. It was scary to be cut off from something you'd always had strengthening you. I knew. I knew, but I didn't sympathize at all.

Tia smiled and looked at Alastor, who hadn't moved save for the lazy flapping of his oversized wings. He sighed. "You meddle too much, Tia."

"What did you *do?*" Brynn demanded. "Why do you look like that?"

Tia looked down at herself, smoothing a dress into existence over her form. She still looked insubstantial and she was still speckled with the pale characters. "I used the dogs as a channel to get into the Horn and you as an anchor to the world. Then I did my best to redirect as much as I could of each ghost that came after me to you." She shook her head. "That Horn is very powerful, though. I don't seem to be quite what I was, do I?"

Before Brynn could answer, Yejun said, "Oh no, what's going on now?" The air distorted around the Horn, so that it seemed to change sides. Strange noises emerged from the bell and the mouthpiece. The distortion spread as the Horn bucked and Yejun backed away.

The Fiddler leapt lightly inside the circle and put a hand on the Horn. It stilled under his touch, but resentfully, as if ready to burst into world-jarring throbbing at any excuse. The Fiddler said, "Come now. You've grown up very fine, but this doesn't suit you anymore. We can do better." He reached his other hand inside the wide bell of the horn and pulled something invisible out.

Invisible, but *noisy.* It was a harsh, jarring piece of music. My dogs whined and covered their ears and I did the same. It was a headache incarnate, and if it didn't stop soon, I'd be cutting my own ears off just for a chance of relief.

Nobody else liked it very much either. "Shh," said the Fiddler, and pulled a miniature trumpet out of his coat pocket. He tipped the song in his hand into the trumpet, and silence fell.

The Horn still glinted angrily, but it had lost the malignant shimmer that had bothered me since I'd first seen it. The Fiddler picked it up and handed it to Jen. "You know what has to happen next."

She looked at him uncertainly. "Sen said..." Then she shook her head. "Not me. This isn't for me to do."

Alastor said quietly, speaking directly to me, "Haven't you ever wondered about what would happen after the Wild Hunt was cut away? The world is accustomed to a Hunt. It will birth a new one in the pattern of the old, unless the void is filled, just as it would if your father was destroyed."

The Fiddler glanced up at Alastor. "Your kind is very bad at understanding endings. I never expected the Horn to bond to this world as it did, but now that it has, I'm sure we can come up with a better structure for the Wild Hunt. We just have to give it a new song instead of having it constantly strain for echoes of what I've taken away." He put his bow to his violin and started to play again.

This song was different than the previous gentle, supportive music he'd played on the roof. It was energetic, with dark twists and many little motifs. It was, I realized, about a journey.

"A new Hunt!" said Amber joyfully. A golden radiance spilled off her skin. "Oh, yes, please. I'll join!"

Amber wasn't the only one glowing. The song the Fiddler played described *us*, and the golden shimmer surrounded Yejun and Brynn and sparked off my fingers. It surrounded Cat and Jen, too.

"It can't just be you," said the Fiddler. "It needs six. Don't be afraid. I won't let it drag you in against your will."

Yejun straightened his shoulders. "Will we still be ourselves? Can we have lives? Or would we have to go back to that crazy city?"

"The Hunt is free now, whoever embodies it," answered the Fiddler serenely. "It will call you to your task, when you are needed. It will, I hope, be an unpleasant one. Necessary, but unpleasant."

Yejun hesitated, then said, "Okay, sure." He stepped forward.

Brynn pulled herself away from Branwyn a heartbeat later. "I have to, Bran. I'm already in." She turned her hands up. The glyphs of the rescued souls were gone, but the stylized horses still reared on her arms. She gave Branwyn a reassuring smile. "It'll be fine. You went out looking for magic and found it, right? My turn." And Branwyn scowled, but let her walk over to stand beside Yejun and Amber.

Cat stood facing Jen, holding both her hands. "Sen wanted you to live," he told her. "She wanted me to save you."

Jen stared down at the ground. "I can't—I can't imagine life without her. I don't want to. All I ever wanted was her." Then she sighed. "But none of you are even old enough to drink. No, not even you, Cat, you're like two months old." And she pulled away from Cat's hands and walked past him into the glow surrounding the other three. Cat stared after her, a wry, pained smile on his handsome face. Then she turned back and held out her hand to him, and he sprang forward to take it.

Alastor stood behind me, whispering. "I have to tell you. This is what your father wants, kid. You think those people are your friends, but this is a scheme, a play by your father to turn you into what he wants you to be. He's Hunter, after all. Once you join them, you will become exactly what he wants, exactly what your dogs were before. Are you going to take them back into that?"

If I could have just ignored him, I would have. I didn't trust him. But what he said tapped into my deepest fears. I knew how much my father wanted me to integrate into his pack, to accept what they wanted from me and lead them on hunts. Wasn't this that? Was this just an elaborate setup, a game he'd arranged to get what he wanted?

I couldn't just ignore him, but I could reject the fears he stirred, over and over again, every day. It would be easier with friends. "This is real," I said, and ran to catch Yejun's outstretched hand.

The Fiddler's song traced out our journey, our fights and flights and shared moments, and the light around us grew until it shone through us, like we were made of hollowed glass. Then the Fiddler's song poured into us, filling us up with ourselves, transfigured. The Horn reached out tendrils of gold and those tendrils merged with the glass of our bodies. For an amazing moment we were all connected through the Horn. We were all beautiful. And the wildness, the alien essence of the Horn wove its way into us. I could hear it, feel it. I could look into the depths of the golden sheen and see truths I barely had the framework to understand. And I was not a puppet, not a celestial's dream or shadow. Just as a golden strand connected me to the Horn, another strand, thick and solid, ran from me to the world. I was a bridge. We all were.

And the world expected certain things of us. It ached, from old wounds and new ones. We would have to deal with those as we found them.

The song ended, but the light didn't fade until Tia moved between us. She was still a dark phantom, pierced with glyphs of light. She wasn't part of what we were, but she picked up the Horn and held it gently.

"The first thing you must do is to deal with those who once occupied your position. They are neither celestial nor human, but shadows come to life, and they are a vector for corruption that *must* be removed."

We looked at each other. The Horn tugged on me gently, and the world pushed, but I set my feet and thought about the order. I thought about what being *removed* meant. There was a blankness within the Horn.

"It's peace," said Jen quietly.

Amber shuddered. "It's oblivion."

"It's *justice*," said Tia firmly.

My pleasure at seeing Tia's return ran up against an iceberg of irritation. Hadn't the Fiddler just explained to us that it was people like her—people the Horn couldn't fully destroy—who had made this mess? I gave her a quelling look. "Shh. You may have started it, but you're not finishing it. You're not contributing."

Cat addressed the Fiddler. "Can't you take them with you, back wherever you came from? It was your abandoned magic that twisted them this way."

The Fiddler tilted his head, his dark hair falling across his face. "I'm not going to do that."

"That'd just be punting the problem to somebody else, anyhow," Yejun said.

Brynn whispered, "They can't help but hurt things. They hurt each other. They even hurt their horses."

Everybody looked at me, including the thousand ghosts that Tia had preserved from the eschaton in the Horn.

I sighed. "It's necessary."

Brynn threw wide her hands and horses galloped off of her, six of them. Golden and black and silver, crimson and earthen and twilight, a river of sparkling ink come to life. Each horse chose a rider, came to us unsaddled and unbridled. The golden stallion came to me. He was not afraid. And as he turned his head to look me in the eye, I saw that was because he was *furious*.

Personally, I was nervous. Horses weren't my thing. But these horses were part of the Wild Hunt, bound by music of their own, not just by Brynn's magic. They were a story far older than my dogs. And they'd spent millennia under those who probably would have been happier with motorcycles.

Whatever the golden stallion saw in my eyes, it satisfied him. A simple saddle shimmered into place on his back. He blew on me and stomped his hoof.

I looked down at my dogs. They recognized the horses. They *re-*

membered, without shame or guilt, what had gone before. Other than the spikes of pain, they'd liked running with the horses.

They were ready. I had to be, too. I took a deep breath and climbed into the saddle. A real Huntsman probably would have done it with more grace. But once I was settled up there, tall and nervous, I looked around. Almost everybody else was in their own saddle, and only Jen and Amber looked comfortable. That made me feel a bit better.

Cat, whose horse was still staring at him, ears flattened, said, "I'm sorry. I'm still learning. I'll try not to be like them."

One ear, then the other, pricked up, and the horse pawed the ground meaningfully.

"Agreed," said Cat. Then, as the horse turned more invitingly, he sprang into the saddle with an assurance that made Jen and Amber's familiarity look babyish.

My horse trotted to the edge of the roof and I looked down. A mist rolled over the roof and obscured the ground below. It was a screen through which the rest of the world appeared only dimly. Only my friends and their mounts seemed real; even Tia was shrouded by a haze of white, and her ghosts were gone entirely.

The world below was just hazed landmarks and streets, except for a single individual, running down a street. It was one of the previous Huntsmen, and he was as visible as we were.

My horse walked off the edge of the roof and plunged downwards.

-twenty-seven-

We flew down from the hotel tower, galloping on mist, the Wild Hunt in pursuit of the world's cancers.

But let's be honest. The horse was doing all the work. He'd neglected to put on any kind of bridle when he'd donned the saddle, so I was really just along for the ride. But, mounted on his back, I could see a little more of his thoughts and the Hunt's history. We'd have to get to know each other later, we'd have to make friends and build a partnership, but for now, this horse wanted to see its previous rider punished. Or at least gone. It was enough for a provisional relationship.

Jen had the Horn and after a moment, she started to play it, a simple, foreboding song. We swept down on the Huntsman known as Atl, born from the sacrifice of an angel, as he ran from us. I'd never known his name myself, but the horse did, and the Horn did. They knew his crimes, too, but even I could see the way the mist pulled away around him and the ground under his feet was raw and bleeding.

We weren't all armed, not yet, but Cat was, and when my dogs had circled him, trapped him, Cat threw his knife and the Horn swallowed Atl down and the angel's sacrifice became no more than an angel's mistake, and something to heal from.

Cat dismounted and picked up the bow and quiver left behind when the Huntsman vanished. He presented them to Amber, who took them solemnly.

After that, we knew the process, which made it easier. When we were close, the mist opened so we could see the wounds and their source, but the dogs led us until then. They learned the scents from the Horn, and they were relentless, because it was a game to them.

Easier, because we knew a little of what to expect, but not actually *easy*. We found Ne in a stable trying to get another horse, and Cle sobbing in a church, and we took two more bows when they were gone. Bows, instead of icy swords, and I wondered if even the form of their weapons was part of their corruption. Ipa, sorcerer of the Wild Hunt, had hidden himself as a tree, and because of that he took more work to find. Yejun had to find him, looking for the reconstruction work on the magic of the world. But once we did, he didn't fight us at all. He gave Yejun a brass sphere, then spread his arms and let the magic of the Horn dissipate him.

We found Tala and Ion together, fighting each other. As we arrived, Ion tried to get away, but she caught him and held him down, then dragged him to his feet. "Die like a hero," she told him, then wrestled him around to face us. She was splendid and beautiful as she held him by his hair and a twisted arm, and I wondered if the wound around their feet hailed from her as much as him. I hesitated, I admit it. She'd fought him off, then held him down. I wanted that kind of power to be free. I wanted to learn from her.

Her fierce gaze went from me to Amber to Brynn, then she shook her head. "It starts so easily." She kicked Ion's spear away from him, toward us. "I have lived for this moment for too long. To take us both out of this world..." She planted a kiss on Ion's bruised cheek. "Together. That's what you wanted, beloved, isn't it?"

His frozen, furious expression was all for Tala, and I felt, just for a moment, irritated. Here I was, in his place. I wanted him to see me and understand. I wanted him to be afraid of *me*.

I was my father's daughter.

Then Tala gave a sharp cry and the horses surged forward and the Wild Hunt swallowed Tala and Ion both, and they were gone.

It was over.

The horses carried us back to the roof again, where Tia and Branwyn and Marley and the Fiddler still stood, waiting. As I slid off the golden stallion's back, I felt numb and exhausted. How long had we been riding? Was it still Halloween?

The Fiddler played our song as we landed, just a snatch, then bowed and vanished before we could speak again. I wondered if he'd gone back to where he'd come from, carrying the malignant song. And I wondered if it had a better purpose, where he'd come from, or if it was always a force for destruction. I wished I'd thought to ask him.

Brynn leaned forward and hugged her horse's neck. When she slid off, her eyes were shining. "I'm a magical girl," she told Branwyn, with both pride and laughter in her voice.

Branwyn didn't share her delight. She sounded like she was ready to cut someone as she asked, "A magical girl who still goes to school and sleeps at home and doesn't terrify her mother?"

Before Brynn could decide on an answer, Amber said uncertainly, hopefully, "If you're a magical girl, does that mean we saved the world with the power of friendship?"

"Sure," said Yejun, stretching. "The power of friendship." He glanced at Jen. Jen smiled back at him. She looked more alive than she had since I'd met her, with a vibrancy and a glow I'd never seen before. Then Yejun looked at me. "Now what?"

"Live your lives," suggested Tia. She looked down at herself, at her dark shimmer and bright markings. "You're still *mostly* who you were before. You just have a new job. Lives are important for maintaining perspective."

"So is school," said Branwyn, with a bright, hard edge to it.

"Yes, Bran," said Brynn with exaggerated patience. "I have a *girlfriend* and the GSA. I can't just abandon them."

"A life," said Jen, as if tasting it. She looked down at Cat's hand holding hers. "I need some time," she began, then pushed Cat away. "I need some time, Cat. We had something before she died, I know. I've never stopped thinking about it. But it's going to take a while before I stop blaming that *something* for what happened. I was distracted when I shouldn't have been."

"I know," said Cat, simply. "If you're alive, I can wait."

"Can I go gloat?" asked Amber. "No, that's probably a terrible idea. I'll hang out with one of you for a while so it's easier to get the gang all together again." She looked at Cat mischievously, and a nervous look crossed Jen's face.

"What about you, AT?" asked Yejun. His eyes were dark, intense, and there was no hiding from them.

Everybody followed his gaze and I looked back at them, surprised. "I'm going home, of course. Back to my father. That hasn't changed. We go back to our lives, right?" I shrugged.

"And we're all going with you?" he demanded. "Right?"

I shook my head. "That would make it harder. I'd be afraid for you. But just knowing that I have you guys to come to when the Horn calls, that does help. And I have my dogs back again." I smiled at them.

Nobody smiled back. Branwyn said, "You don't have to go back to him."

"I do," I said. And I thought about explaining, but I realized I didn't know how. I'd seen myself on our first Hunt. I'd wanted Ion to fear me. I was my father's daughter and I belonged there. He was my father, she was my mother, and I couldn't escape just by walking away. I'd seen that already. Life in his house had shaped me and I didn't know how to live anywhere else, not really.

But I couldn't help glancing at Tia, to see if she was once again disappointed in me. If she was, she didn't show it. She just looked back at me, serene. And that was better than Marley and Branwyn's frustration, the anger I thought I saw on almost everybody's face.

Yejun's face was all hard planes. I went to him, stood on my tip-toes and brushed my lips across his. He didn't move, until his hands were under my elbows and his mouth was no longer a hard line. Then I pulled away. "See you when the Horn blows."

Tia caught my arm. "You lost your phone. You can borrow mine until you replace it." She pressed something into my hand. My fingers closed reflexively.

I went home.

It was just the same as it ever was. I made sure to put my dogs away before I got onto our property, and I shifted the costume I'd picked up so the bag was visible. Sure, it was a full day after I'd left, but all I could really think was *only a day*. And I kept an eye out for Scott, but I didn't see him at all. My father must have really disapproved of how he lost track of me.

I stopped at the clearing of ghosts on my way home. If Emily's ghost was there, she didn't come out. But the other ghost did, the one who had spoken to me before. She looked at me with something that wasn't hatred, before bowing. It wasn't much, but I'd take it.

I walked into the house as my father and his wolves were eating brunch. The news was on, and somebody was exclaiming about the suited black-winged angel who had been hovering over downtown Seattle. I guess nobody had noticed the flying horses. Maybe the mist worked both ways.

My father leaned back when he saw me, putting his feet on the table. "Where have you been, Annalise?"

I lifted the costume bag. "These were sold out everywhere. I had to go on a costume quest."

"I tried calling you," he said, deceptively soft. "We needed some things."

"Phone fell under a bus," I said, a touch nervously.

Looking me over, he said, "You look like you fell under a bus, too." My scrapes had healed but my street clothing was still torn up. I'd forgotten.

I shrugged. "I got mad at the bus."

He gave me a long, steady look. "Your performance tonight had better impress me, or we're going to have to start your training up again with a lot more review than I expected."

"Sure," I said, and went upstairs. I needed a shower and a new set of clothes a lot more than I needed an argument or a broken hand.

I spent a while up there looking at my clothes, wondering which of them worked for the Wild Hunt. Was rocking the Victorian gothic aesthetic an important part of Wild Hunting? Or could I discover my own style? I'd have to, based on my wardrobe.

Eventually, as the afternoon wore on, my father shouted for me and I went downstairs again.

"Where's your costume?" he asked me, his eyes narrowed.

"I'll put it on when it's time," I told him, sitting down on the couch and looking around the living room. It seemed different, somehow. Smaller.

"You're mighty relaxed," he said dangerously, and I straightened up and looked at him. "You seem to have forgotten what thin ice you're on. Maybe I should—"

I stopped listening and really *looked* at him. He seemed smaller, too. I saw him and I remembered Ion, who was just the same. They'd both tried to destroy everything that made me, me.

And I'd survived.

He was just one of so many monsters. He lived in a house of monsters and he cultivated the seeds of monstrousness, and he still couldn't turn me into the kind of monster he wanted me to be.

He's really bad *at this*, I thought clinically, watching him gesticulate and rant. *I'm his daughter.*

I remembered leaping the chasm to catch Amber's hands. I had to run back into the maw of a monster to get enough distance to do that.

"Actually, I'm not going to do the Halloween thing," I told him, cutting him off mid-sentence. "And you should try to behave yourself for once."

He stared at me, his shocked expression rapidly eclipsed by fury. "You need a lesson," he growled. "Give me your hand. Or would you rather I bring in the pack?"

I raised my hand, spread out my fingers, and looked at it. Then I flicked my fingers, and my dogs bounded out of my shadow to surround me.

Leaving them between me and him, I walked to the trophy cabinet, where I slid open the glass and took my mother's locket. I kissed it. "This time, Mama," I told it, and tucked it into my pocket. And I felt better, better than I ever had when I was in LA and under Tia's protection.

I walked back to the living room. My father, in his grand living room where I simply no longer fit, said, "What the hell are you doing?"

"I'm leaving," I told him.

His face twisted and the pack flowed into the room from the rest of the house. I barely glanced at them as they formed up behind Hunter. I could feel my father's wrath billowing off him. He was going to punish me now.

Well, he was going to *try*. But even with his pack behind him, he was all alone.

He lunged, grabbing me. My dogs watched curiously. They didn't attack him. They didn't see the need, but he thought they were afraid of him, and he laughed.

Then he tried to break my arm. I felt him squeeze, felt his magic run through me and ground itself below my feet. I wasn't *just* his daughter anymore. I was part of the Wild Hunt and I would never be alone again.

He stared at me, his face suffused with disbelieving rage. Then he tried again, squeezing my hand, putting pressure on my arm. "Stop," I told him mildly. He didn't listen. So I put my free hand on his chest, and the next time he sent his *fracturing* magic into me, it circled back around into him and it *broke his heart.*

He let me go and staggered back into his pack. Shock and pain wiped away his rage entirely and he stared at me like I was a nightmare come to life.

I walked around him toward the door, then turned back to look at him. "Don't expect me back. Don't try to get me back. If I do come back again, I'm bringing friends. I'm bringing an *army.*"

Then I stepped out into the beautiful autumn afternoon, my dogs flanking me. I walked down the driveway, waiting for the roar from within. I was ready if it came. But there was only a wet, pained noise.

I didn't fit anymore. It wasn't a comfortable thought. I'd have to learn to live on my own. But not *alone.* And now, with my mother's locket in my hand, I was finally ready to go.

I dug out the phone Tia had loaned me and opened the Contacts list. Tia had hundreds, maybe thousands of contacts, and I scrolled through looking for numbers I recognized. They were grouped. There, in Group 1, was Marley and Branwyn and a few other names I knew. And further down, in Group 13, were Yejun and Jen and Cat and Amber and Brynn and myself.

I looked at the list for a while. Then I dialed a number and listened to it ring. When it was picked up, I said, "Hi. It's me. Can I stay with you for a while? I have some things I need to sort out."

a note from the author:

Hi!

Thank you for reading *Wolf Interval*. If you'd like to know when my next book is available, you can sign up for my mailing list at www. dreamfarmer.net, follow me on Twitter at @chrysoula or like my Facebook page at https://www.facebook.com/chrysoula.tzavelas.

Reviews help books and readers find each other. If you want to share your thoughts with others, I welcome all reviews, positive and negative. It's incredible how much they matter.

The next book in the Senyaza Series will be *Etiquette of Exiles*, a collection of short stories documenting the year after the faeries rejoined the world. It's due in June of 2015! And after that, in the autumn of 2015, comes *Divinity Circuit*, a full-length novel about Branwyn and Marley.

--Chrysoula

acknowledgments

Without whom the book would not be: Kate. Kevin. Raymond. Michelle. Jenna. The denizens of the war room, some of whom deserve their own book. Angie and Stacy, Suzanne and Beth.
And all my readers, who keep me writing.

Robin and Killian, you're here too, in your own special space.

about the author

Chrysoula Tzavelas went to twelve schools in twelve years while growing up as an Air Force brat, and she never met a library she didn't like. She now lives near Seattle with cats, dogs, adults, and children. They graciously allow her a few hours to write every day and one day she'll have time to do other things again, too.

She likes combed wool, bread dough, and gardens, but she also likes technology, games, and space. This probably goes hand in hand with liking Jane Austen, Terry Pratchett, and Iain Banks.

follow the author

www.dreamfarmer.net
Twitter: @chrysoula
Facebook: facebook.com/chrysoula.tzavelas
Google+: plus.google.com/u/0/103166129089211811271/posts
Goodreads: goodreads.com/author/show/5049815.Chrysoula_Tzavelas